Carola Dunn is the author o
mysteries. Born and raised in Er
lives in Eugene, Oregon, USA.

ALSO BY CAROLA DUNN

The Daisy Dalrymple mysteries

Cornish mysteries

SUPERFLUOUS WOMEN

A Daisy Dalrymple Mystery

Carola Dunn

CONSTABLE · LONDON

CONSTABLE

First published in the US in 2015 by Minotaur Books,
an imprint of St. Martin's Press, New York

First published in the UK in 2015 by Constable

This paperback edition published in 2016 by Constable

Quotation from Vera Brittain's 'The Superfluous Woman' from
Before You Died © Poetry Vera Brittain Estate 2008,
quoted with permission from Little, Brown Book Group

1 3 5 7 9 10 8 6 4 2

A CIP catalogue record for this book is available from the British Library.

ISBN: 978-1-47211-549-2

Printed and bound in Great Britain by CPI Group (UK) Ltd, Croydon CR0 4YY

Papers used by Constable are from well-managed forests and
other responsible sources.

MIX
Paper from
responsible sources
FSC® C104740

Constable
is an imprint of
Little, Brown Book Group
Carmelite House
50 Victoria Embankment
London EC4Y 0DZ

An Hachette UK Company
www.hachette.co.uk

www.littlebrown.co.uk

Dedicated with thanks to our forebears
who struggled for the rights of women;
and with hope to the present generation,
that they will continue the struggle to
preserve and enhance those rights.

ACKNOWLEDGMENTS

Without Virginia Nicholson's *Singled Out: How Two Million Women Survived Without Men after the First World War* (Viking 2007), I could not have conceived and written this book.

My thanks also, for help on many and varied subjects, to Dolores Gordon-Smith, author of the Jack Haldean mysteries; Malcolm of the Telephone Museum; Christine Jones; Gavin White; D. P. Lyle, M.D.; Allan Mitchinson; Penny Bingham; Eddie Tulasiewicz; Jo Parker; The Centre for Buckinghamshire Studies; Simon GP Geoghegan; and to my brother, Tony Brauer.

. . . far away,
Behind the row of crosses, shadows black
Stretch out long arms before the smouldering sun.

But who will give me my children?

—"The Superfluous Woman,"
Vera Brittain

HISTORICAL NOTE

Britain after the First World War had about
two million more women than men. The press labelled
them "superfluous" or "surplus" women.

SUPERFLUOUS WOMEN

ONE

Daisy awoke gasping for breath. Her racing heartbeat thudded in her ears. For a frightening moment she had no idea where she was.

Just a nightmare, of course. She had dreamt she was shut up in an airless room with no doors or windows where a faceless figure was trying to smother her. As memory returned, her heart quieted, but her breathing was still laborious. Her chest ached. She started to cough.

Raising herself on one elbow, she reached for the glass of water beside the bed and took a sip. She had gone to sleep sitting up, as the doctor had recommended. The hotel's inadequate pillows had slipped off the bed during the night. The chambermaid would bring her a couple more if she asked. The staff of the Saracen's Head had been very friendly and helpful when she arrived in Beaconsfield yesterday.

The pale light filtering through the blue cotton curtains told her she had slept through the night for the first time in weeks.

Getting out of London, out of the Thames Valley, clearly was a good idea. The smog of October 1927 wouldn't count among the worst to afflict the metropolis. However, the southerly breeze that broke it up wafted the noxious mixture of coal smoke and river fog up the hill to Hampstead, usually happily above the miasma. Daisy's mild cold had turned to bronchitis.

The doctor ordered her out of town. She didn't want to impose her illness on friends and she felt too rotten for a long journey. Beaconsfield, a small town on the edge of the Chiltern Hills, seemed ideal.

The air was clean; she was breathing more easily already.

She was about to leave the warm nest of her bed to retrieve the pillows when she heard a tentative knock on the door.

"Who is it?"

"Your tea, madam."

"Come in." Calling out set off another fit of coughing.

"Oh, madam, you don' half soun' ba'." The local speech featured unvoiced final consonants, much easier to understand than some dialects Daisy had encountered. She very soon stopped noticing. "You better have a cuppa, quick."

The maid, a sturdy, sandy-haired, freckled young woman of about Daisy's age, set down the small tray and poured. "Here. Carefu' now. You don' wan' it to go down the wrong way."

Daisy managed to stop coughing for long enough to sip, and then to empty the cup. It soothed her throat a bit. "Thanks. Weren't you waiting in the dining room yesterday evening?"

"That's right. I'm a waitress, really. I don't do the cleaning and such, but I live in so it's easy to help out with early morning teas, and sometimes on reception, to oblige. And to earn a bit extra, too," she confided. "I'm saving up to go to London and learn to type. I want to work in an office."

"Good for you. What's your name?"

"Sally, madam. Sally Hedger. Properly, Sarah. There's another cup in the pot if you want it. And a couple of biscuits. I saw you di'n't eat enough dinner to keep a flea alive."

"I was too tired, and my throat's a bit sore from coughing. I haven't been very well, so I came to Beaconsfield to breathe the country air. It's already doing me good. Would you mind awfully picking up my pillows? I seem to have knocked them off in the night."

"Here you go." Sally plumped them up and put them behind Daisy's back. "That'll be comfier for you."

"I don't suppose you could scrounge a couple more for me? I'm supposed to sleep sitting up."

"I 'spect so. Can you manage till I've done the rest of the teas?"

"Of course. Whenever you have a moment."

"And how about breakfast in bed? You didn't ought to be rushing to get yourself up."

"Sally, could you really? That would be marvellous! You're a treasure."

"Don't tell anyone or they'll all be wanting it, too."

She was as good as her word. Daisy didn't get up till after ten. She was able to take a leisurely bath instead of the usual hotel scramble to get out of the way of other guests queuing up. Back in her room, she went to the window.

Last night she had been too exhausted to bother about the view. Now she looked out over back gardens to meadows where black-and-white cows grazed, and ploughland with winter wheat just beginning to green the pale, chalky soil. A few trees were bare already, but oaks clung stubbornly to the brown leaves they would keep all winter and the bright gold of beeches stood out against the grey sky.

Not the slightest breeze stirred the leaves. Daisy decided she felt fit enough for a short walk. She dressed warmly, a flannel petticoat under her tweed skirt and a flannel vest under her blouse and pullover—her fashionable friend, Lucy, would have been horrified, she thought with amusement. Stout walking shoes, a warm coat, and a blue muffler and hat her stepdaughter had knitted for her, pulled down over her ears: she might well stun the local citizens as well.

She hadn't paid any attention to the town as she was driven through the streets from the station, but she had noticed a church right opposite the Saracen's Head. A stroll round the church-yard would be a good start to regaining her strength.

Dressing had tired her. On second thoughts, she took off the hat and stuffed it into the coat pocket, then tidied her hair. It was after eleven, time for morning coffee.

The residents' lounge had only two occupants, who looked like commercial travellers. Deep in discussion over papers spread on a low table, they scarcely looked up as she passed through to the ladies' parlour beyond. There, three elderly women were seated at a round table by the fire. They glanced at Daisy and, obviously deciding she was a stranger of no interest, returned to their chatter. Not so many years ago, a woman staying alone at a hotel would have caused disapproving stares. With two million more females than males in the country, most of whom would never have a chance to marry, single "girls" were no longer noteworthy.

Coffee and a cream cake restored Daisy's desire for a little gentle exercise. (She didn't even feel guilty about the cream cake as she had lost several pounds while ill. Well, a few at least.)

She went out. Slowly, feeling like a tottery old lady, she crossed the wide street to the church. She stopped to look at an elaborate war memorial. Bronze plaques on all four sides each listed twenty names: eighty men lost from this small town and the surrounding rural district. Daisy noted several pairs of names, including two Hedgers who must surely be related to Sally, the waitress, as well as a few trios, and six surnamed Child—six killed in one family.

Filled with melancholy, she trudged through the churchyard, right round the church. In spite of the grey sky, the day was now warmish for October. She unwrapped her muffler and undid the top button of her coat.

As she completed the circuit, a ray of sun broke through the clouds to strike a wooden bench near the memorial. Daisy accepted the implicit invitation. Though she had coughed only once or twice, her legs felt a bit wobbly. She was glad to rest and contemplate the scene.

Opposite, on the corner, stretched the gabled west front of her hotel, the Saracen's Head, a centuries'-old coaching inn. The exposed timbers of the first floor looked much too straight to be the originals, though. The few other half-timbered buildings in the vicinity looked more genuine; most were typical Home Counties, mellow red brick with red-tiled roofs.

All four streets meeting at the crossroads were unusually wide for a town centre. They formed the intersection of the main route from Windsor to Aylesbury and the London to Oxford road, now the A40. Daisy had often driven through, in fact, without taking any particular notice of the town.

She wondered whereabouts Willie lived. Wilhelmina Chandler, a friend from school, had very recently moved from the North to Beaconsfield. They had exchanged occasional letters over the years, but never met since leaving school. Daisy hoped to call on her and refresh their friendship, once she'd recovered a bit more strength and was sure the coughing spells were a thing of the past.

The letter with the address was in her room. When she felt up to a visit, Sally would probably be able to direct her to the street.

She returned to the hotel. Climbing the stairs brought on another spate of coughs and she was glad to collapse onto the bed. A glass of water followed by a cough pastille did the trick. The taste of horehound, wintergreen, eucalyptus, and menthol lingered in her mouth, making the prospect of lunch unappealing.

In the end, telling herself firmly that she must keep up her strength, she went down to the restaurant just before they stopped serving lunch. Only half a dozen people were there, and most of them were just finishing their meals, so Daisy was able to chat with Sally.

The waitress brought a bowl of oxtail soup. "This'll do you good, madam. If I was you, I'd have the shepherd's pie after. Nothing in it to scrape a sore throat. It'll go down a fair treat. Stewed apple and custard for afters?"

Daisy assented. The soup was rich enough to banish the cough pastille taste, and the shepherd's pie was delicious.

When Sally returned with the pudding, Daisy asked, "Do you know where Orchard Road is?"

"Oh yes, madam. I can tell you how to get there."

"Is it far?"

"Maybe ten minutes to this end, 'bout the same again or a bit less to the other end. Which end was you wanting?"

"The house is called Cherry Trees."

"I know it. There's three ladies just moved in. My Auntie May cleaned for Mrs. Gray, that sold the house, and the new ladies kept her on. Friends of yours?"

"One of them, Miss Chandler. I hope to make the acquaintance of her friends."

Sally looked doubtful. "When you're feeling more yourself, madam," she said firmly. "It's down the New Town end, too far for you to walk yet awhile. Unless you was to hire a car?" She sounded even more doubtful.

Daisy laughed, which made her start to cough. After a sip of water, she shook her head and ventured to speak: "I'll wait a bit."

She waited two days, two days of early nights, late rising, and afternoon naps, eating and sleeping well, walking a little farther each day. On the morning of the third day, Thursday, she wrote a note to Willie Chandler and gave the Boots, a skinny youth, sixpence to deliver it.

An answer came the same evening. Willie was sorry Daisy had been ill. Assuming she didn't like to stay out late, would she care to come to tea the next day, to meet Willie's friends and housemates, Vera Leighton and Isabel Sutcliffe? If she arrived at about half past four, Isabel would be at home. Vera, a teacher, was usually home by five at the latest. Unfortunately Willie herself often didn't get home till six thirty, sometimes seven, but if Daisy felt up to staying that long, they could talk as Willie walked her back to the hotel.

Edward, the Boots, earned another sixpence taking Daisy's acceptance to Cherry Trees.

The next afternoon she set out early, reckoning that Sally's twenty-minute walk would be at least a half hour for her. The weather was still good, cloudy but with the sun breaking through now and then. It was a pleasant walk along Aylesbury End, a slight downhill slope. She hoped she would still consider it slight when she had to walk up it going back.

Once she left the shops and cottages behind her, high beech hedges, bronze-leaved, hid many of the houses and gardens along her way. On the opposite side of the street occasional roofs were visible through treetops. They seemed to be quite big houses, fairly modern. The railway hadn't come to Beaconsfield till the turn of the century. Sally had told her about being taken as a little girl to the opening of the station. The New Town had sprung up around it and now spread to meet Old Town.

Where Orchard Road forked off to the left, Daisy saw a bench on the far side. She crossed and sat down for a minute or two. *Not far now*, she assured herself as she trudged onward.

On either side of the street, the beech hedges continued, allowing only occasional glimpses of largish houses and gardens. At last she came to the green-painted gate she was looking for. A white plaque declared in black script that this was Cherry Trees. She paused for a moment, leaning against a gatepost, to catch her breath.

She had made it, without dropping dead on the way. So much for her doctor's gloomy prognostications!

TWO

A stout, red-faced woman came down the garden path towards Daisy, the yellowish gravel crunching beneath her run-down shoes, bulging with bunions. She wore a lime green, polka-dotted head scarf over greying hair, and a shapeless, shabby black coat nearly to her ankles.

Daisy opened the gate as she approached, and stood aside. The woman gave her a suspicious look and grunted what might have been an acknowledgement.

Mrs. Hedger, Daisy assumed. Sally, without saying anything derogatory, had given the impression that her Auntie May was a bit of a curmudgeon.

As Daisy stepped through the gateway, she saw that the gravel path led to a brick and timber house, the timbers silvery grey with age and the roof tiles lichened. The façade was rectangular but asymmetrical, with the front door off-centre, a small window to its left, a large one to the right. Yellow climbing roses, still in bloom, flanked the door and spread to meet above it. On each side of the path grew a cherry tree. Long, narrow scarlet leaves still clung to the branches, though many had already fallen.

Beneath one tree a woman was raking the debris into a

pile. The gardener was tall and sturdy—robust was the word that came to mind—her dark hair in a severe bob, almost an Eton crop. She was clad in a red pullover, khaki trousers, and stout boots.

At the click of the gate latch, she glanced round in dismay. "Mrs. Dalrymple—I mean Fletcher? Willie still refers to you as Daisy Dalrymple. Good lord, is it half past four already? I'm so sorry." Her voice hinted at a Yorkshire upbringing. She leant her rake against the tree trunk and came towards Daisy, pulling off her gardening gloves. "I'm Isabel Sutcliffe."

"Yes, I'm Daisy Fletcher." Daisy and Isabel shook hands. "How do you do?"

"Come on in. I just don't notice the time when I'm busy, but don't worry, the scones are keeping warm in the oven and it won't take a moment to make tea."

The fragrance of the roses gave way to lingering odours of baking when Isabel opened the front door and ushered Daisy into the entrance hall, floored with redbrick tile.

"Lovely and warm!" Daisy exclaimed as her new acquaintance took off her boots and donned house slippers.

"I made up a good fire in the sitting room because Willie says you've been ill. Let me take your coat, then you can go and thaw out. I'll just put my boots by the back door and dash upstairs and change. I'll be with you in a trice."

"Please don't bother to change for my sake, Miss Sutcliffe."

"Really? Right-oh. Do please call me Isabel."

"And I'm Daisy, of course."

The furniture in the sitting room was Craftsman-style beechwood, upholstered in a modern geometrical dark and light blue print, with blue and white curtains drawn across the wide window. Sinking into a large, well-cushioned chair, Daisy held out her hands to the roaring fire.

The original fireplace had been huge, surrounded by smoke-blackened beams. A good half was blocked off, faced with blue and white Dutch tiles, leaving a good-sized grate in the centre. Looking around, Daisy wondered whether the room had once been part of a farmhouse kitchen. Isabel, having changed boots for house slippers, returned with a tea tray and confirmed her guess.

"The land was once a cherry orchard, as you might surmise from the name of the street and the house." She poured tea. "Here, have a scone while they're warm. Shop jam, I'm afraid, but come again next year and you'll get homemade."

"Thanks."

"This house was the original farmhouse, eighteenth century according to the house agent. The previous owner, a London businessman, bought it in 1904 or thereabouts, knowing the railway was coming. He sold off the land for building and pretty much gutted the house to modernise it. He put in gas, then his second wife made him electrify. They left the gas range, though. I'm glad, because it's what I'm used to, what I cooked on at home, in Yorkshire."

"I'm glad, too, since it produced such light scones." Daisy helped herself to a third. "Delicious! You're a good cook."

"Practice. Mother and I turned our house into lodgings when Papa died. That's how I met Willie and Vera. They were among our lodgers."

"How did you end up here in Bucks?"

"You know Willie went from typist to bookkeeper to chartered accountant?"

"Yes. She was always good at arithmetic at school. We didn't go as far as anything worthy of being called maths—unsuitable for ladies and too taxing for our delicate female brains. Willie was probably the only one who actually enjoyed numbers and would have liked to go further."

Isabel grinned. "Incomprehensible, isn't it? A lot of people at her old firm were green with envy, and one old fuddy-duddy of a partner didn't approve of a woman in that position, so she went looking for another job. She got one in High Wycombe and found digs there. Vera and I decided to follow her south. After my mother died, we sort of became a family. . . . You know the situation, nearly a million men dead and many more disabled in the war. 'Superfluous women,' they call us."

"I was lucky," Daisy said soberly. "Meeting Alec and us falling for each other, I mean. Vera's a teacher, Willie said?"

"That's right. Luckily there was an opening in the junior school here in Beaconsfield. She came down in August. I put my house and furniture up for sale and joined them when it sold. We were in horrible lodgings in Wycombe while I hunted for a place to buy. They'd both saved a bit of money, so we went in together, but of course my share is by far the biggest, which is just as well as I have no skills except housekeeping and gardening! Sorry, I'm talking your ears off."

"No, you're not. I'm interested. Besides, talking still makes me start coughing sometimes, so I'm much better off listening. Yes, I'd love another cup, please," she added as Isabel lifted the teapot in her direction. "And is that parkin? I adore parkin."

"It is. Let me cut you a slice. The thing is, we haven't been here long enough to make any friends, so I'm pretty much alone all day except for the shopping and our char three days a week. And she's not exactly chatty."

"Mrs. Hedger?"

"How on earth did you know?"

"Her niece is a waitress at the Saracen's Head. Sally's chatty all right, very friendly and helpful."

"Oh, yes, she came over to give her aunt a hand one day. Mrs. H is the grim-faced sort, never two words when one will do, but she's efficient. It wouldn't be easy to replace her in a small place like this, so I'm glad she was willing to stay on when Mrs. Gray left. She already knows things like how to cope with the cranky boiler and how to open the desk drawer that always sticks."

"Very handy!"

"We bought the furnishings with the house, you see. Mrs. Gray was going abroad and wanted to get rid of everything. She's recently widowed, poor thing, though I can't say she seemed exactly grief-stricken when she showed us round the house. Mr. Vaughn, the house agent, told us her husband was thirty years older. A lot of us surplus women grasp anything in trousers they can catch." Isabel grimaced. "No, that was catty. I don't know anything about their marriage."

"I know what you mean, though."

"I expect I shall turn into a catty old maid." Isabel seemed unconcerned at the prospect. "The others have careers to occupy their minds, but I—" She raised her head as if listening. "The front door. That'll be Vera. If you'll excuse me, I'll just go and put on the kettle. She'll be dying for her tea."

Daisy heard voices in the hall, then Vera Leighton came in. A wiry woman, she had mousy, frizzy hair pulled back in a knot with exuberant wisps escaping. It was the only exuberant thing about her. She looked tired, and her dark grey skirt and jacket and prim white blouse did nothing to enliven the picture, though doubtless proper for a schoolmistress.

She introduced herself in a low, pleasant voice. Perching on the arm of a chair, she said, "I'm glad you're recovered enough to come to tea. Isabel and I have been longing to meet you. We all read your articles in *Town and Country*, of course, and Willie has told us so much about you."

Daisy wondered how much Willie could find to say about her writing. She was sure she had asked her friend not to mention that Alec was a police detective, and she certainly hadn't disclosed her own unorthodox activities in the detecting line. If that was what Vera was talking about, Willie must have heard through the Old Girls' bush telegraph.

"Well . . ." she temporised.

"One should never say that." Vera smiled, lighting up with amusement so that she became quite attractive, almost pretty. "It always makes me want to ask, 'What exactly did she tell you?' Nothing but good, I assure you."

Laughing, Daisy agreed. "I've never found a response that wasn't either discourteous or defensive. I'll just have to reciprocate in kind. Isabel told me you found a job here just when you wanted it. You must have had excellent references from your last position."

"I was lucky that there was an opening, but yes, I'm a pretty good teacher though I don't like to boast."

"How do you like your new school?"

Vera's face clouded. "The children are marvellous. Two or three naughty ones—there always are; none as bad as the little toughs I had in Huddersfield." She hesitated, then decided not to utter the "but" Daisy was sure hovered on her lips. "Willie is our great success story, of course. The first woman chartered accountant qualified in 1919, and there still aren't many. Where on earth is Izzie with the tea? I'm parched."

"Do go and change if you want to. Don't mind me."

"Are you sure you don't mind? Teachers are expected to look so boringly respectable. Which I dare say I am, but I like to wear a bit of colour at home. I'll be back in two ticks."

Left on her own, Daisy's eyelids grew heavy. She awoke with a start at the clink of china. For a moment she thought she was in her hotel room and Sally had brought her tea. She started to thank her, then, blinking, recognised the room and the two anxious faces looking at her over the teacups.

"Oh dear, I nodded off. How impolite! I hope I didn't snore."

"Not at all, just wheezed a bit," Vera assured her. She had brushed out her hair and wore it in a single loose plait. Though still on the mousy side, she was a trifle more vibrant in a brown skirt and canary-yellow jumper, set off by a short but good string of pearls and lipstick in a brownish red shade. "Are you feeling all right?"

"A bit groggy. I always do if I nod off during the day. The doctor said the wheeze might last a few weeks even after I stop coughing. But I'm all right, really. I'd love another cup of tea."

Isabel now wore a moss-green wool dress, but still no makeup. She lifted the tea cosy and felt the teapot. "It's still hot. You were only out for a few minutes." She passed the cup and saucer and, unasked, another slice of parkin.

They let Daisy eat and drink in peace, discussing household

matters. Isabel was clearly in charge of domestic business, and Vera, at least, seemed grateful not to have to deal with shopping, cooking, laundry, cleaning, and coping with Mrs. Hedger. Sally's aunt was not only grim-faced but pigheaded, it seemed.

"She has her own way of doing things," said Isabel, "and nothing I say can make her stop straightening the stuff on your desk, Vera. You can try talking to her yourself. If that doesn't work, you'll have to put up with it or do your own room."

"I could have killed her when she stacked those books on top of the one paper I needed urgently. I spent half an hour hunting through the other papers, then biked back to school to look for it."

"Perhaps it's revenge for the kirby grips you lose all over the house. I found a couple myself today and put them on the mantelpiece."

"Oh, thanks. Sorry, they *will* fall out, no matter what I do." Vera went to the fireplace, found and pocketed a couple of hair grips, and returned to her chair.

"Well," Isabel sighed, "I'll keep checking the notices in the newsagent's window, but chars are hard to come by here, as I was telling Daisy earlier. We were lucky to inherit her."

"I inherited my treasure of a cook-housekeeper from my mother-in-law," said Daisy, and instantly regretted her words. She hoped she didn't sound as if she were bragging about her marriage, her "treasure," or being able to afford a cook-housekeeper, not to mention other servants. "Mrs. Hedger seems to be a mixed blessing," she added quickly. Perhaps the woman had been soured by losing a close relative in the war, one or even both of the two Hedgers on the memorial.

But that was another topic best avoided. The chances were that Vera or Isabel or both had lost people they loved. Kind and friendly as they were, Daisy had only just met them. They were still strangers. She didn't know what subjects they were touchy about.

Vera sighed. "I suppose it'll teach me to keep my desk clear. I'm glad you're the one who has to deal with her."

"She's more of a holly hedge than a beech hedge," said Isabel, "but I'd rather cope with her than with a classroom full of children. Daisy, you have twins? They must be a handful. Do they go to school yet?"

"No, they're just toddlers. I have help with them, thank goodness, and talking of prickly, their nanny qualifies as a gorse thicket! My stepdaughter is fourteen and away at school except for the holidays. She's a darling, though, not at all difficult."

"I seem to remember being at my worst at fifteen. That's why I trained for primary teaching, not secondary."

"My mother claims I was always difficult," said Daisy, "and still am, come to that."

Vera laughed. "Tell us about your babies, Daisy, if it won't set you coughing."

Daisy was always ready to talk about Oliver and Miranda, and both women seemed genuinely amused by stories of the twin's antics. Given that Vera and Isabel had little chance of becoming mothers, Daisy included a tale or two of naughtiness and illness, to remind them that having children wasn't all sunshine and roses.

"I miss them," she said. "I haven't seen them for weeks, except for blowing kisses from the door, for fear of infection."

Vera shook her head. "Believe me, I'm pretty good at judging when a child with the sniffles is going to spread them to the whole class! I doubt you're infectious still."

"That's what my doctor told me before I came away, or I wouldn't be visiting you."

"Is Daisy here?" Willie breezed in, bringing a breath of cold air. "Daisy, old top, it's good to see you! How are you?" She stood, hands on hips, looking down at Daisy.

"Much better, darling."

Wilhelmina Chandler ran one hand through pale blond curls as exuberant as her personality. Even in her grey business costume, her makeup discreetly unobtrusive, she managed to bubble. "Looking a bit pale and wan, but I see Isabel's been feeding you up nicely. Izzie, pour us a cuppa, would you? I'm parched. Picked up a nail in the front tyre and had to run for the train, pushing my bike."

Isabel felt the teapot. "It's barely lukewarm. I'll make another pot."

"Don't bother. As long as it's wet. Ta." She gulped down the tepid tea. "Now, Daisy, how long are you staying in Beaconsfield?"

"At least till Sunday evening."

"Oh, good, then we'll see you again."

"Izzie and I thought you might like to come to lunch on Sunday," Vera proposed.

"Good idea," said Willie. "Do say you will, Daisy."

"I'd have loved to, thank you, but my husband is coming to join me on Saturday morning, if he can get away."

The other three consulted with a glance.

"He's welcome, too," said Isabel, "if he doesn't mind an excess of female company."

"Of course he wouldn't. I won't be sure he's actually coming, though, till he arrives. Alec's working hours are . . . erratic."

"Never mind," said Isabel, "we'll expect him if we see him. I was thinking, to even out the numbers, we might invite the Cartwrights, but—"

"No!" Vera exclaimed vehemently.

"All right, keep your hair on! It was just a thought."

Willie finished her tea. "Daisy, are you up to staying for supper tonight, or shall we set out?"

"I'd better head back, or you might have to push me in a wheelbarrow."

A few minutes later, with Daisy carefully wrapped up against the night air, she and Willie started up the gentle slope of Orchard Road.

"Who are the Cartwrights?" Daisy asked. "Isabel said she hadn't had time to make any friends here yet."

"Vera's headmaster and his wife. They invited her over for drinks one Sunday soon after the beginning of term, and we haven't returned their hospitality. Partly because we've only just got the house sorted out. Also, we haven't really been able to afford any halfway decent sherry, let alone spirits for cocktails."

"She—Vera—didn't sound frightfully keen."

"No-o." Willie's expression was invisible as they were still some distance from the next street lamp, but she sounded as if she were frowning. "I don't know what that's about. She hasn't talked about any trouble with Mr. Cartwright. Bosses can be difficult in a million ways, though, as I know from experience. Be glad you're your own boss."

"Editors can be awkward, too, believe me, but on the whole I've been lucky. As for Alec's superintendent, the less said the better. By the way, did you tell the others he's a policeman?"

"No, you asked me not to, though I didn't gather why. He's not in some top secret undercover branch, is he?"

"Heavens no, a common-or-garden detective chief inspector."

"Tall, dark, and handsome, is what I've heard."

"Handsome? Well, he has the most adorable hair, dark and springy. It just won't lie down flat as he'd like."

"I'd want to boast about him, to friends."

"It's just that most people badger me about what it's like being married to a detective, or they want to hear about his cases, or they go silent."

"I didn't reveal *your* ventures into sleuthing, either," Willie said, her voice mischievous.

"I'd like to know who told you, because I didn't."

"I can't remember. More than one Old Girl, I think. Always with a 'top secret' caveat attached."

Daisy laughed—and doubled up coughing. Willie helped her to the bench at the end of Orchard Road, and they sat there for a few minutes while she recovered. Few people were out and about at half past six on a chilly weekday evening. A couple of cars passed, going towards the new town; an errand boy on a bicycle zipped by in the opposite direction, whistling, his basket laden and his front light casting a weak and erratic beam.

A moment later, a motor roared behind them. Daisy glanced round to see a black car speeding up Orchard Road, only its side lamps lit. It barely slowed at the intersection, narrowly missing a van as it swung into the main road, towards the old town.

"Something something eight seven four," said Willie.

"What? Oh, the number plate?"

"Yes. If I see him driving like that again, I'll report him. Did you notice the letters?"

"No, sorry. And it's no good asking me what kind of car it was, either." Daisy stood up. "I'm all right now. Let's go."

By the time they reached the Saracen's Head, she was worn out, though pleased with herself. In the brightly lit lobby, Willie took one look at her and said, "Come on, let me buy you a drink."

"My treat. I've already been royally entertained to tea and I have high hopes for Sunday lunch."

Daisy would have gone to the ladies' parlour, but Willie pushed open the door to the saloon bar.

At their entrance, half a dozen men at the bar and three at a table looked round and fell silent. They looked like a mixture of prosperous farmers, shopkeepers, possibly a lawyer's clerk or two, and the better kind of commercial traveller. Every face instantly registered disapproval, from raised eyebrows to scowls.

Respectable women unescorted by a male were still taboo in a barroom. The barman said gruffly, "You ladies'd be more comfortable in the parlour."

Willie gave him a bright smile as she marched over to the bar. "Thanks, but this will do us very well. What's yours, Daisy? A hot toddy?"

"Vermouth and soda, please." She delved into her bag for money.

"And I'll have a half of draught mild."

Stony-faced, the man poured and siphoned Daisy's drink and drew Willie's. Daisy paid. Willie, her point made, carried the glasses to a table as far removed from all the others present as possible. Hidden by the high-backed settle, she burst into giggles.

"They'll learn," she said tolerantly. "These days, there are too many of us to be ignored or shunted off into a backroom."

Next time Daisy saw Sally, the waitress had heard the story and was full of admiration for "that Miss Chandler."

"She put him in his place proper, didn't she, madam! And as polite and ladylike with it as you please."

"She took him by surprise and he was flummoxed."

Sally's giggle sounded just like Willie's. "Men! Too big for their boots they are, the most of 'em. Good for her telling our Mickey where to get off. He's cross as scissors, he is."

THREE

Alec had been sent to Oakham, to help the minuscule Rutland county force. Two simultaneous investigations had overwhelmed their meagre resources. By late afternoon on Saturday, three people had been arrested on a variety of charges. Alec left Detective Sergeant Ernie Piper to deal with the paperwork, his forte. After sending Daisy a wire to say he'd be with her by dinnertime, he set out cross-country for Beaconsfield in his new royal blue Austin Twelve.

Before leaving London for Oakham, he had received two cheerful letters from Daisy recounting the immediate improvement in her health and continuing progress. All the same, he was worried about her. She was so seldom ill she was inclined to belittle her own symptoms, besides not wanting to worry him . . . Yet here he was worrying anyway.

He concentrated on driving, through a light but relentless drizzle, the complicated route from Rutland to Beaconsfield that Ernie had mapped out for him.

It was dark when he reached the Saracen's Head, to find himself expected. The *ping* of the bell on the reception desk brought a young woman from the room behind it. On hearing his name, she exclaimed, "Oh, Mrs. Fletcher will be ever so happy to see you, sir. She's ever so much better than when she came. Hardly ever coughs and none of them terrible coughing fits yesterday."

"Thank you, Miss . . . ?"

"Hedger. Sally Hedger, sir. Mrs. Fletcher's in her room—your room. Number eleven, turn right at the top of the stairs. She has a key, and here's another one for you, in case you need it."

"Thanks."

"Any bags to be brought in, sir?"

"This is it." He hefted his valise. "I can manage, thanks." Luckily he'd taken an extra clean shirt to Rutland. He went upstairs and found the room. Knocking, he called, "Daisy, it's me," while trying the handle.

The door wasn't locked. As it opened, Daisy cried, "Darling!" and jumped up from a chair by the fire, dropping a book on the floor.

He dropped his valise as she flung herself into his arms. Kicking the door closed behind him, he kissed her. Her enthusiastic response lasted long enough to prove she no longer suffered from severe breathlessness.

"Darling, I've missed you. I'm so glad you managed to get away."

"Ernie Piper knows where I am. The Yard doesn't."

"Good."

He held her away from him and scrutinised her face. "You don't look quite as like a death's head as you did." Still a bit wan, but the curl was returning to golden-brown shingled hair that had lain limp and drab when she left London.

"How kind of you! I'm perfectly well, I promise, and trying not to regain too many pounds."

"I like you with the pounds," Alec said firmly, remembering that, at their first meeting, "cuddlesome" had been the word that came to mind.

"That's a great relief, but I'm trying anyway. Did you get my last letter? When did you leave town?"

"I had two letters."

"Then you didn't get the one about the invitation to lunch tomorrow."

He groaned. "I hoped—"

"I know. I rather wish I hadn't accepted, but I did. I told them I wasn't sure whether you'd make it, though, so you could go away again."

"Not till I can take you with me, love. Not till tomorrow evening, that is, or early next day at latest. I have to turn up at the Yard on Monday morning."

"We'll stay over till Monday, then, so we'll have the evening together. I'm sure you'll get a good Sunday lunch, at least. I gather Isabel is an excellent cook."

"I'm glad to hear it. And speaking of food, I'm hungry. I missed lunch today, as usual."

"I'm ready, let's go down."

They went to the saloon bar first for a predinner drink. The barman was surly, and Alec got the impression that Daisy was a particular target of his scowl. When they sat down, she explained.

Alec laughed, but said, "Your friends have just recently moved here, didn't they? I'd have thought they'd do better not to start out by antagonising people."

"Willie said they'll stick to the White Horse in future. They've been in a couple of times without anyone objecting." Daisy bristled. "I don't see why women shouldn't have a quiet drink in a respectable bar just because they don't happen to have a male escort."

"Nor do I, love, so there's no need to look daggers at me! It sounds as if your friend handled it just right."

"That's what I thought," she said, mollified.

"If I'm meeting them tomorrow, you'd better tell me a bit about them," Alec proposed.

Daisy was glad to oblige. The harmonious ménage she described seemed to Alec to be a bit too good to be true. He'd come across quite a few households made up of "superfluous women," and in his experience they were liable to suffer from most of the same sources of discord as the average marriage.

22

Not that he would say so to Daisy.

When they went to the dining room, he noted with amusement that she was on the friendliest terms with the staff, especially Sally Hedger. Obviously the barman's attitude had not affected the others.

As usual, Daisy made friends wherever she went. He regarded her fondly across the table, happy to see the natural colour returned to her cheeks, the bounce and shine to her hair. She hadn't coughed once since he arrived.

The clouds dissipated overnight and the sun shone bright in the pale blue sky. Though it gave little warmth as yet, it promised a perfect autumn day. After breakfast, Alec drove Daisy to Burnham Beeches, where they rambled through the ancient forest, glowing golden in its autumn glory.

Alec found it exhilarating. He was amused at Daisy's awe. She wasn't easily awed. He had to agree that the straight grey trunks of the beech trees gave the impression of a vast cathedral spreading as far as the eye could see in every direction.

It was chilly in the shade of the woodland paths, but when they returned to the open area of heather and birch where Alec had parked the car, the sun was surprisingly warm. Daisy shed scarves and gloves and coat and even, defying propriety, her woolly hat.

"You'll get cold."

"I can easily put them on again. It's hardly any distance back to the hotel, though, and if you drive fast, we'll be there in no time."

"Twenty miles an hour."

"The most disregarded law in the country," Daisy teased.

"But I'm a copper."

She laughed. "And if coppers all drove no faster than twenty, they'd never ever catch anyone."

Alec proceeded at his usual steady thirty miles an hour, keeping an eye out for coppers. Mindful that life is precious and fragile—the doctor had spoken of pneumonia—he held Daisy's hand as he drove except when he needed his to change gears. They didn't often manage to spend more than a few hours alone together. Damn those well-meaning friends of hers and their invitation!

After washing and changing at the hotel, they drove to Cherry Trees.

The ladies welcomed them warmly. As soon as Daisy had introduced Alec, Isabel Sutcliffe, a strapping creature, excused herself to go and see to the gravy. Vera Leighton appeared to be average in every way, the sort of person one met and immediately forgot. Daisy's schoolfriend, Miss Wilhelmina Chandler, was small and fluffy. Alec recalled with a start that she was a chartered accountant.

"Do come into the sitting room," she invited. "We have some just about passable sherry."

"We were hoping the previous owner of the house might have accidentally left a bottle or two of the good stuff in a dark corner of the cellar," said Vera, "but the key is missing and we haven't been able to open the door to find out."

"What kind of lock is it?" Alec asked.

"Just an ordinary old-fashioned one. Not a Yale or Chubb or anything. Isabel fiddled with a wire coat hanger without success."

"Would you like me to have a go?"

"Will you? You're not a burglar by profession, are you? Willie went all cagey when we wondered what you do."

"I did not go cagey, if you must use that revolting term! You'd better take care or you'll find yourself teaching American slang to your kids."

"They already know it from the cinema, all but the littlest."

"Anyway, I was being *discreet*."

"I hope Daisy is sufficiently discreet not to have revealed that I was a burglar—if I were one! My thanks for your discretion, Miss Chandler. I'm a detective officer, Miss Leighton. We tend to learn a few burglarious tricks. Is the coat hanger handy?"

"In the cupboard under the stairs. I'll get it," Willie said promptly.

"Even if there are no bottles in the cellar," said Vera, "Isabel wants to use it to store apples. We have five trees, and the fruit's sitting in crates in a damp garden shed full of spiders and earwigs. The house agent told Iz the cellar's practically airtight, to control the temperature for old Mr. Gray's collection of wines. The old man was fanatical about it, apparently. Mrs. Gray was going to sell the lot, but you never know, we might find something that wasn't carted away."

Willie reappeared with an unravelled coat hanger and a torch. "I'm not sure if there's electric light down there. This way."

Alec followed her across the hall, Daisy and Vera trailing behind. At the rear, an open door revealed a dining room, the table set for lunch. Willie turned into a narrow passage, with a staircase on the right leading up to the first floor. A door in the left-hand wall also stood open. Daisy peeked in and saw the kitchen, with Isabel stirring something on the stove. An appetising smell of roast beef wafted out.

At the end of the corridor was a half-glazed door to the outside. Beside it on the left, a row of pegs held coats, with a shelf above for hats and a row of rubber boots beneath. Willie gestured at a door on the right, under the stairs.

"This is it, Mr. Fletcher. May I watch?"

"Really, Willie!" Vera exclaimed.

"I promise I won't take up burglary!"

"You're welcome to watch, but you won't learn much. It's mostly a matter of feel."

Alec bent the wire to the angle most likely to be helpful. The keyhole had a hinged draught excluder. He swung it to one side and inserted the lock pick. It didn't go right through—there must be another flap on the other side—but it went far enough for his purpose. He was out of practice so it took a couple of minutes, but the wards eventually clicked back.

He stepped back, turned the doorknob, and gave the door a slight push.

"Whew!" Willie retreated, holding her nose.

"Aargh!" Daisy fled, gagging.

"A dead rat," said Isabel, who had come out of the kitchen to see what was going on. At Daisy's heels, she rapidly returned to her stronghold.

"A Hamlin-Town of dead rats!" Vera followed them. "Coming, Mr. Fletcher?"

He shook his head without a backward glance. "Duty calls." The kitchen door thumped shut.

A handkerchief held to nose and mouth, Alec switched on the torch and cautiously set foot on a small landing. To his right, flimsily railed wooden stairs ran steeply down against the wall. The middle section of the railing was broken. He went down a few steps and directed the beam at the floor below the break.

On the pale grey floor lay a corpse, just one, not a horde of rats. It wore a tweed costume, a silk blouse, pearls, and one shoe.

The cellar was airtight enough to keep out blowflies, apparently. But nothing could prevent the ravages of decomposition. Having seen what he needed to see, Alec hastily stepped back into the passage and slammed the door.

FOUR

Daisy, feeling rather green, sat at the kitchen table with Willie and Vera. Isabel had gone back to stirring her gravy. The savoury smell helped banish the sweet, sickly stink of death from Daisy's nostrils.

"Could a badger have burrowed in?" Daisy asked. "Or a fox, perhaps?"

"Don't think so," said Isabel. "I only had a glimpse when the agent and Mrs. Gray showed me round the house, but I'm pretty sure the walls are bricked and the floor is stone."

"Besides," Vera pointed out, "if an animal could get in, it could get out by the same hole."

Willie, her face as green as Daisy's felt, shuddered. "Thank goodness we invited your Alec, Daisy. He'll know what to do."

"I suppose no one's going to feel like sitting down to roast beef," Isabel said regretfully. "Oh well, it can be eaten cold, and the gravy will reheat. I can rescue the potatoes, too, and the carrots, but the Yorkshire pudding'll be a dead loss. Tea, everyone?" She filled and plugged in an electric kettle.

"So, let's face it," said Vera, her eyes filled with horror, "it's a person. But who on earth—?"

Alec came in, opening the door as little as possible to squeeze through and closing it sharply behind him. In spite of these precautions, a nauseating whiff accompanied him. His clothes were probably permeated, Daisy thought in dismay.

"I've opened the side and front doors and all the downstairs windows to air the place out. I checked that all the doors upstairs are shut. I suggest you stay in here for the moment, all together. Are you on the telephone?"

"No, we're waiting for them to connect it," Isabel told him. "There's a phone box just round the corner in Station Road, outside the post office. Three minutes' walk."

"Where's the police station?"

"I think it's in the Old Town."

"Yes," Vera confirmed. "Wycombe End, practically next door to your hotel."

"I'll ring, then, unless I meet your beat bobby on the way. Not rats, as you'll have guessed."

"Would you like one of us to go and phone?" Willie asked reluctantly.

"No, thanks, I'd better. There's nothing to be done until the local force takes over. I haven't attempted to relock the cellar door. I assume none of you is likely to open it."

"No fear!" they chorussed.

"Darling, are you going to tell them you're from Scotland Yard?"

Alec grimaced. "I'd rather not. They won't like it. But on the other hand, they're pretty well bound to find out and then they'll be offended. Best policy is to reveal all up front." He looked round the table. "And that goes for you ladies, equally. They're going to be asking you a lot of questions. For pity's sake, don't hold anything back. I'm off."

"Turn right at the gate," Isabel directed him, "then left on Station Road and it's on your right."

"Thanks."

"Thank *you*! And thank goodness you're here."

With a wave, he departed, once again letting in the horrible stench of death.

"Damn and blast!" said Daisy. Only Vera appeared slightly shocked.

"Why?" asked Isabel, making tea. "We're the ones who are going to be interrogated. At least, I imagine it must have been there since before you even came to Beaconsfield."

"Probably. It's not a subject I've studied intensively, but considering the cool, dry conditions in the cellar, I should think it must have been there quite a while."

"Ugh!" Willie shivered.

"But Alec found the body, so he's a witness. He can't possibly keep it from his superintendent, and Mr. Crane will blame me, as usual."

"Blame you for what?" Vera demanded. "He has no reason to blame you for anything!"

"He doesn't need a reason. Whenever I'm within a hundred miles of a case Alec's involved with, he's convinced I'm interfering."

"That's not fair."

"Fairer than you might suppose," Willie put in a trifle maliciously.

"But never mind," Daisy said hurriedly, to forestall any questions from the other two on the fairness or otherwise of Superintendent Crane's strictures. "It's not likely Alec will have anything to do with the case, apart from giving a statement about finding the body. The local police almost always want to run things themselves, and he can't just butt in without being invited. Their first question's going to be: Who is it? They won't get very far without identification. Any ideas?"

"Except you, Daisy, we haven't had any visitors since we moved in." Isabel had been stowing away the unwanted meal in the larder. Now she came to sit with the others, pouring herself a cup of tea. "Not even the vicar, though Vera goes to church."

"He's a rector, not a vicar," Vera said. "He did drop by once, one evening when you two had gone to the cinema. I didn't mention it because I didn't think you'd be interested. And you were so busy telling me about the films . . . I gave him a cup of tea. He didn't go anywhere near the cellar door."

"Anyway, he hasn't gone missing," said Willie.

"No one else has called," Isabel continued. "I'm here most of the time."

"Do you lock all the doors when you go out?"

"Well, no, not if I just pop round to the shops. But why would anyone come into the house uninvited?"

"To snoop," Vera suggested. "Or burglars, of course."

"In daylight? When I might return any moment?"

"You ought to get a watchdog," said Daisy.

"Anyway, nothing's gone missing and no bag of swag found lying about the house."

"Not to mention," said Willie, "that to get into the cellar a burglar would have to have a key—"

"Not if he had a lock pick," Daisy pointed out, "or a picklock, or whatever it's called. Alec easily managed with a coat hanger."

"He'd have to have locked the door again behind him, barring his own escape route, then fallen down the stairs and broken his neck."

"I remember the stairs being steep," said Isabel, "but we don't know that that's what happened. Maybe he had a heart attack or something."

"He'd still have had to lock the door behind himself. It doesn't sound likely."

"Suppose he heard me coming home," Isabel mused, "he might have thought he could hide there until the coast was clear. Oh dear, you don't suppose he died of asphyxiation, do you? The cellar's supposed to be nearly airtight."

They were all silent for a moment. A slow death from asphyxiation was much more horrible than a quick one from a broken neck or a heart attack.

Daisy broke the silence. "Do you think a burglar would try

a locked cellar before ransacking the house? It doesn't sound likely to me. If he'd collected the loot first—"

"We would have noticed stuff missing," said Willie, "not that any of us has anything of real value."

"There's Vera's grandmother's pearls."

"But I wear them practically every evening," Vera pointed out. "They say pearls lose their lustre if they're not worn. And Isabel's silver."

"It's all present and correct. Besides polishing twice since we moved in, I've been checking it now and then to make sure none of it has wandered off with Mrs. Hedger. So far so good. She has her faults, but dishonesty doesn't seem to be one of them."

"And she hasn't got a key to the cellar?" Daisy checked.

"She said Mrs. Gray never gave her one. Her duties didn't include dusting or sweeping down there. Never set foot in it, she said, and she wouldn't have if asked, being TT."

"I never realised taking the pledge included refusing to dust bottles!" The others laughed, halfheartedly. Daisy went on, "It certainly sounds as if it must have happened before you moved in. How long was the house empty, do you know?"

Isabel frowned. "I'm not sure. Mrs. Hedger went on coming in to dust, so I couldn't tell by that. Just a few days, I think. As we bought it furnished, moving wasn't a major upheaval for either Mrs. Gray or us. Once Willie had everything sorted out with the solicitor, the house agent, Mr. Vaughn, told us we could move in anytime after the first."

"You dealt with the lawyer, Willie?"

"Most of the business. We all had to sign the papers, of course. But I learnt a bit of law in my last job, some of it relating to conveyancing."

"I hope he treated you professional to professional."

"He wasn't too bad."

"What about Vaughn? Was he properly respectful of your eminence?"

"I had very little to do with him," said Willie, tight-lipped. Daisy had a feeling she had wanted to say, "as little as possible."

Isabel said, "Not my cup of tea but he was all right. A bit too polite, if anything; smarmy, especially towards Mrs. Gray."

"Well, presumably she was paying him a commission," Daisy pointed out. "And he hoped to sell you a house. I expect it's a job that calls for a bit of smarm."

Isabel and Vera laughed, then Vera said guiltily, "We shouldn't be laughing. What if the police arrived and heard us?"

"I wish they'd hurry," said Willie.

Meanwhile, as Alec hurried up Orchard Road and crossed Station Road to the telephone box, he was in two minds as to whether to ring the Beaconsfield police, probably a sergeant and a couple of bobbies, or county HQ. Also, since sooner or later he'd have to reveal his credentials, should he do so at once, on the telephone, or wait until he spoke in person to a detective?

It wouldn't make much difference in the end. Some local coppers were happy to have help from Scotland Yard, official or unofficial. Some bitterly resented the implication that they couldn't cope on their own. Might as well tell them right away.

He'd better not disgruntle the local bobby by going over his head, he decided. He asked the operator for the Beaconsfield police station.

"Inspector Neal's on holiday, sir. Sergeant Harris is in charge. He'll be at home, this time of day."

"This is urgent. If he's on duty, or even if he's off, come to that, I don't care where he is."

"Yes, sir."

A woman answered the phone. Alec asked for Sergeant Harris.

"He's just sat down to his dinner," she said crossly.

"I'm afraid it's urgent, madam."

The next sound that came to Alec's ear was a repressed belch. His own stomach rumbled sympathetically and he thought with longing of roast beef and Yorkshire pudding.

"Now then," Harris grumbled, "what's so urgent a man can't be let to eat his dinner in peace?"

"A body, Sergeant."

The ensuing pause somehow conveyed disbelief rather than shock. After a few seconds the voice came laden with suspicion. "And who might this be as I'm speaking to?"

"My name is Fletcher, Alec Fletcher. As it happens, I'm a . . . an officer with the Metropolitan Police." No need to announce his rank nor to mention Scotland Yard. "Let me make it clear: I'm not on duty. My wife and I are visiting friends. It's pure chance that it was I who discovered the deceased."

"Pure chance, was it, sir? Just where exactly was you when pure chance led you to this dead man?"

"Woman." Alec was beginning to feel as if he'd swapped rôles with Daisy. She had more than once complained of scepticism on the part of authorities when she dutifully reported having happened upon a body.

"Ho, a woman, eh? And I s'pose you're going to tell me you've never seen her before in your life."

"I think it extremely unlikely that I've ever seen her before, far less made her acquaintance. But in the circumstances, it's impossible to make a positive statement either way. Perhaps you'd better come and see for yourself."

"I'll do that, sir, and you just stay put till I get there, if you please."

"That wouldn't be much use to you, Sergeant. I'm in a telephone box on Station Road."

Heavy breathing. "And where, sir," said Harris, "*if* so be you don't mind me asking, did you leave the corpse?"

"Where I found it. In the wine cellar at Cherry Tree House— no, just plain Cherry Trees. Orchard Road."

"Cherry Trees. New people. Three old maids, isn't it?"

"I don't think they'd appreciate that description. I'm going back to the house now. I'll see you there shortly."

Striding back up Orchard Road, he hoped the foul stink had

cleared from the house. It would inevitably return when Sergeant Harris opened the cellar door, but with all the room doors in the house closed, and side and front doors left open, the worst of its impact should be avoided. Alec was quite looking forward to the moment when the stench hit the nostrils of the obnoxious sergeant.

Still, as Alec would have been quick to point out to Daisy, the man was just doing his job. And he'd been called out in the middle of his Sunday dinner, not a bad excuse for grumpiness.

A whiff of rotting flesh reached Alec when he was halfway up the garden path. Emanating from the open front door, it was unpleasant but bearable. No doubt it was worse in the house still. He didn't want to ask the women to open the kitchen door.

He stopped and studied the house. The kitchen was on the northwest corner. He walked over to the small, wide-open window framed by blue gingham curtains.

The odour coming from it was mostly roast beef. His stomach rumbled again.

Voices cut off as he tapped on the glass. He heard a clink of china, as if someone had set down a cup on a saucer with a shaky hand.

"Hello?"

"Alec?" Daisy came to the window and peered out, holding back the curtain. "You gave us a shock! Aren't you coming in?"

"I'll wait in front for Sergeant Harris and bring him round to the side door. You ladies can stay put in the kitchen with the door closed, for the present."

"Wouldn't it be better if we all left now, darling? Presumably the sergeant will open the cellar door again, and that foul smell will return to full strength."

"He's going to want to talk to you."

"Of course. Which will mean opening the kitchen door to the stink, unless we decamp to the Saracen. He can talk to us there. Here, we'd be gagging and choking."

"It's a point. You'd better hurry, he should be here any minute. Take the car and go round by Station Road, and with a bit of luck you'll miss him. He won't be happy, but I'll make your excuses."

"Unless he has the most appalling case of catarrh, he'll be as happy to get out of here as we will." She turned away. "Come along, girls, we're hopping it."

FIVE

"*Not the* bar, this time," said Willie as Daisy parked the Austin Twelve in the street outside the Saracen's Head.

"No," Daisy agreed. She sniffed. "For one thing, I think we still smell a bit—gamey's the word. I hope there's no one in the ladies' parlour."

"They'd soon leave," Isabel said dryly, getting out of the back.

"I wish we'd had time to wash and change," Vera moaned.

"I could go up to my room and change, but it doesn't seem fair as you can't. You could all wash, though."

"Do let's!" Willie chimed in as they entered the lobby. "I'd really like a bath but even just scrubbing my face and hands would help. We'll have to be quick, though. Alec and the local police may turn up any moment with a million questions."

"Not Alec." Daisy led the way upstairs. "If they want him on the case, they have to go through a big palaver with the Yard. And the locals won't be along for a while, I expect. The sergeant will have to report to his superiors right away. They'll probably send out an inspector from High Wycombe, or even Aylesbury." Opening the door of her room and ushering the others in, she added, "Listen, I'll have to ring for hot water. Don't for pity's sake say anything about the body in the maid's hearing."

Sally arrived slightly out of breath, with her cap on crooked and no apron. "I've got the afternoon off," she said, and her nose twitched. "I was just leaving when I saw you'd rung, Mrs. Fletcher, so I came, 'cause her that's on duty is answering another bell."

Daisy smiled at her. "I don't want to keep you from your time off. Could you have Edward bring up plenty of hot water?"

"Right away, madam." Peering past Daisy, she added, "Shall I fetch some extra towels and face flannels first?"

"Please do."

"Thank you, Sally," called Isabel.

"Hello, Miss Sutcliffe. Anything else you need?" Sally was obviously bursting with curiosity. She would hear the story sooner or later, doubtless in more detail than most people because of her aunt charring at Cherry Trees, but she'd have to wait.

"That's all just now, thank you." Daisy closed the door as the maid dashed off. "Phew, I think she smelled a rat!"

"I wish it had been a rat!" Vera exclaimed.

They all stood for a moment looking at each other with remembered horror.

Willie asked, "D'you mind if I open the window, Daisy?"

"Please do. A bit of fresh air might help. Won't you all sit down? Two chairs and two on the bed."

"Better not," said Isabel. "The smell might transfer from our clothes to the bedspread and upholstery."

"Oh dear, you're right!"

"That chair's caned, though."

"You'd better sit there, Daisy." Willie lowered the window and perched on the windowsill. "Never mind playing hostess, you're still convalescent. Am I right in thinking they won't let us go back to the house today? Even if we want to? Which I, for one, don't!"

"Nor do I." Vera leaned against the bedpost. "I just hope all our clothes aren't impregnated."

"Alec said the upstairs doors were closed. I'm afraid the

police may open them." Daisy frowned. "I'm not sure whether they'd have to get a search warrant, in the circumstances."

"Search our rooms?" Isabel was outraged. "Why would they do that?"

"I'm not saying they will, just that they may. Depending."

"On what?" Willie asked.

"Well, I suppose, on when the victim died. Before or after you moved in."

In the silence that followed Daisy's statement, Sally tapped on the door and came in with towels and flannels.

"The hot water'll be a couple of minutes." She piled her load on the cane-bottomed chair beside the folding screen that hid the marble washstand. "Will you be all right if I go now? I don't want to leave you ladies in the lurch."

Daisy assured her they'd manage without her and offered her a tip.

She refused it. "I wouldn't've done it for anybody else, Mrs. Fletcher, and that's a fact. I'll be off now." She whisked out.

"You've got her eating out of your hand," Isabel commented with a touch of envy. "I wish her aunt were as tractable."

"She's a nice girl, and ambitious. She's saving to take a typing course in London. I'll give her a good tip when Alec and I leave, to help her on her way. Speaking of which, hadn't you better book rooms for tonight? You don't want to go back to the house, even if the police would let you."

Vera looked anxious. "The Saracen is too expensive for me."

"We'll see if we can share a room with two beds and a truckle," Isabel suggested. "Though if one of us goes down to the reception desk smelling like this, I wouldn't blame them for refusing us!"

"Daisy has clean clothes she can change into," Willie reminded them. "Daisy, would you mind—?"

"Of course not. Here's our hot water." She opened the door to admit the Boots, struggling with several steaming water-cans. "Thanks, Edward."

He disappeared behind the screen and the metal cans clinked on the marble. Unlike Sally, he didn't appear to notice any untoward effluvium. Also unlike the maid, he had no qualms about accepting a generous tip. He went off whistling.

"If I'm to put on clean clothes," said Daisy, "I think I'll have a bath. It didn't seem fair before, but as I'm to tackle the landlord . . ."

"Do," said Isabel. "All the more hot water for us."

Half an hour later, much refreshed, Daisy went down to the foyer. The proprietor himself came in response to the bell. Mr. Whitford was short, round, rubicund, and smiling, like an idealised innkeeper straight out of Dickens. He continued to beam as he affirmed that he had a vacant room that would suit Daisy's friends down to the ground with the addition of a remarkably comfortable folding cot that the Boots would fetch down from the attic.

"And the names of your friends, madam?" he asked, pencil poised over the register.

"Miss Wilhelmina Chandler. Miss Isabel Sutcliffe. Miss Vera Leighton."

He looked up, eyebrows raised. "Miss Leighton? That'd be the new teacher?"

"Yes, that's right."

"Summat wrong at the house?"

The truth and nothing but the truth, but not by any means the whole truth: "There's a nasty smell."

"Drains. That's an old house, that is. The last people were always having trouble with the drains. My cousin, he's a plumber and he knows them drains inside and out, back'ard and for'ard. Here, let me write down his name for the ladies. Not but what May—May Hedger—will tell 'em he's the one they want."

"Thank you, I'll give it to them, but they already have someone . . . looking into the matter. . . ."

"Never mind, eh! They'll end up wanting his help, I don't doubt. Now, here's the key to the room, two of 'em's all I've got."

"I'm sure they'll manage."

"And I'll see the cot's set up within the hour."

"Thank you very much, Mr. Whitford."

The landlord leaned across the counter and lowered his voice confidentially. "Truth is, I wouldn't do it for just anyone, but my daughter's boy as wasn't any too keen on learning his letters, he *likes* going to school since Miss Leighton's come." He nodded and winked.

Not at all sure what his manner was intended to convey, Daisy smiled in response and returned upstairs.

Opening the bedroom door, she took a shallow breath as she stepped in, then sniffed. "It's not half as bad as it was," she announced.

"I can still smell it," Vera said unhappily. "I wish I had a change of clothes."

"I could lend you and Willie frocks, though you'd flounder in them. You're both much slimmer than I am and Willie's shorter."

"It wouldn't be fair. Izzy's too tall to borrow from you."

"I expect I can persuade Alec to go and pick up some clothes for you when he gets here."

"We haven't even got our handbags," Willie pointed out, "and I have to have my briefcase for work tomorrow."

"Alec will sort things out. In the meantime, here's a couple of keys to your own room. They're setting up a cot, which the landlord swears is remarkably comfortable."

Isabel looked sceptical. "Let's hope we won't have to suffer for too long. Daisy, how long will they keep us out?"

"I really don't know, but I doubt if it will be longer than you'll want to stay away."

"I wonder whether Mrs. Hedger will be willing to clean the cellar? We may have to hire—I don't know what sort of person or company." Isabel's domestic mind had already returned to the practicalities of their situation.

Vera shuddered.

"You'll find someone, Iz," said Willie. "In the meantime, as we're now officially residents, I'm off to take a bath, even if I have to put the same clothes on again afterwards."

"Will there be time for all of us to have a bath before the police arrive?" Vera asked.

"If not, they'll just have to wait. Come on. We'll see you in a bit, Daisy."

Daisy decided to put her feet up for a few minutes while she pondered the body in the basement. She was certain her three friends, the old and the new, were in no way responsible for the corpse in their cellar. Nonetheless, they were going to find themselves drawn into the police investigation, always an ordeal. Daisy would have to stay in Beaconsfield and do what she could to give them the benefit of her experience.

She rearranged the pillows, kicked off her shoes, leaned back, and promptly fell asleep.

Harris was not happy. So much was evident as soon as the bulky sergeant stepped through the garden gate, wheeling his bicycle, his podgy face under the helmet creased in a scowl.

Alec wasn't very happy, either. He had been pacing up and down the path for over thirty minutes. He didn't see how even an overweight police officer could take half an hour to bicycle three quarters of a mile downhill.

As Alec strode towards Harris, the sergeant turned his back and wheeled the bike over to a tree, against which he leaned it, his every motion slow and deliberate.

Refusing to let himself be baited, if that was the man's game, Alec walked on to the gate. He looked each way along the street before he closed it and turned back to find the sergeant staring at him suspiciously.

"Mr. Fletcher?"

"Yes. You're Harris, I take it."

"What was you looking for just now?"

"Just to make sure no one followed you here. An elementary precaution."

41

Harris looked puzzled, as well he might. Some of the belligerence had left his voice when he asked, "Now what's all this about finding a corpse?"

"Follow me." Alec spoke with authority. The man was already resentful so any attempt to conciliate him was pointless. At least he didn't argue.

Alec led him round to the open side door. Inside, the smell had mostly dissipated, though an unpleasant trace lingered. If Harris noticed it, he did not comment as the crunch of boots on gravel changed to a clatter on floor tiles.

Alec gestured towards the cellar door. "The body's in here. Would you like to see it first, or shall I explain the circumstances that led to my finding it?"

"Circumstances be blowed! I want to see whether there really is a body."

"All right." Alec held his handkerchief to his nose as he reached for the door handle.

Harris gave him a scornful look. "I thought you Met people were tough."

The door swung open. Before he had even cast a glance downwards, the sergeant gagged, his ruddy complexion taking on a ghastly grey-green tint. At top speed he lumbered to the open side door and disappeared.

Having slammed the cellar door shut, Alec went after him at a slightly more leisured pace. Sounds of retching came from the right, so he turned to the left and moved a few feet away to stand with his back to the unhappy sergeant.

"I would offer to fetch you a glass of water, Sergeant, but I don't intend to go back into the house for a while. Are you ready to hear how it came about that I—"

"Save it for Inspector Underwood," Harris snarled. He smirked as Alec swung round. "He's expecting my call."

"I wondered whether you'd rung in. Underwood, is it? High Wycombe or Aylesbury?"

"High Wycombe. He'll be here in no time."

"Where are you going to telephone from?"

Harris took a step towards the house, shuddered, then hawked and spat. "Not in there."

"They aren't connected yet, as it happens. What are you going to tell Underwood?"

"Why, that it's no false alarm, there really is a body."

"You haven't actually seen it, though."

"How do you know? Anyway, there's no need to tell the inspector. I smelled the reek all right. That's enough for me."

"I'll stay and guard the house while you go and phone."

"No need for that. Just lock the place up before you go. Wait, where are you going? Don't leave Beaconsfield till the inspector's seen you."

"If I were to go, I'd join my wife and the ladies at the Saracen's Head. Unfortunately, they left in rather a hurry and didn't hand over any keys. I can't lock up, besides which the house needs airing."

"Well, don't go mucking about inside."

"If I had any desire to do so, I had half an hour on my own here before you turned up, Sergeant. I'll be here when you return."

"Have it your own way." Sulky-faced, Harris trudged past Alec and round the corner of the house.

Alec wished he could overhear Harris's report. He wondered whether Underwood would press the man about the appearance of the body. Admittedly, he doubted that he himself would be able to give a good description. The stench had been so overpowering, it befogged his memory, obscuring the scene in spite of his deliberate attempt to fix it in his mind.

No blowflies. That was a mercy. But it was odd. The cellar was not absolutely airtight, and carrion flies were exceptionally good at seeking out the smell of death. Although they couldn't find a way in, he'd have expected them to cluster at the keyhole.

He tried to recall the moments before he had swung the keyhole cover aside and inserted his pick. Had he been aware of a faint odour, or was it his imagination, in hindsight?

No, there had been something, but his olfactory memory insisted it had been the smell of disinfectant, not decay. One of

Daisy's friends, most likely Isabel Sutcliffe, must be keen on hygiene—or doing her utmost to diguise the noxious emanations from the cellar.

Alec wanted to know a good deal more about the background of Miss Sutcliffe; of her companions, as well, since Isabel might have tried to get rid of the smell without knowing its source.

However, it was none of his business, he reminded himself. All he had to do was hang about until the obnoxious sergeant returned, and later give a statement to the inspector from High Wycombe.

His pondering had come full circle. What exactly had he seen on the floor below the broken rail?

A woman, lying on her back, her arms flung out, her head at that angle that speaks unmistakably of death, the obscene remains of scarlet lipstick on the devastated mouth. The condition of the body was such that he couldn't begin to guess her age. Though her dark brown hair had shown no grey, these days that meant little. Bobbed hair, or she had put it up in a knot behind her head.

Brown tweed costume; flesh-coloured stockings; one well-polished brown leather shoe, not flat but low-heeled, as if the wearer expected to do a certain amount of walking; he hadn't noticed a second shoe. Pearls, real or imitation closer examination would tell. Gloves? He thought not. He had a vague impression that a hat, the usual cloche-style, had lain on the floor some distance from her head.

She had fallen backwards, or twisted as she fell. As for the space she lay in, it was about the same size as the kitchen above it. Three walls of mortared brick were lined with empty wooden wine racks. The floor appeared to be the native chalk, levelled and compacted. He hadn't looked at the ceiling.

That was all Alec remembered. He was tempted to go and take another look, but repulsion overcame temptation without much of a struggle. It was not his affair.

Except as a witness, he was reminded, as an elderly constable joined him, saying, "I'm the beat officer, sir. Sergeant Harris told me to keep an eye on you."

SIX

The click of the door latch woke Daisy. She blinked at Alec.

"Have a good nap?"

"Darling, I wasn't asleep!"

"Of course not, if you say so. Let me amend that: Are you feeling better for the rest?"

"Much. I didn't dream . . . or rather have a nightmare?"

He laughed at her, then said seriously, "I'm afraid not."

"I take it the local bobby turned up? What did he have to say?"

"He was in a great hurry to turn things over to his superiors. I didn't wait for their arrival. Where are your friends?"

"They've taken a room here and went to do a more thorough job of washing than they could as nonresidents. Darling, they desperately need clean clothes. I don't suppose you could fetch something for them?"

"Not, at least, until Inspector Underwood gives the say-so. In any case, they won't want me rooting through their drawers."

"I wouldn't be so sure, especially if the alternative is letting the locals paw through their undies. Or going into the house before it's been fumigated. Goodness, is that the time? They're probably downstairs by now. Will you go and knock on their door while I splash my face and powder my nose?"

Daisy had to go to the bathroom to wash the sleep from her eyes, as every last driblet of water in the cans had been used. When she returned to their room, Alec was back, having found the others' room empty, gone downstairs, and found out they were in the parlour.

"Whither I dared not venture."

"There's a residents' lounge, too. I'll get them to move so that we can have a confab."

He groaned. "Do I want a confab?"

"Of course. I'm sure you've got dozens of questions you want to ask."

"That's as may be. Allow me to remind you, it's not my case."

"Yet," said Daisy. "Unless you altogether avoid Willie and Company, you won't be able to avoid discussing it."

"We'd better go back to town as soon as I've given my statement to Inspector Underwood. I'm due back to work tomorrow, remember."

"Oh, blast!" Daisy coughed experimentally. "I think I'd better stay on for a few days to make sure I'm completely recovered."

"The air in Hampstead is perfectly good now."

"Perhaps I should go up with you and see what my doctor advises."

"Don't bother. He's completely under your thumb. If you asked him to advise you to go to the Riviera, he'd comply without hesitation."

Daisy laughed. "Luckily I don't want to go to the Riviera. I might go up with you tomorrow just to see the babies, but I do want to be here to support Willie. You must admit I have plenty of experience of surviving police interrogation."

"Which is nothing to boast of! All you can do is advise them to tell the truth—"

"'The whole truth, and nothing but the truth.' I wonder how

46

many times I've heard that?" She kept her reservations on the subject to herself. "Come on, let's go down. It's teatime and I'm ravenous."

"I wonder how many times I've heard that?"

Downstairs, they went to the residents' lounge. Alec flipped on the electric lights, as daylight was fast fading. Overstuffed horsehair chairs and a small sofa, covered in once-maroon rep, formed four or five groups round low beechwood tables. On each were several coasters advertising drinks. A mauve hearthrug with a pattern of orange triangles clashed horribly. Elsewhere, the polished floorboards showed the scratches and scuffs of centuries that no amount of polishing could hide. Inevitably, fox-hunting prints adorned the walls.

Daisy continued through the connecting door to the ladies' parlour. Here flowered cretonne reigned, the prints were of old roses, and the floor boasted an inadequate square of emerald green carpet.

Her friends were the only occupants.

"Daisy, where have you been?" Willie greeted her, jumping up.

"Sorry, I fell asleep. Alec's back. He can't come in here. Let's have tea in the residents' lounge."

"I didn't think I'd ever be able to face food again," said Vera, "but I admit I'm hungry, and a cup of tea would be bliss."

"We must keep our strength up," Isabel said bracingly. "When the police turn up to pepper us with a lot of questions, we'll be glad of it. Pity we didn't eat the roast beef first and look for a bottle of liqueur afterwards."

Daisy was turning back towards the other room when Willie stopped her with a hand on her arm. "We wondered if it's all right to talk to Alec about what happened. To ask him what he saw, I mean; how long the . . . body has been there. That sort of thing."

"Without any gory details," Vera clarified.

"After all, no one's told us not to talk about it."

"The local bobby may have asked Alec to keep quiet. He'll

make up his own mind, though. Ask away. He can but refuse to answer." She went through, relieved to find Alec still alone. He stood leaning against the mantelpiece. "Tea, darling! Everyone's famished."

"I've already rung the bell."

As they settled by the fire, a middle-aged waitress came in. Alec ordered tea for five, with plenty of sandwiches.

The waitress left. Alec went over to the door and made sure it was closed properly. "Is anyone in there?" he asked, pointing to the ladies' parlour. They all shook their heads as he came back to sit down. "We can talk now. But if someone comes in—including servants—we change the subject."

"All right," said Willie. "First, what did you actually see in the cellar? None of us stopped to look. A man or a woman?"

"A woman. Dark hair. That's about all I can tell you."

"Can, or will?"

Alec smiled. "A bit of each."

"Did the local police tell you not to blow the gaff?" Daisy asked.

"Not in so many words, but the only officer I saw was the local sergeant, Harris. He was out of his depth. I didn't wait for the detectives to turn up. I'm treading on thin ice here—"

"And you don't want to fall in up to your neck, but at least you're not quite mixing your metaphors!"

"Great Scott, Daisy, I'm trying to explain my position here to your friends."

"I've already told them, darling." She gave him a sweet smile in exchange for his exasperated look. "What was Sergeant Harris like?"

"Well, let's just say I interrupted him in the middle of his Sunday roast and things went downhill from there."

"Oh dear!"

"Sergeant Harris?" said Isabel. "That's the man who came round a couple of days after we moved in, to introduce himself. He made it very clear he didn't approve of three unrelated single women living together. I doubt if he has a right side to get on."

"If he does, I certainly didn't get on it!"

"He knows who you are?"

"I told him I'm an officer of the Metropolitan Police. I didn't mention the Yard or being a detective, nor my rank. I'll have to tell the inspector, though."

"When are you going to notify the super?" Daisy sighed. "I suppose you have to."

"Can you imagine the explosion if I didn't and he found out? Which he'd be bound to. I won't disturb him on a Sunday evening, but I'll send a wire from here before I go in to work tomorrow, to give him time to simmer down a bit, with any luck, before I see him."

"They'll let us go to work, won't they?" Vera asked anxiously.

"I can't think of any reason why they wouldn't. They might turn up with more questions."

Vera bit her lip. "I'll get the sack, for sure."

"No, why should you?" Willie cried. "You haven't done anything wrong."

"The townspeople won't want their children taught by someone who's been mixed up in a murder investigation. I can't blame them."

"Mr. Cartwright will stick up for you. The headmaster's words must carry a lot of weight."

Looking even unhappier, Vera said, "Yes, but . . . No. I don't know."

"For pity's sake, which?"

"Leave her alone, Willie," Isabel snapped. "She's said she doesn't know. What about *your* job?"

"I'm not worried about losing it. Alec, I suppose it really is a case of murder?"

"She didn't lock the door herself."

"No. And there's no hope of keeping it quiet?" Willie answered her own question: "No, of course not. Even if the press somehow missed it, we couldn't keep it from Mrs. Hedger and she'd have it all over town in no time."

"To do her justice," said Isabel, "she has her faults, but she's not a gossip."

"Until now, we haven't given her anything juicy to gossip about," Willie pointed out.

On this dispiriting note, their tea arrived. For some time no one spoke of the dire discovery at Cherry Trees. When the waitress came to remove the scant debris, Daisy noticed that everyone looked more cheerful. She felt more cheerful herself.

She knew, though, that Alec, despite his announced detachment from the investigation, wouldn't be able to resist returning to the subject that was on all their minds.

Isabel got in first. "I've been trying and trying to think what we can do about saving your job, Vera. No brilliant ideas so far, I'm afraid."

"We'll come up with something," Willie said confidently, "if the issue ever materialises. As long as the children like you and behave for you, I doubt the board, the parents, or the head will want to lose you. Mr. Fletcher, how long is it likely to be before the police let us back into the house? I've got important papers that I need at work tomorrow."

"I really can't say. There are too many variables. You won't want to move back in until it's been thoroughly cleansed and disinfected, of course. Would your Mrs. Hedger tackle a nasty job like that?"

"I don't know," said Isabel. "She might if we paid enough. If not, I just hope I'll be able to find some odd-job man glad to get any work. In the meantime, what am I supposed to do about things like the milk delivery? The post?"

"Sorry, I've never had to deal with that side of things. The inspector might be persuaded to bring out the papers you need, Miss Chandler, after they've been examined."

"The papers are highly confidential."

"Then you'd have to insist that only he see them. Men rarely reach the rank of detective inspector if they're incapable of keeping information confidential."

"All very well, but my boss . . . I'd have to get his permission. Mr. Davis, of Spencer, Mott, and Davis."

"Have it out with DI Underwood."

"I need the children's work papers that I took home to correct," said Vera. "Those are not confidential, of course."

"Will they really rummage through all our stuff?" Isabel asked in dismay.

"Sorry, I would, in the circumstances. I can't speak for the local chap. Now you've had time to think, can you still not recall any visitors since you moved in?"

Isabel frowned. "Not what I'd describe as a visitor. The house agent dropped in one morning. He wanted to check that everything was all right."

"Did you ask whether he had a key to the cellar?"

"Yes, as a matter of fact. He said Mrs. Gray never let him have any keys. She insisted she should always be present when he showed the house."

"What about the solicitors?"

Willie answered: "When we signed the papers, her solicitor handed over a set of keys, all he had. Of course, we weren't to use them before the first. Come to think of it, he should have got Mrs. Gray's set from her when she left, and turned them over. Which he didn't."

"Good point."

"She may have gone off with them by accident."

"Yes, or he may have forgotten to give them to you. I— Underwood must ask him. What's his name?"

"Darling, it's not your case," Daisy reminded him. "No solicitors."

"Right, love. Miss Sutcliffe, are you certain that Vaughn didn't have any keys?"

"I only know what he told me."

"If Vaughn had had them," said Willie, "I wouldn't count on

him to give them up. Assuming his claim is true, I don't blame Mrs. Gray for not trusting him."

"Why?"

But Willie would say no more.

Alec turned back to Isabel. "Vaughn didn't offer to write to her to ask about the cellar key, or keys in general? I assume you haven't got her present address."

"No, and nor did he. He asked me if I had it. In fact, I thought at the time that was the only reason he came. He was disappointed when I said I didn't, and he left pretty quickly after."

"Presumably her solicitor has an address for her."

"Alec!" Daisy said warningly.

He gave her a rueful grin. "Solicitors are out of bounds. I got a bit carried away. Forgive me, ladies."

"I don't mind," said Isabel. "Is there anything else you'd like to know?"

"I'd better not ask any more questions. I'm permitted to wonder aloud, though, am I not, Daisy?"

"It's a free country!"

"All right. I'm wondering, now that I've told you the deceased is a dark-haired woman, whether you have any ideas about who she might be or how she ended up in your cellar."

"Mrs. Gray has dark hair," Isabel told him uneasily. "Short. Crimped."

"Obviously," said Willie, "the most probable person to be involved is Mrs. Gray, whether as victim or as . . . the one responsible for the death. Don't you agree, Mr. Fletcher?"

"I'll go so far as to say that I expect the detective inspector to begin his investigation by checking whether the body is in fact Mrs. Gray."

"So if he doesn't," Isabel suggested, "we'll know he's not much cop."

As she spoke, the door opened. The Boots appeared. "'Tective Inspector Underwood. 'E wansta see Mr. Fletcher."

A tall, thin man in a Sunday black suit and sober tie stood behind the boy, peering over his shoulder. The inspector had the sort of face that could be anywhere from thirty to fifty years old. His glance of dismay swept over the ladies, pausing on Isabel. Had he heard and misinterpreted her last few words? As his gaze settled on Alec, Daisy read in his expression a compound of mistrust, defiance, and uncertainty.

SEVEN

The landlord had lent DI Underwood his snug. The room where Mr. Whitford was wont to entertain friends and favoured patrons was small and cosy, with sagging armchairs long ago faded to an indeterminate brown. The smell of tobacco was all-pervasive, the low ceiling yellowish from centuries of fumes.

Alec sat down by the fire without waiting to be invited. He was in no position to take control of the coming interview, but he was not about to let the inspector imagine that he could be dominated. He took out his pipe and tobacco pouch.

Underwood stood for a moment looking down at him, his face gloomy. Then, sighing, he dropped into the chair opposite, long limbs asprawl.

"Harris says you're from the Met."

Alec took his warrant card from his inside breast pocket and handed it over. "Not so much *from* as *of*. I'm not here on business."

Studying the card, the inspector sighed again. "Detective Chief Inspector, Scotland Yard." He took down the particulars in his notebook, then looked up. "Are you saying you didn't come down about this business, sir? You weren't hot on the trail of a connection to some metropolitan crime, so to speak?"

"Great Scott, no. Whatever gave you that notion?"

"Sergeant Harris as good as told me so." Underwood returned the warrant card and sat back.

"I can't be held responsible for whatever nonsense comes out of Harris's mouth."

"Frankly, sir, there are those who doubt whether Harris is always responsible for what comes out of his mouth. Why he was ever promoted—well, never mind. This sort of thing is above his head. A nasty affair."

"Very nasty."

"Would you mind telling me how you come into the picture, sir?"

Alec was faced with the conundrum Daisy always complained about when he asked her for a coherent narrative: Where to start? Keep it short, he decided.

"I happened to be the person who opened the cellar door and discovered the body."

"Harris got that bit right, then. What exactly is your connection with the family? The household, I should say. This all-female household."

"They are not my harem, Inspector," Alec said dryly, "if that's what you're wondering."

"The thought never crossed my mind, sir!"

"Glad to hear it. My wife came down to Beaconsfield to convalesce. She was at school with Miss Chandler—I take it Harris managed to give you all the names correctly? I spelled them out for him."

"Er, no." Underwood sighed. "He said a mob of spinsters was known to reside in the house but they'd cleared out before he arrived. I'm sorry your wife was subject to such a terrible experience, sir, 'specially if she's been ill. Harris didn't mention her, and wasn't able to give me any of the names except yours."

"Never mind," said Alec, tolerant of the failings of subordinates for whose mistakes he was not responsible. "The sergeant was in pretty poor shape after the shock."

The inspector's snort made a change from his sighs. "Mrs.

Fletcher." The name went into his notebook. "Miss Chandler, was it, sir?"

"Miss Wilhelmina Chandler. Miss Vera Leighton. Miss Isabel Sutcliffe."

"Thank you, sir. Miss Chandler was at school with Mrs. Fletcher. They're not elderly spinsters, then. Some of these 'surplus women' like they talk about in the papers, they'd be?"

"They wouldn't appreciate the epithet, but yes, I believe that's a fair enough description."

"Newcomers to the district, Harris said."

"As to that, I know only what my wife has told me. You won't want thirdhand information. You'll have to ask them."

"Fair enough. Had you ever met any of them before?"

"Never."

"Not even Mrs. Fletcher's schoolfellow? At your wedding, for instance?"

"We had a quiet wedding, just family. Miss Chandler may have been invited to the reception, I don't know. If so, I'm pretty sure she didn't attend. She lived up north, after all, and not in affluent circumstances, and wasn't especially close to Daisy. It's possible she came and I somehow missed meeting her."

"You'll have a good memory for names and faces, no doubt, in our business."

"I do. However, I can't say my mind was running on those lines at the time. Are you a married man, Inspector?"

"Widower. Lost my wife in the flu."

"So did I. My first wife."

After a silent moment of mutual commiseration, an unexpected grin lit Underwood's dour face. "I'll be blamed if I can remember a thing about our wedding breakfast. Right, Mrs. Fletcher's convalescing in Beaconsfield, and she calls on her friend, very natural, even if they weren't close. And you, sir?"

"I came down to see Daisy and to drive her back to town after a pleasant weekend in the country."

"No such luck, eh? Your good lady was eager to introduce you to her friends, I expect."

"Rather the reverse."

"Oh? Why was that?"

Alec was half amused, half irritated to have his own techniques used against him. "Look," he said, "I'll tell you what happened and what I observed. For opinions, wishes, hopes, reasons, you must apply to those concerned. The ladies at Cherry Trees invited my wife and me to Sunday lunch. We reached the house some time between half past twelve and one o'clock."

"You can't be more precise?"

"No. Miss Sutcliffe was busy in the kitchen. They keep no cook. Miss Chandler and Miss Leighton invited us into the sitting room. We were offered sherry. One of them—Miss Chandler, I think but couldn't swear to—apologised for its mediocre quality. One or the other mentioned that the previous owners were reputed to have owned an excellent wine cellar. The ladies had speculated that when it was cleared out, a bottle of something good might have been overlooked. However, the door was locked and they had not been provided with a key."

"They could have sent for a locksmith."

"I daresay they would have in due time, when they'd settled in. But that's mere speculation. I offered to take a look and see if I might be able to help. It's a simple, old-fashioned lock, as no doubt you noticed."

"Easy to pick."

"For anyone with the slightest knowledge and skill, and a suitable instrument. Miss Chandler produced a wire coat hanger. The ladies, including my wife, accompanied me to the door to watch—"

"Including Miss—the cook, Miss Sutcliffe is it?"

"She was there when I opened it. She saw us pass the kitchen, I suppose, and followed to see what was up. Picking the lock took only a few moments. As soon as I pushed the door open, all four ladies fled to the kitchen and closed the door."

"And who can blame them!" DI Underwood said feelingly. "I'd've liked to turn tail myself. How would you account for none of them noticing the stink before? The cellar isn't completely airtight. You didn't get a whiff as you approached?"

"Nothing suggestive of decay, but . . ." He flared his nostrils, remembering. "Carbolic!"

"I knew it! They did smell it and tried to conceal it."

"Hold on. It's more likely, wouldn't you say, that they smelled something vaguely unpleasant and tried to eliminate it with disinfectant."

"Speculation, sir." Underwood's face was bland. "We better get this straight, sir, so we understand each other. I hope you won't take it amiss. You're a superior officer, I'm not questioning that, but this is my patch. Unless I decide I can't cope, and my super agrees, this case is my pigeon. I won't say you couldn't be useful to me. But when all's said and done, you're a witness. Even was I to call for the Yard to help, chances are it wouldn't be you they sent."

"For witness, read suspect. You're quite right, Inspector," Alec acknowledged ruefully.

"At least at this stage of the game. I hope you won't hold it against me, sir. Seems to me, though, for the present we'd better stick to the facts, as you said."

"Meaning a description of what I saw when I opened the cellar door. All right, here goes. For a start, you must realise that all I had to see by was a small torch. If there's electric lighting down there, I didn't care to look about for the switch."

"I don't blame you. Proper pongy that was. I'd go so far as to say the most revolting pong I've ever smelt."

"Far be it from me to contradict you."

"Having warning, we brought an arc light. As it happens, there is an electric bulb in the cellar, but the switch is awkwardly placed, an arm's length from the door. A quick look with a torch—You wouldn't have taken in much beyond a very dead woman, I suppose."

"A bit more. I'm a copper after all, even if beyond my bailiwick, and a detective to boot. I noted the broken rail on the left, of course. The woman was lying on her back, just below it. She appeared to be well dressed, in tweeds, a silk blouse, and pearls, whether real or imitation I couldn't tell from above."

"But you could tell her blouse was silk?"

"The material had a sheen. Could have been artificial silk, to be sure, but the rest suggested otherwise. She was wearing one shoe, well-polished, again judging from the sheen."

"Not much dust down there."

"No. The cellar is supposedly nearly airtight. I didn't see the second shoe."

"It was found on the floor, directly below the landing."

"Hmm. It must have come off as she fell."

"Or as she hit the floor."

"Could be."

"It's hard to see what could have made her lose her balance, don't you think?"

"You're asking me to speculate, Inspector?"

"No!" Underwood paused, with a sheepish look. "Well, yes, I suppose I am. On second thoughts, it would be a bit silly not to take the opportunity to pick your brains. You've got much more experience in this sort of thing than I do."

"I've never come across anything quite like this before. I take it you're convinced the death is a homicide?"

"Oh yes. It seemed obvious at first, because of the door being locked, then I realised she might for some reason have locked it behind her and put the key in her pocket, then stepped back from the door and took dizzy as she started down those steep, narrow stairs. She'd likely have fallen on her face, though. Besides, the doctor checked her pockets and there's no keys at all."

"You're quicker than I was. I didn't think of the pocket possibility until just now, when I was describing her clothes to you. It's a bit odd that she was on her back, whichever direction she was going in."

"My guess is, when she lost her balance she twisted to make a grab for the rail attached to the wall, and missed it."

"I missed it, too," Alec said ruefully. "Missed seeing it, that is. My attention was all in the opposite direction and in trying not to breathe. Was the doctor able to say how long ago she died?"

Underwood grimaced. "Very vague, given the unusual conditions: cool, dry, no flies. At a guess, two to four weeks. The local sergeant says the ladies moved in about a fortnight ago."

"At the beginning of October."

"Just so. Lots of coming and going and general confusion that someone took advantage of. The victim was, you might say, a moving target."

"Ouch!"

"Sorry, sir. Bad pun."

"An excellent pun."

Underwood looked gratified. "I have a go at *The Observer* crossword every week. Puns are the least of Torquemada's tricks. But wouldn't you agree, about the coming and going?"

"The change of residents would account for the long delay before the finding of the corpse, but whether that was planned or was a lucky happenstance for the killer remains to be seen. No reports of local people missing?"

"None. The first thing we have to do, of course, is identify the victim." He hesitated. "According to Sergeant Harris, rumour had it that the previous owner of Cherry Trees, Mrs. Gray, was going abroad. I can't help wondering whether she ever arrived."

"Supposing it's her body, then you'll know she didn't. I don't know how long she lived here, but you should be able to find someone who'd recognise her."

"Once she's been cleaned up a bit, maybe. She's a mess, though. I don't like to ask a woman to do it. I suppose the ladies who bought the house would have met her?"

"You'll have to ask them," Alec said firmly.

"All right." Underwood sounded quite cheerful. "Just finding out where the boundaries are. A couple more questions for you, sir. You couldn't see the second shoe under the landing. Fair enough. Was there anything else down there that you noticed?"

Alec frowned in thought. "A hat. An ordinary sort of cloche hat, as far as I could see, lying not far from her head."

"That's all?"

"I'm pretty sure, though I had only a small torch and didn't linger, remember."

"No handbag, for instance?"

"Not that I saw."

"Gloves?"

"She certainly wasn't wearing gloves."

"Rings?"

"Her hands were grossly swollen, and they lay palm up. Chances are I wouldn't have been able to see the shanks of wedding and engagement rings, or even a large gemstone, if any."

"You didn't go down the stairs?"

"No. She was so obviously beyond needing help. Was there a handbag?"

Underwood shook his head.

"A hat and no handbag," Alec commented. "It's odd."

"Maybe it'll turn up somewhere in the house."

"Perhaps one of the ladies found it and put it aside to be kept till called for."

"Possible," the inspector allowed grudgingly. "You see, you've already given me an idea or two. I don't suppose you'd care to sit in on my interviews—some of them, at least—on an informal basis? Not taking part, of course, but passing on any hints afterwards: questions I should have asked, inconsistencies I missed, that sort of thing. No, you won't want to spoil your holiday with your lady wife."

"My 'holiday' ends at nine tomorrow morning."

"You're going back to London?"

"Duty calls."

"And Mrs. Fletcher?"

"She's thinking of staying on a few days."

"It's only half an hour by train. You could come back evenings. I'll be working day and night till I've got my man. Or woman."

"I may well be working day and night, if a big case comes up. And not necessarily in town. I could be sent anywhere in the country."

"I daresay I'd have to ask officially for your help." Underwood sighed. "I'd rather try to tackle it myself."

"While unofficially picking my brains," Alec said dryly.

"While learning from an expert. What if there isn't any important case waiting for you at the Yard? I'm sure Mrs. Fletcher would appreciate you rejoining her, and being here anyway, surely you'll want to help me exonerate her friends."

"Or incriminate them?"

"I'd be less likely to make a mistake that'd fix the blame on an innocent person if I had your advice."

"My super would blow a fuse! Oh well, I can't withold from him that I'm a star witness in a murder case, so he's going to blow a fuse anyway. I'll put it to him. And you must ask your super's consent. He may be less convinced of my innocence than you appear to be."

"I'll tell him it's the best way to keep an eye on you," the inspector said slyly, "which is no more nor less than the truth."

EIGHT

Vera made sure the door was latched behind Alec and the inspector, then turned and said, "He heard you, Izzie. I'm sure he heard you say he's not much cop."

"That's not what I said," Isabel pointed out. "Besides, I'm sure he has more important things to worry about, and so do we. For a start, I'd better write a note to Mrs. Hedger telling her not to come tomorrow. If she turns up and finds a constable stationed at the door, there's no telling who'd come out the winner. Where do they keep the writing paper in this place?"

"Over there." Daisy pointed to a dimly lit corner of the lounge. "There's a desk lamp. Edward will deliver your note. He's very reliable."

"Edward?"

"The Boots."

Willie laughed. "Typical Daisy! Only you would know the name of the Boots. And you've taken Sally Hedger under your wing."

"She took *me* under *her* wing when I was ill. She's a sweetie."

"I defy anyone to say the same of her aunt," said Isabel gloomily, switching on the lamp on the writing table. "She'll probably demand to be paid for tomorrow. Well, it's not her fault she won't be working. But it won't surprise me if she quits because of the murder."

Vera shuddered. "I wouldn't blame her."

"I doubt she'll give up the job," said Willie. "After all, before we moved in, she went on cleaning Cherry Trees without knowing whether we'd pay or continue to employ her."

"Very set in her ways, our Mrs. Hedger," Isabel agreed, sounding a bit more cheerful. "Let's just hope she'll stay. *And* agree to clean the cellar."

"I bet she'll be the first person the inspector wants to talk to," Daisy pondered aloud. "After you three, that is. You obviously know very little about Mrs. Gray. Mrs. Hedger must know plenty, having worked for her for years. Did she have other servants?"

"A woman answered the door when Vaughn brought us to see round the house," said Isabel. "She was a cook-housekeeper, I think. She didn't apply for a job with us, not that I need a cook or housekeeper. I'm pretty sure there was a lady's maid, though I never met her face-to-face. The Grays' gardener did ask me to keep him on. He worked for the Grays full-time and wanted to stay, but I had to tell him I'd do all but the heaviest stuff. He didn't want part-time work. He recommended a jobbing gardener, Lassiter, who's available pretty much whenever I need him. I've no idea where the other fellow went, nor the women. He didn't live in so presumably he was local."

"Do you remember their names?"

"Haven't the foggiest. I'm sure I never heard the maid's. The gardener was Smith or Brown or Jones or something equally unmemorable."

"Lassiter would know," Willie suggested.

"Yes, tell the inspector about Lassiter, Isabel."

Willie grinned. "You've gone into sleuth mode, Daisy?"

"Sorry! I can't help it."

"It's all right," said Vera. "After practising with you and Alec, it will be easier to face the police. Not that I have anything to tell them."

"You don't hear any gossip at school?"

"Not really." Vera flushed vividly. "There's just Mr. Cartwright. He doesn't gossip."

"Most men don't, not with women, at least." As she spoke, Daisy wondered, why the blush? Did Vera have a crush on Cartwright? "They share rumours only with other men, usually in a pub. It's very inconvenient! You don't have mothers coming to pick up the little ones after school?"

"A few. Most either live nearby or have older siblings. The ones who do come mostly want to talk about little John or Jane."

"We just haven't been living here long enough," Willie reminded Daisy. "I hear a bit of gossip in High Wycombe, but it's local, not about Beaconsfield people. I'm afraid we're really not going to be much help to the police."

"They won't think we're being deliberately uncooperative, will they, Daisy?" Vera was by far the most anxious of the three.

"I can't see why they should, but so much depends on what they've found out so far and the character of the detective in charge."

"What—" Willie broke off as a couple of men entered the lounge.

For a moment Daisy assumed they were plainclothes police, but they looked taken aback to find four women in possession of the room. Detectives would have expected to find them there.

"Excuse us, ladies," one said breezily. "Just want a quiet drink. We won't disturb you." But he looked meaningfully at the LADIES' PARLOUR sign.

"We're waiting for my husband." Daisy hated to find herself on the defensive. She hoped the others didn't often feel they had to excuse their lack of a male escort. "Don't mind us."

The second man rang the bell, then they sat down as far away as they could. The bell ringer had a quiet voice, but from what the other said, they were commercial travellers from London planning calls on local shopkeepers in the morning, before moving on to High Wycombe and beyond.

"We can't talk here," Willie whispered. "Should we go through? Or up to your room, Daisy?"

"No. We'd better wait till Alec or the police come back. In the meantime, we'll just have to talk about our knitting."

For some reason, that struck all of them as excruciatingly funny. They exploded in laughter, eliciting curious stares from the two men.

Daisy had to admit she was no knitter. She attempted it so rarely that she always forgot how to purl. She extolled her step-daughter's skill, however. The others were all enthusiasts and managed to keep a conversation going. It filled in time and lessened the tension they had all been feeling.

The arrival of a hefty young man in a brown serge suit and police boots set them on edge again. After a swift glance round the room, he came over to them.

"Mrs. Fletcher?"

"I'm Mrs. Fletcher."

"Would you mind coming with me, please, madam?"

As Daisy stood up, Willie asked, "Where's Mr. Fletcher?"

"I believe he's stayed with the inspector, miss, to have a word with Mrs. Fletcher."

"Will he be rejoining us?"

"Not right away, miss, far as I know. If you was to feel more comfortable in the other room, that'll be all right."

"You can be writing out lists of what you need from the house," Daisy suggested. She accompanied the officer through the lobby and several twists and turns of passages. "May I ask your name?"

"Um," he said, as if he wasn't sure whether it would be proper to give such information to a witness. Or a suspect.

"Never mind. I'll call you 'Officer'. But I assume there are several officers about, so it would be easier—"

"Pennicuik, madam," he informed her hastily. "Double N-I-C-U-I-K."

"I bet lots of people spell it wrong. Hard luck! Detective Sergeant?"

His ears turned pink. "Not yet, madam. Detective Constable. Maybe next year. DI Underwood thinks I show promise."

"Good for you."

"Some of the time," he added with painful honesty.

Daisy laughed. "Never mind. Practice makes perfect. Good luck! What's Mr. Underwood like?"

"Tricksy. I mean, he's all right. As a gov'nor. Madam, is it true Mr. Fletcher is a DCI at Scotland Yard?"

"It's true."

"Gosh!" In the ill-lit passage DS Pennicuik's expression was not readable, but his voice changed from awed to businesslike as he opened a door. "This way, if you please, madam. Mrs. Fletcher, sir."

Alec came to meet Daisy, took her hand, and introduced her to DI Underwood.

As they didn't appear to be at daggers drawn, she said with a warm smile, "How do you do, Inspector? I hope I can help you, but I can't imagine how."

"My job is to find out, Mrs. Fletcher." Underwood shook the hand she offered, his clasp cool and firm. "Do take a seat. Would you prefer to have the chief inspector stay?"

"Oh no, there's no need. Darling, I'm sure the others would be grateful for your reassurance that the inspector is not an ogre."

"Sorry, Mrs. Fletcher, I can't allow that. Sir, I'd prefer you to stay away from the rest of the ladies until I've spoken to them."

"As you wish, Mr. Underwood. You're in charge." They exchanged a faintly amused look that puzzled Daisy. "I'll be in the bar, Daisy. I've earned a whisky."

He left. Underwood sat down opposite Daisy, and she was aware of Pennicuik settling in a corner slightly behind her, with his notebook at the ready. It was a position she had adopted more than once, when Alec was desperate for someone to take notes.

"Tell me all about it," the inspector invited. "Let's start with how long and why you've been staying in Beaconsfield."

"I arrived on Monday evening." Daisy explained about

bronchitis and getting above the Thames fogs. "And being close to town, in case Alec should be able to come down for the weekend, as he did. Beaconsfield rather than Surrey because I'd recently heard from Willie—Miss Wilhelmina Chandler—that she'd moved here. She lived in the North, and I hadn't seen her for ages. We were at school together."

"You had the best part of a week, then, to renew your acquaintance. Did you—"

"I was too ill the first few days. Everything set me off coughing. I went to tea on Friday."

"So you didn't spend much time in the house," Underwood said regretfully. "Pity. You'd never been there before?"

"No. I wouldn't know the previous owners from Adam. Or Eve. I've never been *to* Beaconsfield before, only through it, on the A40."

"Did they show you round Cherry Trees on Friday?"

"I was feeling so much better, I walked over and—I hate to sound feeble, but by the time I got there I was pretty much done in. Isabel—Miss Sutcliffe—plunked me in a chair by the fire and went to make tea. The others weren't back from work yet. All I saw of the house was the entrance hall and the sitting room."

"That's a pity. From my point of view. What did you all talk about?"

"Our work. My children. Umm . . . to tell the truth, I dozed off for a while."

"Quite natural, after your illness."

"Oh, we talked about servants, I remember. The usual thing. And why the three of them came south."

DI Underwood pounced. "Why did they?"

"Shouldn't you ask them?"

"I will. But I daresay, like most people, they'll be a bit nervous being interviewed by the police, as you, Mrs. Fletcher, obviously are not. If you'll give me what one might call an overall view, I shan't take up their time with irrelevant questions."

Daisy had a feeling his rationale was somewhat specious, but she was always a bit muddled about what was hearsay, what was speculation, and what counted as reporting her own knowledge and observations.

"This is what I remember," she said cautiously. "I couldn't swear I'm getting it right."

"No swearing involved at present, and it won't go in your official statement."

That made her even less certain that she ought to be telling him. She couldn't see what harm it could do, though. "All right. Let's see, where should I start?"

"I'll leave that up to you, Mrs. Fletcher."

"In a nutshell: Miss Sutcliffe had a large house in Huddersfield and not much money, so she took in lodgers. Willie—Miss Chandler—and Miss Leighton had rooms there and they became friends. Miss Chandler worked as a secretary and bookkeeper. She studied and took the exams and became a chartered accountant."

"Did she now! A bright young lady."

"Very. But there was some ill feeling about her success at the firm she worked for, that made her uncomfortable."

"Some people are jealous of success, even when it's taken hard work."

"That, and I gathered one of her bosses believed women had no business becoming professionals. She found a good job in High Wycombe, so she had to move. The others decided to stick with her. Miss Leighton's a teacher and luckily St. Mary's school here in Beaconsfield had an opening. Miss Sutcliffe sold her house and bought Cherry Trees. She's housekeeper, cook, gardener—and landlady to some degree, I think, but I'm a little vague about that."

"Then Miss Sutcliffe must be about the house much of the time? She's the most likely to know something about the previous residents."

"I can't answer for her. That you will have to ask them."

"Of course. Now, would you please tell me what happened at Cherry Trees today."

"Alec and I were invited to lunch. We—"

"Just a minute. When did you receive the invitation?"

"When I went to tea. They invited me, then included Alec when I told them he was coming. If he didn't mind being outnumbered four to one, they said."

"Did they know then that he's a police officer? A detective chief inspector?"

"Willie did. Miss Chandler. She didn't tell the others. I prefer to keep quiet about it, in general. I expect your wife's told you how people look askance at a copper's wife."

"She did." He grinned. "Often and often. Go on."

"Where had I got to?"

"Nowhere as yet. I interrupted. Sorry."

"Oh, yes. Alec and I arrived at the house at about half past twelve; I don't know exactly, but I can't see that it matters. It's not as if she'd just died. Willie and Vera showed us into the sitting room and offered us sherry."

"Can you remember which of the two actually made the offer?"

"No, but a tray with a bottle and five glasses was set out already, so it wasn't impromptu. One of them apologised for the quality of the sherry. I'm not sure who first mentioned the wine cellar and their hopes that they might find an overlooked bottle or two of something good, if they ever managed to open the door. Willie, I think. I wouldn't swear to it, though."

"Where was Miss . . . hm, Sutcliffe while this was going on?"

"In the kitchen, putting the finishing touches to the meal. It smelled wonderful." Daisy sighed. "But of course we never got to eat it."

Underwood clucked in sympathy. "Miss Chandler asked the chief inspector to have a go at the lock?"

"Alec offered. Willie produced a bent wire coat hanger that Isabel had already used to try to open it, in vain. We all trooped along to watch Alec. Isabel came out of the kitchen, too. He jemmied the lock in just a few seconds and opened the door. It was horrible!"

"I hate to ask you this, Mrs. Fletcher, but can you describe the body for me? The way it lay, the clothes and so on."

"Not me. The stench made me turn tail before I caught so much as a glimpse."

"And your friends?"

"I passed Willie. The others reached the kitchen scarcely a step behind us, though, and one of them slammed the door. Vera. After asking Alec if he was coming."

"Presumably he said no."

"I didn't hear. Anyway, he didn't join us for several minutes. He said— But that's hearsay, isn't it?"

"Not exactly, not if you're telling me what he said about his own actions."

"Oh." She nearly asked if he was sure, but it didn't seem tactful. "He said, as far as I remember, that he'd opened the front and side doors and lots of windows, for which we were duly thankful, and that he had to ring up the police."

"He didn't tell you what he'd seen?"

"No. Obviously it was a human body, or he wouldn't have gone off to notify the local coppers. The GPO hasn't put the phone in yet."

"They've been known to dally. What did you ladies talk about while he was gone? Any theories as to who it might be?"

"Not from me. Except, I did wonder if it might be a burglar, but they hadn't seen any signs of burglary. Do you know yet how long she'd been there?"

Underwood frowned. "Mr. Fletcher told you it was a female? Just you, or all four?"

"All of us. I think he wanted to see how they'd react." Wrong thing to say, she realised at once.

The inspector looked thunderous. "He did, did he!"

"That's only my guess. It's instinctive with Alec. He's been a detective a long time." To deflect him, she asked again, "Do you know when she died?"

"Not till the autopsy, if then. How long have the ladies lived at Cherry Trees?"

"A couple of weeks. I don't know the exact date. Someone said they were free to move in anytime after the first of October. Again, that's something you'll have to ask them. Or her lawyer, or the estate agent."

"Do you happen to know the names of those two?"

"Not the lawyer's." She kept quiet about Alec having asked for it. "The agent is Vaughn."

"Donald Vaughn, that'd be, of Langridge's in High Wycombe?"

"Don't ask me. Anyway, the neighbours probably know when they moved in, even though they haven't exactly been friendly."

"No?"

"Not actively unpleasant, I gather, just not welcoming."

"Yes, well, we'll be talking to them in any case."

"Of course. You'll want to know when they last saw Mrs. Gray."

He gave her an odd look, part annoyance, part curiosity. "Indeed. You seem familiar with police methods."

Not for the world would Daisy reveal that she'd been mixed up in more than a few cases. "I *am* married to a copper."

A muffled snicker came from DC Pennicuik. Daisy didn't dare glance his way. She wondered just how the inspector and Alec had worked out their relationship in this case. Usually it was easy to tell whether the local man resented or welcomed the assistance of Scotland Yard, official or not. Insofar as she could judge without observing their interaction, Underwood seemed ambivalent.

"We seem to have got sidetracked," he said mildly. "You mentioned talking with your friends about servants. Have they any?"

"Not live-in. Just a char three days a week. Mrs. Hedger—she'd be the best person to ask about the date they moved in. She worked for the previous owner and just stayed on, taking care of the house, when Mrs. Gray . . . left. If she left. Sorry, but one can't simply turn off one's brain!"

Underwood heaved a deep sigh. "No, I suppose it's too much to expect of the modern young woman."

"It seems pretty plain to all of us that the chances are she's either the body or the murderer."

"Mr. Fletcher's suggestion?"

"As I remember," Daisy said dryly, "Miss Chandler was the first to voice the probability. No doubt Alec had already considered it, being a policeman."

NINE

$\mathcal{DC}$ $\mathcal{Pennicuik}$ escorted Daisy back to the lounge. She was glad not to have to find her own way through the passages. Suddenly she was very tired.

Six men were in the residents' lounge now. A third had joined the original two; another pair, one smoking a cigar, consulted over a map spread on a table before them; and one solitary sat hunched over a mug of beer, contemplating his sorrows by the look on his face.

"Looks like the ladies moved to the other room," Pennicuik said uneasily, "unless they've scarpered."

"Nonsense. They have no reason to run away." Daisy trudged over to the connecting door. "If they're not here, they'll have gone up to their room. They're staying at the Saracen's Head, you know."

"Oh. Umm." The young detective turned bashful. "Umm, would you mind taking a look, madam? I didn't ought to go into the ladies' parlour, not without it's urgent. Mr. Underwood wants to see Miss Leighton next, if you wouldn't mind asking her to come out."

She took pity on him. Besides, it would be silly for him to

knock and wait for someone to respond when she was going in anyway. And it never hurt to get on the right side of a copper, however junior.

"Hold on half a mo, then."

The three looked round as Daisy entered and closed the door behind her. In her absence, they had all acquired drinks, which did not seem to have cheered them up.

"What's he like?" Willie asked.

"Not bad." Daisy plumped into the nearest chair. "He doesn't bite."

The feeble witticism made them laugh more than it deserved.

"We were just talking about whether we ought to get a dog," Isabel explained, "thus locking the stable door after the horse has been stolen."

"I would. Sorry to interrupt, but Mr. Underwood would like to see Vera."

"Me? Why me? I mean, why me first?"

"I've no idea. A random choice, I imagine."

"Oh. Yes, I suppose so. Couldn't Willie or Iz go first, then?"

"He asked for you. You'd better go."

"Buck up, Vera, don't be such a drip," Isabel admonished her. "Daisy said he won't bite."

"He doesn't suspect Daisy, and she's married to a chief inspector. Daisy, would you come with me? *Please!*"

"I doubt he'd let me."

"What about Alec? If he—"

"He didn't stay with me, and Mr. Underwood told him not to come and talk to you, so that's even less likely. All right, let's see if he chucks me out." She struggled wearily from her seat.

"You're worn out," said Willie with concern. "Vera, I do think you might—"

"It's all right," Daisy repeated. "I don't mind, honestly."

"Here." Vera picked up the glass beside her. "I haven't taken a single sip. You drink it."

Daisy didn't ask what it was, just took a couple of swallows.

75

Gin and tonic, which she didn't much like, but the warmth that coursed through her brought a smidgen of energy.

"Come along." As she opened the door, a mutter of voices in the residents' lounge ceased. She noticed that all the residents present were watching PC Pennicuik, who shifted uneasily from one foot to the other. In a low voice, she introduced Vera: "Miss Leighton, Officer. I'm going with her."

"Uh, I don't know if the gov'nor . . ." He looked round at the avid listeners. "We'll talk outside."

Their footsteps sounded loud on the bare boards. Behind them, the muttering started up again.

Pennicuik almost slammed the door behind him.

"They're talking about us," Vera said despairingly.

"They're strangers," Daisy pointed out, "or they wouldn't be in there."

"I'm sorry," Pennicuik blurted. "I wish I didn't look so much like a copper."

"It'll wear off," Daisy consoled him, "the longer you're a detective." She had kept walking fast while they spoke, and they had nearly reached the landlord's snug before the constable realised it. She shepherded Vera in.

"Mrs. Fletcher?" Underwood rose. "Did you remember something—?"

"'Fraid not, Inspector. Miss Leighton asked me to come and support her. With your permission, naturally, but I can't see why not."

"You can't?" He gave her an incredulous look and glared at Pennicuik, entering after the ladies.

"Sir, I couldn't—"

"I didn't give him a chance to stop me, so don't berate him. Go on," she said persuasively, "let me stay. I promise not to say a word, just to hold Vera's hand. Metaphorically."

"Miss Leighton?"

"Oh, please! I've never had anything to do with the police. . . ."

Not for the first time since he'd made Daisy's acquaintance, Detective Inspector Underwood sighed. He waved them to seats.

The edge that had been in his voice when questioning Daisy completely vanished as, in a most prosaic tone, he requested Vera's full name and address. Next he asked for her previous address, the temporary lodgings in High Wycombe, and before that, in Yorkshire.

"I grew up in Yorkshire," she volunteered, already much more comfortable with the situation, to Underwood's credit. "My father is a canon at York Minster."

"I expect he would have liked you to stay at home?"

"Yes. He didn't want me to train as a teacher in the first place, but Mother coaxed him round. I didn't want to spend my entire life in the Minster close, and I knew I'd end up living at home if I worked in a school in York, so I looked for a position in Huddersfield. You won't have to tell him about . . . this, will you?"

"You're an independent adult, Miss Leighton. I can't foresee any reason why I'd have to approach your family, though I can't promise. Why did you—all three of you ladies—choose to move south?"

Daisy knew he had to ask everyone more or less the same questions so as to compare their answers. Moreover, so far he hadn't obtained this particular information from those concerned, only from Daisy herself and possibly from Alec, at one further remove. Hearsay, she told herself. Vera's account was no different from her own. Boring. Her eyelids drifted downward and the voices seemed to come from a long way off.

She wouldn't be much comfort to Vera if she fell asleep. Blinking hard, she tried to concentrate, as the inspector obliquely approached the happenings of the day.

Vera was distressed in spite of the kid glove treatment. Altogether natural, in Daisy's view. She herself would prefer not to talk or think about the discovery of the body. It had been a horrid experience, even though Alec had borne the brunt. But Vera's upset now was of a different nature from her near-panic at the prospect of the interview with the police. Puzzling over the difference, Daisy missed another chunk of Vera's evidence.

Talking about the murder evoked in the schoolmistress

horror, pity, and a certain detachment. There had been nothing detached about her fear of stepping alone into the lion's den.

DI Underwood had turned out to be not such a lion after all, and Vera seemed quite at ease.

So was it just fear of the unknown, her lack of experience dealing with the police, that had sparked her earlier alarm? Or was the cause deeper, something that had happened to Vera. . . . Daisy had a feeling that if she could remember everything everyone had said today and at tea on Friday, she would have a clue to . . . to what?

She must have nodded off for a minute or two, because the next thing she heard was the inspector saying incredulously, "Nothing?"

Vera's response sounded defensive: "Why should they gossip about their neighbours to someone they barely know? All they want to talk about is their children."

"The children don't tell you things?"

"About their own families, yes. Since I've been here, I've heard nothing I can't handle myself, nothing that would make me report to the authorities."

"You don't overhear the mothers talking to each other?"

"I don't listen," Vera said primly, with a hint of rebuke. "What they say to each other is none of my business."

Underwood coughed, raising his hand to his mouth—to hide a smile, Daisy suspected. "Very proper, I'm sure. What about your colleagues? You don't chat with them?"

"No." The single syllable was adamant, but Vera's voice trembled as she explained, "The only other teacher is the headmaster."

The inspector looked at her with narrowed eyes. "His name?"

"C-Cartwright, Roger Cartwright."

Underwood didn't pursue the subject, to Daisy's disappointment. She wanted to know what was going on between Vera and the headmaster. On the other hand, she didn't at all want Vera crying on her shoulder, so it was just as well that DI Underwood decided to end the interview.

Perhaps he, too, was keen to avert tears if possible. Alec always had a couple of extra handkerchiefs in his pockets in case of weeping witnesses, suspects, and even villains.

Underwood thanked Vera for her assistance, warning her that he'd probably have more questions for her later. He told Pennicuik to escort her back to the others and return with Miss Chandler. When Daisy started to stand, he said to her, "Just a moment, if you please, Mrs. Fletcher."

Daisy examined her conscience. "I didn't utter a single word!" she said indignantly.

"Not so much as a word," he agreed. "I appreciate your . . . self-control. I wondered whether Miss Chandler, too, is likely to insist on your presence."

On the verge of admitting that she couldn't imagine Willie needing support, Daisy bit back the words and said instead, "You'll have to ask her."

"There's no point in you leaving and coming back. You'd better just stay. While we wait: Miss Leighton's account included a few details neither you nor the chief inspector mentioned, as is only natural. Would you say it was accurate? Off the record."

"I didn't notice any discrepancies." She wasn't about to confess that she hadn't listened half the time. She swallowed a yawn.

"Did it spark any ideas? Remind you of details you left out before, perhaps?"

The only noteworthy point was Vera's marked aversion to Cartwright, surely not relevant to the murder. Daisy shook her head. "Not immediately. I'll think about it. Something may occur to me later."

The brief exchange made her wonder more than ever on what terms Underwood and Alec had parted. Rare indeed were the police officers who recognised that her opinion might prove useful. She was sorry she had no suggestions to offer.

The brisk tap of footsteps approached the door. Willie came in, her tread light, and glanced round the room as Pennicuik trudged in after her.

"Hello, Daisy. Still here? But no Alec?"

"It's not his case, darling. Detective Inspector Underwood is in charge. He kindly let me stay with Vera."

"How do you do, Inspector." Willie stepped forward with a friendly smile, her hand held out. "I'm Wilhelmina Chandler."

Underwood shook hands and invited her to sit.

"It was good of you to let Daisy support Vera. I'm sure you did your best, but she's absolutely shattered anyway, poor thing. She doesn't do well under fire."

"I assure you, Miss Chandler, in no sense was Miss Leighton under fire!"

"Badly phrased. Vera deals better with children than adults, as I'm better with numbers than words. Now that we've got that out of the way, let's get going."

"Would you like Mrs. Fletcher to stay?"

"I don't need support, but don't make Daisy leave. By the look of her, she'll never move again."

"Thanks for nothing!"

"You've been ill. You're entitled to look as if you're at death's door."

"You're welcome to take a nap, Mrs Fletcher," said Underwood, and mouthed silently, "again."

Daisy glared at him. She had hoped he hadn't noticed. While she'd been snoozing, he'd been disconcertingly wide-awake, it seemed.

"Let's get down to business, Inspector," said Willie. "If you want to know what I saw, you're out of luck. If you want to know what I smelled . . ."

TEN

This time Daisy listened carefully, in case the inspector quizzed her afterwards. It was easier to keep her mind on what was said because Willie's voice was bright with interest, and she fenced with Underwood, just as Daisy had.

"Why on earth do you want to know why the three of us moved south?" she demanded.

"The more I know about those involved, the quicker I'll be able to solve the case."

"'Those involved?' We're not involved. Someone took the liberty of using our house to dispose of—"

"That's as may be, Miss Chandler. Supposing you to have nothing to do with the murder, it was probably committed by someone who knew the house was empty."

"The neighbours."

"Or the house agent, or someone who was aware of your plans. I'm still asking you to tell me why you moved."

Willie grinned and complied. "Not many firms are willing to hire a woman accountant," she finished. "I couldn't afford not to take the position."

"I've never had anything to do with accountants," Underwood admitted. "What's the difference between them and bookkeepers?"

"We're the ones who check the books, to make sure they're properly kept: accurate arithmetic and accounts balanced, no errors, no fraud. That's my job for the present. Senior partners advise companies on the law and so forth."

"Fraud, eh? Anyone in your sights?"

"That's confidential."

"In other words, yes."

"I can't say any more. It's an interesting theory, though."

"What is?" Underwood asked irritably.

"I assume you're proposing that someone either intended to kill me and botched it, or hoped to intimidate me into botching an audit."

"Or just to distract you from doing a thorough job," Daisy suggested.

"Rubbish!" The inspector frowned at her. "I'm not proposing any such notion, Miss Chandler, especially your second theory. Killing someone just to intimidate a third person may be something that goes on in the East End, or in Huddersfield for all I know, but not on my patch!"

"Good. Then you won't keep pestering me to disclose confidential information."

"Let's see if I have better luck with nonconfidential information. What date did you move into Cherry Trees?"

"The afternoon of Saturday the eighth. Isabel came over on the first and spent the week making sure everything was ready for Vera and me. I don't know how much time she spent at the house, but I assure you, she didn't use any of it to push a stranger down the stairs."

Underwood eyed her narrowly. "Put like that, it does seem unlikely," he conceded. "But perhaps the victim was not a stranger. I'm not going to be making any headway until she's been identified. You didn't recognise her?"

"I didn't see her. To put it crudely, I smelled her, and that was quite sufficient. I can't express how grateful I am that Mr. Fletcher was present to take charge." Willie smiled at Daisy.

"Tell me about it. Start with why you invited him to the house."

As far as the facts relating to the dinner invitation and the corpse's discovery were concerned, Willie's statement differed little from Daisy's own and what Daisy had heard of Vera's.

"When Mr. Fletcher came back," she finished, "he said we could leave, and we did, as fast as possible."

"Who can blame you? Mrs. Fletcher says you were the first to suggest that the previous owner of the house is likely to be either the victim or the killer. Is that correct?"

"I can't remember whether I was first. It seems a reasonable proposition."

"Did you ever meet her?"

"Briefly. Twice, actually. Miss Sutcliffe found the house and liked it, but of course she didn't make any decisions without us— Vera and me—looking it over and giving our approval. Mrs. Gray was present when we called, and the house agent, too. I was far more interested in the house than in its owner. She didn't make much impression then. And when I met her again, to sign the papers at her lawyer's, I was concentrating on the contract."

"Do you recall her lawyer's name?"

"Ainsley. Ours is Butterworth."

"Would you recognise Mrs. Gray, if you saw her again?"

"I doubt it. I'm not good at faces. If she's the body, judging by what I've gathered about its condition, definitely not!"

"You ladies didn't find any of her effects in the house when you moved in? A handbag, clothes, suitcase, nothing at all?"

"I assume Isabel would have mentioned it if she had come across something other than the household effects that were part of the deal. She certainly would if she'd found a handbag with anything of value in it."

"Does Mrs. Gray have any relatives that you're aware of?"

"For all I know, she could have swarms. I haven't the foggiest. Surely Mr. Ainsley must know."

"The solicitor? Yes." Underwood asked a few more questions in a desultory way: Where Willie had lived before the Huddersfield lodgings, how long she had lived there, whether she'd known the other two previously, the name of her firm in High Wycombe.

Having provided the last, Willie begged, "Please don't talk to the partners before I've had a chance to tell them what's happened!"

"We may not have to see them at all, certainly not before you go to work tomorrow. I'll have more questions for you at a later date. We'll wrap it up for now, though. Thank you."

"Not at all, it's been interesting. By the way, I really must have my business suit for tomorrow."

"If you and the other ladies each write a list of necessities, I'll see what I can do. Pennicuik, fetch Miss Sutcliffe now, with apologies for keeping her waiting."

Daisy was half eager to see whether any new information would emerge, half dying to go and have a drink with Alec. She doubted Isabel would need support any more than Willie had; on the other hand, her chair was much more comfortable than anything in the bar. She had sunk into its embrace to the point where getting out would be quite a struggle. "Would you like me to stay again?" she asked,

"Why not?" said the inspector sardonically.

From the doorway, Willie waved to Daisy. Pennicuik followed her out.

Underwood cocked an eyebrow at Daisy.

"Nothing," she said regretfully. "I hope Alec doesn't hit the roof when he finds out I'm attending your interviews, especially as he isn't."

"It's highly irregular. Please blame it on your friends, not on me!"

"Don't worry, I will. I just wish I was being more helpful. I'm glad you didn't ask Vera about identifying the body."

"It's a nasty job to ask anyone to do, even when the person is strong-minded and the body's in reasonably good shape. Failing a belated 'missing person' alert that fits, I expect we'll have to rely on the cleaning woman. Not the most desirable kind of identification, always supposing she agrees to do it and doesn't go off into a fit of hysterics. Which," he added, his thin face gloomy, "she probably will."

Isabel arrived. She had no objection to Daisy's presence. "Vera asked me to thank you for staying with her, Daisy. She was too shattered to remember when she was allowed to leave the room." She glared at Underwood.

Daisy jumped to his defence. "Not the inspector's fault," she said.

"Perhaps you can tell me, Miss Sutcliffe, why Miss Leighton was upset when I asked whether she had heard any gossip at school?"

"Well, she disapproves of gossip on principle. But she really was pretty upset when she came back, and I've never known her react so strongly before."

"Talking about murder and finding decayed bodies isn't exactly soothing to start with," Daisy pointed out. "Besides, she's afraid gossip about it will result in her losing her job."

"Thank you, Mrs. Fletcher. She told you that?"

"She told all of us," said Isabel, while Daisy was examining Underwood's gratitude for sarcasm. In her experience, detectives were sparing of thanks, especially directed to her. He seemed sincere. She decided she rather liked him.

All the same, she kept quiet as he went on questioning Isabel.

After the formalities of name, past addresses, dates, and so forth, and her description of the afternoon's events, the inspector said, "You've spent a good deal of time in the house for the past two weeks. You never noticed a smell in the passage by the cellar door?"

"Yes, but it wasn't the smell of death and decay. Mrs. Hedger, our char, scrubs it with carbolic every time she comes. I've told her she's overdoing it. She insists that what with the drains and my coming in from the garden with manure on my boots, it's

85

necessary. She's one of those people it's a waste of time to argue with. Stubborn and set in her ways as they come. I wouldn't have chosen her, but she did for Mrs. Gray before so it was easiest just to keep her on."

"Not so easy to find cleaning women these days," Underwood sympathised. "Mr. Fletcher also smelled carbolic. Which days does Mrs. Hedger oblige?"

"Monday, Wednesday, and Friday."

"Today's Sunday, and the carbolic smell was still evident. No wonder none of you noticed any odour that escaped from the cellar. You have no other servants?"

"No. That reminds me, though. The Grays had a live-in cook-housekeeper and lady's maid, and a full-time gardener. I can't recall their names, but the gardener recommended a jobbing gardener to me. Chap called Lassiter. Presumably Lassiter would know the name of the man who sent me to him, if not where to find him."

"This Lassiter's a local man?"

"I don't know his address. I've only needed him once. I left a message at the newsagents in Station Road, as the other man advised, and Lassiter turned up next morning to do some digging for me."

"We'll find him." Underwood made a note. "Miss Sutcliffe, as well as spending more time in the house than either of your friends do, I gather you saw more of Mrs. Gray in the course of buying the house. Tell me about her."

"Medium height, good figure, dark hair, bobbed but longer than mine and expensively waved," Isabel said promptly. "Thirty-five or so at a guess, but looked younger. She dressed well, expensively: nothing fancy that I saw, just a bit too smart for a country town, in my opinion. So was her makeup. I don't use the stuff. Not much jewellery, but what she wore looked good. Not that I'm much of a judge. Usually pearls, both necklace and earrings, and a largish ruby on her ring finger."

"You have an observant eye, Miss Sutcliffe."

"Running a boarding house—or private hotel if you want to doll it up—teaches you to notice people."

"I daresay. Have you heard any gossip about her from the neighbours? I take it you're not as unalterably opposed to gossip as Miss Leighton."

Isabel grinned. "Heavens no. As the neighbours have yet to call, they're no help. I did find out a bit from Mrs. Gray herself and from the house agent."

"Oh? What did they have to say?"

"The agent told me she was much younger than her husband, and his second wife. Albert Gray had plenty of brass." She pronounced the word with the short Yorkshire vowel. "He was tight-fisted, though. His only extravagance was his wine cellar. He'd pay for her fancies to a point and then shut the spigot. She wasn't at all happy. Mr. Vaughn had no qualms over gossiping about his client."

"You didn't like him," Underwood stated.

"Not much, I admit. I wouldn't have chosen him to deal with, but as it happens he's a relative of one of Willie's bosses, who recommended him."

"Ah. Nor you didn't like Mrs. Gray?"

"Discontent sours people, don't you think? Even though he'd died—last April, I think it was—and she'd inherited a fortune, she stayed sour. That was my impression. She told me herself she'd been married to a miser and couldn't wait to get out of the place. A long holiday abroad was her immediate aim, before deciding where to live."

"Did she mention where exactly? 'Abroad' is a big place."

"Paris to start with—Albert Gray had refused to spring for a holiday in Gay Paree. Then she was going to stay with friends on the Riviera, possibly followed by Italy."

"No names for the friends?" he asked unhopefully. "Or which Paris hotel?"

"She had no reason to mention them as there wasn't the slightest chance I'd know them."

"Cannes? Monte Carlo?"

Isabel shook her head. "Just 'the Riviera.' Boasting."

"That sort." Underwood nodded his understanding. "If you remember anything else about her destination . . ."

"I'll let you know, of course. Not likely, though."

"Did she have any relatives?"

"Not that she mentioned, but why should she?"

"All right. Can you tell me any more about Vaughn?"

"Not about *his* relatives, other than the one I mentioned, who's in Willie's firm. He's Donald Vaughn's brother-in-law, I think she said. Vaughn married his sister. Vaughn's pushy, but I suppose house agents have to be. Flashy and full of himself. A bit of a bounder, perhaps. I don't want to traduce him. You'll talk to him yourself, Inspector?"

"Most certainly."

"You may decide I'm talking through my hat." She hesitated. "It seemed to me there was something between them, Vaughn and Mrs. Gray. Something more . . . personal than his finding a buyer for her house."

"Indeed!"

"Nothing definite. Nothing I could swear to."

"A place for me to start. You're a detective's dream, Miss Sutcliffe." They smiled at each other.

At once, Daisy wondered if there was a possibility of "something between them" in the future. Not much chance. At Underwood's age, he was probably married, and Isabel would remain a surplus woman.

Had Mrs. Gray been a member of the superfluous ranks? Had she, like Daisy, beaten the odds to find a husband? Unlike Daisy, though, it didn't sound as though she had found love, or even contentment, far less happiness.

More to the immediate point, had she found death in a dark cellar?

ELEVEN

Alec had taken a seat in the corner of the saloon bar most distant from the bar itself. Two wooden settles against the walls met in the corner, and two spindle-back chairs occupied the other two sides of the small table, its top marred by countless rings in spite of a scattering of coasters. Like most police officers, Alec preferred to sit where he could see the whole room, especially the entrance, whether or not he was expecting someone—or trouble.

He had opted for a pint of home-brewed bitter rather than whisky. He might be glad of a clear head later. DI Underwood was sure to want to talk to him again. After a gulp of the excellent brew, he nursed his beer and sat back to watch and listen.

His fellow imbibers looked to be a moderately prosperous lot, from various walks of life: tradesmen, clerks, farmers, commercial travellers, a professional or two. There were two women, staid matrons obviously out with their husbands.

Nowhere appeared the excitement inevitable if any were aware of the murder.

Sergeant Harris had struck Alec as a man not to be trusted to hold his tongue, but these were not the sort of people to whom he'd chatter. His friends would be in the public bar, where Alec would stick out like a sore thumb. Tom Tring, his sergeant of many years, would be the perfect man to find out what was being talked about there, but Tom had retired just a month ago. Not to mention that this was Underwood's job. Alec was finding it deuced difficult to keep the fact in mind.

The saloon bar drinkers were not likely to be the sergeant's confidants, but they were the sort the Grays might have consorted with. Alec, in his oft-assumed guise as a civil servant, was more one of them than DI Underwood was likely to be. Chatting to them, he might learn something useful about the Grays.

So Alec was welcoming when a newly arrived couple, after greeting two or three people and glancing round the room for seats, came over to his table.

"D'you mind if we sit here?" the man said. "Quite a crowd tonight."

"My pleasure."

"Thanks. The usual, Alice? What's yours?" he asked Alec as he pulled out a chair to seat his companion.

"Bitter, thanks. But I'm not in need." He hoisted his half-full tankard.

"Get it while you can. A few more crammed in here and you won't be able to catch Mickey's eye for love nor money. Well, money might work. . . ." He went off to battle the swarm at the bar, shaking hands here and there as he went.

"I'm Alice Barnes," the woman introduced herself. She was fiftyish, round faced with smile lines, dressed in good but well-worn clothes. "That's my husband, Brian, that was. He won't be back for at least twenty minutes."

"Fletcher. It's obvious Mr. Barnes is on good terms with everyone here."

"It's Doctor. Most of them are Brian's patients, or their wives and children are," Mrs. Barnes said dryly.

Alec wanted to ask whether the Grays had been Barnes's patients. However, if he gave in to temptation, the inspector would have every right to be incensed.

The doctor's wife continued, "You're not from these parts, Mr. Fletcher?"

"London. Just visiting. An old friend of my wife's moved here recently, from the North."

"Ah, so you've escaped the reunion. Sensible man. I don't believe I've met anyone who's recently moved here from the North. . . ." She paused invitingly.

Alec saw no reason not to oblige. "Miss Chandler. She and two friends have bought Cherry Trees, in Orchard Road."

"Oh, yes, someone did mention that three ladies had moved in. About a fortnight ago, wasn't it? You'll think it disgraceful, Mr. Fletcher, that I haven't called on them yet. I'm afraid I'm very bad about introducing myself to newcomers. I tend to wait until I meet them at someone else's house. I'm a nurse, you see, and though I don't work full-time, I'm kept pretty busy in Brian's practice."

"Two of them are working women, so they'll quite understand."

"Now I remember. Teachers, aren't they?"

"One is. Miss Chandler is an accountant, duly chartered."

"Is she! How enterprising. One is reminded that until the Crimean War, nursing was not considered a suitable occupation for a respectable female. It seems a pity that it takes war to persuade men of our capabilities. I really must make Miss Chandler's acquaintance."

Hoping he'd been helpful in breaking the ice for Daisy's friends, Alec was afraid he was merely meddlesome. As a policeman he ought to know better, when they might yet prove to be involved in the murder. But he'd taken a liking to the three women, bravely making their own way in what was still a man's world. It was one of Daisy's attributes that had first drawn him to her.

The doctor returned, two tankards in one hand and a sherry glass in the other. He set them down as his wife introduced Alec, and they shook hands.

"From London," Mrs. Barnes added.

"Then you won't be interested in the latest local rumour."

"Brian, you can't say that and just stop there," she protested. "Mr. Fletcher won't mind." She cast a questioning glance at Alec.

"Not at all," Alec said, hoping he looked politely resigned, not all agog. The subject of the rumour was not difficult to guess.

"Apparently the police have taken over Whitford's snug."

"That bumptious Sergeant Harris? What's wrong with the police station?"

"It's an inspector from High Wycombe, dear. He's interviewing witnesses."

"Witnesses to what?"

The doctor shrugged. "No one seems to know."

"A decent rumour should have more meat to it," Mrs. Barnes complained, laughing. "Don't you agree, Mr. Fletcher?"

"Some rumours are best fleshed out," he said cautiously, thinking of those that aid the police. "Others are better left to die."

"Unmourned," Dr. Barnes agreed. "This one, I suspect, is true, and when the details are revealed in the fullness of time, we may well wish it wasn't."

"A police investigation is bound to bring bad news to someone." His wife firmly changed the subject. "Now that's enough of that. Mr. Fletcher has been telling me about his wife's friend who recently moved here. Miss Chandler. She sounds like an interesting—"

"And here she comes," Alec interrupted, standing and waving as Willie entered the bar and looked round.

"Oh, good!" Mrs. Barnes exclaimed. "You will introduce us, won't you?"

Willie's face lit up as she saw Alec. She started to come over, but hesitated as she realised he was not alone.

It was not the best time for her to meet the Barneses, but once she had appeared it was inevitable. Alec waved again, wondering where Daisy was and what she was up to. He couldn't ask Willie in the presence of the others.

The doctor stood up as she arrived. Alec made the introductions, and Barnes asked, "What are you drinking, Miss Chandler?"

"My turn," said Alec, seating Willie, though he didn't really want to leave her alone with them.

"Not at all, it's still my round."

Willie looked as if she was in need of a brandy, but she glanced at Mrs. Barnes's glass and opted for sherry. The doctor went off. He wouldn't be gone long: The crowd was thinning as dinnertime approached. With luck, the Barneses would soon join the exodus.

The ladies were making small talk, Willie careful of what she said, Mrs. Barnes with apparently genuine friendliness.

"I hope you'll enjoy living here," said the latter, "you and your friends. I'm looking forward to meeting them. And to making your wife's acquaintance, Mr. Fletcher." She turned back to Willie. "Mrs. Fletcher will be joining us, I imagine?"

"I . . . I'm not sure. She's . . . rather tired. Thank you," she added as Dr. Barnes returned with her drink, saving her from further explanation. Or further evasion, Alec thought, trying not to show his misgivings.

"What a pity. Some other time, perhaps. London's not far, and we have excellent train service. It's very easy to get up to town for concerts and the theatre."

"Not to mention shopping," the doctor teased.

"Well, the choice here is very limited," Mrs. Barnes said indignantly, "and not much better in High Wycombe. I don't go shopping in London very often. Have you had a chance to look round our shops here, Miss Chandler?"

"Not much. I'd be glad to know which you recommend."

They chatted for a few more minutes, then Mrs. Barnes told her husband to finish off his beer, as they had to go. "I left jacket potatoes in the oven," she explained, searching through her handbag. "Bother, I've left my diary at home, but I'll be in touch when I have it beside me."

The Barneses left. As soon as they were out of earshot, Alec turned to Willie.

She spoke first, gloomily. "Not a chance, when news gets about. It's a pity; I liked them."

"Nice people. You never know."

"I expect they knew the Grays. Will the inspector talk to them?"

"I imagine so. Where's Daisy? I know prevarication when I see it. I don't believe for a moment that she's too tired to come and have a drink!"

"It was the first excuse that came to mind. And true, besides. Vera said she kept nodding off, though she seemed quite alert when I was interviewed."

Alec groaned. "Great Scott, how the deuce does she do it? And what the deuce is Underwood thinking of to let her?"

"Does she make a habit of sitting in on police interrogations?"

"Yes. Give her an inch . . . My fault, I suppose. When I first met her, I was short of men, and I let her help me. She took short-hand notes and typed them up for me."

"Nothing so formal for Inspector Underwood. Vera wanted her hand held, which he allowed. Then she stayed to see if I needed support. I didn't, but she looked so comfortably ensconced in her chair that I couldn't bear to oust her! Not that I minded her being present. She must have stayed with Izzie, too, or she'd be here by now."

"Where's Vera?"

"She went upstairs. She was pretty upset in spite of Daisy's support."

"Not everyone can be as blasé about a police 'interrogation' as you appear to be."

"It's not just that." Willie frowned in thought. "She's been—"

"Hold on a minute. Someone's coming over."

A corn-blond young man had just walked in, scanned the room, and spotted Willie. After a moment's hesitation, he headed for Alec's table. In spite of his cocky stride and a gleaming smile, he looked worried.

As he came closer, Alec saw that he wasn't as young as he'd appeared through the haze of smoke in the bar. Thirty, or even thirty-five. Nonetheless, he was extremely good-looking. His navy suit was in the latest style, double-breasted, with pencil stripes, wide trousers and sleeves, slightly tailored waistline, and wide lapels with rounded tips. His tie was striped with a hideous shade of mauve.

Alec said in a low voice, "A secret admirer?"

"Certainly not!" Willie snapped.

"Miss Chandler. I've been hoping to run across you."

"Hello, Mr. Vaughn," she greeted him, coldly polite.

The estate agent, Alec recalled.

"Sorry to butt in, old chap. I won't be a moment. How are you liking the house, Miss Chandler? No problems?"

"None that we can blame on you," Willie said sarcastically.

"Oh. I . . . Good. Heard from Judith yet? Mrs. Gray?"

"No, and we hardly expect to."

"She might send her address, so that you could forward anything she left behind."

"She didn't leave anything that wasn't included in the contract of sale, and she hasn't sent her address. Sorry." Willie didn't sound in the least apologetic.

"Sorry to bother you. You will let me know if you get her address?"

She sighed. "I'll tell Miss Sutcliffe you're asking for it. She's the one who sorts the post."

"Thanks ever so. It's just—"

"I'm sure you want to go and join your friends, Mr. Vaughn. Good-bye."

He went off at last, disconsolate.

"What was that all about?" Alec asked.

"I'm not sure. He came to the house one evening. I was the only one at home—I was tired and the others went to the cinema. I didn't invite him in."

"You don't like him, do you?" It was more of a statement than a question.

"I don't think you should ask me that."

"You're right. I apologise."

Willie waved away his apology. "I forgot to tell the inspector he called. Does it matter?"

"Shouldn't think so, but do tell him when you get a chance. Vaughn asked the same questions at that time?"

"Yes, but I don't remember that I bothered to mention it to Izzie. For all I know, she did find something from Mrs. Gray in the post and chucked it away, not having any use for it."

"I'll ask—I'll suggest that Underwood ask her. No, I've got to keep my finger out of this pie! You ask Isabel and if she says yes, advise her to report it to Underwood."

"It would eliminate Mrs. Gray as victim and possibly save a lot of effort, I suppose."

"Especially if she remembered the address, or could find the paper. The Sûreté—No! Stop me meddling."

"As long as you don't actually get in touch with the Sûreté or tell Underwood what to do, it's not meddling," Willie assured him. "One can't help thinking about it."

"But I shouldn't be talking about it."

"Let's talk about something else, then. When do you think we'll be able to move back—"

"I don't think you should ask me that," he quoted her own words.

She laughed. "Oh dear, there really isn't any other topic of conversation at the moment, is there?"

"Would you like another sherry?"

"What I'd like is a large B and S. I'm not sure mixing the two is a good idea, though."

"It won't hurt you. One B and S coming up."

While he was at the bar, Daisy and Isabel came in. Daisy did look tired, as Willie had claimed. Barely convalescent, yet she couldn't keep her nose out of a murder investigation, he thought with exasperated fondness. No point in trying to exact her promise not to get involved, but he would make her promise to take care of herself. He hoped her friends would keep an eye on her when he went back to London, if she insisted on staying.

Isabel saw him and they came over.

"What would you like?" he asked.

"Sherry, please," said Isabel.

"Not something stronger?"

She grinned. "I was brought up Methodist. I still feel slightly guilty drinking sherry. I never developed a taste for cocktails, and beer is unladylike. I hope their sherry is better than what we offered you."

"Mrs. Barnes, the doctor's wife, seemed to find it acceptable. Daisy, the usual?"

"Yes, please, darling. But let's take our drinks to the dining room. I asked them to reserve us a table. I'm so hungry I could eat a horse. Where are the others? Not still in that dismal parlour?"

"Willie's over there." Isabel nodded towards the corner. "I'll fetch her."

Alec added a sherry and a vermouth with soda to his order and asked the barman to have them brought to the dining room. The man grudgingly agreed.

"Vera's gone upstairs," Alec told Daisy. "Willie said she's upset."

Daisy frowned. "She was in quite a state, and I can't work out why. I'll go and see if she wants to come down for supper."

"Let one of the others go, love. You're not altogether yourself yet."

"I do feel rather like a wet rag, but I'm sure it's just missing lunch. Tea was good but didn't make up for it." She paused as the others came up, then said, "Sally Hedger is waiting in the dining room this evening. I'm sure she'd take a tray up to Vera if she doesn't want to come down."

"I'll try to persuade her to come," said Willie. "It's not good for her, brooding alone. Besides, we need to talk."

"No talk about the m—the case while we eat!" Alec commanded.

"All right, but I still think Vera should join us. If she hides herself away, Inspector Underwood is bound to find it suspicious."

97

TWELVE

Willie went upstairs to talk Vera into coming down, while Daisy, Alec, and Isabel made their way to the dining room. Sally, a neat figure in her black frock and white apron, met them at the door with a smile and showed them to a table.

"Miss Leighton and Miss Chandler will be down in a minute," Isabel told her.

"I heard you ladies are staying the night here, Miss Sutcliffe," Sally said diffidently. More concerned than curious, she went on, "I hope there's nothing wrong at Cherry Trees, what with the police from Wycombe in the snug and all."

"Don't worry, Sally, nothing involving your aunt."

"Auntie May can take care of herself, miss. It's you I was worrying about. You're all right, then?"

"Except that we're hungry," said Daisy. "What's on the menu?"

"It's cold roast beef or lamb, with salad and baked potatoes," Sally said apologetically. "We don't get that many people Sunday evenings."

"It's more choice than I'd be offering at home this evening," said Isabel. "I'll have the lamb. And I might as well order the same for the others."

Daisy and Alec both chose the cold beef. Daisy offered to swap with Willie or Vera if they preferred it.

They arrived just as Sally went off to fetch the soup. Vera was red-eyed and subdued. She hardly ate anything and spoke only when directly addressed, though she appeared to be interested when Alec and Willie talked about making the acquaintance of Dr. and Mrs. Barnes.

Sally had just brought apple crumble and a pitcher of custard when DC Pennicuik entered and came over to their table.

"DI Underwood would like to see you, sir, when you've finished your supper."

"In the snug?"

"Yes, sir."

"Five minutes."

"Thank you, sir." The constable departed.

"Oh dear," said Daisy. "I have a nasty feeling—"

"Daisy," Willie exclaimed, "you don't think Underwood suspects Alec, do you?"

"I doubt it. No, I have a feeling Alec's going to end up more involved in the investigation than he claims to want to be."

"I'll do my very best to avoid such a fate," Alec said dryly. "Daisy, make sure your friends' meals are put on our tab."

That provoked an outcry, but he insisted that it was a fair return for their offered hospitality at lunchtime. It wasn't their fault they'd been unable to carry out the offer.

"It's my fault," Vera lamented. "I wish I'd never mentioned the locked cellar!"

Daisy had misremembered who had been the first to bring up the subject. She still couldn't see why it mattered, but the inspector had asked her. Alec looked interested, though no one who didn't know him extremely well could have guessed it.

Perhaps they both assumed the person who drew attention to the inaccessible cellar could not be aware of what would be found when it was opened. On the other hand, whoever had shoved the victim down the stairs—assuming that was what had killed her—must have been on tenterhooks, waiting for the body to be found, so perhaps she'd prefer the inevitable discovery to be hurried up. Daisy could imagine Vera being unable to stand the suspense. However, she could not imagine Vera doing the shoving.

Unless the victim had died of poison, or stabbing, or something else, and had then been dumped in the cellar. . . .

Of course, only Willie had had the slightest idea that Alec's skills might include picking locks. Yet she was the one who had blithely fetched the wire for him to make the attempt. Even given her fundamentally cheerful disposition and the inevitability of eventual discovery, Daisy found it inconceivable that she would have shown no signs of uneasiness.

The likeliest culprit of the three was Isabel, without question. She spent more time in the house, so had more opportunity. Tall and sturdy, she was physically capable of the deed. Her choice to sell her family home in Yorkshire and move to Buckinghamshire showed her decisive and resolute. Daisy hadn't witnessed her losing her temper, but it wasn't difficult to envision.

Angry, Isabel would be formidable. But Daisy had no idea what, if anything, would make her angry enough to resort to violence.

Not that it mattered. Far more likely was that the murder had occurred before the friends moved in. Daisy hoped Detective Inspector Underwood was of the same mind.

At this point in her musings, Alec excused himself and stood up to leave. Daisy realised she'd consumed half her crumble without tasting a bite.

"Eating in your sleep, love?" Alec teased. "Better not stay up late."

"How long do you think Underwood will keep you?"

"Your guess is as good as mine."

"How annoyed is he about your being on the spot?"

"Your guess is as good as mine."

"Darling, you must have some inkling!"

"Ambivalent, if you insist."

"That's no help."

"Sooner or later, he'll come down on one side or the other. I mustn't keep him waiting." He departed.

"Daisy, is there any chance Alec will be put in charge?" Willie asked.

"I very much doubt it, whether the inspector wants him or not."

"Underwood can't suspect him!"

"You never know. He's a witness at least. He can't very well investigate himself."

Willie giggled. "No, it sounds ridiculous, and unethical, if not actually against the rules."

"The press would have a heyday. I wonder how long it'll be before they arrive."

Vera quailed. "Oh, no! Not tonight, surely?"

"People must have seen the police at Cherry Trees. Someone will have notified the local paper by now."

Vera heaved a sigh of relief. "The *Bucks Free Press* doesn't come out till Friday, thank heaven."

"If they have a single enterprising reporter, he'll sell a tip to one of the nationals. But they'd have to get here tonight to publish the news in tomorrow's morning papers."

"Let's go and have coffee in the parlour," Isabel proposed. "Nobody can bother us there."

Except a female reporter—but Daisy kept quiet not wanting to sow further alarm and despondency. If she were a newspaper editor, she'd consider the story of a murder in a house inhabited by three single women to call for the feminine point of view.

Sally arrived to clear the table. "Will you have coffee?" she offered.

"Could we have it in the parlour?" said Isabel.

"Yes, of course, Miss Sutcliffe."

As the others trailed out, Daisy said, "Sally, put everyone's dinner on our bill, please."

"All right, Mrs. Fletcher. That's ever so nice of you." She lowered her voice to a whisper. "That Sergeant Harris is in the public. He's telling everyone the detective that's in Mr. Whitford's snug won't let the ladies go home."

"Has he said why?"

"Not outright, just nasty hints. That's his way."

"Oh dear! Thank you for telling me, Sally."

Daisy hurried after her friends.

As soon as the door of the ladies' parlour shut behind her, she warned them that rumours were already flying, no doubt growing more shocking with every repetition.

"Inevitable," Isabel said. "We're the obvious suspects. In fact, the only ones, as far as I can see."

"Oh!" Vera moaned.

"We've got to face the facts, Vera. There isn't anyone else."

"I'm not so sure of that," Willie argued. "What about Donald Vaughn?"

"Methinks the gentleman doth protest too much?" said Daisy.

"Yes, and he wasn't his usual bumptious, obnoxious self this evening. All that show of enquiring after her could be a ruse to divert suspicion."

"Could be. As far as the investigation is concerned, it's very early days yet. The police don't know yet what they're looking for or whom to ask. For a start, we seem to be taking it for granted that the remains are Mrs. Gray's. Admittedly, she doesn't sound like a particularly pleasant person, though I don't know enough about her to judge. When they begin to dig into her background, they may find she has dozens of enemies."

Willie grinned. "Dozens?"

"All right, several. Not to mention friends who would know when she left town."

"And *whether* she left town."

"If they saw her off, or have heard from her since. When did you see her last?"

"We signed the papers on September the sixteenth. I didn't see her after that."

Vera nodded agreement.

"Neither did I," Isabel confirmed, "nor hear from her. I was a bit surprised. I'd expected a few last-minute adjustments to what she wanted to leave for us."

"Such as?" Daisy asked.

"Oh, for instance, in the linen cupboard there's a set of initialled silver-plated napkin rings that look like a family heirloom. She might have forgotten those and decided she wanted to keep them after all. I didn't really think too much about not hearing from her, just assumed she was satisfied."

"From what little I saw of her," said Willie, "she's the sort who's never satisfied."

"That's why I was a bit surprised. She was impatient, too, and liable to make up her mind without due consideration."

"In any case, she's not necessarily the victim," Daisy reminded them. "We already decided she could have been the murderer. Or it could be someone else entirely, nothing to do with her, someone taking advantage of the house being empty to dispose of an inconvenient body."

"Do you write fiction as well, Daisy?" Isabel enquired. "That sounds like a plot for a thriller."

"No," Daisy said crossly.

"I feel as if we're stuck in a shilling shocker." Vera's voice was shaky. "I don't know how you can be so calm about it."

"Getting all het up doesn't help," Isabel pointed out. "In fact, it makes everything seem ten times worse than it really is."

Willie stuck up for Vera. "She can't help it. You have nerves of steel, and I can usually see the funny side. Daisy, do you think the police will seriously consider the theory of the empty house used as a dumping ground by strangers?"

"It's not a theory, only a vague hypothesis. What Alec would call wild speculation. But they have to take all possibilities seriously, especially when they have so little to go on."

Sally came in with a tray of coffee cups and a pot. "I brought a cup for Mr. Fletcher, too," she said, "just in case."

"He's still with the inspector?"

"Yes, madam."

"Thank you, Sally."

Daisy heaved herself out of her chair. "I'm going to tell Underwood about Sergeant Harris spreading rumours. The sooner that's put an end to, the better. Not to mention trying to find out what's going on between Underwood and Alec!"

"Sit down and drink your coffee first," said Isabel. "You don't want to fall asleep in the middle of your sleuthing."

"I'm not sleuthing." Daisy subsided and took the cup Isabel handed her. "Not really. And don't you dare suggest to Alec that I am. He hates to admit that sometimes I'm helpful, not just interfering."

THIRTEEN

"*What's yours,* sir?" DI Underwood greeted Alec.

A promising beginning; Alec decided to reward his earlier abstemiousness. "Whisky and soda, a small one, thanks."

"Off you go, Pennicuik."

Alec took a seat. "What can I do for you, Inspector?"

"For the present, nothing, sir. Nothing official, that is. I've spoken to my super on the telephone and he says he can't make any decisions till he's talked to your super. Superintendent Crane, I told him. That's right?"

"That's the man."

"Have you informed him of the situation, sir?"

"I thought I'd wait till the morning and catch him at the Yard. He gets a little testy when disturbed on a Sunday evening."

"I persuaded Mr. Parry to wait till tomorrow." Underwood and Alec exchanged a smile of complicity. Managing superior officers was part of being a copper.

"What did he have to say when you told him about me?"

"'Blast,' followed by 'damn' as he absorbed the implications. Those weren't the actual words he used, mind you. He was in the Navy and he has some salty profanity at his command. But once I'd got him to consider my plan calmly, he was all in favour."

"Somehow, I'm not surprised. In essence, your plan is to use the services of the Yard without the county having to pay for them."

Underwood grinned. "Yes. Do you think your super will go along with it?"

"It's . . . not impossible, if I'm not urgently needed elsewhere. You'd have to stop the nonsense about keeping your eye on me as a material witness. Save it for Mr. Parry if you must. Crane wouldn't like it a bit. Casting aspersions on one of his officers isn't going to win his cooperation."

"I already dropped that line. What *would* help?"

Alec eyed him appraisingly. "Can I trust in your discretion? And Parry's?"

"If we can trust in your innocence . . ."

"Touché. May I take it you're prepared to extend the same belief to my wife?"

"Unofficially, by all means. I'd be astounded if Mrs. Fletcher played any rôle in the crime. But I'm sure you realise that officially she can't be dismissed so easily, as accessory after the fact, at least. She's known one of the women for many years, and appears to be on intimate terms with the other two. It's plausible that she might help them to cover up the murder."

Alec had no answer for that. He himself had more than once suspected Daisy of just such a misdeed, and even accused her. In at least one case, he knew full well she had helped a killer to escape. She always had what she considered an excellent reason.

"Yes, I suppose it's plausible," he said cautiously. "I'm sceptical, though, about the ladies being involved in the death."

"I have my doubts," Underwood admitted. "I'm afraid Mr. Parry was on about spinsters going peculiar and getting funny ideas into their heads. I tried to explain they're too young for 'the change,' but he's not convinced."

"Pity. Never mind, when we—*you* find out who's dead, you'll doubtless have plenty of suspects on your hands. The same goes if it is in fact the Gray woman, once you start investigating her background."

"Still, we'll have to look at those three very carefully. Both Miss Chandler and Miss Leighton are hiding something, that's for sure. What do you think about this Vaughn fellow, the house agent?"

"Nothing, pending your identifying the victim."

Underwood puffed out his thin cheeks and issued a long sigh through pursed lips. "That's the first order of business, all right. Mustn't take it for granted it's Mrs. Gray, even if she's the only person who's disappeared."

"With a perfectly good explanation."

"That," said the inspector, sighing again, "is the fly in the ointment. So what *will* help persuade Superintendent Crane?"

"My wife," Alec said reluctantly. "Mention that Daisy's here and he'll—"

He was glad to be interrupted by Pennicuik's entrance, bringing their drinks, whisky for Alec, a pint of mild for Underwood, and a modest half pint for the detective constable himself. "Sorry it took so long, sir. After-dinner crush." He sounded wistful.

"No dinner for us tonight, my boy. We've work to do."

"They've got Scotch eggs and pickled onions at the bar, and potato crisps."

Underwood turned his eyes ceiling-ward and rolled them. "Is he under the illusion that he's still a growing lad?" he demanded rhetorically. The constable's ears reddened. "All right, I daresay we'll think better with something in our stomachs. Here." He handed back the change Pennicuik had just given him. "But don't take so long about it. You need to cultivate that air of authority."

"Yes, sir. Thank you, sir." The young man departed at a trot.

The inspector shook his head. "I have high hopes for Pennicuik, but sometimes . . . Where were we?"

"Contemplating Mrs. Gray's proposed travels. Pondering the odds of tracing her to an unknown hotel in Paris and thence to unknown friends in an unknown part of the Riviera."

"Let's hope it doesn't come to that. Not that I wish her dead!"

"Let's hope she has friends we can unearth to whom she's given details of her plans. If it becomes necessary. How do you propose to go about identifying the body?"

"The char, don't you think? Not necessarily to view the corpse, but she should know something about who her friends were. Or are. And she might be able to pin down the date, if we're really lucky."

Alec nodded. It was just the sort of job his retired sergeant had excelled at. DS Tom Tring had been at his best with servants, especially female servants, and labourers, and in public bars, in a way that Ernie Piper was unlikely ever to emulate. Ernie was brilliant at organising information, though, and at remembering details. . . . But unless Alec was officially called in, DS Piper would not be coming down to Beaconsfield.

"Going to approach her yourself?" he asked.

"Unless you think she might succumb to Pennicuik's boyish charm."

As Underwood spoke, the constable came in again, bearing two plates. His beetroot-red ears made it plain he had heard. Without a word, he set one plate beside the inspector, then turned to Alec. "I didn't bring any for you, sir, seeing you had dinner. I hope that's right."

"Yes, thanks. That's not a bad idea, Inspector. From everything I've heard, Mrs. Hedger is an awkward customer. Any sign of coercion and she's liable to dig in her heels. You might do worse than to send in a junior officer. If she doesn't come across, you can always bring in the heavy guns."

"Hmm. Maybe I should have a word first with that niece of hers who works here. Fetch her here, Pennicuik."

The constable bolted a bite of Scotch egg and resignedly set down the remainder on his plate. "Yes, sir." He tramped out.

"What do you bet she asks Mrs. Fletcher to come with her?"

"I'm sorry. Daisy assures me she doesn't do it—whatever it is—on purpose. It just happens."

"This isn't the first time? That's a relief. I was afraid I was somehow encouraging her."

Alec thought it politic not to point out that Underwood had in fact done so, by letting Daisy stay after he had let Vera go. He very much doubted that either Willie or Isabel would have claimed to be unable to cope without her.

"I do wonder what's making Miss Leighton so touchy," Alec said.

"We'll find out in due course."

"And very likely it will have nothing to do with your case."

"And digging into it will upset her more. Can't be helped. It's part of the job."

Pennicuik returned sooner than expected, his face as studiedly impassive as the best of detectives—or butlers. "Miss Hedger, sir. And Mrs. Fletcher." He held the door open for them.

Rising, Alec and Underwood exchanged a glance of resignation and sighed, quietly and simultaneously.

"Thank you for coming, Miss Hedger. We won't keep you from your work for long."

"They can manage without me, sir." If Sally was perturbed by the summons, she didn't show it. "The worst's over."

"Do sit down. Mrs. Fletcher . . . ?"

Uninvited, Daisy dropped into a chair, and Sally followed her example, as did the men.

"I think you ought to know, Inspector," said Daisy, "that Sergeant Harris is in the public bar, busy spreading nasty rumours about what happened at Cherry Trees."

"I heard people repeating what he said," Sally confirmed emphatically. "It was me that told Mrs. Fletcher."

Underwood jumped up. "The flaming idiot! I've had trouble with him before. How he made it to sergeant I'll never understand. Excuse me a moment." He strode out.

"Anything else to report, Daisy?" Alec asked sardonically.

"Not to report, exactly. I wondered whether you and Underwood have seriously considered that the murder might have nothing to do with the house. I mean, someone who happened to have a body to dispose of found out that the house was unoccupied . . . No, it sounds silly now."

"It's a possibility Underwood and I have discussed, though not in depth."

"Oh, good. Not complete bunkum, then."

"No. Only local people would know about the house, though, and no one local has been reported missing."

"Blast!"

Alec was about to invite her in no uncertain terms to remove herself, when Underwood returned.

"He's left already, which means a written report instead of a private dressing down. Along with his failure to view the body, it's inexcusable." Still standing, he addressed Sally. "Miss Hedger, I gather you have worked at Cherry Trees?"

"Just a bit, sir, on and off, like, to help Auntie. Only once for Miss Sutcliffe, but when Mr. and Mrs. Gray lived there."

"I may have to interview you later, but for now, it's your aunt I want to ask about. I've got a few questions to ask her, and I'm told she can be—hmm—stubborn."

"Pigheaded is what Auntie May is, sir, and she don't hold with gossip. Nor with the police, neither."

"Do you think she'd be more likely to cooperate with me or with DC Pennicuik?"

Sally laughed. "If you're thinking she has a soft spot for a young fella, you're out. I'm not saying she don't mourn my cousin Sammy that was killed in the war, but they fought cat and dog when he was alive. She used to cuff him round the ear when he was a kid, and he gave her a black eye once when he grew. No, the only one she might mind is Mr. Fletcher, 'cause he's a gentleman and she does have some respect for the quality. Not much, mind. I couldn't promise."

Alec didn't dare look at Underwood. "I'm just a copper, like Detective Inspector Underwood."

"Well, you talk posh, like Mrs. Fletcher. Don't tell Auntie and she won't know the difference."

"Thank you, Miss Hedger," said Underwood. "You've been very helpful."

"Anything I can do, sir. Nobody—not even Mrs. Gray—deserves to be beaten to death with a poker."

"Good gracious," Daisy exclaimed, "is that what the sergeant's been claiming?"

"Hinting's what he does, madam, and there's other hints worse nor that."

"The identity of the victim is not yet known," Underwood informed her. "I'd take it kindly if you were to pass the word."

"Then I will, sir. That Mr. Harris ought to be told off good and proper. I hope you'll take him down a peg or two, sir."

As soon as the door closed behind Sally, the inspector remarked, "That young woman has a sensible head on her shoulders. Too bad she's stymied our—my plans."

"If you ask me," Daisy said wearily, "which I know you do not, I'd wait till tomorrow. Sleep on it. Whoever she is, she's been dead a long time. In the morning, your super, Inspector, and Mr. Crane will sort out Alec's status in the case, and then you'll be able to go full steam ahead with or without him."

Underwood looked at Alec. "She's got a point."

"Once in a while, every now and again, she does hit the nail on the head."

"Thanks for the vote of confidence, darling! If you can manage without me, I'm off. Oh, that reminds me: Inspector, don't forget my friends are badly in need of some clothes and papers from the house."

"I hadn't forgotten. Pennicuik, you go along with Mrs. Fletcher and get the details. Thank you, Mrs. Fletcher."

Alec waited till Daisy and the constable had left before he asked, "You're going to take my wife's suggestion?"

"It makes sense, and not only because of your position. I've got a couple of men talking to the neighbours. If Mrs. Gray was friendly with any of them, we could have much of the information tonight and only need to confirm it with Mrs. Hedger tomorrow. Should be easier than trying to dig it out of her."

"But she's still our—your best bet for pinning down the date of death."

"Very likely. At least two weeks, the doctor said, and probably not more than four, but given the unusual conditions—"

"They always find an excuse for waffling."

"Don't I know it! This time, though, I doubt we'll get anything useful from the autopsy."

"Unless Daisy's other suggestion proves true: She was killed elsewhere and dumped in the empty house."

"Miss Chandler was the first to propose that theory, I believe."

"Lividity will . . . Except that lividity might not survive the decomposition. I'm not sure about that. The pathologist may even have trouble telling whether the broken neck was the cause of death or occurred postmortem."

"I hadn't thought of that," Underwood said sheepishly. "She could have been poisoned or stabbed or something, and the neck was broken when the murderer chucked the body over the edge." Underwood sighed. "One way or the other, it's as nasty a business as I've come across in a long time. Believe me, if my super wants to call in the Yard, I won't kick against the pricks."

FOURTEEN

Preceding Pennicuik along the narrow passages, Daisy considered the state of affairs with satisfaction. Underwood was not bent upon closing the case quickly by pinning the guilt on one or more of her friends, as she had feared. He was open to other solutions, even one that excluded their house as anything worse than a convenient place to dump a body.

She wondered to what extent Alec had influenced the inspector. They had taken to each other; so much was clear. If they had not been on friendly terms, Alec would never have teased her in the other man's presence.

What was more, he had admitted that she was helpful, even if he had qualified the statement in wholly unnecessary terms. Such an acknowledgement was rare enough to be prized.

They found Willie in the residents' lounge, glancing through a somewhat tattered copy of the *News of the World*. She dropped it when they entered. Daisy glanced round the room. The rest of the residents must be at dinner still, or in one of the bars.

"Where are the others?"

"Vera decided to go back upstairs. Iz went with her."

"DC Pennicuik has come for your lists of stuff you need for tomorrow. Did they leave theirs with you?"

Willie produced three lists from a pocket, and Pennicuik went off.

"All right," said Daisy, sitting beside her, "what's up with Vera?"

"That's what Izzie's hoping to find out. Given that Vera's more sensitive than either of us, and a body in the cellar is enough to upset anyone, it doesn't seem to be the murder per se that's upsetting her. It seems to be something to do with Cartwright."

"The headmaster, right? She wasn't upset about him before the murder?"

"All we were aware of was that she didn't want to invite the Cartwrights for a drink. She doesn't talk about her troubles much, just stews over things."

"So she sees or suspects some connection between Cartwright and the murder?" Daisy mused.

"So it would appear. Let's hope Iz gets it out of her. She's far more sympathetic and patient than I am. If she fails—"

"If she fails, the inspector will have to start digging, and he won't be half as sympathetic and patient. He didn't miss much, you can count on it."

"And if Isabel succeeds, will Alec listen to her and advise as to whether Underwood needs to be told?"

"I'm sure he'll listen. If there's anything in it, I'm sure he'll insist on telling the inspector. Alec has no standing—"

"I should have thought by now the inspector would have asked for his help."

"It's not up to Underwood. Didn't I explain the chain of command?"

Willie sighed. "Don't bother. I can't wait to go to work tomorrow and have something to concentrate on other than murder! Some nice, solid, straightforward numbers. Though . . ." She didn't pursue the thought.

Daisy did. "Though? There's something going on at work, isn't there? This isn't the first time you've hinted."

"I know. I should keep my mouth shut. I'd tell you if I could, Daisy, honestly."

"I'm more concerned about your keeping it from the police."

"It's nothing to do with them." Willie sounded unconvinced, and unconvincing. "Not yet."

"What do you mean? The sooner they know—"

"I meant it's nothing to do with the murder."

"Are you certain?"

The door was flung open. "Dammit!" roared the large man in a dinner jacket who appeared on the threshold. "Where's the—Oh, excuse me, ladies. The tapster sent me off on a wild goose chase." He glared malevolently at the connecting door to the saloon bar. "I see I'm right back where I started. Can either of you by any chance direct me to the landlord's private room?"

"It is complicated," Daisy said sympathetically. "You turn— No, perhaps I'd better show you the way."

"My dear lady, I wouldn't dream of disturbing you."

But Daisy was already on her feet, ignoring Willie's expression of surprise and doubt. She suspected that the tall, stout gentleman was Underwood's superintendent and she wasn't about to let him get away without making an effort to hear what he had to say.

"That's all right. It's easy to get lost in old buildings like this." As, looking baffled, he stood aside to let her pass, she asked, "You're here to see Detective Inspector Underwood, Mr . . . ?"

"Parry," he said grudgingly.

"Superintendent Parry? I thought you must be. I'm Mrs. Fletcher."

"Fletcher? You're the Yard chap's wife? The one who found the body? Those three spin . . . ladies are your friends!" he accused her.

"DI Underwood has already sorted out all that. Doubtless he'll be writing a report for you explaining everything he didn't tell you over the telephone."

"Hmph."

Daisy decided no response was called for. In fact, as the

super appeared to be in a bit of a temper already, she might well make things worse. Whether he was annoyed with Underwood, with Alec, or with Daisy herself remained to be seen.

They reached the den. "Here you are." She stepped back to let the superintendent barge in, then sneaked in behind him as the others stood up. Taking a seat in a dark corner, she knew Alec, Underwood, and Pennicuik had all spotted her, but as she had hoped, they chose not to draw Parry's attention to her.

The inspector introduced Alec.

"How do you do, sir."

Parry stared at him. Daisy couldn't see his expression, but wasn't surprised when he said in an exasperated voice, "So you're the man responsible? I suppose you want to be responsible for the investigation, too."

"Not at all, sir. I'll have more than enough work waiting for me at the Yard tomorrow. Besides, it's a matter for your chief constable and my assistant commissioner."

"The CC will follow my advice."

"I can't say the same for the AC."

"Hmph!"

"Usually my superintendent would make the decision. However, in the circumstances, I'm certain Mr. Crane will take it to the AC. And even if your CC should ask for the Yard's assistance, sir, they could well decide I'm not the right man for the job."

"'In the circumstances.' Hmm." This time his interjection was a thoughtful sound, not irritable.

"Chief Inspector Fletcher has been very helpful already, sir," put in Underwood.

Parry rounded on him. "But would you want help if it wasn't Fletcher, eh?"

"It depends, sir. As I mentioned on the telephone, there's a chance we may have to ask the Yard to request the Sûreté's assistance with enquiries in France."

"All right, I'll—"

The door was flung open and a stranger burst into the room,

a man in an overcoat, with salt-and-pepper hair cropped short and a bristling moustache to match. His hands, one holding his hat, the other a pair of leather gloves, were large, out of proportion to his narrow shoulders. He looked around wildly as Parry swung to face him.

"Who the dev—" Parry caught sight of Daisy and scowled at her. "Who the deuce are you, sir?"

"Cartwright's the name. Whatever she told you about me, it's lies, all lies! She's a—"

"I haven't the slightest idea what you're talking about." The superintendent pointed at a chair and Cartwright sank into it. Parry himself sat down at last, Alec and Underwood thankfully following his example.

Daisy held her breath, but the three policemen were all too interested in the intruder to remember that she ought to be chucked out. Pennicuik, catching her eye, kept his mouth shut.

"Cartwright?" said Underwood. "The headmaster?"

"You know of this man?" Parry demanded.

"I've heard the name mentioned, sir."

"In connection with this case?"

The inspector gave his superior a warning glance. "Not exactly. Tangentially, as you might say."

Daisy was delighted with Underwood's unexpected erudition. Her dear friend, DS Tom Tring, retired, had an extensive vocabulary and enjoyed displaying it. She warmed still further to Underwood.

Parry turned to Cartwright. "I am a superintendent of police. Who do you assume has told us lies about you, and why?"

"Why might she lie? Or why do I assume she has lied?" the schoolmaster asked, prissily precise.

"Either. Both. And why do you think there's a connection with our investigation?"

"I don't . . . I . . ." Agitated, he stood up, dropping a glove. "Clearly I am mistaken."

"So it would *appear*. Detective Inspector Underwood will send someone to take a statement—"

"I was mistaken! I have nothing to say that's of interest to the police."

"All the same," said Underwood, "I'm afraid we can't just drop the subject now you've brought it to our attention. I'll need a statement, sir."

"Not at the school!"

"As you prefer, sir. Constable, escort Mr. Cartwright out and get his address and the hours when he can be found at home. That will be all—for the moment."

Cartwright practically bolted, forgetting his dropped glove. Pennicuik picked it up and hurried after him.

"He's got the wind up all right." Parry nodded with satisfaction. "One of your spinsters is a teacher, isn't she? That'll be who he's talking about, I bet. They go funny, spinsters."

Daisy opened her mouth to object. Alec and Underwood both glared at her.

"Sir," said the inspector, "I'd—"

"What, you're still here, Mrs. Fletcher? Thank you for your help. We won't keep you any longer."

For once, she didn't mind being chased out. She had managed to stay much longer than she expected, and to learn much more than she ought, thanks to Cartwright's intrusion. What was more, her dismissal had been so abrupt, no one had ordered her not to talk about what he'd said.

With any luck, by now Vera would have told Isabel her side of the story. Putting the two parts together, they might work out whether it had anything to do with the murder, or at least bring some comfort to Vera, in that whatever had happened troubled him just as much as her. More so, in fact: She hadn't been driven to make wild accusations to the police.

The residents' lounge was inhabited solely by men. Several stared as Daisy walked through to the parlour to see whether Willie had been driven to take refuge there. She had, and Isabel was with her.

"Who was that?" Willie asked.

"The superintendent, as I guessed."

"That's why you were so keen to show him the way! They let you stay in the snug?"

"I sat down in a corner and stayed quiet as a mouse. Parry forgot me and Alec and Underwood weren't keen to draw his attention."

"Is Parry going to ask Alec to help?"

"They hadn't really decided when I left."

"You were kicked out," Isabel guessed.

"Yes, but before that . . . The most extraordinary thing happened. Cartwright came rushing in, babbling—"

"Wait a minute," said Willie. "Cartwright? Vera's Cartwright?"

"Her headmaster, yes. He insisted that 'she' was lying about him, which rather baffled the coppers as he'd barely been mentioned."

"'She' being Vera?" Isabel asked.

"He refused to say, once he understood that no one had been saying anything, true or false, about him. But I'm certain Alec and Underwood assumed it was Vera, and the superintendent was pretty quick on the uptake. Underwood must have told him on the phone about you three. He knew Vera was a teacher, so he put two and two together. By that time, Cartwright had backed down and denied any connection with the case. He departed with as much haste as he'd arrived."

"He never explained what he was talking about?"

"No, but they're going to take a statement from him. Did Vera tell you what he did that started the fuss?"

Isabel frowned. "Yes. She said I could tell Willie, but she couldn't make up her mind about you, Daisy. Sorry, she feels she doesn't know you well enough."

"Never mind." Daisy did her best to repress her bursting curiosity. "I understand."

"Iz, we ought to tell her—not what he did, since Vera is so embarrassed about it, but what Cartwright said afterwards."

"Well . . . all right. He threatened that if she reported . . . what he'd done, he'd easily convince people it was all her fault.

Everyone would take his word over hers. She'd be disgraced and she'd lose her job."

"And all three of us would have to leave the district," Willie added. "The trouble is, he's right. He's a pillar of the community. We're strangers, and 'superfluous women.' No one would believe her."

Daisy couldn't deny it. "However, the situation has changed. I still can't see what it has to do with the murder, but the police are going to dig until they're sure of that. I doubt they can keep it quiet, even if they try. If you ask me, Vera should make a clean breast of it."

"That's what I told her," said Isabel. "She refused to go to the police—the inspector or even your husband—so I persuaded her to go and talk to Mr. Turnbull, the rector. She can't postpone it till tomorrow because of school. She was putting on her hat as I left."

"Oh good! At least someone will know the truth before the rumours start flying."

"And someone with plenty of credibility," Willie pointed out.

"One would hope so!"

"What's more, it's a church school, for what that's worth, so the rector is probably on the board of governors."

"What still baffles me," said Daisy, "is why Cartwright assumed the police were investigating his misbehaviour towards Vera. I suppose he walked or drove past Cherry Trees, fortuitously or because he's been keeping an eye on her."

"He hasn't got a car. Teachers in church primary schools aren't paid at all well, even the head in such a small school. In fact, before what happened, Vera told me he'd been complaining to her that his wife nags him for wasting his talents for such low pay. One of the things she wants is a car, apparently. He claimed to Vera to be dedicated to teaching. Vera says he's dedicated to power, even if it's just power over a classroom full of children. He's a great knuckle-rapper, is Cartwright."

"If he bullies children, it's not surprising he would bully his subordinate." Daisy returned to her theory. "He could have

120

walked past the house. He would have seen the police there, and then he heard they were here, too."

"Or vice versa," said Willie.

"Or vice versa," Daisy agreed. "But was whatever happened with Vera so criminal as to require so large a police presence?"

"No," said Isabel. "I'm certain the police would have taken no action whatsoever if she had reported it."

"Guilty conscience, then. And now it's his own fault that it will all come out. It does seem to me, though, that it rules him out as the murderer."

"Yes," Willie said sadly. "Much as I'd love to see him arrested, he'd hardly have drawn attention to himself if that were the case."

"Unless," said Daisy, "it's a deliberate red herring, as Vaughn asking for Mrs. Gray's address may be. Cartwright might hope that bringing attention to the lesser offence will throw them off the track for the greater."

"Could it work?" Isabel asked.

"Unlikely. The police—the CID, that is—see through much more complicated ruses. But he may have a low opinion of the local police—"

"Not surprising if he takes Sergeant Harris for an example!"

"Or Cartwright may just be really, really stupid. Not unintelligent, perhaps, but lacking in common sense. At any rate, having thrust himself into the middle of a murder investigation, he's going to find himself thoroughly investigated."

FIFTEEN

Vera scurried into the parlour. Daisy suspected it had taken a lot of nerve for her to brave the residents' lounge on her own. She was dressed for outdoors.

"Did Izzie tell you?"

"I told them you're going to see the vicar. Rector. And I told Willie why, but not Daisy."

"Oh."

"Isn't that what you wanted."

"Yes. But . . ." Vera dithered.

"But what?" asked Willie with a hint of impatience.

"Daisy, are you C of E?"

"Yes. At least—"

"Would you mind awfully coming with me? Izzie's Methodist, and Willie never goes to church."

"I hardly ever go," Daisy admitted.

"But you're not Mr. Turnbull's parishioner. Willie is."

As Daisy actually wanted to accompany Vera, she stopped raising objections. "I'll get my coat."

"It's very kind of you, Daisy," said Isabel, "but are you sure you're not too tired?"

"Not at all." Curiosity outweighed weariness every time.

"It's just across the street," Vera pointed out, "beyond the church. I'll run up and fetch your coat and hat if you like."

"I'll go," Isabel offered, and she hurried out.

Taking her cue from Willie, Daisy didn't tell Vera about Cartwright's irruption into the middle of things. It might well change her mind about confiding in the rector.

Five minutes later, Daisy and Vera crossed the road, free of traffic on a Sunday evening. The grass in the churchyard sparkled with frost and the church stood silhouetted against the star-filled sky. Daisy started to turn left, towards the Old Rectory, an ancient building she had noticed on her peregrinations.

Vera put a hand on her arm and gave a little tug to the right. "It's this way. The new rectory is to the north. Not that it's very new—mid-eighteenth century."

"Much more comfortable, I expect. Look, there's a light in the church. Could it be the rector?"

"I doubt it, not so long after Evensong. Probably the sexton clearing up."

"What sort of person is the rector? Is he married?" A nice, sympathetic clergyman would be an ideal match for Vera, Daisy thought.

"He reminds me of my grandfather."

Too bad. "In what way?"

"He looks like him. Grandpapa was a clergyman. They run in the family. But he was also a hard-headed, practical Yorkshire-man. He spent all his life as vicar of a poor parish in Bradford and he was more concerned with alleviating poverty than climbing the church hierarchy, like my father. He was the kindest man I ever met."

"And Mr. Turnbull is kind?"

"Well, I don't really know, but he looks kind and he was very nice when he called."

Daisy crossed her fingers for luck. Vera's optimism seemed a bit premature, but at least she had cheered up.

A frowning maid opened the door of the rectory and asked

their business. Daisy gave their names and asked to see Mr. Turnbull. Grudgingly the woman invited them to step into the hall, then went away to ask her master if he could see them, muttering audibly about "people who never give the poor man a moment's peace."

"Should I offer to come back in the morning, before school?" Vera whispered. "Or after school?"

"No." Daisy was adamant. Given time to worry, Vera would not easily be brought back up to scratch. Besides, delay would give Cartwright a chance to get his story in first.

The maid returned, with a martyred air that Daisy hoped was not a reflection of the rector's. She led them to a pleasant, shabby living room, Daisy with a firm grip on Vera's arm to prevent backtracking.

The man who came to meet them was short and plump, with a broad pink face and thick, wavy silver hair. He had changed his clerical black for an ancient blazer with the threadbare crest of a Cambridge college on the pocket.

"My dear Miss Leighton, what can I do for you?" He turned courteously to Daisy. "I'm afraid I didn't quite catch your name, Mrs . . . ?"

Vera seemed tongue-tied so Daisy said, "Fletcher. A friend from London. We're sorry to disturb you so late on a Sunday evening."

"Not at all, not at all." He beamed at them benevolently, then glanced behind him, where a plump, grey-haired woman was gathering up her knitting. "My wife."

No hope for Vera, then, even if he weren't thirty years too old. Daisy exchanged polite murmurs with Mrs. Turnbull.

"Don't move, dear," said the rector. "I'll take the ladies to my study."

"There's no fire, dear. It will be icy."

"No matter, no matter. They are young and dressed for out-of-doors, and you know I don't feel the cold."

Vera found her voice. "Mrs. Fletcher has just recovered . . ."

"Come and sit by the fire, Mrs. Fletcher," said Mrs. Turnbull placidly. "I'll make cocoa." She went out.

When they were all seated, the rector asked Vera how he could help her. She looked pleadingly at Daisy, beside her on a sofa.

Daisy knew only half the story. Also, she wanted to avoid all mention of the murder, let alone suggesting any link between it and Vera's troubles. She opted for brevity and candour.

"I just happen to be in Beaconsfield for a few days. I'm not really familiar with the situation, but I gather something that happened at the school upset Miss Leighton. She—"

"Indeed!" The rector leaned forward, fixing an intent gaze on Vera. "I'm sorry to hear it, Miss Leighton. And extremely interested."

Alarmed, Vera faltered, "B-but I . . . You already know?"

Had Cartwright spread his version of events? If so, Daisy thought, the fat was in the fire. She could only hope she'd be able to smother the flames.

"The fact is," the rector continued, reaching over to pat Vera's hand, "we have had great difficulty in keeping teachers for the infants. It is some time since any have stayed longer than a single term. Naturally we—the board and I—suspect a common factor. However, not one of the young women has been willing to speak out, to give any but the vaguest of reasons for resigning. Without facts, we cannot act."

"Go on, Vera," Daisy urged.

"It was last month," she began hesitantly, "a couple of weeks after the beginning of term. Before we moved to Beaconsfield. The children had left and I was tidying the room, preparing lessons for the next day. I was at the blackboard copying out a poem from *When We Were Very Young*. Children respond so well to Mr. Milne's verses. They want to learn to read them for themselves." She fell silent.

"My little ones love them," said Daisy. "You were writing one on the board when . . . ?"

"When Mr. . . . The headmaster came in. I thought . . . I assumed he wanted to make sure I had everything I needed, to ask if I had any questions or wanted advice, as he had once or twice before. I said hello and went on writing on the board. He came up behind me and put his arms round me, and he . . . he . . ." She shuddered. "I'd rather not describe—"

"No, no, by all means!" exclaimed the rector.

"I broke away from him and ran to the door. I told him I was going to report his . . . advances. He said I was a . . . a typical frigid old maid and it was no wonder no one had ever loved me. It's not true! I was engaged. It's different when someone you love kisses you, when you *want* to be kissed." Her voice cracked.

"He didn't come back from the war?" the rector asked gently.

Vera nodded. Daisy couldn't speak, a lump rising in her throat as she relived the moment when she'd heard that Michael wasn't ever coming back. She took Vera's hand in hers.

As if taking strength from her clasp, Vera went on: "Mr. Cartwright threatened that if I told anyone, he'd say I tried to . . . to seduce him and had hysterics when he wouldn't . . . cooperate. He said I'd lose my job and never teach again."

"Darling, that's a threat that would only work if he had done it right away. Telling his version now will lead to his having to explain why he let you go on teaching innocent children after your misbehaviour. Wouldn't you agree, Mr. Turnbull?"

"Why, yes. I hadn't thought about it in precisely those terms, but yes, I see your point, Mrs. Fletcher. He would be most unwise to come forward now."

Daisy realised it was pointless to try to keep Vera's personal troubles separate from the murder. "That seems to be just what he's done."

"What? He hasn't come to me."

"He went to the police."

"Surely this is not a matter for the police!"

"I doubt it. But 'the wicked flee when no man pursueth.'" Daisy was pleased with herself for producing an apt biblical quotation. "You've heard about the police investigation in Beaconsfield?"

"I have heard a doubtless garbled version of something of the sort," the rector said severely. "More than one, in fact, so one or the other is necessarily inaccurate."

"Yes, well, the details are not important just now. As to what brought Mr. Cartwright into the picture, I can only speculate. My theory is that he was passing the house where Miss Leighton lives, saw the police there, learned that she was helping with their enquiries, and jumped to the conclusion that she'd reported him. At any rate, I witnessed his bursting into the inspector's room declaring wildly that an unnamed 'she' was lying. When the inspector obviously didn't know what he was talking about, he withdrew his words. And his person."

"Good gracious!" the clergyman exclaimed.

"Daisy, you didn't tell me!"

"No, you weren't there when I told the others, and as you'd already made up your mind to report him to Mr. Turnbull, I decided his antics might scare you off."

"They might. I'm such a coward."

"Some of us, myself included, would be scared stiff to face a classroom full of children."

The rector asked, "You say Cartwright's not going to pursue the matter?"

"The police will. He has no choice. One can't make wild accusations to an officer investigating murder, and expect—"

"Murder? Then that part of the story was true. I didn't want to believe it, in our quiet little town."

Daisy was about to speak, but he bowed his head in silent prayer over his clasped hands. She was wondering whether she too ought to pray, and if so for whom, when he looked up.

"What should I do, Mr. Turnbull?" Vera asked desperately.

"Sit tight, my dear. Go to school in the morning. Have as little to do with the headmaster as is consonant with courtesy and the necessities of your profession. I'm going to do a little investigating myself. I have the addresses of two of your predecessors who left unexpectedly. I shall write at once and ask them to reveal why they felt unable to stay with us."

"It might be better to look them up in person," Daisy suggested, "if they are within reach. They may not care to put the experience on paper."

"Why should they speak up now," said Vera, "when they wouldn't before?"

Daisy thought fast. "Because, before, they would have just put their reputations and careers in danger, but now they'd be helping you, who find yourself in the same position. Or so we can reasonably assume."

"You're right, Mrs. Fletcher. One is in Croydon, I believe, and the other also south of London. Surbiton? I'm sure there are buses," he added vaguely.

"Oh, Mr. Turnbull, I'm sure writing to them will be enough. I can't ask you to traipse about—"

"My dear Miss Leighton, you are not asking, I'm offering. I keep Mondays as clear as I can, in case anything should come up. 'Traipsing about,' as you put it, will be a pleasant outing."

"I'll drive you, Mr. Turnbull," Daisy proposed. "I'm going up tomorrow to see my babies. I'll pick you up at Marylebone Station in my car."

"That would be most enjoyable, Mrs. Fletcher, if you can spare the time. Let me find my address book and the train time-table." He toddled off to his fireless study.

"It's very sweet of you, Daisy, but—"

"Don't worry, darling, it shouldn't take long, and besides, I have an ulterior motive. You've probably already realised that my besetting sin is curiosity. I'd like to see your predecessors for myself. Also, they may be willing to tell me what they find embarrassing to spell out to the rector."

"I couldn't bring myself to confess to him that I smiled at Mr. Cartwright when he came in."

"Why shouldn't you? The previous time, he'd come to help you."

"Yes, but he probably thought I was encouraging him."

"Admittedly you're particularly attractive when you smile, but if one has to consider every time one feels like smiling that it could inflame the passions of the nearest male, life would become impossible. You mustn't think for a moment that his boorishness was in any way your fault, Vera."

"I used to smile a lot more before, I think."

"Well, start smiling again. It suits you."

As she spoke, a tap on the door preceded Mrs. Turnbull's entrance with a tray of steaming mugs. "Here we are. Now where's my husband disappeared to?"

"He went to get his Bradshaw's, Mrs. Turnbull."

Without comment or questions, the rector's wife—properly discreet in public, though he might tell her everything in private—passed round the cocoa and offered a plate of custard creams. She sat down, saying, "I'll leave you in peace when Jeremy comes back."

"It's all right, Mrs. Turnbull." Vera managed to smile at her. "We've just about finished my . . . our business."

The rector returned, happily waving a large diary, the larger train timetables, and a map book. "Here we are. Let us plan our travels, Mrs. Fletcher."

While they discussed train times and pored over the maps, Vera talked to Mrs. Turnbull. Daisy didn't hear much of what they said, but to her relief, they appeared to be getting on well together.

Daisy and Vera left the rectory half an hour later. Vera walked with a much springier step. Daisy plodded. All she wanted was her bed.

SIXTEEN

When Alec at last went upstairs, Daisy was already in bed and half asleep.

"Darling, have they decided?" she asked drowsily.

"Decided what?"

"Whether they want your invaluable assistance."

"They want me, if they can get me. Go back to sleep, love, we'll talk in the morning."

For once, she obeyed orders. When, having donned his pyjamas and brushed his teeth, he slipped in beside her, she didn't stir.

Alec was tired, but questions and concerns swirled in his restless mind. First and foremost was the super and the AC's possible reaction to the peculiar predicament he found himself in. He would have to testify at the inquest as a private person. If his superiors decided to accede to Buckinghamshire's request for his services, he might find himself on the stand as a detective officer as well. The coroner would have good reason to be outraged.

All Alec could do was employ his persuasive powers to convince Crane and the AC that they must send someone else. Surely the fact that the three most obvious suspects were Daisy's friends would be sufficient.

Wilhelmina Chandler, Vera Leighton, Isabel Sutcliffe: suspicion inevitably fell on them. Alec was fairly certain they were not responsible for the woman's death. He didn't think that conclusion was influenced by his undeniable bias in their favour. Years of experience told him anyone was capable of killing, under the right—or wrong—circumstances. But equally, his experience of judging character made him doubt that any of the three was capable of behaving as she had since the discovery if burdened by a guilty conscience.

Nonetheless, Vera's emotional collapse and Willie's refusal to break a confidence would have to be investigated. As for Cartwright's extraordinary outburst and Vaughn's repeated efforts to trace Mrs. Gray—or to pretend to want to trace her, the two men had moved themselves from the periphery to the centre of the case.

Tomorrow . . . No, no point planning for tomorrow until he heard whether he was to be involved or not. He lay listening to Daisy's quiet breathing, thankful that the horrendous, laboured wheeze had completely disappeared. If he had lost her as he'd lost Joan—

It didn't bear thinking of. Holding her close, he fell asleep.

When the chambermaid tapped on the bedroom door in the morning, Daisy went on sleeping soundly. Alec washed and dressed quietly, then kissed her good-bye. She smiled, mumbled, and turned over. He went down to breakfast, intending to catch an early up-train.

As he ate, he changed his mind and decided to drive up. He hoped Daisy would have the sense to stay in Hampstead once she got home, and he had no idea whether he'd be returning to Beaconsfield. He might need the car for a job elsewhere in the country.

Daisy didn't get down to breakfast until the last possible moment before they stopped serving. Isabel was in the dining room, dawdling over a cup of coffee.

Joining her, she asked, "How is your room working out?"

"Not bad. Cramped, but we don't have much stuff. Vera said the truckle bed was quite comfortable—Sally put an extra mattress on it for her. Vera and Willie went to work. Last night, DC Pennicuik brought us Willie's briefcase and Vera's papers, and our handbags and some clothes, thank goodness. He was no end embarrassed about the clothes! I saw Alec, but just to say good morning before he dashed off. He went up to town?"

"I presume so. I hope the super doesn't hit the ceiling. No other coppers about yet?"

"Not that I've seen. I need to know when they'll let me get the cellar cleaned. I can't stand not having anything to do. They won't object if I go and get some work done in the garden, will they?"

"I doubt it, unless they take it into their heads that another body might have been buried in a flower bed."

"Daisy! Surely they can't—Oh, you're joking. Aren't you?"

"I was, but you never know."

"I do hope Alec comes back. Though I was quite impressed with Inspector Underwood. He seems intelligent, especially in comparison with Sergeant Harris. I hope Underwood hasn't left Harris to guard the house."

"More likely a constable, who won't care two hoots if you work in the garden. It's worth asking, anyway, if you're dying for something to do."

"The alternative is to go and try to persuade Mrs. Hedger to take on the cellar."

"You're pretty certain she won't?"

"I don't know, she might, if I offer her enough money. One thing's certain, she'll be offended whether I ask or not. She'll make sure I realise it's not part of her duties and go about baleful and tight-lipped for hours, if not days."

"Tell her she can use as much carbolic as she likes."

Isabel laughed. "That's a notion. I'll try it. Oh well, it'll have to be done, but I can put it off until the police give the word."

Sally Hedger arrived with Daisy's breakfast. "More coffee, Miss Sutcliffe?"

"No, thanks, Sally. I'm just keeping Mrs. Fletcher company."

The waitress hesitated a moment, then said, "Mrs. Fletcher, d'you mind if I ask . . . Was it really Mrs. Gray that was killed, like they're saying?"

"I don't know, Sally." Better not to mention that no one knew as yet. It was the stuff of nightmares. "Did you like her?"

"Her! No, I did not. Married Mr. Gray for his money, she did, and made him cut his son out of his will, they say."

"A son? He had a son?" Daisy wondered whether Alec and DI Underwood knew.

"Yes, madam. There's them as says worse of her: She did the old man in. She used to talk to him really nasty, but I can't believe she was that wicked, to kill him. 'Sides, the doctor said he died natural. Natural causes."

"Miss!" called a man on the other side of the room. Sally, having dropped her double bombshell, bustled off.

"Gosh!" said Isabel. "Do you believe any of it, Daisy?"

"That Gray had a son, yes. It's the sort of thing people would know. About the will: It wouldn't be surprising if father and son quarrelled over the second marriage. As for Mrs. Gray murdering her husband, I don't suppose we'll ever know. He was elderly, so the doctor wouldn't have looked very hard, so he probably didn't test for poisons."

"Couldn't they exhume his body?"

"With nothing but rumour to go on, I don't think the police could get permission for an exhumation, even if they wanted to."

"Not much point, anyway, with her dead."

"You're assuming she's the body in the cellar."

"Aren't you?"

"Well, yes. I dreamed last night that it turned out to be some-one else and Alec was sent to France to find her and I went with him. . . ." She sighed. "Too much to hope for. I wonder whether Inspector Underwood is aware of the son. Ought I to tell him?"

"He can hardly fail to find out. The lawyer must know."

"You're right. Alec would say it was unwarranted interference. Besides, I haven't time. I'd better stop talking and finish my breakfast or I'll have to run for the train."

Alec reached the Yard at nine. On his desk was only routine paperwork.

"How's Mrs. Fletcher, Chief?" his sergeant, Ernie Piper, en-quired.

"Much improved, thanks. What's up?"

"I dotted all the i's and crossed the t's in Rutland. Inspector Mackinnon took care of everything that came in here over the weekend. There's nothing new to hand."

"That's what *you* think," said Alec, but he didn't explain. Time enough for that when he found out what his position was. He read reports, signed a few letters, initialed memos, all the while waiting for a summons.

It didn't come till shortly before eleven. Ernie answered the internal phone. His end of the brief conversation consisted en-tirely of "Yes, sir." He hung up. "The super wants to see you, Chief. He sounds unhappy."

"For once, he has cause."

Crane's secretary said only, "Go straight in, Chief Inspec-tor," but her moue and her eyebrows told Alec to watch out.

As if he needed a warning.

He stepped through the door. As he approached the desk, the super regarded him in stony silence and did not wave him to a seat. Alec remained standing, trying his best not to come to at-tention.

"Explain."

Alec explained. His story did not change with repetition, but it sounded more and more unconvincing to his own ears each time he told it. At least the super had no interest in the details, only in the broad picture.

His face brought to mind a dormant volcano preparing to erupt. In due course, he erupted.

"It's the devil of a mess your wife has dragged you into now!" He grabbed a fistful of papers from his desk and shook them at Alec.

"Sir, she didn't exactly—"

"Don't quibble, Fletcher. *Her* friend's house. *Her* friend's invitation. *Her* friend's cellar."

Alec let the flow pass over him unanswered. It trickled to a halt.

"Yes, sir."

"It's a pretty kettle of fish! I trust Mrs. Fletcher is back at home with no intention of venturing to Beaconsfield again unless her presence is officially required."

"I—ah—I'm not sure exactly what her plans are, sir."

"Dammit, man, she's your wife! Can't you control—"

"Sir." The secretary's voice came over the interoffice phone. "The Assistant Commissioner will see you and the chief inspector now."

The AC was not given to lengthy or intemperate speech, and he didn't put up with it from his subordinates. "Be seated, gentlemen. Mr. Crane, I have received a brief wire from the chief constable of Buckinghamshire requesting the 'informal' assistance of Mr. Fletcher in a murder investigation. Please explain."

"Mr. Fletcher was visiting friends, sir, with his wife." The super kept his tone even, but the AC winced perceptibly at the mention of Daisy. "He discovered a body hidden on the premises, so he is a vital witness. Nonetheless, the detective inspector in charge has been treating him more like a colleague than a witness, let alone a suspect."

"You confirm that, Fletcher?"

"Yes, sir."

"And has the inspector good reason not to regard you as a suspect?"

"I've never in my life been near the house before, sir, nor met the ladies."

"Ladies?"

The super fielded that one. "Three spinsters sharing lodgings, I gather, sir."

"These surplus females turn up under every stone," the AC commented.

Alec held his peace, with a mental apology to the ladies in question.

"In the circumstances," said Crane, "Buckinghamshire hesitates to put in an official request for DCI Fletcher specifically. But as he's already familiar with the case, they won't have to waste time briefing him."

"True." The AC thought for a moment. "Mrs. Fletcher is also a witness, I take it?"

"Yes, sir," Alec admitted reluctantly. "I doubt she'll be called at the inquest, though."

"And does the local chap consider her a suspect?"

"Not seriously, sir, I'm pretty sure. He can't disregard her altogether. She was in Beaconsfield for a week, and had previously called on her friends. I can't see how she could be suspected of the murder itself, but accessory after . . ."

Simultaneously, Crane and the AC sighed.

"You'll have to go," said the AC. "As unofficially as I can manage it, which means the local man remains in charge and you are helping him, not running the investigation. Understood?"

"Understood, sir."

"See to it, please, Mr. Crane." The AC nodded dismissal.

Alec felt he'd got off lightly. At least they hadn't openly blamed him for Daisy's involvement, though, in spite of the evidence of the past, they appeared to harbour a lingering feeling that he was able to control her.

Walking at his side, the super said, "I didn't think he'd go for it. You're going to have to watch your step, Fletcher. This Bucks DI may think he wants you holding his hand or looking over his shoulder, but don't count on it lasting. Good luck."

"Thank you, sir." Recalling Underwood's blushing baby-faced detective constable, he ventured: "I'd like to take my sergeant if I may. He's good at the sort of detail work provincial forces often can't cope with, and the sooner I get this business cleared up, the happier we'll all be."

"Piper? I suppose so, as the villains seem to be quiescent for a change. Mind, if anything blows up I might recall him. Might recall you, too, come to that. If they want it unofficial, they shall have it unofficial. Mrs. Fletcher all right, is she?"

"Yes, thanks." Or so he assumed. He should have wakened her and asked her plans. He didn't even know whether she was staying in Beaconsfield or had come home.

First things first: he went to tell DS Ernie Piper to prepare for an out-of-town assignment.

"Train or car, Chief?"

"I'm not sure yet. It's an easy journey by train, but the local inspector doesn't have a motor assigned to him at present, so it might be useful. Get me my house on the phone, would you? Daisy, if she's there."

In his brief absence, another stack of papers had appeared on his desk. He started looking through them while Ernie put the call through.

"It's DS Piper, miss. The Chief would like to speak to Mrs. Fletcher if she's at home." He listened a moment, then covered the mouthpiece with his hand. "Mrs. Fletcher's just leaving, Chief. Halfway down the front steps."

Alec picked up his receiver. "Elsie?" he said to the parlour-maid. "Ask Mrs. Fletcher to come back, please."

"She's in a bit of a hurry, sir, but I'll tell her."

A moment later, Daisy was on the line. "Darling? I can't stop to chat. I promised Mr. Turnbull I'd meet him at Marylebone."

"Who?"

"The rector."

"What? Why?"

"That's what we're trying to find out. Are you being sent back to Beaconsfield?"

"Yes. I hope you're staying here."

Daisy laughed. "I got a day return."

"You don't have to use the return half."

"They're expecting me. I can't let them down. Nor Mr. Turnbull. Oh, by the way, did you know Mr. Gray had a son?"

"Daisy, how the—"

"I must run, darling. I'll see you at the Saracen. Toodle-oo!"

SEVENTEEN

Miranda had greeted Daisy with, "Is Mama all better now?"

"Kiss Mama better." Oliver had suited action to his words and they both smothered Daisy with kisses.

Nurse Gilpin grudgingly admitted that they had missed her while she was ill, but they didn't seem to realise how long she'd been missing from their lives. It was nearer three weeks than a fortnight since the doctor had forbidden any contact.

She read to Miranda, who absorbed books like a sponge, helped Oliver put together his wooden train tracks, and played hide and seek with both of them. Then she took them and the dog for a walk on Hampstead Heath. On the way back, they stopped at the garage in the alley to get her Gwynne Eight.

The twins were thrilled to ride in the car for the twenty yards back to the house. Daisy turned them over to Mrs. Gilpin and made ready to depart, only to be called back to speak to Alec on the phone.

After talking to him, Daisy drove down the hill to Marylebone, the smallest of the great London terminals. The rector came out just as she pulled up in front. Spotting her, he waved away a hopeful cabbie and hurried over.

"My dear Mrs. Fletcher, this is very kind."

"Hop in, Mr. Turnbull. We mustn't dawdle if we're going to catch both our targets during their lunch hour. Miss Perry in Surbiton first, I think, and then Miss Mason in Croydon. They're quite close to each other."

They crossed the river by the Hammersmith Bridge and soon reached Surbiton, so quintessentially suburban that it was sometimes referred to as Suburbiton. Daisy stopped at a newsagent's to get directions to the school. They arrived at ten to one, perfect timing.

The building was much larger than the Beaconsfield school. With more people about, Miss Perry ran little risk of finding herself alone and cornered in her classroom by an objectionable superior.

The clergyman went in search of the head teacher, leaving Daisy to wait on a chair in the entrance hall. She hoped she'd be sent for but doubted it. Miss Perry was unlikely to desire the presence of a complete stranger at what must be at best an awkward interview, even a stranger who was young, female, and sympathetic, as Mr. Turnbull would surely inform her.

A couple of minutes passed, then the din of feet and childish voices came from somewhere beyond the hall. Gradually the noise faded. A couple more minutes passed. Evidently Miss Perry didn't need Daisy. She got up and went to study the row of portraits on the other side of the hall. The local dignitaries hanging there were notable only in their fondness for a wide variety of beards and whiskers, and the lack of any trait other than worthiness in their expressions.

At last the rector returned. He, too, looked worthy. He also looked worried, yet with a touch of complacency.

"You were right? Miss Perry had the same experience?"

"Yes. I wish I'd been wrong. How could I be so blind?"

"How could you guess, if she didn't tell anyone?" Daisy consoled him. She took his arm, and gently steered him towards the front door. "I presume, like Vera, she didn't think she'd be believed?"

"She left us at the end of the spring term. Even now, she's very upset and was reluctant to speak out. I had to tell her about Miss Leighton, in strict confidence of course, and point out that she might save future victims from the same . . . unpleasantness." He stood by the car, lost in thought.

"Do get in, Mr. Turnbull, or we'll be late."

Climbing in, he observed, "The two are rather alike, Miss Perry and Miss Leighton, both diffident. Timid, even, though they cope well enough with children."

Daisy pressed the starter. The Gwynne obligingly started on the first try. Engaging first gear, she wondered aloud, "Was either of them timid before being cornered by Mr. Cartwright?"

The rector turned his head to stare at her. "You think not?"

"I haven't the foggiest. Do you remember interviewing them?" She glanced at him.

His brow wrinkled in an effort to recall. "Not clearly, I'm afraid. Just that they both had excellent references."

"They were probably a bit nervous about the interview, anyway. What is Miss Mason like?"

"Rather different, as I recall. More . . . more poised, and determined. When she left, I concluded that she was moving on to a better position, not fleeing in distressing circumstances."

"What a pity!" Daisy was disappointed. One statement confirming Cartwright's actions wouldn't be half as convincing as two.

"However," the clergyman added humbly, "I failed to observe any signs of distress in Miss Perry when she tendered her resignation, so my ability to judge is unreliable, at best."

Daisy made soothing sounds. Being the sort of person people confided in, though often interesting, was sometimes exceedingly embarrassing.

She drove on through the Surrey suburbs and the short, shrinking stretches of countryside between what had once been villages. Croydon now sprawled in all directions, in part because of the aerodrome. When they reached the outskirts, Daisy again stopped at a newsagent's.

"What's the name of the school, Mr. Turnbull?"

"The Old Palace school."

"I've heard of it. It has an excellent reputation. In fact, we thought of sending my stepdaughter there. After teaching infants in a village school, Miss Mason does seem to have moved onward and upward."

"So this part of our journey may be in vain." He went into the shop and returned with directions.

The school was in the ancient summer palace of the Archbishops of Canterbury. Though the buildings had been through hard times in the nineteenth century, much remained as it had stood for centuries. The medieval great hall, through which Daisy and the clergyman were escorted, was a marvel.

However, the room they were shown into was nothing out of the ordinary. Daisy had offered to stay outside, but Mr. Turnbull, demoralised by his encounter with Miss Perry, begged her to stay with him. "Unless Miss Mason specifically asks you to leave."

Miss Mason came in. She was younger than Daisy, tall and svelte, not exactly beautiful, but striking. Even without makeup, doubtless forbidden by the school, she looked well groomed, something Daisy struggled to attain.

"Hello, Mr. Turnbull." Her voice was self-confident and warmly welcoming. "How very pleasant—and unexpected—to see you again." Eyebrows raised, she turned towards Daisy. "And . . . ?"

"Mrs. Fletcher, who has kindly acted as my chauffeur."

The ladies exchanged polite greetings.

"And what brings you to Croydon, sir?"

"Er . . . hm . . ." Mr. Turnbull sent Daisy a pleading glance. He appeared to regret having embarked on his voyage of discovery.

Daisy was sure forthrightness was the way to approach Miss Mason. "The rector finds himself obliged to ask a rather personal question. If you'd rather I wasn't present, I'll take myself off, but . . ."

The schoolmistress's eyebrows rose again, almost as expressive as Alec's. "But? How intriguing. Do ask, Mrs. Fletcher, and then I'll decide—whether to answer the question and whether to answer in your presence."

"Fair enough. We—Mr. Turnbull, that is—has just found out that both the infant teachers who succeeded you at St. Mary's suffered harassment—" Daisy glanced at the rector to make sure he approved of the word; he nodded. "By a certain person."

"That snake, Cartwright," Miss Mason said calmly. "I should have known if I didn't report him, he'd try it again. I rapped his knuckles for him, you can be sure. And that's another thing I dislike about him: He's too free with the ruler and the cane for my taste."

"It was because of him you left?" the rector ventured.

"Partly. I could handle him. But the young man I was seeing at the time was insanely jealous. I shouldn't have mentioned it to him. He took to following Cartwright. The old goat started making up to a young—youngish woman married to a rich old man, I gather, so my young man stopped worrying about him."

Daisy wanted to pursue the subject of the youngish woman, but Mr. Turnbull was so appalled, she didn't like to.

"Scandalous!" He gasped. "I can hardly believe my ears."

"She sent him packing, apparently. As I did my young man. I didn't like his possessiveness. Another reason to move on. I always intended to end up here eventually. My aunt is the headmistress and she promised me a place once I had some experience. When she heard what had happened, she hurried things along."

"My dear Miss Mason, I'm so very sorry—"

"Don't be, Mr. Turnbull. I'm quite happy here. Is there anything else? My children will be returning to the classroom any moment."

"We won't keep you. Allow me to thank you most sincerely for your frankness."

"I regret not having spoken at the time." In a low voice, for Daisy's ears alone, she added dryly, "I hope I shan't regret having changed my mind at this late date."

Daisy felt guilty. Some, at least, of what she had heard she must pass on to Alec, and once in the hands of the police, one could never be sure where information would lead. Miss Mason hadn't been warned that she was on the periphery of a case of murder.

Warning her, Daisy was sure, would have constituted interference from the police point of view. Already it was going to be touchy deciding what she had to tell them and what could be decently suppressed.

Mr. Turnbull preceded the ladies to open the door for them. Behind his back, Daisy whispered, "I don't suppose you'd like to tell me the name of the youngish woman?"

"Oh, something very ordinary. Grove? Or Green, or—Gray, that's it."

Daisy hoped she didn't look too obviously triumphant. "And your friend who saw Cartwright visiting her?"

Miss Mason shook her head. "No, we may have parted brass rags, but that wouldn't be fair. Sorry."

All the same, Daisy mused as she and the rector returned to the car, she had news for Alec. She could explain why Vera had been evasive when questioned and whom Cartwright had in mind when he asserted that "she" was lying about him. She could also offer a motive for Cartwright to have killed Mrs. Gray.

If necessary, the police should be able to trace Miss Mason's jealous boyfriend and get his evidence that the widow had rejected the schoolmaster. Cartwright was apparently a singularly unsuccessful would-be philanderer.

He had a propensity for violence. Both Vera and Miss Mason had remarked on his penchant for beating the children in his class. He was impulsive. He hadn't waited to find out what the police were investigating before he rushed to try to exculpate himself. If Daisy had a list of suspects, he'd be at the top.

"What's Mrs. Cartwright like, Mr. Turnbull?" Daisy asked, starting the car and turning left into the street.

"I was just thinking about her. A difficult woman, I'm afraid.

But I mustn't speak ill of her; no doubt she has her reasons. And besides, it's no excuse for Cartwright's shocking behaviour."

"Very true. Oh dear, I think we're going the wrong way. I'd better concentrate on driving."

They had to circle around to get onto the right road. From that point it was fairly straightforward. Daisy's thoughts wandered again.

Her whole edifice, she realised, was based on the premise that the body was Mrs. Gray's. Surely she must be? After a fortnight or more, anyone else would have been reported missing.

Unless—Could Mrs. Gray have had a prospective travelling companion? Suppose they had planned to set out from Cherry Trees for the Continent, had quarrelled, and Mrs. Gray had pushed her friend down the cellar steps. In that case, the victim would not be missed for who could guess how long?

But that line of speculation was equally fruitless until the corpse had been identified. Daisy was going round in mental circles, and if she didn't watch where she was driving, she'd be going round in literal circles again.

EIGHTEEN

As Alec was leaving the Yard, he heard Tom Tring's voice and glanced into the room he was passing.

"Tom!"

"Hello, Chief. I just popped in for a chat."

The officer with whom he was chatting developed a sudden diligent interest in the papers on his desk. DS Tom Tring, retired, came out into the passage, closing the door behind him. His huge bulk was clad in one of his more subdued suits, a dark grey and forest green check. The bald dome of his head was as shiny as ever and his face no longer had the greyish tinge of permanent tiredness it had worn his last few weeks in the force.

"It's good to see you, Tom. Can't stay away from the old place?"

"Retiring's harder than you'd think, for both me and the missus. She's got her ways, and I try to stay out from under her feet."

"I expect it will grow easier with time. Most things do."

"I haven't got enough to do, that's the beginning and end of it. You know how it is on the job, Chief. You can't start an allotment garden or join a bowling team or suchlike because you may be called away any moment. How are my godson and Miss Miranda?"

"Flourishing. You and Mrs. Tring must come and see them one of these days."

"Any time. And give my best to Miss Belinda when Mrs. Fletcher writes to her at school."

"I write to Bel, too!"

"But not as often, I bet. I know who writes most letters in my family, and it isn't the men. What are you working on these days?"

"A murder in Bucks. I found the body, which has complicated matters. I'm sort of officially unofficial on the case."

"Ah. Mrs. Fletcher involved, by any chance?"

"Well, yes."

Tom grinned. "Ah!"

"You know, I was thinking about you last night. What we needed was someone not obviously a cop to mingle in the public bar. Come to that," he added thoughtfully, "we still do. Also someone to chat with servants in hope of tracing a gardener and a maid. But no, that wouldn't be at all according to Cocker."

"Come on, Chief, you can't dangle the carrot and then whip it away! Unofficial, you said. What could be more unofficial than me and the missus taking a little holiday in the country? Wouldn't it be a coincidence if we ended up in the same place as you and Mrs. Fletcher?"

Alec's turn to grin: "I can't stop you, Tom. We're at Beaconsfield—pretty country. Come on up to the office—no, better not."

"Too official-looking?"

"Much too. It's just on opening time; let's go over to the Feathers. I'll buy you a pint and explain the situation."

When Alec and Ernie Piper reached the Saracen's Head, Sally Hedger was at the reception desk.

"Mrs. Fletcher isn't back from London yet, sir," she said to Alec. "You're staying on?"

"For the present. I'm not sure how long."

"I'll see if you're still in the book." She opened the big ledger. "No, Mr. Whitford wrote you down as checked out. Here's your key. And Mr . . . ?"

"Piper," said Ernie. "Ernest Piper, Detective Sergeant, miss. I don't know how long I'll be staying neither, sorry. Likely as long as Mr. Fletcher."

"I'll put you in Twelve, Mr. Piper, next to the Fletchers." Sally smiled at him. "Stay as long as you want. You're from London, too?"

"That's right."

"I'll see the Boots takes up your bags, gentlemen. By the way, Mr. Fletcher, Inspector Underwood has set up at the police station today. It's just down the road. Turn left outside the door and go on round the corner into Windsor End."

"Thanks."

"Miss Sutcliffe spent half the morning there. Mr. Underwood asked her not to see Auntie May about cleaning the cellar till after he's talked to her."

"Miss Hedger, I know you sometimes help your aunt. Please don't offer to do so on this occasion."

"Is it as nasty as they're saying, then?"

"Who's saying?"

"Everyone, but it was Sergeant Harris as started it."

"Today?"

"No, sir, last night, like I told the inspector. I haven't seen hide nor hair of him today."

"Good," Alec said grimly, hoping Underwood had put the sergeant firmly in his place. "It's quite as nasty as anything I've ever seen. Stay away. If my wife comes in before I return, please tell her I'll be at the police station." He almost added, "and she's not to join me," but decided that was carrying familiarity a bit too far.

As he and Ernie turned left into Windsor End, Ernie said, "That young woman seems to know a lot about our business."

"Rumours have been flying, as you heard, but more to the point, Daisy has taken a liking to her."

"I see."

"Sally was very good to Daisy when she was ill." Alec tried not to sound defensive.

"Well, that's different then, isn't it." Ernie had always been a staunch admirer and defender of Daisy, even after he at last realised that she wasn't always right. "A nice young woman. Miss Sutcliffe is not the lady Mrs. Fletcher was at school with, right?"

"Right. She's the one who runs the household. But they're all Daisy's friends now."

"If that isn't Mrs. Fletcher all over! This is an odd position we're in, and no mistake, being unofficial. What are you going to do if this DI Underwood starts ordering you about, Chief, and telling you to do things you don't agree with?"

Alec had told Ernie all the facts of the case, but hadn't attempted to explain his tenuously amicable relationship with the local man. "Let's not borrow trouble," he temporised. "Here we are."

Beaconsfield's police station was an ugly brick building that also housed the magistrate's court. DI Underwood had appropriated a good-sized room with a couple of desks. He was the sole occupant, seated at one of the desks, gloomily reading the top page of a neat pile. When Alec and Ernie entered, he sprang up.

"Chief Inspector, glad to have you back, sir." He looked enquiringly at Ernie.

"DS Piper, my right-hand man. Superintendent Crane suggested he might be of assistance."

"Happy to meet you, Sergeant."

"Likewise, sir." They shook hands. "I hope I can help."

Underwood waved them to a couple of rather battered wooden chairs and sat down on a similar one behind the desk. "The two of you have doubled my detective force, though I have a few PCs and a uniform sergeant at my disposal."

"Not Sergeant Harris, I hope," said Alec.

"Lord, no! My super gave him what-for for gossiping and he's lying low. Sergeant Levin and his men are talking to neighbours who weren't at home when they called yesterday or this morning. They'll try the shops on Station Road, too. You never know, someone may have seen her with an identifiable companion, or been given an address to forward a final account."

"Delivery people may even be able to put a date to her demise—or departure. Any luck with the neighbours?"

"So far, nothing. With those damned high hedges all along the street, nosy neighbours are scarce! Not one of the residents of Orchard Road admits to having been better acquainted with Mrs. Gray than to say good morning."

"Too soon to give up," Ernie observed cheerfully. "You never know what they'll remember with a bit of digging."

"True, Sergeant. Maybe I'll set you onto them. Two or three did say they think she's spent a good deal of time in London since her husband died. So far we haven't found a local doctor or dentist. They're cagy about giving information about their patients on the telephone, so DC Pennicuik called on all the Beaconsfield practitioners—both, rather, one of each. Dr. Barnes was her husband's practitioner, but not hers. I sent Pennicuik to High Wycombe to make the rounds there. If she went to a London doctor or dentist, though . . ." Underwood looked thoroughly discouraged.

"Her dentist could be all-important," said Alec. "Dental records may be the only way to get a positive identification of the victim. Have you seen her lawyer yet? He's in Beaconsfield, isn't he?"

"Mr. Ainsley, yes." The inspector glanced at the wall clock. Standing, he took his hat from the knob of his chair. "I've got an appointment with him in fifteen minutes. He was away for the weekend, his secretary told me, and wasn't expected back till after lunch. You'll come with me, won't you, Mr. Fletcher?

Solicitors are always tricky to deal with and he might be a bit more forthcoming to a high-ranking Scotland Yard man."

"I'll come. In the meantime, I suggest Piper go through those reports you have there. He's a demon for spotting easy-to-overlook details."

"Go right ahead, Sergeant. I wish you better luck than I've had."

A chilly breeze from the north had arisen. As Alec and Underwood passed the Saracen's Head, Alec was tempted to drop in to find out whether Daisy had returned already. But Underwood was walking briskly, so he resisted temptation. They crossed the main road, and continued down Aylesbury End towards Station Road and the new town.

The thought of Daisy reminded him of her inexplicable errand. "Was Mrs. Gray a churchgoer?" he asked.

"I don't think so. The pastor of the Congregational was sure she'd never attended his services. The rector of St. Mary's wasn't at home when I called, but his wife was pretty sure Mrs. Gray wasn't a member of the congregation, even on an occasional basis."

"The rector is the Reverend Mr. Turnbull? I . . . uh . . . I ought to tell you that he was picked up at Marylebone station this morning by my wife. Don't ask me why. I haven't the slightest idea."

"She wouldn't tell you why?" Underwood asked, disbelieving.

"She told me on the phone, said she was in a hurry, and hung up before I could ask."

"You wouldn't have mentioned it if you didn't think it's something to do with the case."

"Nothing so clear-cut. It just occurs to me that the school Cartwright and Miss Leighton teach at is a church school. The rector, one may assume, is one of the governors. Miss Leighton lives in the house where the woman died; she was evasive and emotional when questioned. Cartwright's behaviour last night needs to be investigated: Who does he think told us lies about him, and why?"

"And today the reverend gentleman enlists Mrs. Fletcher to escort him about London? Hmm."

"There may be absolutely no connection with the case."

"But it's fishy, if you'll pardon me saying such a thing about your wife."

"You won't be the first, Inspector. No doubt we'll find out in due course what it's all about."

"We've got Miss Chandler hiding something, too, something about this Vaughn chappy who keeps asking after Mrs. Gray, not to mention Miss Sutcliffe claiming he fancied her—Vaughn fancied Mrs. Gray—maybe was even her lover. Here we are."

He stopped at a newish brick building separated from the pavement by just a couple of steps. Beside the green door, a brass plate, worn by much polishing as if it had been transferred from an older building, announced the presence within of Ainsley & Barrett, Solicitors and Commissioners for Oaths. Underwood reached for the electric doorbell.

Alec put a restraining hand on his arm. "If he isn't aware that we haven't yet identified the body," he advised, "don't be in a hurry to tell him. He'd probably refuse to talk about a living client."

"It wasn't in this morning's papers. Local rumours all assume the body is Mrs. Gray's." He pressed the bell.

"I expect they're right."

"The surgeon's doing the autopsy this afternoon. If nothing else, her rings will help."

They were ushered straight into the lawyer's office. Mr. Ainsley was a small, dried-up man, dwarfed by a large room furnished with a huge Victorian desk and heavy glassed bookcases. He didn't stand when they came in or offer to shake hands.

Underwood introduced himself, "Detective Inspector Underwood, sir, of the Buckinghamshire Constabulary. And this is my colleague from Scotland Yard, Detective Chief Inspector Fletcher."

Ainsley bowed his head in acknowledgement and invited them to be seated. "How may I be of assistance, gentlemen?"

"I daresay you've heard, sir—"

"My secretary informed me that Mrs. Albert Gray's lifeless body has been found. Is it true that she was murdered?"

"The circumstances indicate a case of murder, yes, sir. You'll appreciate that the more information we have about a victim the better, and nobody we've spoken to hereabouts seems to have been more than barely acquainted with Mrs. Gray."

Neatly worded, Alec thought; Underwood had avoided stating outright that the body was Mrs. Gray's, though the solicitor still might raise a stink if he found out it hadn't yet been officially identified.

The lawyer nodded. "I was given to understand that her friends are, or were, I should say, mostly in London."

"And her family?" Underwood asked. "We have to get in touch with her family."

"I fear I cannot help you there. Neither she nor her late husband, when he was alive, ever mentioned her family to me."

"She left them nothing in her will?"

Ainsley steepled his fingers and studied the two detectives over this barricade, not inconsiderable for one of his stature. "Strictly speaking, I am not at liberty to discuss Judith Gray's will until it is probated. I can tell you this: When I drew it up after Gray's death, I asked her if she wanted to leave any little remembrances to family members and she refused without explanation. She has . . . had little enough to leave."

"Really? Everyone says Albert Gray was wealthy!"

"He was."

"How long were they married?"

"About five years. Judith Gray was certainly entitled to provision for life. However, acting on my advice, Albert left most of his property in trust to her, as long as she remained unmarried, with reversion to his son by his first wife, and his son's descendents per stirpes."

Underwood looked baffled.

"You mean," Alec intervened, "she enjoyed the income for her lifetime but couldn't touch the capital?"

"Precisely."

"But she was able to sell the house?"

"Oh yes. Gray foresaw that she'd want to move to a flat in London."

"Or to an unknown address in France?"

"That neither of us foresaw, I regret to say. Nothing in Gray's will disallows such a move, so I was obliged to authorise a letter of credit to a French bank, for almost the entire proceeds of the sale."

"Drawn on what bank, sir?" Alec put in.

"The local branch of the County and Midlands. Retrieving the sum from France is going to be complicated, to say the least," Ainsley added peevishly. "And I have several personal letters waiting for her to send her address. I suppose I'll have to open them."

Underwood's eyes gleamed. "They'll probably give us the addresses of some of her friends."

"I shall need legal proof of her demise, first."

One of those frustrating vicious circles, Alec thought. They needed a close friend to confirm identification of the body but they couldn't find a friend until . . . "Does the estate include Mrs. Gray's ruby ring?"

"It does, though not her pearls, which she left to a friend."

"To a friend!" Underwood exclaimed. "Then you must have that friend's particulars?"

"I'll have my clerk look out the name and address for you."

"Thank you, sir. Also Albert Gray's son . . . ?"

"Of course, of course. Robert's the name. Though you may not find him at his London flat. He's in the Foreign Service, a diplomat. He's often abroad."

"Does he know the provisions of the will?"

"Yes indeed. You mustn't think he's been unprovided for. His father bought the flat for him and set up a small trust so that he will never starve. However, Albert felt a young man should make his own way in the world, as he himself had." The lawyer took out his pocket watch and opened it.

154

Underwood looked at Alec, who said, "Just one more question, sir. You would recognise the ruby ring? Beyond a doubt?"

"Certainly. Why?"

"Not having any family members to identify the body, we can do with as many confirmations as possible."

"Her stepson will recognise her." Ainsley let out an unexpected chortle. "With pleasure."

The inspector opened his mouth. Alec shook his head. They took their leave, with proper expressions of gratitude, and stopped on the way out to tell the secretary someone would be sent later that afternoon to fetch the promised names and addresses.

Out on the pavement, Underwood said, "Why . . . ?"

"He was more helpful than he should have been, than he intended to be, but he would never have explained what he meant by 'with pleasure.' We can assume the son didn't care for his stepmother."

"Not to mention, he stands to inherit a lot of money! I'd say he's suspect number one."

"I won't argue with that."

"He has a huge motive. The means are right there on the spot. Opportunity is all we need."

"And evidence," Alec said dryly.

"We didn't ask about keys."

"An excuse to go back. What's next on the agenda?"

"What would you suggest?"

"The bank, don't you think?"

"We'd better step on it. It's nearly closing time, if the Beaconsfield branch is the same as High Wycombe." Underwood took a plan of the town from his pocket and consulted it.

The bank was just a couple of minutes' walk along Station Road. It was a small branch, with just two clerks. Underwood asked to see the manager.

Over his half spectacles, the clerk frowned at them. "We close in ten minutes," he pointed out. "The manager won't be seeing any further customers today."

"Police." Underwood showed his warrant card. Though he spoke quietly, the second clerk and the three customers present turned to stare.

The frown became a scowl. "No need to announce—" Catching sight of Alec's raised eyebrows, an expression known to stop even Daisy in her tracks, the clerk pursed his lips. "Very well, I shall ask Mr. Torrance whether he is able to assist you." He took his time closing down his station, then disappeared into a backroom, from which he quickly reappeared. "Please come this way."

Mr. Torrance was stout and red-faced, with bulging eyes. "What do you want?" he demanded aggressively.

Alec placed his warrant card on the desk in front of the man. "To ask just one question, sir."

He picked it up and studied it for a moment. "Scotland Yard. Well?"

"Mr. Ainsley, the sol—"

"Yes, yes, I know who Ainsley is. Get to the point."

"Mr. Ainsley, as trustee of the estate of the late Albert Gray, provided his widow with a letter of credit for a large sum, drawn on this bank. Has it been presented at a bank, here or abroad, and if so where?"

"That's two questions. And now I've one of my own. What business is it of yours?"

"Murder is our business," Alec said bluntly. "Your evidence could prove that the victim is not Mrs. Gray."

Torrance's eyes popped more than ever. "Mrs. Gray murdered?"

Alec left it to Underwood to explain. He was still uncertain of his colleague's abilities. This was a good test. The inspector passed, giving the bank manager just enough information but no more.

"Oh, very well," said Torrance petulantly. "Such a large transaction would have landed on my desk. As it has not, you can take it that the letter has not been presented for payment or deposit at any bank in the United Kingdom within the past two or three days. A Continental bank should have notified us immediately, or enquired about the validity, but of course one can't count on them, and it would take longer."

"How long, sir?"

"Any of the more civilised countries, no more than a week. If that's all . . . ? The bank may close to the public but I still have work to do."

"You'll let us know if and when the letter of credit is presented, of course, sir," Alec said in a tone that took for granted a positive response.

Emerging on to the pavement, Underwood blew out an emphatic breath. "Phew! I reckon we were lucky to get anything out of him. Not that his answer solved the question. Just another hint suggesting the deceased is Judith Gray."

"Better than the reverse," Alec pointed out.

"What do you mean?"

"If he'd provided evidence that Judith Gray was alive no more than a week ago, we'd have a corpse on our hands without the slightest idea whose."

NINETEEN

Daisy reached the Saracen's Head at teatime. Edward the Boots informed her that Miss Sutcliffe was in the parlour.

"Oh, good. Please tell her I'll join her shortly. Is Mr. Fletcher in?"

"No'm. He went to the p'lice station, him and Mr. Piper. That 'tec that was in the snug, he's there today."

Bother, Daisy thought crossly. It would be much more difficult to find out what was going on at the police station. She thanked Edward and went upstairs for a wash and brush-up, pondering Ernie Piper's unexpected arrival. Then she headed for the ladies' parlour.

A welcome fire burned in the grate. Isabel sat by it, alone, paging in a desultory way through a gardening magazine.

"Daisy!" She tossed the magazine onto the nearest table. "I'm glad you're back. I'm feeling like a leper in here. Women I've seen at the shops, who've never appeared to notice my existence, keep peering in and instantly recognising me as connected with the murder. And going away again."

"Never mind. Don't let them stop us ordering tea. I'm

parched." She rang the bell. "I'll tell you about what the rector and I found out, as soon as I've wetted my whistle."

Sally came. "Edward said you're back, Mrs. Fletcher. Tea?"

"Yes, please, Sally."

"We've got lots in for tea, so it may be a little bit. The ladies are all going in the dining room, though. You've got it nice and peaceful here."

"They're all talking about us, aren't they, Sally?" Isabel asked.

"About the murder, miss, yes. I'm listening out for anything about Mrs. Gray, being as I know Mr. Fletcher needs more information. That Sergeant Piper, madam, do you know him?"

"Oh yes, I regard him as a good friend. He's staying here?"

"That he is. Seemed like a nice young man."

"He is. And not married."

"Oh, madam, that's not what I meant at all," Sally said, rosy-cheeked. "I'll fetch your tea, ladies."

Daisy waited till the door closed to say with a laugh, "Ernie's made quite an impression there!"

"Do you really . . ." Isabel fell silent as the door opened again.

Two women came in—all the way in, and closed the door behind them. As the pair came over Daisy recognised Mrs. Turnbull.

"May we join you, Mrs. Fletcher?"

"Please do. This is Miss Sutcliffe."

"Mrs. Barnes," the rector's wife introduced her companion. Everyone murmured, "How do you do."

"I met your husband last night, Mrs. Fletcher," said Mrs. Barnes, "and Miss Chandler also. Your mutual friend, I believe?" She looked from Daisy to Isabel.

"As is Miss Leighton, of course," Mrs. Turnbull added. "Miss Sutcliffe, I must apologise for not having called at Cherry Trees. I was away when you moved in and then I got swamped with catching up. I'm afraid the three of you are going through a time of troubles."

"That's one way of putting it!" said Isabel.

"If there's anything I can do to help or advise . . ."

"I don't suppose you have any influence over Mrs. Hedger? The cleaning lady?"

"None whatsoever," the rector's wife admitted tartly. "She's not an Anglican."

"But I doubt the Congregational pastor can help you either," said Mrs. Barnes. "She's a thoroughly cross-grained old woman."

Isabel laughed ruefully. "She seems to be notorious."

"I daresay she's done the odd job now and then for just about everyone in town. She's a hard worker but she does things her own way. She's not refusing to work at Cherry Trees, is she? She's been there forever. I wouldn't have expected her to give up one of her regular jobs like that."

"She's not. But I'm going to have to ask her if she'd clean up the . . . Well, I won't go into distasteful detail. I doubt she'll agree, even for extra pay. I couldn't really blame her, but if she refuses I don't know where to turn."

"My dear, the Labour Exchange, in High Wycombe. These days there are so many young men looking for casual work. Since the war, you know. They don't seem to be able to settle to anything. And some of them must have seen things as bad as . . . as what you need cleaned up."

"You don't think it would bring back terrible memories?"

"One can but ask."

"How does one go about it?"

As Mrs. Barnes explained the system, Sally came in with tea for four. Mrs. Turnbull took on the task of pouring. Daisy handed round cups and saucers before settling herself with a plateful of watercress sandwiches.

"Mrs. Fletcher," said the rector's wife, "I want to thank you for shepherding Jeremy about London this afternoon."

Daisy couldn't very well admit she'd been motivated as much by curiosity as any benevolent impulse, the latter in any case being directed towards Vera, not the rector. She muttered something deprecatory.

"Whatever he found out," Mrs. Turnbull went on, "has disturbed him greatly. He can't make up his mind what to do about whatever it is."

If Daisy correctly understood the situation, the rector had only two choices. He could confront Cartwright himself, or he could consult the Board of Governors and make them share the dirty work. For either alternative, he'd have to work out how to present his case persuasively, but persuasion should be a clergyman's forte.

"I hope he decides soon," she said, thinking of the uncomfortable position poor Vera was in.

"It's something to do with Miss Leighton, I take it, as you and Jeremy laid your plans when she came to consult him." Mrs. Turnbull's tone was noncommittal, but Daisy realised she was being genteelly pumped.

"It was a great relief to Vera to be able to talk to Mr. Turnbull," she said. "His sympathy gave her hope." Hope of what, she didn't specify.

"Vera's much more cheerful since seeing the rector," Isabel confirmed. "And I'm much more cheerful since Mrs. Barnes has told me how to hire workers to clean the cellar. Daisy, pass those Shrewsbury biscuits, would you?"

Mrs. Turnbull offered refills of tea.

Daisy took a Bakewell tart and ate a bite of the almond-paste-topped pastry before succumbing to a different kind of temptation. "Did you know the Grays?"

"Not well." Mrs. Barnes exchanged a glance with Mrs. Turnbull. "At least, Albert Gray and Ruth, his first wife, were sociable enough, but after she died he withdrew rather, stopped entertaining and refused most invitations. As his doctor, my husband must have seen more of him than I did."

"We were all glad when he remarried, though a woman so many years his junior . . . Younger than his son, in fact. Well, that was none of our business, of course."

"When was that?"

"Two or three years ago?"

"Nearer four," said the rector's wife. "They didn't get married at St. Mary's. A registry office in London, I believe."

Daisy instantly felt guilty for having done the same—chiefly to dodge the worst of her dowager viscountess mother's recriminations for marrying a middle-class policeman.

"Judith Gray wasn't at all interested in mixing with local people," Mrs. Barnes elaborated, "not even the younger crowd. She had—has—friends in London and it's so quick and easy to get into town from here."

"I'm sure it was her London friends who gave her the idea of moving to the South of France," put in Mrs. Turnbull. "A visit to Paris, then off to stay with friends in a villa on the Côte d'Azur until she finds a place to buy. Or so rumour has it."

Daisy was dying to ask whether rumour ever spoke of the possibility of Judith Gray having deliberately hastened her husband's end. Assuming Dr. Barnes had been his doctor, Mrs. Barnes would surely be aware of any such insinuation. Such a query would be crass, however, much worse than just asking whether they had been acquainted with Mrs. Gray.

How neatly they had all avoided mentioning that the subject of their gossip had more than likely been murdered!

Mrs. Turnbull regarded the scant remains of their tea with a sigh. "What an excellent tea the Saracen's Head does, and how lucky I come here rarely. I must be going. Jeremy will be wondering where I've got to."

With much goodwill expressed, the older ladies prepared to depart. Scarves were knotted, hats straightened, gloves donned, handbags gathered. As they moved towards the door, Sally entered.

"Are you going? I'm ever so sorry I didn't come and ask did you want more hot water or anything else. We've been that busy, I've been run off my feet."

"We had all we needed, thank you, Sally," said Mrs. Barnes. "And more," Mrs. Turnbull added ruefully.

Sally saw them out, then turned back to Daisy and Isabel and started collecting the tea things. "They're nice ladies, aren't they? But we got a right lot of ghouls in the dining room. Asking nosy questions about you ladies, miss, you and Miss Leighton and Miss Chandler, and you, Mrs. Fletcher, and the chief inspector."

"What did you tell them?" Daisy asked.

"Not a blinking thing, madam, nor I wouldn't have if I'd got anything to tell."

"I'm sure you do, so thank you for keeping quiet."

"Happy to oblige, madam." Grinning, she picked up the tray and left them.

"She must have enjoyed foiling the busybodies," said Isabel, adding ruefully, "Is that why Mrs. Barnes and Mrs. Turnbull were so pleasant? Just to persuade us to pass on the details?"

"I don't think so, though it was a bit of a fencing match at times. At least, I'm pretty sure they wouldn't have asked any awkward direct questions. Sally's pretty sharp and she called them 'nice.' Remember, last night Mrs. Barnes met Willie and Mrs. Turnbull met Vera. They realised they couldn't possibly be murderers, so they wanted to meet you—"

"To 'vet' me."

"Don't we all vet new acquaintances?"

"True. Then you believe they really will call once we've got things straightened out?"

"Definitely. And with the doctor's wife and the rector's wife both on calling terms, the rest will soon come round."

"I expect so." Isabel gave a sigh of satisfaction. "I must say, it'd be nice if people smiled and said good morning when I go shopping. Escape from Coventry. Not that I've ever been to Coventry—I don't suppose it's any worse than Huddersfield."

Daisy laughed. "I couldn't say, I've never been to either. Now, let me tell you what the rector and I found out and then I'm going to lie down for a while, if you won't think it frightfully rude."

"You must be exhausted, Daisy. You've been dashing about as if you weren't still convalescent."

"I do feel a bit limp. It was worth it, though. Listen!" She described the visits to the two schools. "So the rector has no reason to doubt Vera's story and Cartwright hasn't a leg to stand on. I'm off. Tell Vera when you see her, if the rector hasn't."

"I will! And I can't thank you enough—"

"Please don't. I'll see you later."

On her way upstairs, Daisy met Vera coming down. She looked tired—as who wouldn't after a day in a classroom full of small children—but as if a burden had fallen from her back.

"Daisy, I'm—"

"Dying for your tea, I'm sure. Izzie's in the parlour. I'll see you later." With a wave, Daisy escaped and trudged on up the stairs.

She was pleased with her day's work. Vera's problem was well on the way to being solved, and the prospects for an end to Isabel's isolation looked good. What was more, she could confirm to Alec and DI Underwood that Cartwright was a ladies' man, with a tendency towards violence.

He had physically assaulted three women. Had he attempted the same trick with Mrs. Gray? Unlike the three junior teachers, she would have had no reason to keep quiet, so he'd have felt he had to silence her.

Alternatively, Miss Mason's young man was mistaken and Cartwright and Mrs. Gray actually were having an affair. She might somehow have found out about his behaviour with the others, leading to a quarrel. Unless she was having an affair with Vaughn . . .

By this point in her musings Daisy had kicked off her shoes, put her feet up on the bed, and leaned back against the pillows. She fell asleep.

TWENTY

Daisy awoke feeling much refreshed. With more than enough
time to wash and change before dinner, she stayed put, watching
in a detached way the curtains flap in a determined breeze blowing through the part-open window. ("Less than four inches is a
draught," her nurse had always said; "More than four inches is
fresh air.") She was thinking drowsily about getting up when
Alec came in.

"Daisy, are you all right?" he asked in alarm.

"Perfectly all right, darling." She sat up. "Why shouldn't I be?"

"It's not like you to take a nap between tea and dinner!"

"I'm still sort of convalescent, according to Isabel, at any rate.
Besides, I've had a busy day."

"So I've heard."

"Oh, blast, have you been talking to the rector? I wanted to
tell you myself."

"No, he was out when we called, as was his wife."

"Must have been teatime. She joined us for tea, Izzie and me.
The doctor's wife, too. It's no good asking either of them about
Mrs. Gray, though. They barely knew her." Daisy passed on what
the two had said.

"Thanks. That's much the impression we've been getting from everyone. But what I really want to know is what the dickens you and the rector were up to?"

"Mr. Turnbull had some questions he wanted to ask Vera's two predecessors at the school. I offered to drive him so that he wouldn't have to work out the underground and buses and so on."

"Nothing to do with the case, then?"

"Just some information he hoped would help Vera." Daisy added cautiously, "But we did come across something that might help you, too."

"Oh yes?"

"You needn't sound so sceptical!"

"You must admit it's a bit odd that the rector's quest to help Miss Leighton just happened to result in *you* finding evidence for the police."

"Serendipity. Well, I did hope—the very vaguest of hopes . . ."

"Otherwise, no doubt, you wouldn't have offered Mr. Turnbull your services as chauffeur."

"But so vague, I was sure it wouldn't count as interfering. You were going to interview Mr. Cartwright, weren't you? After he barged in on you and Underwood and the superintendent?"

"Of course. Though we were pretty certain his outburst was irrelevant as the victim couldn't have told lies regarding an investigation that didn't start till long after she died."

"So you wouldn't press him too hard. Have you seen him already?"

"Underwood sent someone to get a statement." Alec considered for a moment. "I can't see any reason not to tell you. Cartwright said he'd had one too many whiskies and thought he saw his wife going into the snug to complain to the landlord about letting him run up a bill he couldn't afford. His wife confirms that he spends far too much on drink but swears she wouldn't demean herself by speaking to a common publican."

"At that point, Sally had left and I was the only woman in the snug. Does she look at all like Sally or me?"

"Hm, I wonder if . . . The constable who called on her described her as a sour-faced shrew with a bad perm."

"Darling, really! It's a clever story, though. It puts him in a bad light so you wouldn't be inclined to investigate any further."

"All right, what did you discover?"

"He never misses an excuse to cane or rap the knuckles of the unfortunate children he's supposed to teach."

"Many schoolmasters do that, and schoolmistresses, too."

"Many don't. At the least, it shows he's not averse to violence. Also, he's a lady's man, given to forcing unwanted attentions on defenceless females."

"Is he, now! Including Miss Leighton, I presume."

"You'll have to ask her, and the others."

"Others? Miss Sutcliffe and Miss Chandler?"

"I wouldn't call them defenceless, would you?"

"Who, then?"

"I can't tell you that. Ask the rector. But Mrs. Gray could have been one of those he approached. Perhaps he was rougher with her than he dared to be in the schoolroom, and she fought him. Or perhaps he was actually her lover, and they quarrelled."

"Pure speculation," Alec scoffed automatically, but he looked thoughtful.

Daisy let him think for a moment, then went on, "Or perhaps the sour-faced shrew found out about their affair and attacked Mrs. Gray."

He groaned. "I can't dismiss any of your wild guesses out of hand. You'd better change your clothes if you want any dinner."

"Are you insinuating that I'm a mess?"

"Yes, love. Stating rather than insinuating. Better than being sour-faced but you look exactly as if you've been sleeping in that dress. As you have."

This Daisy could not deny, so she let the dress be crushed a little more in his arms, and they went down late to dinner.

Willie, Vera, and Isabel were already on the main course, so Daisy and Alec waved but didn't join them. The room was

167

packed, but Sally had saved a table for the Fletchers. She brought steaming bowls of soup.

"Mulligatawny; I hope you like it. Then there's veal and ham pie or Dover sole. I heard you went and saw Auntie May this afternoon, Mr. Fletcher. Did she snap your head off?"

Alec smiled at her. "I have a tough head, don't worry. Daisy, what will you have?"

"The sole, if it's really fresh?"

"I wouldn't offer it to *you*, Mrs. Fletcher, if it wasn't. Come straight from Billingsgate this very morning, on ice all the way."

Alec chose the pie. Sally left, and Daisy asked, "What's she like? Mrs. Hedger? I saw her briefly the first time I went to Cherry Trees. She was just leaving."

Typically, he tossed the question back. "What did you think of her?"

"Morose. Suspicious by nature. That's just from her looks, and I saw her only in passing. I didn't chat with her. She didn't look as if she wanted to be sociable. I can't comment on what Isabel said about her being hardworking, but I can well believe she's obstinate."

"Obstinate, obdurate, and obstructive. Apparently my accent isn't posh enough to impress her. She just kept repeating that her job is cleaning, not spying on her ladies nor paying attention to their looks or their comings and goings. She doesn't hold with 'carryings-on' and wouldn't have stood for anything of the sort."

"She doesn't live in, so that doesn't mean much. When did she last see Mrs. Gray?"

"She can't remember. She pays no attention to her ladies' comings and goings."

"I'd expect her to remember when she was last paid."

"I daresay she does, and is just being difficult."

"Perhaps Mrs. Gray gave her a farewell bonus. She refused to attempt to identify the body, I take it?"

"Her job is cleaning, and one lady looks much the same as another."

Daisy laughed. "Oh dear! What a pity she isn't one of those chars to whom their employers lives are of all-absorbing interest. What about Vaughn?"

"He was out of the office all day, showing houses, inspecting houses, dealing with tenants of houses the agency manages." Alec shrugged. "Whatever house agents do. Underwood made an appointment to see him tomorrow in case we can't catch him this evening. Miss Chandler hasn't dropped any further hints about him?"

"Never a murmur. He must have spent quite some time with Mrs. Gray, going over the house and showing it to prospective buyers. Surely ought to be able to identify her, even if they weren't having an affair. Are you any closer to proving it's her body?"

"Not to proving, but the odds are improving."

They had finished the mulligatawny soup, tasty but a bit heavy on the curry powder. Sally brought the main course.

"Mr. Piper's just come from the police station, sir, and'd like a word when you can. I'm giving him his supper in the kitchen. He said he'd rather."

Was that a touch of pink on her cheeks? Daisy wasn't sure. The waitress was a very self-possessed young woman.

"That's kind of you," Daisy said. Did the pinkness intensify?

"Tell Piper I'll be with him as soon as I've finished eating." Alec sounded morose. "Thanks."

"Mr. Whitford says you can use the snug again, sir, if you need to. You're bringing in a lot of new customers." Sally whisked off to serve another diner.

"Were you expecting the rest of the evening off, darling?"

"Not really. I just hoped to dine in peace. Did I tell you Tom Tring is coming down to Beaconsfield? He may be here already."

"But he retired!"

"He's missing the job. I happened to run into him at the Yard, chatting with an old crony. He asked after you and the children, of course, then he wanted to know what I was up to. I told him my presence on this case was strictly officially unofficial. Naturally, he immediately guessed that you were involved."

"Darling!" she protested.

"So we hatched a plot whereby he would go undercover even more unofficially—"

"His missus won't appreciate that a bit."

"She's coming too, I hope. Just a city couple taking a few days' holiday in the country. They'll stay elsewhere and he'll patronise the public bars, here and elsewhere, keeping his ears open."

"I'm sure his pub-crawling will reconcile Mrs. Tring to the business," Daisy said ironically.

"We'll see. If you happen to come face-to-face with her or Tom, pretend you don't know them."

"I'll try. I suppose there's no way you can introduce him to Sally's Auntie May? I bet he'd get her talking."

"Probably. That's a good idea, if I can come up with a way to get them together."

"I'll try, too."

Alec's face expressed severe misgivings. "Daisy, you are absolutely not to—"

"Oh, I won't try to bring them together, darling, just think of a way for Tom to do it himself."

"If you come up with a suggestion, don't approach—"

"You've already told me not to show I know them. I presume you have a way to contact him in secret? Signs and passwords? Leave a message in the hollow oak at midnight? This is beginning to sound like a children's adventure story!"

Alec grimaced. "For pity's sake, don't say that to Underwood."

"Does he know about Tom?"

"No. If Tom comes up with anything useful, I'll find a way to feed it to the inspector without letting on where it came from. I'd better skip pudding and go and see what Ernie wants. I may very well end up back at the police station, so don't wait up for me."

He rose, bent to kiss Daisy's cheek, and departed in the direction of the kitchen. Half the people in the room stared at Daisy.

Sally hurried over to her. "Would you like me to serve your

afters in the parlour, madam? Miss Sutcliffe and Miss Chandler are having their coffee in there."

"Yes, please, Sally, if it won't be too much trouble."

"Not a bit of it, madam. It's treacle tart tonight, or plum compote." In a whisper, she added, "That's Cook's fancy name for bottled plums."

Daisy opted for the plums and made her way to the ladies' parlour. A stout elderly woman and a younger one who addressed her as "mama" had taken the sofa by the fire. They displayed no interest in Willie and Isabel, so Daisy guessed they were not locals. She joined her friends.

"Where's Vera?" she asked in a low voice.

"There was a note for her from the rector," said Isabel. "She went to see him."

"By herself?"

"By herself," Willie confirmed. "She's a changed woman."

"Thanks to you, Daisy."

"Oh, nonsense!"

"You went with her to see Mr. Turnbull. You went with Mr. Turnbull to see the other teachers."

"And now," Isabel said, "if you've recovered from your strenuous day, I'm hoping to persuade you to come with me, to talk Mrs. Hedger into cleaning the cellar."

"Me? Why not Willie?"

"Sally said her aunt is impressed by posh accents."

"Willie has a posh accent."

"Not any longer. I used to when we were at school but it didn't survive a few years in Huddersfield."

"When I listen for it, I can hear odds and ends of Yorkshire creeping in," Daisy admitted. She didn't bother to tell them Alec had had no luck at all with Mrs. Hedger. He spoke the King's English as well as anyone, but her own voice—though not as acutely upper-class as Lucy's, she hoped—definitely retained the timbre of her upbringing. And she was quite good at putting on her mother's almost majestic hauteur, when it seemed called for.

"Never mind," said Isabel. "You must be shattered after all your running around."

"Not really. I had a good snooze before dinner. All the same, couldn't we put it off till the morning?"

"I'd rather not. Mrs. Hedger will be off early to whoever she works for Tuesdays, and if I have to go to the Labour Exchange, Mrs. Barnes says it's better to get there early before the most respectable workers are snapped up. It's not far. Her cottage is just off the Wycombe Road."

"All right, I'll go with you."

Willie laughed. "Confess, Daisy, you're dying to meet her."

"Not dying. But I must say I'm curious to find out if she's really as impossible as I've heard."

"What's up?" Alec asked as he and Ernie Piper stepped out into the rain and walked briskly towards the police station. "New information?"

"Not exactly, Chief. Nothing new, just putting things together from statements taken this evening and the ones that came in earlier. And Mr. Underwood wants to talk to you about who interviews who tomorrow."

"It sounds as if I'm going to be glad I decided to drive down!"

They turned in at the door beneath the blue lamp.

As they entered the room, Underwood stood. "Thank you for coming back, sir. I'm sorry to disturb your evening."

"Comes with the job, doesn't it?" He tried not to sound grumpy. The poor bastard wasn't married and very likely had nothing better to do with his evening than pore over his case, though no need for haste was apparent. The trail had been cold before the starting point was discovered.

Alec sat down. Ernie went to the desk and produced from his pocket a wax paper–wrapped packet.

"Veal and ham pie, sir. Miss Hedger put it up for you. She said all you had for supper yesterday was pickled onions and crisps."

"And a couple of Scotch eggs, but it's very thoughtful of her. Please give her my thanks."

"I will."

"What can I do for you, Mr. Underwood?" Alec asked, suppressing his impatience over these courtesies. He'd gone without dinner often enough to know how much it was appreciated if it turned up unexpectedly.

While waiting for Underwood to finish his mouthful, Alec debated internally whether to tell him about Daisy's unsanctioned outing with the rector. The inspector was bound to find out, if he hadn't already. Better to get it over with, but perhaps he could keep Daisy out of it.

"While you're eating, let me tell you what I've just heard. It seems the rector has spoken to three young women, unknown to each other, all of whom describe Cartwright as a ladies' man, given to pressing his attentions where they're not wanted."

"Miss Leighton told you?"

"No, and my source refused to give names. Miss Leighton's a fair bet, though."

"Dead cert. That sort of bully always picks on those in a position of weakness."

"Which makes an attempt on Mrs. Gray's virtue less likely, however."

"True," Underwood admitted reluctantly. "It calls for a second interview, though, with a bit more to go on than his story and his wife's. And of course, I'll have to talk to the rector."

"And Miss Leighton."

"After we find out what the rector has to say, and after school's out."

Alec nodded. "What else is on the agenda?"

"Your sergeant here has turned up a couple of points that need looking into. Three of the neighbours have mentioned seeing a black closed saloon car parked outside Cherry Trees, several times in the past few months and at least once in the last fortnight. And a couple who take a stroll every evening have twice seen a similar car drive up the street, pause outside Cherry Trees, and then drive on quite fast. The man thinks it was a Jowett."

"They noticed it because of the odd behaviour, Chief, but didn't think to mention it until they were asked specifically about a car of that appearance."

"No licence plate number, I suppose?"

"The letters, BH, which is Bucks. No surprise. They contradict each other on the numbers."

"Too much to hope for," said Underwood. "It's pretty good luck to get that much, considering the high hedges. Not the sort of street where every neighbour knows everyone else's doings."

"I haven't actually seen the street or house yet," Ernie reminded them.

"Nor you have, Sergeant. You'd best take a walk over there first thing tomorrow, so that Miss Sutcliffe can get on with the cleaning. You've read the reports. Take a look round, see if you think we've missed anything. Then you can go and show the rings to Mr. Ainsley—"

"The rings!" Alec exclaimed. "Mrs. Gray's rings?"

Underwood grinned. "Who else's? They were delivered by a motorcycle officer while you were at dinner." From an envelope he shook out on to the desktop a plain gold wedding band and a rather flashy ruby ring. Picking up his piece of pie, he took a large bite.

Alec reached for the rings, but held back. "They've been checked for dabs? And cleaned?"

His mouth full once again, the inspector nodded.

The rings smelled faintly of formalin. Inside the band were engraved initials, APG and JJG. "Albert Gray and Judith Gray. What were their middle names?"

"Albert Peter and Judith Jane," Ernie said instantly.

"Not much doubt there. And the ruby is distinctive, in the heart-shaped setting with those diamond chips."

Underwood swallowed his mouthful. "Not ruby. It's paste. Well, he was known as a skinflint. Mr. Ainsley should be able to make a positive identification of the ring, don't you think?"

"Oh yes. Which means we're close to certainty on the identity of the deceased. Did they say what killed her?"

"Broken neck, as far as they can tell. Dislocated vertebrae caused by a fall. The doc is pretty sure it wasn't broken postmortem and the . . ." He looked down at the top paper of the pile in front of him. "The hyoid bone is intact, so no strangulation. He thinks the back of the head may have been bruised, but probably from the fall, not severely enough to suggest she'd been hit. No bone damage, at least. And that's about all he's willing to say, because of the condition of the body. The worst is, it's impossible to clean up her face to make her recognisable."

"Damn! Time of death?"

"Still two to four weeks, probably the middle of that range. I'll have Pennicuik follow up with all the most promising neighbours, see if he can dig out anything the uniformed men missed. He can man the station here while you run your errands, Sergeant, then you'll take over here while he does his part."

"Yes, sir."

"First thing, though, catch the ladies at breakfast, before the two of 'em go to work. Ask if any of them ever noticed a vehicle like the one reported. If that's all right with you, Chief Inspector?"

"We're at your disposition, Mr. Underwood. What's on the agenda for me?"

"I wondered if you happen to have any acquaintances at the Foreign Office. I'd very much like to know the stepson's whereabouts in the past couple of months. Also, this friend who inherits the pearls has to be run to earth, and her address is in London."

"As it happens," Alec said dryly, "a friend of mine from Manchester University managed to squeeze through the swarms of Oxbridge men into a position at the FO. I expect he'll be able and willing to help. Anything else to be done while I'm in town?"

"Not that I can think of. I don't suppose Mrs. Fletcher would like to go with you?"

"And stay there? I'll put it to her, but I doubt it. She seems to be comfortably settled at the Saracen's Head and determined to support her friends, though she might pop up for a few hours to see the twins."

"Ah well." At least Underwood apparently didn't delude himself that Alec was able to control Daisy's movements. "Myself, I'm going to start in High Wycombe. I'll send someone up to the county offices in Aylesbury to get a list of owners of cars with the BH registration. You never know, if it's not too long it may be useful. Then I'll call on Mr. Butterworth, the ladies' solicitor, and whatsisname, Miss Chandler's boss—"

"Mr. Davis, sir," Ernie put in.

"Thank you, Sergeant. And see if I can catch Vaughn at his office. If not, I'll talk to *his* boss and set up an appointment."

"Langridge's, in the High Street."

"Then back here to have a word with the rector. Depending on what he has to say, I may ask you to come with me, Sergeant, to see Cartwright. Depends on the time, too. I won't fetch him out of his classroom if he turns out not to be a serious suspect. Have I covered everything?"

"It should clear the ground nicely," said Alec, "which is about the best we can hope for at this stage, considering how little we have to go on."

"One thing, sir." Ernie hesitated. "It's not strictly relevant, but it's kind of a loose end you might want to tie up."

"What's that, Mr. Piper? Go ahead."

"Well, Miss Hedger told me there's a rumour Mrs. Gray did away with the old man. There's likely nothing in it, and even if it's true, it wouldn't have a direct effect on finding who killed her. Unless . . ." His voice trailed off uncertainly.

"Spit it out, man," Underwood encouraged him.

"It's pure speculation, sir, as the Chief would say, but supposing her stepson guessed she'd murdered his dad—"

"Or came home for his funeral and heard the rumour—You'd better ask where he was at that time, too, Mr. Fletcher. April, wasn't it?"

"He died on the twenty-fourth of April, sir, and was buried on the twenty-eighth."

"Not much time to return to England from the farthest reaches of Empire," Alec observed. "But a friend who attended the funeral and heard the rumour could have passed it on in a letter. In any case, I'll check the dates."

"Because," said Underwood, "it would give him a whopping great motive, on top of the money, for doing in his stepmother."

TWENTY-ONE

Umbrellas raised, Daisy and Isabel made their way along the Wycombe Road. They passed the Fire Engine House, then turned off into a narrow, muddy alley. Sally had told them her aunt's cottage was the fourth on the right. The drizzle, scarcely pierced by the lamp on the far side of the main street, made it difficult to tell one tiny cottage from the next. Lath and plaster, ancient and ramshackle, they opened directly onto the mud.

At one front door, a pale paving stone caught a glimmer of light. One resident, at least, had made an effort to prevent the muck from being tracked in.

"That will be it," Isabel guessed.

Daisy stood back, peering, and counted. "Yes, that's the fourth. It seems to be completely dark, though. She probably goes to bed early."

Isabel, closer, said, "No, there's an oil lamp or a candle burning downstairs. I can just make it out through the curtain. Come on."

Failing a door knocker, she used her hand. Her glove muffled the sound so she took it off and rapped with bare knuckles.

After a moment, a suspicious voice asked, "Who's there?"

"It's Miss Sutcliffe, Mrs. Hedger."

"What d'you want, Miss, disturbing a poor ol' hardworking woman this time of night?" Despite her complaining words, her voice was flat.

"You didn't work today," Isabel pointed out. "I promised to pay you anyway, so I've brought your money."

"Devious," Daisy murmured, "and clever."

The door creaked open. Mrs. Hedger, a brightly multicoloured shawl over her head and swathed round her shoulders, appeared with her cupped hand already held out. Her back to a dim oil lamp, her face was shadowed.

Isabel reached into her coat pocket and took out a purse. "It's too dark out here to see to count." She stepped forward, so that the charwoman had to retreat.

Daisy followed them in. The room was tiny, and very clean, from the brick floor to the shabby wooden rocking chair, the whitewashed walls, the mantelpiece above the meagre fire, and the tarnished looking glass above the mantelpiece.

Coins clinked into the waiting palm. "Also," said Isabel, "I wanted to talk to you about earning some extra cash."

Mrs. Hedger was staring at Daisy. "Who's she?"

"A friend. She walked with me for company. No doubt you've heard what happened at Cherry Trees? There's some cleaning needed, and I can't pretend it won't be—"

"No!" Her vehemence was so much at odds with her usual surly reticence as to startle Daisy. "Not that I haven't laid out a corpse or two in my time, but . . . *her*! No, I won't do it, and that's flat."

"The body's not there any longer," Isabel said coaxingly. "The police removed it. It's just that it's left rather a nasty mess. Or so I'm told. I'd pay extra, of course."

"Not for nothing I won't."

Daisy didn't blame her a bit, but she said in her mother's tones of utmost displeasure, "You may regret disobliging, the next time Miss Sutcliffe has a job to be done for extra pay."

Mrs. Hedger was unmoved. "I've said all I has to say, Miss,

and I'll thank you to leave me in peace. I'll be in Wednesday, same as usual, to do my usual."

"That depends on the police," said Isabel. "I'll let you know. Good night."

They walked in silence to the end of the alley. Daisy was piqued by her failure, but she laughed. "It would seem my voice isn't posh enough."

"It was worth a try."

"Perhaps I'd have had more success as myself, not my mother."

"Never mind. I didn't really expect her to agree, even if she has 'laid out a corpse or two.' I just hope I can find someone willing at the Labour Exchange."

"You'd better check with Underwood before you hire someone."

"Oh, yes. I wonder—There's the church clock. Half past nine. He'll have gone home by now."

"Don't be so sure. The police work all hours on an investigation like this. Though this case is rather different, of course. They're usually in a hurry to find clues before they disappear, but this time if they were going to disappear they'll be long gone by now."

"I might as well pop into the police station anyway."

"The Saracen's Head first. Alec may be there, or Underwood himself, and able to give you an answer."

"It's a very unsettled life, isn't it?"

"I never know whether Alec will be home for dinner. He's sent all over the country, though. I imagine Underwood rarely has to leave the county."

"What does Alec think of him?"

"He hasn't told me directly, but judging by how well they're working together, I'd guess he respects his competence."

"That's good. All the same, I'm glad Alec's on the case."

They crossed the Wycombe Road and were halfway across Windsor End when the door of the Saracen's Head opened and a very large man stepped out into the light from the lamp above.

Spotting them, he stopped and held the door for them, raising his hat to reveal a hairless dome immediately bedewed with glinting raindrops. Isabel passed him with a nod of acknowledgement.

Daisy paused with a smile. He winked at her.

Wondering whether Tom had heard any new and useful rumours, she followed Isabel.

They returned to the parlour, where they found Willie and Vera.

With the burden of her secret lifted, Vera was a new person. She'd never have Willie's sparkle or her drive to succeed, Daisy thought, nor the inner strength that enabled Isabel to cope calmly with what life threw at her. But Vera had a quiet charm that showed more clearly now that she wasn't living in fear.

Daisy was glad for her. She had run out of steam though, too tired to stay and celebrate with them. She turned down the offer of a drink and went upstairs.

Her mind was restless and wouldn't let her fall asleep. Her friends seemed to have put behind them the horrible discovery in their cellar. Ought they to be worrying about DI Underwood? Had the inspector really concluded that the murder had nothing to do with the present inhabitants of the house where it had occurred?

Perhaps Alec would tell her whether they were still under suspicion. He might not, fearing that Daisy would warn them. And he might be right at that.

She thought back over the past week. Nothing she'd seen or heard since arriving in Beaconsfield gave the slightest ground for suspecting any of the three women had the least idea a body was slowly decomposing in their cellar. Nothing in their characters gave the slightest grounds for supposing any of them capable of killing someone and concealing a guilty conscience for a month or so.

Nor had they even the slightest hint of a motive for the murder. The legal papers had been signed; the house was theirs. Mrs. Gray couldn't have refused to vacate it. Nonetheless, doubtless all sorts of rumours about Willie, Isabel, and Vera were flying round the town. Daisy wished she had been able to chat with Tom Tring, to ask him what was being said.

As far as Daisy knew, the police had only two real suspects, and neither Vaughn nor Cartwright looked very promising.

She was still awake when Alec came in.

"Still awake, love?"

"Your powers of observation and deduction are astounding, darling. I'm not sleepy, just feeling a bit limp."

He sat down on the bed and took her hand. "Not a relapse?" he asked anxiously.

"No, I haven't coughed once. I rather overdid things today, I suppose."

"Won't you go home and let yourself be spoiled by Elsie and Mrs. Dobson? I have to go to London tomorrow. I could drive you, so you wouldn't have to tackle the train journey."

"You're going up to town again? What for?"

"You won't let it go, will you?"

"Not as long as there's any chance of helping Willie and company. Did the super call you back?"

"No, it's an errand for Underwood. Do you remember Eric Bragg? I think you've met him."

"Your friend from Manchester? The one whose Mancunian accent somehow survives at the Foreign Office? Oh, no, don't tell me you've proved it's not Mrs. Gray and have to go looking for her on the Continent!"

"No, no. We're about as sure as we can be without finding her dentist that it is her. Underwood, very properly, wants to know what her stepson's been up to recently."

"I'd forgotten about him. He's at the FO?"

"That would make things too simple. He's a diplomat. We can only hope Bragg knows or can find out where he is and where he's been."

"Surely they must keep track of their people? Though I expect there are still places where communication's pretty difficult: parts of Africa and China and the Northwest Frontier, for instance. Well, give my regards to Mr. Bragg. You'll come back here when you've talked to him?"

"Eventually. I also have to call on the only friend of Judith Gray whose name and address we've found."

"Who's probably on the Riviera, waiting for her to turn up."

"Very possible."

"Unless she's actually already there . . . You said you can't find her dentist? What about her doctor? She didn't go to Dr. Barnes?"

"No, though Albert did."

"Have you talked to Dr. Barnes about her? Mrs. Barnes didn't know her, but the doctor might have discussed her husband's illness with her, at least when he was dying. He might have a better idea of what she was like than anyone else you've found."

"Could be," Alec said thoughtfully, taking off his jacket and tie. "He struck me as pretty shrewd. As far as I'm aware, Pennicuik was told only to ask whether he was her practitioner. We ought to find out whether he saw enough of her to gain an impression of her character."

"You see?" Daisy crowed. "I *am* sometimes helpful!" Before he could retort, she went on, "I saw Tom this evening."

"You didn't—"

"Of course not, darling. He was coming out of the hotel—this hotel—as Isabel and I were going in."

"Where on earth had you been?"

"Isabel had to tackle Mrs. Hedger about cleaning the cellar."

"Don't tell me she needed your support to make a request of her own char!"

"Well, no, not Isabel. Though she is a fearsome old woman."

"She is indeed. You wanted to see for yourself?"

"And Sally did say her aunt respected people with posh voices, so when she adamantly refused Isabel, I tried Mother's voice on her. It didn't work. Meeting her made me very thankful for Mrs. Twickle, who's good-natured even though Mrs. Dobson has to stand over her to keep her going. I still think Tom would be able to get round Mrs. Hedger."

"You could be right. Any ideas yet on how to bring them together?"

"I've been too busy to think. Or thinking about other things. Do you still need her evidence?"

"At least as to the date she last saw Judith Gray. I should have pressed her harder on that question."

"You'd think she'd remember, if only because she can't have been paid after that. Unless—I wonder whether Isabel paid her for the days she worked when no one was in residence?"

"Dammit, Daisy, I wish you'd thought of that before I started to undress!" He unbuttoned his pyjama jacket. "I hope she's still up."

"Darling, for pity's sake, it can wait till the morning, can't it? *If* Isabel paid, and *if* she remembers for how many days, she won't forget overnight."

"I bet her household accounts are in perfect order, with Willie looking over her shoulder."

"Bound to be." Daisy recalled with guilt her own accounts, left in Mrs. Dobson's hands—competent, fortunately—for close to a month now. "So if Izzie's forgotten, she'll be able to look it up for you. In the morning. Or as soon as she can get back into the house."

"Good point. I'll pass it on to Underwood. You're in good form tonight."

Daisy smiled smugly. "Thank you, kind sir."

"What else have you been mulling in that overactive brain?"

"Whether DI Underwood—and you, for that matter—still suspect Willie and friends."

"You know they can't be crossed off our lists until we have far more information. As far as I'm concerned, they're at the bottom. I can't speak for Underwood."

"Who's at the top? Cartwright and Vaughn? And the stepson?"

"Yes, but we have nothing definite on any of them. What we need is a few good suspects!" He crossed to the window, opened the upper sash a few inches, and peered out into the darkness, as if he might spot the murderer lurking outside.

"It's early days yet, darling," Daisy consoled him. "Come to bed."

TWENTY-TWO

Daisy was up in time to have breakfast with Alec, if only because arriving at the Foreign Office before ten was pointless. None but lowly clerks and typists started work before that hour.

The dining room was half empty, so Daisy and Alec had their choice of tables. Most of the occupants were already eating. Sally came in with a laden tray, delivered heaped plates to two solitary men, more toast to another, and hot water to a couple's teapot. Then she hurried over to say good morning to the Fletchers and take their order, as well as that of someone who had entered after them. On her way back to the kitchen, she cleared dirty dishes from three tables.

"I'm glad I'm not a waitress," said Daisy. "She never stops running, and with those heavy trays! No wonder she wants to train as a typist."

But by the time Sally returned with their food, the rush was over. She served the last-comer first so that she could talk for a few moments with Daisy and Alec.

"Miss Sutcliffe said to tell you, Mrs. Fletcher, she went to High Wycombe with Miss Chandler. She's got to find someone to clean up the cellar. I'm sorry Auntie is so disobliging."

"I don't blame her." Daisy looked at Alec. "I suppose—I hope—the inspector said she could go ahead?"

"He dropped in last night, on his way to catch a train, to tell her in person. The cellar can be dealt with, once Ernie's looked over the place, but the rest of the house is still out of bounds. Miss Hedger, have you seen Sergeant Piper this morning?"

"He already had his breakfast, sir, and a word with Miss Sutcliffe and the others. He asked me to tell you Miss Chandler gave him a number the inspector wanted. The number of a car, he said, that might be the one you've been looking for."

"A car?" Daisy recalled Willie memorising the licence plate number of a vehicle that had passed them at a dangerous speed the other evening. "If I'd known you were looking for it, I could have told you she knew."

"*Might* be," said Alec.

"Whose car is it, darling?"

"That's what we want to find out."

Sally said hesitantly, "Ernie—I mean Mr. Piper—told me Miss Sutcliffe knows who owns a car just like that one. I can't tell you, though, because he wouldn't tell me."

"I'm glad to hear he has so much discretion," Alec said dryly.

"He's gone off to the police station already. He's a hard worker."

"Yes, he is. Thank you, Miss Hedger."

Sally went off to answer a call from another table.

"Why do you want to know about that car?" Daisy asked.

He wasn't listening. "Ernie? She called him Ernie?"

"Love at first sight."

"No, really, Daisy!"

"Call it attraction at first meeting, then."

"If DS Piper's going to be mooning about instead of—"

"Darling, Ernie isn't the moony sort. He's much too serious about his work. It's time he settled down with a nice young woman, and Sally would be perfect for him. Now eat your breakfast before it gets cold." Applying herself to her bacon and scrambled eggs, she pondered Sally and Ernie's future.

Alec ate half his meal before he spoke again. "I'm going to drive up to town in case I have to chase the woman down."

Slightly confused by what to her was a change of subject, Daisy said, "Woman?"

"Mrs. Gray's friend. For all we know, she may be visiting anywhere in the country. Or out of it."

"You're not going to follow her to the Continent!"

"No. If I get an address for her, I'll send a wire. If not, I'll have to ask the Sûreté to trace her."

"Unless she's gone to Italy—"

"I'll cross that bridge if and when."

"Could you drop me at home? It's not too far out of your way to Whitehall. If the rain holds off, I'll take the twins and Nana for a walk. If not, I'll tackle my account book. And I'll bring back the article I started writing before I fell ill. I ought to try to get some work done."

Far from attempting again to persuade her to stay at home, as she expected, he said, "If you want to bring your portable typewriter, get a taxi to Marylebone. And don't carry it from the Beaconsfield station, up that steep approach. Leave it there and I'll pick it up when I get back."

"Thank you, darling. I hope you don't have to go haring off to Scotland because the mysterious friend has joined a shooting party."

"Judging by what I've learned of Mrs. Gray, no intimate friend of hers would be a sporting type."

"Even the unsporting can get inveigled into a country house visit that involves shooting. You're right, though, she's more likely to be on the Riviera."

"Lucky her. If you've finished, you'd better go and get your coat."

"I must write a note to Isabel, to let her know I'll be back. I hope she's managing to find someone willing to clean."

———

Alec had only once before called on Eric Bragg at the Foreign Office. Bragg had since been promoted. He was now Private Secretary to the Deputy Secretary to the Permanent Under-Secretary, or something of the sort—he was vague about his exact rank. He had even acquired a secretary of his own, a spruce, alert young woman, and an office that retained some of its Victorian grandeur.

He was the same scruffy, wild-haired chap Alec had first met at university, in Manchester. The son of a couple of Lancashire cotton-mill workers, he had inherited the determination that had enabled them to survive childhood labour in the "dark, Satanic mills," and move up to owning a corner shop in the city.

In Eric's case, he had made good use of the help of a teacher who recognised his abilities. He had won a scholarship to Manchester Grammar, where his affinity for languages from classical Greek and Latin to modern French and German emerged. A second full scholarship, to the Victoria University of Manchester, added several more languages to his repertoire.

That was sufficient to overcome the FO's built-in bias toward Oxford and Cambridge graduates. Bragg started as a lowly translator, acquired a fair understanding of another couple of dozen languages, and made himself indispensable despite his humble background, farouche appearance, and ineradicable Mancunian accent.

"Robert Gray?" he said now. "Yes, I know Bob."

"You do? I didn't expect that."

"He's a colleague, and a friend. When he's home, we work together, do a bit of fencing, go out together for a pint now and then. He can speak colloquially more languages than I can read. No degree. He's a rolling stone, and he picks up the lingo like a native, wherever he goes."

"Which is what I'm interested in: where he goes, or rather, where he's been. I hoped you could get the information I need from whoever would have it, but perhaps you already know his movements?"

"No one knows Bob's movements. He's . . . sort of extracurricular."

"A spy?"

"A seeker of information. Like you. What are these enquiries of yours about? I don't see how he can be in serious trouble. In this country. He doesn't spend enough time here, especially since his father remarried. It is an official criminal case, I presume?"

"Sort of extracurricular, but that's beside the point. It's a murder case. The victim is Robert Gray's stepmother."

"Oh lord!"

"You said he has avoided England since his father married her."

"Yes. He referred to her as 'the witch.' Sometimes with a different initial letter, depending on the company. When he was in England on leave, he'd meet his father in town rather than risk coming face-to-face with her."

"Why did he so dislike her?"

"He never really talked about her—just the odd mention. The usual thing, I suppose: She was on the hunt for a wealthy husband, and old Gray was the sap she got her claws into."

"If she made him happy . . . ?"

"D'you know, I'd swear Bob never talked about his stepma, but I definitely have the impression that she made his pa very unhappy. Don't quote me on that."

"I won't, but it adds to the opinions we've heard from others. When did you last see Robert Gray? You know his father died in April?"

"April, was it? Bob turned up in June, a couple of months later. He'd been in—well, I'd better not say, even to a high-up copper. It was several weeks before the news reached him, and it took him several weeks to get home."

"You saw him then?"

"Oh yes, he was in and out of the office for a fortnight or so, though he came back only to see his lawyer."

"Damn, I knew there was something else we should have

asked Ainsley. Lawyers have a way of getting rid of unwelcome visitors."

"If Ainsley's in Beaconsfield, Bob didn't see him. He communicated through his own lawyer, here in town."

"But he was in England for a couple of weeks in June. You're certain he left the country afterwards?"

"Absolutely certain. He sent in a despatch, via the British consul in—somewhere in the Middle East, in September? It's dated in his own atrocious handwriting, and the date of the consul's seal is two days later. I can't remember exactly; I can find out for you. Of course, that doesn't mean he couldn't be back in England by now. In fact, he is. But he came home with one of those eye conditions common in that part of the world. To my knowledge, he's been under a doctor's care with his eyes bandaged for the past ten days."

"You could have told me right away!"

Bragg grinned. "I could have. Just prolonging the pleasure of your company, mate. You see, though: He couldn't have done in the witch."

"That rather depends, doesn't it, on when the witch was killed."

"Oho, so that's it! Not in the last ten days, I take it. When?"

"We can't be sure of the exact date. Be a good chap and get me the date when he wrote that despatch."

"All right, but I'll have to go and beg on bended knee. Coffee?"

"Is it any good?"

"Oh yes, none of your police canteen muck for us. I'll be back shortly." He sauntered out. Alec, remembering him as a brisk mover, assumed he was aping the languid manners of the well-bred young men whose families had pushed them into the FO for want of anything better to do with them.

The rattle of the typewriter in the outer room stopped and Alec heard his friend ask his secretary to bring coffee for two. He addressed her as "chuck," not what she would be accustomed to from those languid young men. The Mancunian endearment didn't hold any significance; Bragg addressed thus any female less than a decade older than he was, and the secretary was about Daisy's age.

She brought in a tray with two cups of coffee and a plate of Marie biscuits. Having set it on the desk, she lingered. "I hope Mr. Bragg isn't going to be too long. His coffee will get cold, as usual."

"As usual?"

"He gets so wrapped up in his work, he often doesn't even notice I've brought it. He'd never eat any lunch, either, if I didn't remind him."

"How long have you worked for him?"

"Since May. He's such a hard worker, he keeps me busy, but that's better than being bored. And lots of what I type is pretty interesting. Top secret, of course. I'm not allowed to talk about it at all, not to anyone. Have you known Mr. Bragg a long time?"

"About twenty years."

She nodded. "I thought you must be an old friend. All the same, it's lucky you arrived first thing. He never sees anyone without an appointment, even his boss. He says interruptions pull him out of whatever language he's translating and then he wastes time switching back from thinking in English. Part of my job is keeping people out. Well, I'd better get back to work. I'm sure he won't keep you waiting, sir."

Alec was less sure, given Bragg's mention of begging on bended knee, often a lengthy process. However, he needed the information. It was worth waiting a few minutes in the hope of crossing a suspect off the list, especially the suspect with by far the best motive.

He wondered how Underwood and Ernie Piper were getting on, and whether Tom had come up with anything of interest.

Bragg returned to cold, scummed coffee, as predicted. He pushed it aside without appearing to notice it, and sat down. "The sixth of September," he announced. "How does that fit in with your murder?"

"Damn. I'll have to check travel times, but I'd say it leaves the question open. Depends exactly where the despatch came from, of course."

"Which I can't tell you."

"And damn again! Would you tell me if it meant saving Gray from the hangman?"

"Ask me again if you're about to arrest him."

"I shall. How is he, apart from his eyes? Not suffering from a raging—or raving—fever, I trust."

"Not when I called to see him. You're going to talk to him?"

"Of course. He's the closest relative, if only by marriage, to a murder victim. In fact, the only relative we're aware of. If there are others, he may be able to direct us to them. In any case, on her death, he becomes a wealthy man."

"He never mentioned that. Did he know?"

"So his father's lawyer says."

Bragg was silent for a moment, then sighed. "All right, I see your point. At least tell me you have other suspects?"

"A couple. But none with half as good a reason for wanting the woman dead as Robert Gray."

TWENTY-THREE

Gray's flat was in a large, Edwardian redbrick block on Marylebone Road. Its many numbered entrances were set back between pairs of bay windows rising the height of the first three storeys. By the looks of the place, Albert hadn't stinted his son in the matter of accommodation.

As he climbed the stairs, Alec reflected that dates and the distance travelled didn't tell the whole story. It was unlikely that Gray should have somehow found out that his stepmother was moving and therefore might not be missed for some time—unless the lawyer, Ainsley, had written to him. Another question to put to the irritable little man.

Even then, to travel all that way hoping that Judith Gray was still in Beaconsfield was to draw the bow at a very long shot.

Yet the man was a spy, presumably used improvising on the spur of the moment and to taking chances for far less personal reward than a sizable fortune. If circumstances did not conspire to favour him, he might have reckoned to be able to trace Judith and rid himself of her in her new abode.

Alec reached the third floor. The passage leading back into the depths of the building was ill-lit, narrow, but carpeted and clean. Several doors opened onto it, each bearing a letter. He found Gray's and pressed the electric bell.

Nothing happened.

He waited a minute, then rang again. This time, he heard a male voice within calling, though he couldn't make out the words. Again he waited. No footsteps, but his patience was rewarded by the click of the Chubb lock. The door opened to reveal a diminutive cleaning lady in carpet slippers and a flowery overall.

"Was you wanting Mr. Gray?"

"Yes, please. I'd like a word with him. Would you give him my card, madam?"

"Ho, madam, is it? I'll give him your card but it won't do 'im a lot of good, seeing he's got a bandage over his eyes."

"Perhaps you could read it to him."

"Forgot me glasses, di'n't I."

"Tell him I'm a police officer."

"Who is it, Mrs. Dee?"

"A rozzer, sir," she called back. "Leastways so he says, but he ain't wearing no uniform."

"Even without his uniform, I daresay he'll relieve the tedium. Show him in."

The voice was educated, though not, Alec thought, at the best schools. Gray and Eric Bragg must have been drawn to each other because neither sported a Public School tie or accent.

Mrs. Dee—Mrs. D.?—stepped back and Alec followed her over the threshold. On his right a door stood open to a pleasant, masculine sitting room, well-lit by the tall bay windows. The charwoman led him the other way, down a corridor even narrower than that at the stair top, its left wall being shared with the common passage beyond; a comfortable flat, but not extensive.

The next door was ajar. She tapped and pushed it open. "'Ere 'e is, sir."

The room was darkened, illumined only by a lamp concealed behind a folding screen, and what little light came from the corridor. Alec made out a bed against the far wall, with a man's figure lying on his back on top of the counterpane. His upper face was hidden by a folded napkin.

"Mr. Robert Gray?"

"That's me. You're the 'rozzer,' I take it."

"Detective Chief Inspector Fletcher. May I come in?"

"Please. You'll excuse me for not getting up: doctor's orders. Find a seat and tell me what a high-up copper wants with me. I'm already intrigued. It's as boring as hell—Don't you think hell must be the ultimate eternal boredom? None of those raging fires!"

"It's certainly a possibility, if you believe in hell."

"Not really," Gray admitted. "All the same, the tedium is driving me mad. I have to lie here for a couple of hours twice a day, with this damn lotion-soaked cloth swathing my eyes, and I'm not allowed out of the flat at all for fear of getting grit in the irritable orbs."

"What's the trouble?"

"Keratoconjunctivitis. Aren't you sorry you asked? It's quite a common ailment in the Middle East—dry air and blowing sand. I suppose you know I've been in the Middle East."

"Eric Bragg told me."

"Eric!"

"He didn't specify where."

"Then neither shall I. Is this an interrogation?"

"I have some questions I'd like to put to you. You're at liberty to refuse to answer, though your refusal will be noted and may—"

"And may be used in evidence against me?" He sounded amused. "What am I supposed to have done? Not a traffic accident, I assume!"

"Rather more serious. Before I explain, would you mind telling me when you reached England?"

"About ten days ago. The fifth, I think. I was rushed straight to the Hospital for Tropical Diseases, in case my eyes were infectious. Which, I'm thankful to say, they are not."

"Was your passport stamped?"

"I've no idea. At that point, I couldn't see at all. My eyes were bandaged very thoroughly whenever there was the slightest chance of light reaching them."

"How did you manage?"

"I can't tell you how I reached a consulate in a port city, nor which city, come to that. But they had someone help me aboard, and then the steward took good care of me. The purser had one of the crew deliver me to the passport people, who sent me to the hospital."

"We'll check with the hospital."

"I wasn't travelling under my own name," Gray said dryly. "As I arrived under the auspices of a passport official, I was admitted . . ."

Alec sighed. "I suppose, in your profession, you have several passports."

The man on the bed grinned, an odd sight with the cloth hiding the rest of his face. "And they've all been turned in to the FO pending my next assignment."

Abandoning that line of questioning as unprofitable—after all, he didn't really need to know about Gray's most recent arrival—Alec asked, "And your previous trip home? When was that?"

The spy's mouth hardened. "June. As soon as I heard of my father's death in April. I still can't believe your lot didn't think there was anything fishy about it."

"'Our lot' asked for an inquest, even though Albert Gray's doctor said he died of a heart attack that was not unexpected, in view of his health. The coroner's jury ruled his death natural. In the light of the verdict, the police had no grounds on which to proceed. What grounds have you for suspicion?"

"What grounds had the police for requesting an inquest?" he parried.

"Nothing but gossip. The 'better safe than sorry' principle. People were saying Mrs. Gray fed him arsenic. That always resounds in the public's imagination, but there were no symptoms of arsenic poisoning and no significant trace in the body. He had a weak heart. You knew that?"

"Yes. He was taking some sort of pills that kept it beating."

"The other prevalent rumour was that she'd substituted dummy pills—difficult, if not impossible, to prove."

"It didn't take rumour to make me suspicious. The bitch he married led him a dog's life."

The pun was unintentional, Alec thought, certainly not intended to amuse. "Why did he marry her?"

"He missed my mother. They'd hardly been apart for a day all their lives. Even as children, they'd grown up in the same street. And he was lonely. I was away too much."

"Your stepmother was very much his junior."

"But reaching the age when she'd begin to be regarded as a spinster, not a 'Bright Young Thing.'" His voice was full of scorn. "She was too desperate for a husband to be particular. Except where money was concerned. She wouldn't have married a poor man. She had expensive tastes, had my stepmama."

"So I've heard."

Gray's grimace was wolfish. "What she hadn't realised was that Dad grew up quite poor and he regarded extravagance as a sin. He didn't stint on clothes or housekeeping, but he refused to dissipate what he'd worked so hard for to buy useless baubles or expensive cars, let alone to throw house parties for people he didn't even like."

"You disliked and despised her."

"From the moment we met. That was several months after the wedding, because I'd been out of touch. She'd cajoled him into tying the knot as soon as possible, though Dad said he wanted to wait for my return. I could have saved him if I'd been here."

"I doubt it. Or if you had somehow prevented the marriage, he would always have resented your interference. You remained on good terms?"

"Oh yes. He was still infatuated with her, but it was too late to open his eyes, so I was polite to her in his presence."

"What made you dislike her instantly?"

"I suppose it was her manner towards him," Gray said slowly. "There was nothing I could pin down. I tried to persuade myself it was the instinctive mistrust that's essential to my job. Yours, too, I would imagine. Then I overheard her talking to a friend about my father and that dispelled all doubt. She despised him, and I hated her."

"So you ceased to be polite?"

"I ceased to meet her. Dad came here, or we went to my club. He was completely disillusioned by the next time I was in England. Why am I blabbing to you?"

To deflect suspicion? Or because he didn't know Judith was dead? "You tell me."

Gray was silent for a moment. "I haven't been able to talk about it to anyone else. No one else has shown any interest, of course. Maybe some of his friends in Beaconsfield cared, but I don't know them. My parents moved there long after I'd left home." He paused. "Partly, it's because I can't see you. Damn my eyes!"

"When can you take the bandage off?"

"Permanently? A couple more weeks at least, the doctor expects. Depends on progress, which is why I obey orders. This session, you tell me. I set the alarm for half past eleven." He gestured at the clock on the bedside table. "Should be soon, but it always feels like forever."

"Just a couple of minutes." Alec wanted to see the man's whole face. In general, the eyes were far less capable of concealing emotion than the mouth.

"The hell with it!" He sat up, taking off the cloth and dropping it with a slight splash in a basin beside the clock. His eyes were reddish, half-open. He blinked, and raised his hands with forefingers crooked, then froze. "Damn, it's so hard not to rub them. Make me think about something else. Why are you interested in my father's second marriage, anyway?" Through slitted eyes, he stared at Alec.

"Your father's second wife is dead."

199

Gray's eyes opened fractionally wider. "Dead! Good riddance! But she was my age, a year or two younger. What did she die of? Motor smash? Wait a minute, you came to bring me the news? A detective chief inspector, didn't you say? She was murdered! And you presume I did it."

"I don't presume you did it. I have to consider the possibility. You have a very strong motive. Are you aware of how your father left his affairs?"

"He told me he felt obliged to provide for his widow, if that's what you mean. He apologised, poor old chap! But everything was to come to me if she remarried or died. At the time, the former seemed far more likely."

"Did the solicitor, Mr. Ainsley, write to tell you Mrs. Gray proposed to sell the house, Cherry Trees, and did in fact do so?"

"He may have. My letters are held for me when I'm abroad, and I haven't been able to read anything since I got back. It doesn't surprise me, though. She was never cut out for life in a village. I expect she's bought a flat in town."

Alec chose not to enlighten him. "You don't mind?"

Gray shrugged. "As I mentioned, I didn't grow up in that house, and I haven't even visited in years. I have no emotional attachment. I do see what you mean about motive, though. I assure you, I've been unable to leave the flat since I was discharged from the hospital. I'll give you my doctor's name."

"Thank you, that won't be necessary. You see, she died a month ago."

"A month? Mid-September? I was in—I was a long way from England, and a long camel ride from the nearest port."

"I've heard camels aren't the easiest ride in the world."

"They're not, particularly when you can't see."

The alarm clock rang shrilly. Alec took it as his cue to leave.

He returned to Whitehall, but not to the Foreign Office. They weren't going to give him an answer unless he called in the heavy guns. The question was, in view of his unofficial status in the case, would the super cooperate?

Several colleagues greeted him on his way up to Crane's office. Word of his present situation had spread, inevitably. Some were inquisitive; some teased him about his penchant for odd cases. Only a couple knew about Daisy's frequent involvement, and they were too discreet to mention her.

Superintendent Crane was fatalistic. "As soon as I heard Mrs. Fletcher was involved, I knew there'd be complications."

"Sir, you can't blame my wife for the Foreign Office's reluctance to divulge where one of their secret agents spent September!"

"When you put it like that . . . But I bet she has relatives in the FO."

"A cousin, on her mother's side. Would you like me to appeal to him for assistance?"

"Heaven forbid! I'll see what I can do. What's the man's name, again?"

"Robert Gray, sir. The victim's stepson."

"Ah yes, difficult relationship. Not that I mean to suggest . . . How are the children doing these days, Fletcher?"

Alec assured him that Belinda loved her boarding school and the twins were growing by leaps and bounds.

"Good, good. I'll be in touch when I get the information. Or not, as the case may be. Never can tell with those Foreign Office Johnnies."

Alec made his way to Belgravia. Judith Gray's friend, Elizabeth Knox, lived in a fashionable maisonette in a row of fashionable maisonettes with pretentious columned entrances. All the curtains were closed. He rang the bell.

Again, an overalled cleaning woman opened the door. "Not at 'ome," she said, and started to shut it.

"Just a minute!"

She stopped and fixed him with an incurious gaze. "Nobody's 'ome, like wot I said."

He lifted his hat. "Is Miss Knox out for the day?" he asked hopefully.

"Mrs. They've both gone off."

"When will they be back?"

"Dunno."

"Can you tell me where they went?"

"Dunno. They don't tell me, do they. I comes in three days a week like always. Don't make no odds to me, savin' there's more work when they're 'ome."

"They must leave a forwarding address with someone?"

"Dunno. If that's all, I've got me work to do."

The door started to close again, and Alec found no reason to arrest its progress. Where, oh where were all the inquisitive, garrulous charwomen of England hiding?

TWENTY-FOUR

The twins were rolling down the hill. Though the sun shone, it had rained in the night. Miranda's pinny and Oliver's corduroy rompers were covered with mud. Daisy decided she'd better add a tip when she paid the laundryman's bill.

Nana was pretty muddy, too. Luckily it was the gardener's day, so he could wash her. Elsie would do it if necessary, but she didn't consider it any part of a parlourmaid's duties—and of course she was quite right. A less obliging girl would refuse.

"One more time, my pets," Daisy called as the children toiled up towards her again. "Then we must go home. Don't pout, Miranda. The wind will change and your face will get stuck. What would Nanny say?"

The dog suddenly charged up the hill, barking.

"Daddy!" Oliver shouted, his short legs pumping harder.

Daisy turned to see Alec coming down. He fended off Nana, who danced about him, whining her delight. He might as well not have bothered, as he then swept up Oliver in his arms, transferring a goodly quantity of mud to his jacket, and placed him, shrieking with joy, on his shoulders.

Miranda arrived. Alec bent to pick her up, eliciting further shrieks from Oliver, but she said, "No, Daddy, I'm being a lady. I'll hold your hand, like Mummy does. Mummy, you can have his other hand."

"Thank you," said Daisy, laughing at the muddy little lady as she took advantage of her generosity.

Oliver piggyback, Daisy and Alec walking slowly to allow for Miranda's short stride, they turned homeward.

The children chattered about the fun they'd had. Oliver's speech was still unclear, but his sister understood every word and interpreted when necessary. Back at the house, they went off with Bertha, the nurserymaid, happily repeating their story, which doubtless would be told a third time, to Nanny Gilpin. Mrs. Gilpin wouldn't scold them too much for their condition, knowing perfectly well who was to blame.

"You'll have to change everything you're wearing, Alec," said Daisy, following the twins and Bertha up the stairs. "Oliver even got his grubby little hands on your collar."

"Your skirt isn't exactly what I'd call pristine."

Daisy glanced down and laughed.

Mrs. Dobson had lunch waiting when they came down. Alec was in a hurry to get back to Beaconsfield, so they didn't linger over the meal. He carried her Remington "portable" typewriter out to the car and they set off.

"Did you talk to Mr. Bragg this morning?" Daisy asked. "How is he?"

"Flourishing. It turns out Robert Gray is a friend of his."

"So he was able to tell you all about him?"

Alec shook his head. "Not much more than that he's in England. His travels are strictly hush-hush."

"He's a secret agent?"

"I didn't say so!"

"No, but really, darling, a hush-hush 'diplomat' can hardly be anything else. So they wouldn't tell you where he was when?"

"I've had to put the super on to it," Alec said gloomily.

"I suppose he thinks it's all my fault?"

"Not exactly your *fault*. Just, if you weren't involved in the case, the situation wouldn't have arisen. He doesn't really believe it, of course."

Daisy snorted in a most unladylike manner. "I should be used to him by now. He is going to find out about the spy for you, is he?"

"He's going to ask. Whether he'll get an answer remains to be seen. Gray is in England at present, and having talked to him, I'm inclined to doubt that he killed his stepmother."

"You're always telling me my personal belief in someone's innocence is of no significance. Especially if it's someone I like. Did you like Robert?"

"I didn't dislike him. He's a quirky chap, interesting."

"And obviously plausible. A prime requirement for a spy must be plausibility."

Alec laughed. "He didn't strike me as a plausible liar, but you're probably right."

"Is he willing to identify the body?"

"I didn't ask. The doctor who did the autopsy said it would be impossible to make her face presentable—Sorry, I shouldn't have told you that. You're not going to be sick, are you?" He slowed down, prepared to stop.

"No, I'm all right. I just need to shut down my imagination."

"Sure?"

"Sure."

"In any case Gray came home with a serious eye complaint."

"Oh, poor man! What about the woman, Mrs. Gray's friend?"

"Departed for parts unknown. The daily professed to be unaware of her destination, and it wasn't the sort of neighbourhood where women chat on the doorsteps. A bobby or two making house-to-house enquiries might turn up something. It's up to Underwood to decide whether he wants to request that level of assistance from the Met."

"Beneath the dignity of a detective chief inspector?"

"Very much so. Not to mention a waste of my time."

Messages awaited both Daisy and Alec at the Saracen's Head.

"Oh, good," said Daisy, reading hers. "Isabel managed to hire a couple of men to clean the cellar. She's over at the house now, supervising—from a distance—and doing some gardening. I think I'll walk over to see how it's going. What about you?"

"Underwood has finished his enquiries in High Wycombe for the moment. He suggests I join him and Piper at the police station—"

"Here, or in Wycombe?"

"Here. To discuss our various findings and plan the next moves. I'll see you later, love."

"Expect you when I see you? All right. I hope the inspector had more luck this morning than you did!"

Alec had covered half the short distance to the police station when it started to rain. Thinking about the case, he hadn't noticed the increasingly threatening clouds. He almost turned back to tell Daisy not to go to Cherry Trees, to remember she'd been ill. Whatever he said, she'd make her own decision, though.

Glancing back, he saw her red umbrella bobbing as she walked in the opposite direction. With any luck, he thought with a sigh, the cellar would have been cleaned already to the point where she and Isabel could take refuge in the house.

He found Underwood dictating his report to Ernie, who had studied shorthand before becoming a detective officer, with the aim of attaining that branch of the service. Pennicuik was laboriously writing his own report longhand. They all looked up as Alec entered, Pennicuik with an air of profound relief.

"Any news?" Underwood asked.

Alec told them the indecisive results of his morning's travails.

The inspector grunted. "Good job we don't want him to take a look at her face. Nor the friend neither, if she wasn't traipsing about on the other side of the Channel in any case!"

"How about you, Mr. Underwood? Any luck? What about the rings?"

Underwood gestured at Ernie, who said, "Mr. Ainsley recognised the fake ruby right away as Mrs. Gray's. Not a doubt in his mind."

"Thank goodness."

"While I was there, I asked him about the stepson, whether he'd come back after his father's death. I didn't know you were going to see him yourself, Chief."

"He did come back to England, in June. I didn't ask him whether he'd come down to Beaconsfield. I slipped up there, though Bragg said all communication about the will was through Gray's own London solicitor."

"That agrees with what Mr. Ainsley said," Ernie confirmed.

"I can't see it matters, Mr. Fletcher," said Underwood, "because he told you he thought his father's death suspicious, even without hearing local rumours. I reckon he's still got the best motive by a mile and a half."

"So it still comes down to what the FO will reveal about his whereabouts. Let's hear the rest of your news, Inspector."

"I'll start with the last item, so that Sergeant Piper can finish taking down my report. In official language, please, Mr. Piper. I called on the rector, the Reverend Jeremy Turnbull, regarding enquiries about Cartwright. He told me he had spoken to three young women, quite independently of each other. All had been approached with 'lascivious intent including physical contact'—his words—by Roger Cartwright, the headmaster of the church school."

"My wife . . ." said Alec. Damn, he'd meant to keep Daisy out of this particular business. "My wife knows, of course."

"So she was your source?" Underwood perked up. "I wondered! I asked Mr. Turnbull whether Miss Leighton was one of the three but he refused to answer."

"So does Daisy. Given Miss Leighton's upset nerves and the rector's involvement, we can be pretty sure of her. I'd guess the others were her predecessors at the school. We can find them if we need them. Is the rector taking any action?"

"He's spoken to the governor of the school board, who'll be calling a meeting of the trustees."

"We ought to interview Cartwright before that, if possible."

"Yes. I'll let DS Piper tell you the rest of our news, while I ring up my super about the stepson. He's already worried about stepping on Foreign Office toes." The inspector left the room.

"Go ahead, Ernie. You walked over to take a look at Cherry Trees?"

"Yes, Chief. All those high hedges, I can see why they wouldn't be keeping tabs on their neighbours. I went round the house—Cor, what a pong!—without finding anything the locals missed. And it was Mr. Tring taught me to search, so I reckon it's all square and above board with the ladies."

"Good. Now, that mysterious vehicle. Miss Hedger told me you'd unravelled the riddle."

"I talked to the ladies about it, Chief, this morning before I went to look at the scene of the crime. Miss Chandler and Mrs. Fletcher witnessed a black saloon driving dangerously last Friday night. It sped past them up Orchard Road and turned into Station Road without pausing to look for cross traffic. Miss Chandler didn't catch the letters but she memorised the numbers—eight seven four—so's she could report it if she ever again saw it posing a threat to life and limb."

"We already had possible letters, didn't we?"

"That's right, Chief. BH 874. Made it easy for the county to look it up. It's a Jowett. As for the owner, they confirmed what Miss Sutcliffe guessed, it's Vaughn's."

"Vaughn's! No surprise, really. He's known to have been hanging about Cherry Trees, first to sell it, then to try for news of Mrs. Gray."

"DC Pennicuik talked to some of the neighbours again, and managed to get a bit more out of them than they'd offered to the uniformed officers."

"Well done." Alec's nod of approbation turned the young detective's ears bright red.

Ernie Piper, not so many years his senior but much more experienced, resumed his report. "Several of them had noticed the car parked outside Cherry Trees for extended periods, longer than the business of selling the house would account for. One had seen it a couple of times, in the evening, driving up the street, slowing in front of the house, then dashing on. She thought it was driven by a woman. Right, Pennicuik?"

"That's it, Sarge. She was pretty certain."

"The Jowett is actually registered to Myra Vaughn, Chief, not her husband."

"Is it, indeed. What, if anything, do we know about her?"

"Only what Mr. Underwood found out from Vaughn's employer, Mr. Langridge. She's older than he is and she's the one with the money. The car is available to Vaughn when needed to show a property to a client, which is not often as most of their business is in High Wycombe. Mr. Langridge hasn't met her, though he hired Vaughn on the recommendation of her brother, a highly respected local accountant."

"That would be the partner in Miss Chandler's firm, correct? What's his name?"

Ernie, as always, had the information at his fingertips—or rather, on the tip of his tongue as he didn't have to consult the notes in front of him. "Mr. Spencer, of Spencer, Mott, and Davis. Davis is the partner Miss Chandler answers to."

"So the inspector talked to Davis?"

"Yes, Chief, but you're getting ahead of me."

"Sorry. Do it your way or we might miss out something vital."

"DI Underwood asked Mr. Langridge whether Vaughn was a satisfactory employee. Langridge said, on the whole, yes. Mr. Underwood thought he was being evasive and pressed a bit, but he wouldn't say any more except that Vaughn is very good at hooking buyers and tenants, which is, after all, their business."

"What sort—" Alec paused, as the inspector returned.

"I got through right away," he grumbled, "only to find Mr. Parry's gone to a meeting in Aylesbury. At least he can't say I didn't try. What were you asking?"

"Piper said you thought Langridge wasn't telling the whole story about Vaughn. I wondered what kind of man he is?"

"Hail-fellow-well-met. I should think he was good at the business in his time but he's now too stout to budge from behind his desk without much huffing and puffing. In fact, while I was there, his secretary brought in a paper that urgently needed signing, and simply leaning far enough forward to put his name to it was a hard job of work."

Langridge sounded like an easy job for Tom Tring, Alec thought. He and his missus could go in with vague enquiries about looking for a place in the country and move on to the shortcomings of the younger generation. "He refused to explain his reservations about Vaughn?"

"I didn't push it. We can always go back. But as it happens, I got a clue to Vaughn's failings at Miss Chandler's firm. I talked to her boss, Mr. Davis. He speaks very highly of her, incidentally. They wouldn't have hired her if she hadn't had an excellent reference from the partner in Yorkshire who encouraged her to qualify as an accountant."

"Did Davis say why her previous boss didn't keep her on?"

"He couldn't talk *his* partner into it. Partly because she'd started there in a lowly position so he didn't think she'd have the authority, partly just what Davis described as typical Northern stick-in-the-muddishness, just as the ladies told us. Mind you, I gather Davis had trouble with his own partners, but he persuaded them it was the forward-looking, go-ahead way to get a march on their competitors. Full of clichés, our Mr. Davis."

Alec and Ernie Piper laughed. Pennicuik ventured a tentative smile.

"And what did he have to say about Vaughn?" Alec asked.

"Nothing direct, though I was pretty direct with him, given Miss Chandler's hints of a connection. He admitted that Langridge is a client, who's presently having his books audited. He wouldn't confirm that Miss Chandler is handling the audit, nor that Langridge requested the audit because he suspects the books have been cooked."

"They're trying to keep Vaughn in the dark," Ernie suggested.

"That's how it looks to me," Underwood agreed. "Maybe trying to keep his wife's brother in the dark, as well. Assuming he's been cooking up the books, could Mrs. Gray have found out?"

"You're thinking blackmail?" Alec suggested. "Conceivable, though I can't imagine how she'd have found out."

"It might've been obvious, Chief, from what he said when they talked about the price of the house. I don't know how it'd work but if he's skimming a bit off the top . . . Miss Chandler's the one to ask."

"If she'll answer. I'm more inclined to consider an affair gone wrong. You haven't interviewed him yet, I take it, Inspector."

"No, sir. His work is the perfect excuse to keep out of our way. His wife was out, too, when I called at their house. I left a note with the maid setting an appointment for six this evening. I hope you'll join me. Unless you'd rather do it yourself?"

"No, the two of us should impress him with the necessity of cooperation. What about Mrs. Vaughn? We'll need to talk to her, as well."

"I hope she'll be there. If not, we'll have to catch her tomorrow. But if *he* doesn't turn up, we'll find him one way or another and bring him into the station. We need to have a chat with Mr. Vaughn."

"Good enough. Which leaves Cartwright."

"How about all four of us waiting at the school gate when the children get out?" Underwood grinned. "I don't mind giving the slimy bastard a bit of a scare."

"It's an attractive thought." Alec considered. "But on the whole, better not. We don't want all the children hanging about asking questions. If we lurk behind the yews in the graveyard, we can watch the school until they have left, and then go in."

TWENTY-FIVE

Daisy hurried along Orchard Road through the rain. By the time she reached Cherry Trees, it was coming down hard, with no signs of letting up. At the gate, an elderly bobby was buttoning his cape.

"Is Miss Sutcliffe in, Officer?"

"Are you press?" he countered.

"A reporter? No, a friend."

"They told me to watch out for girl reporters. Haw! I never seen such a thing."

"Have you had many reporters turn up?"

"Yes'tiddy. Jus' the one today. Not much interest in a body in a cellar since Delores Wendover, the actress, shot that lord yes'tiddy."

"Good heavens, what lord? I've been avoiding the newspapers."

"Can't rightly remember the name, madam, but I dessay he deserved it. Anyways, if it keeps them newshounds away from here, I'm right grateful to Miss Wendover."

"You have a point," Daisy agreed. Her ankles were getting

wet. "I hope you don't have to stand out in the rain much longer."

She stepped forward and, with a gloomy mutter about Sergeant Harris, he moved aside to let her through the gate.

Isabel couldn't possibly be gardening in this downpour. Daisy hoped the house had been disinfected enough to be bearable by now. She rang the bell.

From the open kitchen window to her right came Isabel's voice. "Daisy? Just a minute. It's locked, and I'm just scrubbing the soil out of my fingernails."

"Weeding?"

"That's right."

A minute later, the door opened. Daisy couldn't restrain herself: she sniffed as she stepped across the threshold. "Sorry! That's rude. But it's much better, isn't it?"

"I'm glad to hear it. I wasn't sure if it was wishful thinking."

"It's more disinfectant than . . . anything else."

"Better enough for a cup of tea, if we go into the sitting room and close the door?"

"Definitely. Can I help?"

"No, go and sit down. I already put the kettle on. It won't take a moment."

Only five days had passed—four if one didn't count Friday itself—since last time Isabel had gone to make tea while Daisy waited in the sitting room. She chose the same chair by the fireplace. No fire burned in the grate now, though the room was chilly. She kept her coat and hat on.

Isabel still wore her gardening jacket and a woolly hat, when she came in with tea and biscuits. "I think they're all right," she said doubtfully. "They were in a tin with a tight lid. But don't eat any if you're suspicious. I'll light the fire."

"Not just for me."

"It'll help freshen the air. Besides, we'll probably move back in this evening. The hotel's getting a bit expensive."

"Will Inspector Underwood let you?"

"Yes. He popped into the Saracen's Head at lunchtime to tell me we can come home as soon as we're ready. I don't think he really suspects us, do you?"

"I don't think so. You three have no motive. Of course, the police don't have to prove motive. But without at least the shadow of one, they have to have more incontrovertible evidence than they're ever going to find in this case. I've seen no signs that any of you are under suspicion."

"That's a relief. That and getting the cleaning done. I thought I'd do some baking this afternoon. It always makes the house smell good."

"Good idea. It's really not bad, though. You must have picked good workers."

"A couple of ex-soldiers who just can't settle to a steady job, as Mrs. Barnes said. One of them gets bad spells, and the other can't cope without his pal."

"Poor chaps!"

"They even dug out the floor a couple of inches deep to get rid of . . . It's chalk, you know. Absorbent. I'll have to put down paving stones to fill the space or I'll keep tripping over the edge. They said they'd try to come back tomorrow to help, but not to count on it. I gave them the best letters of reference I honestly could."

"That reminds me, did Mrs. Hedger give you a written recommendation from Mrs. Gray?"

"No, as a matter of fact. I could see how well she'd been keeping up, with no one telling her what to do. Also, frankly, I didn't care to ask for one. You know what she's like. That reminds me, I must go and pick up the post. The police wouldn't let the postman deliver yesterday and the post office said they'd hold everything for us until they heard otherwise. Why do you ask?"

"Because if Mrs. Hedger had a signed and dated letter, the police would know Mrs. Gray was still alive then. And in England."

"They still don't know when she died?"

"Not as far as I know. They aren't even a hundred percent

sure it's her, the last I heard. Ninety-nine and a half percent, but she could be living the gay life in France."

"Surely they must have asked Mrs. Hedger when she left."

"I presume so, but whether they got an answer . . ."

"True," Isabel agreed. "At any rate, if she had a reference letter, I didn't see it. Shall I get some more biscuits?"

"Oh!" Daisy was dismayed to find crumbs on her saucer and the nearby plate empty. "I honestly didn't mean to eat any. No, please don't fetch more! But I'd love another cup, thanks. I wonder whether Sally would know whether her aunt had a reference letter?"

"Ask her."

"I'd better not. I'll mention it to Alec, though."

"I can't see why Mrs. Hedger would have kept it if it was bad, or why she wouldn't have shown it to me if it was good."

"Good in parts, perhaps, like the curate's egg. She'd prefer not to show it if you didn't demand it. But as you didn't, she probably has thrown it out by now."

"More than likely. You know, I can't help feeling Mrs. Gray must have gone to France. Otherwise, why hasn't anyone found her handbag? And even if she sent her trunks ahead, she must have had overnight things, a small suitcase at least, mustn't she?"

"You'd think so."

"I couldn't have helped noticing if they were anywhere in the house. I even went up to the attics. There were some things she sold us that we didn't really need, just cluttering up the place, so I stored them up there. So she must have taken her bag and a suitcase, or where are they?"

"They could have been dumped anywhere," Daisy protested, "and the police have had only two days. They can't go off hunting in all directions for something that may be in Paris, or at the bottom of a pond somewhere, not until they have much more information to go on."

"I suppose not."

"All the same, I wonder whether they've checked at the station here. Mrs. Gray might have left something in the left

215

luggage office, though they'd surely have reported it to the police by now. If she forwarded her trunks, though . . . They'd probably remember where to."

"Wouldn't Mr. Underwood or Alec have checked that?"

"They might not have thought of it. Men seem to be able to manage with a tenth of the luggage."

"You could go and ask at the station, couldn't you?"

"In theory. But Alec and the inspector would probably be furious."

"No need for them to know, unless you found out something useful, and then they ought to be grateful."

"*Ought* to be. Alec is seldom as grateful as I feel he ought to be. Still, if it weren't raining I'd be tempted."

Isabel glanced at the window. "It's stopped raining. And I have shopping to do, as well as the post office. I hate to turn you out— in fact, you're welcome to stay put—but I'd like to go before it starts pouring again."

"I'm coming. I just can't resist enquiring at the station, now that I've thought of it. It's a great trial, being subject to insatiable curiosity."

"Like the Elephant's Child? I loved the *Just So Stories* when I was little." She sighed. "I always thought someday I'd read them to my children. Oh well, what can't be cured must be endured. I'll just take the tea things to the kitchen and wash up later."

Daisy's thoughts turned from Mrs. Gray's luggage to Isabel and Inspector Underwood. She was pretty sure they had taken to each other. The trouble was, supposing their liking became friendship, grew warmer, and ended in marriage? What would happen to the amicable household of the three women?

Not to mention that, although she had somehow gathered the impression that Underwood was a bachelor, she didn't actually know whether or not he already had a wife. . . .

Alec would say, "Don't interfere." And this time, he was probably right.

Carrying umbrellas, Daisy and Isabel walked down Orchard Road and crossed Station Road to the post office. Isabel went in. Daisy went on towards the station. At the near end of the bridge over the railway cutting, she stood aside to let a couple of women with shopping baskets go by in the opposite direction: The footway on the bridge was so narrow pedestrians could pass each other only with difficulty. Once the way was clear, she crossed the bridge and had just reached the far end when she heard hurried footsteps following her.

She glanced round and saw Isabel, practically running after her and about to call out. With a wave, Daisy turned right and moved a few feet down the slope to the station, where the pavement was wider.

Isabel caught up. She clutched Daisy's arm with one hand, the other flapping an envelope with a foreign stamp. "From France!"

"Gosh! From Mrs. Gray? Hold it still, do. I can't read it."

"No, *to* Mrs. Gray." Isabel handed it to Daisy. "I can't make out the postmark, can you?"

Daisy peered at the blurry impression. "St. Tropez, I think. It's taken a long time to get here. It's dated the fifth."

"The post office has held it for a week, expecting her to write with a forwarding address. They should have given it to the police, shouldn't they?"

"Yes, but never mind. You can hand it over in person to the inspector."

"I . . . Or you could give it to Alec."

"He'd be bound to think there was something fishy about my having it. Better that it go straight from your hand to Mr. Underwood's. I'll go to the police station with you, if you like, but first I want to ask about her luggage."

"All right. I'll come, too." Isabel tucked the letter into her string bag and they set off down the hill. "The stationmaster is in charge of left luggage, and he knows me from when I was constantly dashing back and forth to Wycombe. I bet he knows I bought the Grays' house, so he won't be surprised if I ask about her trunks."

"Whereas if I do, he'll either guess that I'm just being nosy or assume the police sent me to ask—if he knows about Alec—which could lead to trouble when he finds out they didn't."

Isabel grinned. "It sounds as if you're often in trouble with the police."

"Only because they regard any attempt to help as interference. I don't know why I bother."

"Insatiable curiosity? There's the stationmaster now, looking portentously at his watch. Must be a train due."

The burly man in the smart uniform frowned at his gold pocket watch and peered down the line towards High Wycombe. The wail of a whistle came to Daisy's ears. The stationmaster's frown vanished; he stowed away his watch and prepared to welcome the up-train to his station.

Daisy and Isabel waited until the train had made its brief stop, allowing two women, laden with loot from the Wycombe shops, to alight. As the stationmaster turned back towards his lair, Isabel accosted him.

"Good afternoon, Mr. Jenkins."

"Afternoon, miss. Summat I can do for you?"

"I hope so. I'm Miss Sutcliffe. I daresay you heard I bought Mrs. Gray's house recently?"

"That I did," he responded cautiously. "And I heard Mrs. Gray was foully done to death in that same house."

Isabel turned to Daisy. "Is it all right if I explain?"

"You'll be Mrs. Scotland Yard?" asked the stationmaster.

"I am. I'll tell you what happened, if you promise not to pass it on."

"I won't. The comp'ny don't put gossips in charge of stations. We see things and we hear things and we keep our mouths shut. Not like the county police. That Sergeant Harris, he's in a mint of trouble on account of not holding his gab."

"So I believe." Daisy wanted to give him as little information as was necessary to persuade him to help. "The thing is, the death occurred before Miss Sutcliffe and her friends moved in. The body was in the cellar and they didn't have a key. Because it's been several weeks, it's . . . not easy to identify, so the police are not absolutely certain it's Mrs. Gray."

"Is that so! I'd reckernise her, surely. Always popping up to town, she was. Come through this very station four or five times a week, sometimes."

"Do you think you would? Of course, you'd be willing to try, a responsible person like you. Shall I mention it to the inspector?" Best to keep Alec out of it as much as possible, though his profession had given her a chance with Mr. Jenkins.

"Happy to help, madam. I wouldn't put meself forward, but if they was to request, I wouldn't say no. Now, what is it I can do for Miss Sutcliffe?"

Isabel retrieved the letter from her shopping bag. "I just picked this up at the post office. It's addressed to Mrs. Gray. It ought to be sent on to her if she's alive, or returned to the sender with an explanation if . . . if not. But there's no return address on the envelope. I'm sure you'd have told the police if she'd left any bags with you."

"I would, natural."

"I wondered, though, whether she forwarded a trunk from here, and if so, whether you remember the address it was sent to."

"There was three." Mr. Jenkins visibly went through an internal debate. "Reckon it can't hurt to tell you ladies. Not that I remember the addresses, mind, just the towns. She sent two trunks to some place in France with a saint's name. Not one of our English saints. I 'spose the Frogs have their own saints."

A saint on the Riviera? "St. Tropez?" Daisy asked.

"Like that, but with a zed on the end. Trop-pezzzz," he buzzed, "that's it. What the street was I can't tell you after all this time. Six weeks, must be, or more. The comp'ny'd have records, though."

"I hadn't thought of that! Of course they would, in case the trunks didn't arrive, or were damaged in transit."

The stationmaster nodded sagely. "Happens. T'other trunk,

that one went to Paris, a fortnight or so later. Now what was the hotel? A king—not a name, something like 'His Majesty'."

"The Majestic?"

"That's it. If there's nothing else I can help you with, the down-train is due in two minutes."

Daisy left it to Isabel to thank him, as another layer of protection against being accused of interfering. They left the station and trudged up the hill.

"If you don't mind," said Daisy, "would you tell Mr. Under-wood you made enquiries with the intention of re-addressing the envelope, then realised that it ought to be turned over to him right away? And leave me out of it?"

"If that's what you want. He . . . They should be pleased, shouldn't they? They can get in touch with the hotel. If Mrs. Gray never turned up, she must be dead."

"Not necessarily, but it would be another nail in her coffin, so to speak. I wonder what the letter says. I expect it's from the friend she was going to stay with, asking why she hasn't arrived yet."

"More than likely. It's a pity we haven't got a full address. There must be millions of English people in St. Tropez. Well, dozens."

"Probably hundreds. But Alec says the French police are far more efficient—or fussy, if you prefer—about keeping track of who's where, especially when foreigners are concerned. With the name, they'll be able to find her if they need to."

Drizzle started falling again as they walked up the curving lane towards the Old Town. Daisy opened her telephone-box-red umbrella and Isabel her conventional black. It was only about a mile, and after the steep slope up from the station it wasn't much of a hill, but Daisy began to flag. She still hadn't regained all her strength after her illness.

They crossed London End to the Saracen's Head and went on past the hotel along Windsor End. Just before they reached the police station, Isabel stopped suddenly.

"What on earth are they doing?" she exclaimed, staring across the road.

"What? Where? Oh, good gracious, I didn't spot them."

In the graveyard, half visible through the rain, Alec, Underwood, and Ernie Piper stood among the trees and tombstones. They appeared to be solemnly discussing one of the stone memorials.

"Daisy, could they be going to exhume Mr. Gray?"

"Is that his tombstone?"

"I have no idea."

"I doubt it. They can't prosecute a dead person. The school's just behind those yews, isn't it? What do you bet they're going after Cartwright?"

TWENTY-SIX

Running footsteps on gravel. Alec swung round to see a small boy in grey shorts and a green blazer, without his cap. Satchel in hand, he dashed along the path from the school, towards the street. With his free hand he seemed to be rubbing away tears. One of his dark grey knee socks had sagged down to his ankle and on the skinny calf two dark red weals were clearly visible.

Alec decided he was going to enjoy confronting Cartwright.

Pennicuik emerged from the shrubbery. "That's the last of 'em, sir, poor little blighter." He aimed the announcement halfway between Alec and Underwood, uncertain to whom he was meant to report.

"Let's go." The inspector took the lead.

Alec glanced back to see if anyone had observed them. On the far side of the street flaunted a bright red umbrella. He sighed. Still, Daisy was preferable to a crowd of curious locals.

The sound of four determined men tramping along the gravel path was very different from a scared schoolchild fleeing. Intimidating, Alec thought with pleasure. He reminded himself that they had no firsthand evidence against the schoolmaster, nothing to justify a charge of indecent assault, far less one of murder.

An alarmed face peered out through the schoolroom window, then disappeared.

Leaving Pennicuik outside to ward off interruptions, Underwood marched straight in without knocking. Cartwright had his back to the door, standing at the blackboard, cleaning it with a feverish motion. He turned slowly, trying to look surprised.

"To what do I owe the visit, gentlemen?" His voice quavered.

"Acting on information received, sir," said Underwood, at his most stolid, "and pursuant to our enquiries regarding the death of Judith Gray, widow of Albert Gray, of Cherry—"

"I know where the bloody woman lives! Lived."

"'Bloody'?" Alec repeated. "You disliked her?"

"I hardly knew her," Cartwright said sullenly.

"Hardly?" asked Underwood.

"I suppose we may have spoken once or twice, at a dinner party or some such occasion."

"It strikes me as a bit odd that you know her address if you'd only met once or twice, casually."

"Someone must have mentioned it in my hearing. I have an excellent memory."

"Good, good." Underwood rubbed his hands together. "Nothing better than a witness with excellent memory, don't you agree, Chief Inspector? You'll have no difficulty, then, Mr. Cartwright, remembering whether you've ever been to Cherry Trees?"

"Nev—I . . . hm . . . Possibly." From adamant to peevish in two and a half words. "In my position in the community, I and my wife receive many invitations. I can't be expected to remember everyone who's asked us over for drinks before dinner."

"In spite of your excellent memory. Ah well, perhaps Mrs. Cartwright will be able to tell us."

And now he was alarmed. "There's no need to bring my wife into this!"

"'This'?"

"This . . . This nonsense. Insinuating that I was involved with Judith. With Mrs. Gray. Why would a smart, well-off young

223

widow like that want anything to do with the likes of me? A penniless schoolmaster with no prospects and twenty years her elder . . . But she married a man thirty years her elder and more!" Now he was disgruntled.

"Judith?" Eyebrows raised, Underwood let the name hang in the air. The silence stretched for all of twenty seconds, that must have seemed an age to Cartwright.

He capitulated. "All right, I admit I called at Cherry Trees, just to offer neighbourly condolences. Mrs. Gray was very friendly, invited me in, offered a drink. She *asked* me to call her by her christian name."

"She was friendly, so you called again."

"Only once or twice."

"Mrs. Gray was friendly still, perhaps a little flirtatious? The sort of manner more appropriate to her gay circle of London friends, perhaps."

"She led me on."

"You tried to kiss her. She rebuffed you. You quarrelled, and—"

"No! It's not true."

"You didn't try to kiss her?"

"I—No, of course not. I'm a married man, with a position to uphold."

"You weren't considering that," said Alec, "when you made advances to the others."

"W—" Cartwright moistened his lips. "What do you mean?"

With distaste, Underwood told him, "Three young women have affirmed that you attempted to fondle them against their will."

"Liars! They're all the same."

"Relying, no doubt, on your position to give you greater credibility than them. However, they're unknown to each other and they all tell the same story."

The schoolmaster sank onto the tall stool behind his lectern desk. "How—how did . . ." His voice failed him.

"You must realise," said Alec, "we can't ignore the possibility of your having behaved in the same way with the murder victim."

"I didn't kill her."

"We'd like you to come across to the station—"

"People will see! The rector—"

"The rector already knows about those three incidents."

Cartwright buried his face in his hands.

"Here comes Vera," said Isabel.

Vera scurried across the street, almost running. "Your umbrella caught my eye, Daisy." She was very pale. "Oh, it's awful. Alec, and his sergeant and Inspector Underwood marched into the juniors' classroom. Are they going to arrest Mr. Cartwright?"

"I doubt it," said Daisy, "unless they've uncovered something I don't know about. Which, of course, they may have. Come on back to the Saracen and have a cup of tea. We've had ours but you look as if you need it."

"Don't let his fate worry you, Vera." Isabel patted her friend's arm. "If he's arrested, it's no more than he deserves. Go and order tea and I'll join you in a minute. I just have to deliver this letter to the police station."

"I wouldn't if I were you," Daisy advised. "We know none of our lot are there and for all we know, Harris is back. I wouldn't trust him not to lose it, or even open it."

"That's a point. All right, I'll come with you two." They all started walking towards the hotel. "I mustn't stay for another cup of tea, though, if I'm to get the shopping done. We can go home, Vera! The cellar's been cleaned thoroughly, and Mr. Underwood says we're allowed to move back in."

"Thank goodness. I can't wait to be back in my own room. I'll pack up all our stuff."

"I haven't told them yet that we're leaving. I hope they won't charge us for tonight."

"I'll sort that out for you," Daisy offered.

"Thanks. They won't want to offend you in case you move

out, too. Would you mind taking charge of this letter, as well? I'd like to go straight home with the shopping, and you can give it to Alec."

"Yes, but I think we ought to give each other proper receipts for it."

"What do you mean?"

"Well, I don't want Alec to think I somehow wangled it out of you, or worse, the post office. And you'll want something saying I've accepted responsibility for handing it over to the coppers."

"What letter?" Vera, her woes forgotten, was bursting with curiosity.

Isabel quickly explained as they entered the hotel. The lobby was empty. Vera, forgoing the cup of tea she had needed so badly a minute ago, made for the stairs.

"Tea at home. Bliss!"

Daisy went to the reception desk, where she found a pad of paper and a pen stand. She and Isabel each wrote out a suitable receipt, then signed and swapped them.

"You go and do your shopping. I'll sort things out with Mr. Whitford. Don't worry, I'll make sure he doesn't charge you for tonight."

"I don't know what we'd do without you, Daisy."

"Oh, nonsense. You'd manage. Just a minute, I keep forgetting to ask you . . . No, never mind. It'll be better if Willie's there. I'll drop round later, if that's all right?"

"Of course. Anytime."

Daisy tracked the landlord to his den. He grumbled a bit at her request but soon let himself be persuaded, as long as the ladies cleared the room before six o'clock. That gave them plenty of time, but Daisy went up to see if Vera needed any help.

"No, thanks, we have hardly anything here. That's what has made it so difficult. We'd have had to start washing things in the hand-basin and hoping they'd dry overnight. Daisy, how much tip should we leave? It's been so long since I stayed in a hotel, I've no idea what's proper."

This weighty question was settled at twenty percent plus six-pence for the Boots, "and a bit extra for Sally, because she's been so helpful. Do you have enough cash?"

"Plenty for the tip, and my cheque book was in my handbag, the one that Pennicuik brought, thank goodness." Vera sat down suddenly on the nearest bed. "It's all very well, but what about Mr. Cartwright? What are they saying to him? Are they asking him about me? What will he say about me?"

"Vera, honestly, you have no need to worry. The rector is on your side, and he heard what those others said about Cartwright."

"But he, or the school board, may decide it's easier just to get rid of another infants' teacher."

"They'd never find a man to teach the infants, so they'd just put themselves in the same situation all over again. At least, they can't be sure he'll be chastened enough not to repeat his offence."

"They could find an older woman."

"I'll be very surprised if they don't give him the sack. He ought to go and teach in a boys' school where there are no young women to tempt him. If, that is, he's not arrested for murder."

"Do you think that's why they descended on him?"

"I'm sure of it. I'm afraid the police wouldn't think what he did to you and the others a serious matter if it weren't for the possibility he tried the same ploy on Mrs. Gray. I wish I could hear what they're saying. And what he's saying."

Vera shuddered. "I don't." She got up and closed the one small suitcase Pennicuik had brought them from Cherry Trees. It had so little inside, it didn't need sitting on, as Daisy's suitcases almost invariably did.

Musing on Mrs. Gray's missing suitcase, Daisy retired to her room for a nap.

TWENTY-SEVEN

Cartwright didn't resist being taken to the police station. Finding out that the rector knew of his misdeeds took the stuffing out of him. Even his moustache looked limp. He forgot to take his overcoat and hat from their hook as they passed. Ernie Piper retrieved the hat and plonked it on his head, then helped him into the coat. The schoolmaster had wit enough left to jerk down the hat brim to shadow his face.

To Alec's relief, Daisy's umbrella was no longer visible. In fact, no one was about except a constable trudging away towards the crossroads, presumably on his beat.

Pennicuik bringing up the rear, the five men crossed Wycombe End and entered the station. Cartwright stumbled on a step. Ernie caught his arm and steadied him.

Sergeant Harris was at the entrance desk. He looked up, glared at Alec, and without a word started to write busily. Underwood ignored him. They went through to the office. The inspector motioned Cartwright to a chair. He sat down as if his knees had given way.

"I'll be with you in a moment, sir. Chief Inspector, I'd like a quick word." Leaving Ernie and Pennicuik to loom over the schoolmaster, Underwood and Alec stepped out of the room. Closing the door, Underwood nodded gloomily towards the front of the building. "I'm sorry he's back. We needn't expect any more cooperation from him than is necessary to keep his nose clean."

"No, I'm afraid not. With luck we won't need much from him. Piper and your chap are good men." And then there was Tom, busy behind the scenes.

"Pennicuik's still wet behind the ears, but he tries. Quite quick on the uptake. I was thinking someone ought to catch Mrs. Cartwright while we've got hubby here."

"And you're wondering whether Piper could handle it? I take it you're not ready to stick Cartwright in a cell to cool his heels?"

"No, and nowhere near ready to arrest him."

"I'm glad we agree. Ernie could handle it, but on the whole I'd rather you or I did."

"You. We've already impressed him with your rank—"

"Oh, is *that* my function?"

Underwood laughed. "Among others. Pity to waste it. Do you want to take Piper?"

"I'll leave him for you. Better just one person, for a first interview, especially with a woman."

"Do you want to take your wife to hold her hand?"

"I think I'll manage without," Alec retorted, grinning.

The inspector nodded. "Right. You know where they live?"

"Ernie found the address among your reports and told me how to get there. That's the sort of detail he excels at. It's just five minutes' walk."

"Don't forget we have an appointment with the Vaughns at six, and you offered to drive."

"I'll be back."

The Cartwrights lived in a small, newish house of the local brick. The small front garden with its white picket fence was very neat: the lawn closely mowed and dandelion-free, the two beds well weeded and still colourful, boasting chrysanthemums, Michaelmas daisies, and a couple of rose bushes bearing a few late blooms. On one side of the house, a hawthorn flaunted its crimson berries. A flock of chattering chaffinches were busy wrecking the display.

A net curtain twitched as Alec opened the gate and set foot on the crazy-paving path. Peripheral vision informed him of twitching curtains in the houses on either side. If a canvas of the neighbourhood should prove necessary, it would be much more fruitful than the struggle to elicit information from the residents of Orchard Road. He rang the bell.

Had Alec been asked beforehand what he expected of Mrs. Cartwright, he'd have described her almost to a T. She was about her husband's age, possibly a year or two older. Her brown hair was set in over-stiff marcelled waves and her makeup was minimal. Her maroon woollen afternoon dress was of good material, well-cut, but not in the current style, nor that of the past couple of years—Alec was conscious of fashion because clothes tell a good deal about character and circumstances. Her face was set as stiffly as her hair, in lines of discontent.

Her look was hostile. "If you're selling Hoovers, I already have one." She started to close the door.

Alec was tempted to offer her the latest model, but he curbed his tongue. "I'm a police officer, madam."

The hostility remained, but she said grudgingly, "What do you want?"

"A few minutes of your time." He glanced to left and right. "Perhaps I could come in?"

"If you must." She stood aside, and shut the door emphatically behind him, as if defying her neighbours. "Well, what is it?"

"Could we sit down, do you think?"

Her mouth tightened, but she led the way into a very conventional sitting room, the furniture well-chosen though inexpensive. Over the mantelpiece hung an oil painting of a colourful garden. Alec went to take a closer look.

"I wish I had more time to spend on my garden," he said, and turned in time to catch an almost wistful expression.

"It's a lot of work. If I had time and money, I'd have a big garden and help—and if wishes were horses, beggars would ride." Impatiently, she added, "What is it you want to say to me?"

He introduced himself.

"Scotland Yard." She raised plucked eyebrows. "Indeed. To what do I owe the honour of your call? Do get on with it. I have to go and supervise in the kitchen. The girl simply can't do anything right."

Alec decided he had to crack her shell of indifference if he was to get anywhere. "I must inform you that your husband is presently helping my colleague with his enquiries, at the police station."

She paled beneath the rouge and she sat down at last, but her voice remained indifferent. "Sit down, Chief Inspector. I don't like people towering over me. What has Roger done now? Set his heart on some underage enchantress? Not one of his pupils, I trust!"

"You're aware of his . . . straying."

"Obviously. Don't tell me he's gone beyond making overtures this time." She took a cigarette from a silver-plated case, the silver worn to show the brass beneath, and tapped it on the lid before lighting it with a match.

"We're investigating."

"He makes us both ridiculous," she snapped, driven at last to overt anger, viciously stabbing out the cigarette after one puff.

"Please tell me how he came to be a church-school teacher."

"I can't imagine what that has to do with anything, but if you want. . . . He was a promising young barrister when I married him. He was in first-rate chambers, a criminal practice—you'd recognise the name, I daresay—and he bore out the promise, until the war came along. When he was demobbed, he just couldn't settle back into his work."

"Not uncommon."

"Which made it no easier to deal with."

"No. I beg your pardon." Alec noted her self-satisfied look. Scoring a point off the questioner made people feel superior and, oddly enough, sometimes caused them to open up. "Please continue."

"In the end, he resigned from his chambers. Our savings ran out and we went to live with—and on—my parents. He found work occasionally, but never stayed long. If he didn't quit, he was given the sack."

"Was there a pattern? I mean—"

"I know what you mean. He usually quit because he considered the work meaningless or demeaning, or both. He was dismissed sometimes for drinking, usually for losing his temper once too often."

"He has a bad temper."

"He flies off the handle at the least little thing."

"And lashes out?"

"Sometimes." Mrs. Cartwright regained a measure of caution. "Not with me, not since I fended him off with a hot poker. This isn't anything to do with his philandering, is it? You think he killed that woman, what's her name . . . Gray?"

"Did you know he was . . . interested in her?"

"I'm not saying another word."

"Do you want to ring up your lawyer?"

"My lawyer? On a schoolmaster's salary, one doesn't have a lawyer at one's beck and call."

Alec didn't press her. He was inclined to feel sorry for her, particularly as her husband was almost certain to lose yet another job. On the other hand, he wasn't convinced that she hadn't known about Judith Gray. Given that knowledge, she herself might have been tempted to push the woman downstairs, with or without the aid of a hot poker. Though, as far as Alec knew, she hadn't attacked any of Cartwright's previous amours, everyone had a breaking point.

"The female of the species . . ." In less than two decades, Kipling's line had become a cliché. Alec's years of policing, not to mention the war, had taught him otherwise: the male human was far more deadly than the female. But one must not discount the female. What of Mrs. Vaughn? Walking back to the police station through the damp dusk, he called to mind what he knew of her.

She was the one who had brought money to the marriage, according to Willie Chandler's boss, Davis, who had it from his partner, Myra Vaughn's brother. Her income was sufficient to run a car. The money was under her own control, and she wasn't particularly generous with it, as evidenced by her "lending" the car to her husband.

Her stinginess might be responsible for his holding a job, though possibly her income was insufficient to keep them both in comfort, or perhaps he just enjoyed the work. His employer said he was good at it.

Yet, to all appearances, what he earned from commissions didn't satisfy him. He was fiddling the books.

Had Judith Gray found out? Was Vaughn himself aware of the audit?

Back at the station, he rejoined the others. As he entered the room, Cartwright looked round apprehensively. He was seated facing the desk. Pennicuik stood behind him and Ernie, notebook and pencil in hand, sat against the wall.

Underwood, behind the desk, stood up. "Might I have a word with you outside, sir?" To Ernie Piper and Pennicuik, he said, "Keep an eye on him."

In the corridor, the door closed, Alec said, "I take it that was a rhetorical warning. He hasn't tried to leave or turned obstreperous, has he?"

"No, he seems pretty cowed. He's admitted to having kissed those three schoolmistresses against their will, but unless they decided to bring charges, we can't do a thing."

"And they won't."

"No. That sort of trick calls for a sock on the jaw . . . but Miss Leighton has no one entitled to administer it. 'Superfluous women,' my arse! If you'll pardon the expression. Sniggers in the press and wanting to send them to the colonies! They're victims like the boys who should have lived to marry them, aren't they?"

"Not quite as final," Alec said mildly. "What else did Cartwright have to say?"

"He repeated that they led him on, and all he wanted was a bit of affection. Pathetic, really. His wife sounds like a right—"

"I wouldn't be too quick to judge. A question of the chicken and the egg. Anything more?"

"Not much. He still denies having anything to do with Judith Gray beyond a call of condolence. That would be more credible if he was a clergyman, or if he hadn't referred to her as Judith."

"And if he hadn't the history with the other women. Possible witnesses to his visiting her would be Mrs. Hedger or her niece, or Vaughn. Vaughn can't deny having been in the house himself, whether his calls were all business or not."

"Or Miss Sutcliffe," Underwood reminded Alec. "She was in and out of the place while deciding whether to buy it, and then going over the inventory with Mrs. Gray. Though I would have expected her to mention it to me if she'd seen Cartwright there."

"Not necessarily, given Miss Leighton's emotional reactions to his name. Now that we've cleared that up, though, you can ask her."

The inspector looked a little self-conscious. "I will. I don't know how much point there is in asking the charwoman, though. Might as well talk to a brick wall, from what you and Miss Sutcliffe say."

"If Sally Hedger hasn't seen Cartwright there herself, she may be able to get an answer from her aunt."

"DI Piper can talk to Miss Hedger," said Underwood, getting a little of his own back. "Now, what's this about chickens and eggs?"

Alec told him what Mrs. Cartwright had related of her husband's sorry history. "So, impossible to tell who was reacting to whom, but I'm inclined to blame the wreck of their marriage on the war."

"Very likely. Not that we need worry about that, only about

the effects. But it's time we were off to see the Vaughns. They live out in Hazlemere. We'd better get moving. I'll have to let Cartwright go." Underwood sighed.

Cartwright, warned that if he left Beaconsfield he must provide an address where he could be found, scuttled out. Pennicuik was left holding the fort. The other three detectives walked to Alec's Austin Twelve, on the way seeing the schoolmaster dive into the Saracen's Head, doubtless to find a meagre solace in alcohol.

Alec drove, with Underwood beside him and Ernie Piper behind, leaning forward to offer directions. He had, as a matter of course, studied the appropriate map. Though the hedged lanes wound hither and thither and crossed each other at frequent intervals without benefit of fingerposts, Ernie was never at a loss.

They reached Hazlemere; they found the correct street. It was less a street than another lane, winding downhill. Turning into it, Alec could see lights indicating several large houses at considerable intervals, set well back from the road.

"And no numbers," Ernie said apologetically. "It's a dead end with a manor at the end."

"I imagine the lord of the manor sold off the land for building," said Alec. "Sorry, Ernie, you're going to have to hop out every time we come to a gate."

Ernie had to hop only twice; most of the gateways had signs readable from the car, set where headlights illuminated them as they crawled by. The Vaughns', Manor Lodge, was the last on the left. Its position close to the lane with a minuscule front garden suggested it had in fact been the manor's lodge.

Alec turned into the drive, which led along the side of the house to a wooden garage at the rear. The old house was built of brick and flint, two stories with low ceilings. No lights showed in the front or side windows, only a dim lightbulb above the front door.

"Dammit," said Underwood, "I left a message with his boss and both message and a note with the secretary. Pennicuik rang here and left a message with a servant." He checked the luminous dial of his watch. "It's past six. Don't tell me he's done a flit!"

"Ernie, go and check round the back."

Piper returned after just a minute. "Just one light on. I think it's the kitchen. It has a window at the back and door on to the drive. There's a new wing back there, but it's completely dark. At the far end, it has French doors to the garden."

Underwood marched ahead to the front door and rang the electric bell. After what seemed a long wait, he rang again and knocked as well. This time, the fanlight above the door lit up.

The door opened on the chain. A youthful face, half-excited, half-apprehensive, appeared in the gap. "You the p'lice?"

"Yes, miss. Detective Inspector Underwood. I have an appointment with Mr. and Mrs. Vaughn."

"They ain'—aren' here. Mrs. Walker, tha's the housekeeper, said to tell you they've gone off to Lunnon. London."

With an obvious effort, Underwood said pleasantly, "Then we'll just have to have a word with you and Mrs. Walker."

"An' Mr. Grissom, too? Dilys ain'—isn' here. She went to the picshers with her young man."

"And Mr. Grissom, too. Open the door, there's a good girl."

"I'll 'ave ter ask."

"Very proper. You go ahead and ask."

The next face to appear was male, elderly, and truculent. "Where's yer 'elmets? That's what I wanna know."

The inspector explained that they were detectives who seldom wore uniform. When Grissom closed the door to take off the chain, Underwood said quickly, "If we can separate them without making it too obvious, will you take the housekeeper, sir? Sergeant, the girl for you, and I'll tackle this fellow."

He stopped the manservant in the tiny entrance hall to ask a question. Alec and Ernie followed the sound of female voices to the kitchen. Here they were in luck, as Mrs. Walker promptly sent the girl to the scullery to peel potatoes for their supper, whither Ernie unobtrusively slipped out to join her, leaving Alec with the stout housekeeper.

The kitchen smelled of roasting mutton. A vivid flash of olfactory memory took Alec back to the smell of roasting beef in Isabel's kitchen and the revolting sequel.

Banishing it, he introduced himself.

"You can't blame me," said Mrs. Walker.

Alec raised his eyebrows. Elucidation followed.

"I told the mistress, myself, I did. Dilys—she's parlourmaid—she took the telephone call as is her duty, and she told me, and I told the mistress. The perlice are coming to see you and the master, I said. They rang up on the telephone, I said, and made an appointment for six o'clock this very evening. And you know what she said? 'We're going to the theatre in London,' that's what, and it's no use arguing with the mistress."

"Difficult, is she?" Alec sympathised.

Mrs. Walker considered this proposition. "Not *difficult*, I wouldn't say. It's just her growing up in the Manor, till her pa died, she knows times has changed but she don't rightly feel it inside her, if you know what I mean."

"I know just what you mean, and that's very neatly put, if I may say so."

Tom would be proud of him, he thought, as she preened. "*I* don't mind. Would you like a cup of tea?"

"That's very kind of you, but not just now, thank you."

"I'll put on the kettle in case you change your mind." She lit the gas burner under the kettle. "Yes, off to the theatre they went, the both of 'em, though I did ought to tell you as the master thought they ought to stay home. Leastways, that's what he said, but it don't always do to take what he says for gospel."

"No? For instance?"

"Like the Manor, f'rinstance. It's let to an American, a millionaire. The master handles the rent and such, him being in the business. Now, maybe he's counting on how the gentry don't talk about money, what they've got and what they spend. But these here Americans, seems like they never stop talking about money. My friend Mrs. Golightly—which she don't, being a large woman—she's housekeeper over to the Manor, and she heard them arguing over could they get a better house for the same rent. One of 'em mentioned the amount, and Mrs. Golightly just happened to mention it to me. And I just happened to notice, doing the household accounts like I do, the mistress not being brought up to it—I just happened to notice that what she's getting isn't what they're paying!" She ended with a sort of triumphant gasp, having run out of air.

"Mr. Vaughn, as agent, is entitled to a commission, you know."

"I know that! It's written down as is right and proper. But it don't add up right, and that I'd swear to."

"Did you tell Mrs. Vaughn?"

"I did not, not being one to come between husband and wife. I lost my own in the war. I'm not saying he didn't have his faults, same as anyone, but—"

Underwood's entrance saved Alec from a recital of the late Mr. Walker's desirable qualities. Though he had intended to broach the subject of marital infidelity, he judged that Mrs. Walker would not take such a question kindly, so the interruption was not unwelcome.

Mrs. Walker went to the scullery door. "Not finished them 'taters yet, my girl? This rate, we'll be eating at midnight."

"They're all done, Mrs. Walker." The maid appeared with empty hands, followed by Ernie, gallantly carrying the heavy cast-iron saucepan for her. Grissom had likewise followed Underwood into the kitchen.

The inspector addressed Mrs. Walker: "You'll excuse me, madam, if Mr. Fletcher has already asked, but can you tell me what time Mr. and Mrs. Vaughn are expected back?"

The housekeeper shook her head regretfully. "The mistress said not to wait up. It's a first night, seemingly; why she was so keen not to miss it. There'll be a party afterwards. They won't be home till well after midnight."

TWENTY-EIGHT

When Daisy lay down for her nap, she didn't fall asleep, but she grew so somnolent that a very soft tapping on the door startled her.

"Who's there?"

"It's me, Sally, Mrs. Fletcher."

"Come in. What time is it?"

"Just after six, madam. I hope I didn't wake you."

"I was just resting my feet. It's been over an hour? Today seems to have lasted a very long time already. What is it?"

"There's two messages come, madam, that I thought might be urgent." She came over to the bed and handed Daisy a pinky-buff telegram envelope and a double-folded note on lined paper. "The telegram's for Mr. Fletcher, sent over from the post office. The boy said it's from Scotland Yard. I told him to take it to the police station, but he said it's addressed to the Saracen's Head and that's where he was told to take it."

Holding up the telegram to the light, Daisy wished she could see what Crane had to say. It must be from him, though she knew she had no hope of reading it. She could, however, deliver it to Alec herself. If she sent Edward the Boots to deliver it to the police station, the same difficulty applied as with the letter from France: If Alec was not there, both might get into the wrong hands.

"I'll see he gets it, Sally." She laid down the telegram and picked up the note.

"Constable Pennicuik brought that one, madam. The telegram came just after he went off, so I couldn't give it to him."

"This is from Alec." She recognised his handwriting. "Let me see what he says." She untucked and unfolded the paper. "Oh, bother, he won't be back for dinner. I don't suppose DC Pennicuik mentioned whether they're all at the station or buzzing about questioning people?"

"No, but Mr. Piper wrote a note to me," Sally said, blushing. "He asked if I—we would be so kind as to send over sandwiches for four at half past seven."

"So they should all be there at seven thirty. Good. I'd better get moving and go over to Cherry Trees right away."

"Mr. Whitford told me the ladies are going home tonight. Miss Leighton rang up Miss Chandler at work to tell her. Miss Leighton gave me ever such a good tip."

"You deserve it, Sally."

"Thank you, madam. I do my best."

"And a very good best it is."

Sally went off, beaming. Daisy hoped all would go well with her, whether the future held a job in London or marriage to Ernie. Or to someone else, she allowed.

She got out of bed and washed her face and hands in the basin. Shedding the creased blouse she had worn to bed, she decided to put on a dress instead of the costume she had been wearing. As she brushed her curls into place, she wondered whether to go straight to Cherry Trees or drop in at the police station to see whether Alec, Underwood, or one of their minions was there. It was just a hundred yards or so. But in the wrong direction, possibly fruitless, and she hadn't found out yet about the possible payment to Mrs. Hedger. She might as well wait until she had collected all her snippets of information. That way, she'd have to suffer through only one ragging for her interference.

The walk back from Cherry Trees was uphill, though not steep. Daisy considered taking Alec's car. If she did, however, he was bound to need it. She left a note telling him where she had gone and asking him to pick her up in the car if possible.

At least it had stopped raining.

The royal blue Austin Twelve was not where Alec had parked it. How lucky she had decided against driving, or she would now be feeling aggrieved at its absence!

About to turn into Orchard Road, she saw a large man walking towards her up Station Road. His hat brim hid his face from the light of the street lamp, but his walk was unmistakable. Daisy glanced round to make sure no one was about, then hailed him.

"Hello, Tom!"

He tipped his hat. "Good evening, Mrs. Fletcher. The ladies have been allowed to return home, I take it."

"Once a detective, always a detective. Are you in a hurry, or will you walk along with me?"

"My pleasure. The Chief explained why I'm here, I assume."

"Because you're bored stiff with being retired." Daisy tucked her hand under his arm.

He chuckled. "Haven't found my civilian feet yet, and that's the truth."

"Also because you're the best at certain aspects of the job that no one else available is good at. You're very unofficial and I'm not to recognise you in public."

"You did nicely when we ran into each other in the doorway last night. Not a blink."

"Just a wink," Daisy retorted, "which was your doing. Have you found out anything useful."

"Ah." Tom pondered. "I don't see why I shouldn't tell you a bit of it. I've traced the gardener and, more important, the housekeeper who used to work for Mrs. Gray."

"Already? Did you talk to them? What did they say?"

"I had a chat over a pint with the gardener, but I'm too

unofficial to go asking nosy questions. Not unofficial enough to tell you what he said, anyway! The housekeeper's moved away. The Chief'll have to go after her. The missus heard some gossip that likely came from her in the first place, I can tell you that much."

"But not what the gossip is?"

"Right." His tone told her he was grinning, and she visualised the way his sweeping moustache twitched when he grinned.

"It sounds as if you've both been busy, and successful. I suppose you won't tell me how you communicate with the Chief, either."

"Not if he hasn't, though I can't see why he wouldn't. Well, here we are." He stopped at the gate of Cherry Trees. "All right to walk home, are you?"

"Yes, thanks. 'Night, Tom. Give my regards to Mrs. Tring."

Daisy went up the path and rang the bell. Vera came to the door.

"Come in, Daisy. Sorry about the smell, but carbolic is better than . . ." Her voice faltered.

"Infinitely better."

"Isabel's left the cellar door open to air it out. We're keeping the rooms closed off as much as possible, but it seeps in everywhere. Do you mind coming into the kitchen? Izzie's cooking."

"Of course not."

"She said there's plenty, so you're welcome to stay for supper, but doubtless Alec is expecting you."

"Actually, no. He's too busy this evening. It's part of being a copper's wife, never knowing quite when he'll turn up. Often he can't even let me know in advance."

Vera opened the kitchen door; they hurried through and she closed it behind them. The kitchen smelled slightly fishy, but much less obnoxious than the hall or passage.

"Hello, Daisy." Isabel was at the sink, scraping and slicing carrots. "I decided I'd better bung out the beef, though it seemed to be perfectly all right. I just couldn't face it. We're having fish pie. I hope you'll stay."

"Yes, thanks."

"Willie said this morning she'll probably work late today, so we're not waiting for her."

"Alec's working late, too." Daisy sighed. "No such thing as regular hours for coppers."

While the carrots cooked and a delicious smell emanated from the oven, they sat at the kitchen table with a glass of white wine. Isabel had splurged to celebrate their return home.

"I know it's been only two days, but it seems like forever."

"It's a pity Willie isn't here," said Vera.

"We'll save a glassful for her. Daisy, did Alec tell you what the letter from France said?"

"Sorry, I haven't actually seen him yet, and I didn't want to leave it at the police station for him in case it got lost. I've got several other things to tell him—"

"About Mrs. Gray's trunks?"

"That's one. Also, I wanted to ask you whether you paid Mrs. Hedger for the time she worked between when Mrs. Gray disappeared and you moved in. If you know how long that was, it would help the police pin down the date she died."

"No, I didn't pay her. It may seem mean, but I hadn't asked her to work and there were so many unexpected expenses just then. We all agreed we weren't morally obliged, even Vera."

"So it won't be in your account book. That's a pity. Did she ask to be paid?"

"Oh yes. And that's another thing: I had no way to tell if she was honest about how long she'd worked unpaid. For all I knew—or know, for that matter—she could have added a few extra days, though now I think she's pretty honest, whatever her other flaws!"

"What date did she claim she was last paid?"

Isabel frowned in concentration, then shrugged. "I can't remember."

"I bet Willie remembers," said Vera. "She always remembers even the most insignificant numbers."

"True." Even the numbers on a half-seen licence plate. "Will you ask her?"

"I hope she'll be home before you leave." Isabel got up to test the carrots. "Just a couple of minutes more." She opened the oven door and took out a haddock pie topped with crispy mashed potatoes. "We were going to eat in here tonight, Daisy. Do you mind?"

"Not at all." Having been properly brought up, she would have said exactly the same even if she abhorred the thought of dining in the kitchen.

Apple charlotte followed the delicious fish pie. Willie still wasn't home by the time Isabel served coffee. They were taking their first sips when the doorbell rang.

"Not Willie," said Vera, getting up, "unless she's lost her key." She went out, to return a moment later with Alec.

"Good timing, darling. I wasn't looking forward to walking back."

"All good policemen have a well-developed sense of timing. Good evening, Isabel."

"Good evening. Have you eaten?" asked Isabel, ever practical.

"Yes, thanks. The Saracen sent us in some sandwiches."

"Coffee?"

"Please. Vera—or Miss Leighton, if you prefer it in the circumstances—I'm going to have to ask you to describe to me your unpleasant experience with Cartwright."

"No!" Vera shot an accusing glance at Daisy. "I trusted—"

"Inspector Underwood talked to Mr. Turnbull, who, incidentally, did not give him your name when he spoke of Cartwright's misbehaviour. It wasn't too difficult to deduce that you were one of his victims. We don't expect to run into any difficulty in finding the other two."

"Daisy said the police wouldn't be interested, it wasn't bad enough for him to be arrested."

"Judging by what the three of you told the rector and assuming he reported accurately to the inspector, that is correct. Our only interest is in whether the details of his actions towards you

244

indicate a pattern of behaviour that might have subsequently escalated."

"In other words," said Daisy, "he might have gone on to push Mrs. Gray downstairs."

Alec frowned at her. "Miss Leighton?"

"I can't!"

"Don't be a jellyfish, Vera," Isabel said bracingly. "Just imagine how you'd feel if Cartwright went on to kill someone else, or even just assaulted another woman, because you wouldn't help catch him."

"If you'd rather," said Alec, "you can tell Daisy and she'll take it down in shorthand. However, Underwood and I will both be reading her report. We may in that case have further questions, and in the end—either way—we'll have to have your signature on it, stating that it's correct."

"You never know," said Daisy, "talking about it may help you to put it in perspective."

"Here or elsewhere?" Alec asked remorselessly. "With or without Daisy or Isabel?"

Vera gave Isabel a pleading look. Isabel got up and poured her another glass of wine. "Have a little Dutch courage."

Twisting the stem of the wineglass in nervous fingers, Vera fixed her eyes on the pale liquid. She began to speak very fast. "The children had all left. I was writing on the blackboard when he came in, through the connecting door. A poem: 'How do you like to go up in a swing?' Do you know it? The little ones love it. I looked back to see who it was, and I smiled at him. I wish I hadn't!"

"For pity's sake," Isabel exploded. "That doesn't make it your fault."

Alec gave her a look of the sort that could shut Daisy up in full flow, no mean achievement. "Did Cartwright say anything, Miss Leighton?"

"I don't think so. I can't remember."

"It doesn't matter."

"I turned back to the board and went on writing, and I explained to him that I was going to have the children copy the poem as best they could and memorise it. He came up behind me—"

"You didn't hear him coming?"

"I was talking, as I said. Besides, he wears rubber-soled shoes so that the children can't hear him creeping up on them. He shouldn't be a teacher. He's a bully." Indignation trumped modesty. "He put his arms round me and felt my . . . my bosom! And kissed my neck. It was horrid. I got away and ran to the outside door. That's when he called me—horrible names."

"You need not repeat his words. Did he pursue you?"

"Just a few steps. He stopped and threatened me."

"Threatened violence?"

"No. If I told anyone he'd deny it and I'd lose my job."

"He made no attempt to attack physically? To give you a push or a slap?"

"He shook his fist," Vera said doubtfully. "I could have been outside before he reached me. Someone might have seen. He went back into his classroom and slammed the door."

"Has he tried anything since?"

"No. But I've been afraid he might."

"You'll be all right now. I'll be very surprised if Cartwright doesn't leave at the end of term, if not before. Thank you for being brave enough to tell me." Alec took a last mouthful of coffee and stood up. "Daisy, are you ready to go?"

"Yes, I'll just get my—" Intercepting a disappointed look from Isabel, Daisy changed direction. "But there are a couple of things I must give you. . . ." She dug in her handbag for the letter from France.

"Later, Daisy. I've got to get back to the station."

Once in the car, she returned to the subject. "Darling, I really do have some important information for you. Perhaps I'd better come with you to—"

"How important?"

"Very."

"Daisy, what have you been up to?"

"Nothing! Mostly just taking messages for you."

"Messages?"

"A telegram from Mr. Crane, for one."

"Great Scott, Daisy! What does he say?"

"*I* don't know. It was delivered, not telephoned, and I didn't read it."

"How do you know it's from the super, then?"

"The boy told Sally it's from the Yard. There's a message from Tom, too."

"I told you not to—"

"I met him in the street, in the dark. He walked me to Cherry Trees. Do you want to know what he said?"

"Of course," Alec said crossly. "That can't wait till we reach the station. Underwood doesn't know about Tom."

"He didn't tell me any details." She related the snippets the retired detective sergeant had passed on. "Does it sound helpful?"

"Might be."

"How about what Vera said?"

He sighed. "A washout. It tends to suggest Cartwright was likely to confine his anger at rejection to verbal abuse. A suggestion is not evidence. Your friend Willie wasn't home yet?"

"No, she'd let them know she'd probably be working late."

"With any luck, finishing up the job. Perhaps we'll be able to clear up that side of things tomorrow, if not tonight."

"Vaughn's defalcations—if that's the right word? Did you see him tonight?"

"Not yet. We had an appointment with him and his wife, but they went off to the theatre in town before we arrived. We left poor Ernie there—not that he wasn't being spoiled rotten by the servants—to phone in when the Vaughns return, however late."

"Does that mean you'll be getting up at one in the morning to go off and interview them?"

"If I get to bed at all. Underwood is no slacker and he's on his mettle."

"Treading the fine line between competing and cooperating with Scotland Yard, poor man! Well, I won't tell you any more until I can tell him at the same time. Anyway, here we are."

TWENTY-NINE

Alec preceded Daisy into the room. "Mr. Underwood, my wife has information for us. May she come in?"

"Yes, of course." The inspector came to the door. "Good evening, Mrs. Fletcher. What have you discovered?"

Daisy was unwontedly nervous. Underwood's presence would deter Alec from blowing her up, but he might himself take a dim view of her activities, though he was too polite to accuse her of meddling—she hoped.

The telegram first, she decided. She couldn't get into too much trouble over that.

"This is addressed to Alec," she said, handing it over. "Miss Hedger gave it to me to give to him. She told me the boy said it's from Scotland Yard."

Alec took a steel paper knife from the inkstand on the desk, slit open the envelope, and scanned the enclosed form. "Damn! Er, drat."

He gave it to Underwood, who read it and said, "Pity. We've lost one of our suspects. I suppose the Foreign Office couldn't be mistaken?"

"They could, of course, but I for one am not about to challenge them without a good deal of other evidence."

"Which we haven't got. Nothing but motive. All right, Mrs. Fletcher, what's that?"

Daisy held out the French envelope. The foreign stamp made both Alec and Underwood sit up and brought Pennicuik to his feet for a closer look.

Underwood reached for it. "From France, and addressed to Mrs. Gray!" He picked up the paper knife.

"How did you get hold of it, Daisy?" Alec's tone was ominous.

The inspector looked up with a glance of mild, slightly amused enquiry.

"I was about to tell you. It's addressed to Cherry Trees. The bobby at the gate wouldn't let the postman deliver there on Monday, so he left the post at the post office, and they kept this morning's delivery, too. I was with Isabel—Miss Sutcliffe—when she went in to fetch it. Of course she showed it to me. She didn't know when she'd see you, Alec, or DI Underwood, and she assumed I'd see you sooner, so she asked me to pass it on. I gave her a receipt. And she gave me a note saying she'd given it to me on the understanding I'd hand it over to the police." Daisy found the bit of paper and laid it on the desk.

"Very thoughtful," Underwood approved. He slid the knife under the flap, trying with a delicate touch to open the envelope undamaged.

"Daisy, you'd better go," said Alec.

"Oh, but I've got more to tell you."

"What on earth—"

"'Where on earth are you, Judith darling?'" Underwood interrupted, reading. "'We've been expecting you for *weeks*. Gee-gee is biting his nails, sure you've had an accident. I told him you're just enjoying the fleshpots of Paris, which only makes him bite his nails the more. Darling, you didn't say which hotel you're staying at so I hope the horrid people who bought your house will forward this. Love from all of us. Do hurry.' I can't read the signature. Here, take a look." He passed it to Alec.

"Could well be Liz, don't you think?"

"Let me see," Daisy requested. "Yes, I'd say it was Liz, then either a K or an X, an initial or a kiss."

"Elizabeth Knox," said Alec.

Daisy handed the letter back to the inspector. "The address is quite legible."

"An address in Sang Tro-pay—"

"And I know the hotel in Paris," Daisy said triumphantly.

All three men stared at her.

"You do?" Underwood was incredulous.

"How the deuce—?"

"Darling, Isabel was naturally anxious about not being able to forward the letter to Mrs. Gray, and—"

"This was before the two of you realised she ought to give it to us, I suppose," Alec said ironically.

"It must have been, mustn't it? Anyhow, it seemed to me it might be worth asking at the station—the railway station—whether she'd sent on any trunks by train, and if so, where to. The stationmaster said the records will be at the railway company offices in London, but he remembered two going to St. Tropez, and a third was shipped to Paris, to the Majestic Hotel."

For a moment, silence reigned. Then Underwood said, "I can't believe I didn't think of asking the railway."

"We've been pursuing other leads," said Alec, "and it's been only two days . . . but you're right. We should have thought of it. Well done, Daisy, though it would have been better to mention your brilliant idea to us and leave it to us to follow up."

Daisy decided to accept the praise and ignore the second part of this. "There's something else . . ." She paused, waiting for exclamations of astonishment, dismay, congratulation, or disapproval. Apparently she had exhausted Alec and Underwood's capacity for such emotions. They just looked at her, so she continued. "All I need is a scrap of information from Willie—Miss Chandler. She wasn't home yet."

Alec frowned. "If you're expecting her to discuss her work with you—"

"Nothing to do with her work. She's silent as the grave about that. She has no reason to keep quiet about what I want to find out."

"What might that be, Mrs. Fletcher?" The inspector sounded resigned.

"A date. It should narrow down the date of death." Both men opened their mouths. Daisy hurried on. "I was thinking about it, thinking that Mrs. Hedger's in the best position to say when Judith Gray was last seen alive. Assuming she's dead."

"You may be sure we'll be questioning her again."

"And will you get any answers? I gather she was no more willing to talk to Alec than to me and Isabel. It struck me that she very likely wanted to be paid for the work she did while the house was unoccupied, and that Isabel probably keeps the household accounts and so would know how long that was."

"What strikes me," said Underwood, "is we could do with a few women on the force. A different point of view, they have. How long did she work without pay?"

"They decided they weren't responsible for what they hadn't asked for, so it's not in the account book. However, both Isabel and Vera are sure Willie must remember the last date Mrs. Hedger said she had been paid. It's a number, you see."

"Miss Chandler never forgets numbers."

"Exactly. That's everything I had to tell you, so if you'll excuse me, I'm going back to the hotel."

Alec walked her out to the street door. "I have to say well done, love, and I'm trying not to say don't meddle. But you must realise that the more helpful to us you are, the more likely the killer will put two and two together and do his utmost to stop you."

Daisy reckoned a grudging compliment was better than a stinging rebuke. "I can't see how he'd ever find out. I don't go round interrogating people—except the stationmaster, and that was really Isabel, who had a good reason for asking."

"If he has his wits about him, he'll have noticed or heard that you're spending more time here than being a copper's wife can explain."

"Oh no, darling, I'm the clingy kind of wife that just can't let her adored husband alone." She reached up to put her arms round his neck and kiss him, and he obligingly responded in kind. Anyone observing them through the glass of the door might well have believed her words.

Alec watched Daisy go off towards the Saracen's Head, wondering whether she'd heed his parting warning, "Stay out of it, and be careful," or had even heard it. She'd do what she considered right, no matter what he said.

He returned to the others.

"I'm sorry," he said to Underwood.

The inspector shook his head, grinning. "The unstoppable Mrs. Fletcher. Well, she's done all right by us. Mrs. Knox being British, I take it I can just send her a wire. Are we required to go through the Yard and the Sûreté for the Majestic Hotel?"

"In the ordinary way, I'd get in touch directly with one of the French officers I've dealt with before. But given my officially unofficial status, we'd better do it by the book. You'll want Superintendent Parry's permission, I imagine."

"I rang him while you were outside, to report the latest news. He's not available. We'll go ahead on my own authority and if he doesn't like it, he can lump it. Will you deal with the Yard?" He pushed the telephone across the desk.

Alec asked the operator for the superintendent on duty at New Scotland Yard. As a police call, it had priority, but even so ten minutes passed before she rang back and connected him.

To his relief, Superintendent Rossiter had the night watch. Rossiter was a friend of Crane and already knew about Alec's peculiar unofficial mission. In fact, he was easier to deal with than Crane would have been. He simply authorised the contact with a foreign force without asking any of the awkward questions about Daisy that Crane would surely have posed.

Ringing off, Alec said, "We've got the go-ahead. You'd like me to compose the telegram?"

"I would. You speak French, I take it."

"Speak, read, and write reasonably well, but I've never mastered French telegramese. You're right that it would be polite and politic to use French, if you think your county budget can hold up at tuppence ha'penny per superfluous word."

"Hang the budget."

"Very well, hang the county budget. Let me get straight exactly what you want to find out."

"Is Judith Gray there. If not, has she been there. If so, has she left a forwarding address, and what is it."

"Admirably succinct."

"Have I left anything out?"

"I'd say you've covered it. Let me get on with it."

Alec wrestled with turning the message into an abbreviated yet clear and comprehensible French version. He left off the accents, as he suspected an English telegraphist wouldn't be able to transmit them. The result looked unfinished; he was engaged in adding them—acute, grave, circumflex, and cedilla—when a constable came in with a note for him.

"The Boots from the Saracen brought it, sir."

"Mrs. Fletcher doing our job for us again?" Underwood asked as Alec unfolded it. His tone was not altogether pleased.

"No, it's anonymous." Tom, of course. "About Mrs. Gray's servants. Our informant met the gardener who used to work for the Grays, in a pub. In Seer Green?"

"Next stop up the line. Just a couple of miles."

"The pub is the Jolly Cricketers, according to Mr. Anon, our informant. The gardener's name's White. Half the patrons were talking about the murder, of course, so White spoke up. He said he wasn't surprised someone did for Mrs. Gray. She was quick to complain when something wasn't to her liking, but never gave a word of praise or thanks. Anon asked whether all the servants disliked her. It seems the housekeeper, Mrs. Clark, had already registered with a London agency before she was given notice."

"Mrs. Clark, eh? Doesn't sound too easy to trace."

"No, a lamentably common name. We might have to try, though. According to Anon, she told White there were 'goings-on' in the house she disapproved of, but she wouldn't name names."

"Does Anon mention the lady's maid?"

Alec consulted Tom's note. "There was a high turnover of lady's maids. The last was a Miss Lewis. High and mighty, didn't consort with gardeners. According to Mrs. Clark, though, she was furious when told she was to be turned off because Mrs. Gray wanted a French maid. She departed the next day without serving out her notice."

"Lewis," Underwood said gloomily. "Be a job tracing her, too, and nothing to be done till the servants' agencies open tomorrow. It's all very second and third hand," he added with dissatisfaction.

"Anonymous letters commonly are. This last bit is equally unverified. All the same, it could be more immediately useful. Anon says—"

A knock on the door. Not waiting for a response, Isabel Sutcliffe opened it, stopping on the threshold. "The officer at the desk said to go straight in. I hope I'm not interrupting."

The inspector smiled at her as he rose. "Not at all. You're very welcome." He hurried round the desk to hold a chair for her. Catching Alec's amused eye, he quickly added, "I expect you have information for us?"

"Daisy explained about the significance of the date Mrs. Hedger was last paid?"

"Yes," said Alec. "We ought to have thought of it ourselves."

Isabel absolved them. "It's only natural. It's usually women who pay the cleaner."

"I have no excuse," Underwood admitted. "As a widower, I'm the one who pays the charwoman."

Eyes brightening, she consoled him, "You've been busy. Well,

Willie came home soon after Daisy left. She remembered right away. Mrs. Hedger claimed the last day's work she was paid for was the seventeenth of September."

"Thank you, Miss Sutcliffe. That may prove extremely useful. And thank you for coming out so late to tell us."

"Does Miss Chandler usually work so late?" Alec asked.

"She's usually home by half past six. She finished the job she's been working on today and Mr. Davis asked her to stay on and go over the figures with him."

"What figures were those?"

"She was auditing some company's accounts, she wouldn't say whose. Frankly, neither Vera nor I was particularly interested."

Alec laughed. "And who can blame you. Would you like me to run you back to Cherry Trees in the car? If the inspector can spare me for ten minutes . . ."

"Of course." Underwood looked a bit wistful, as if he'd prefer to escort Isabel himself. Knowing nothing of his driving skills, Alec didn't offer to let him. "Good idea. Take fifteen and see if Miss Chandler will open up to you about the audit. Sergeant Piper isn't likely to ring for at least a couple of hours."

"Will do. You can send off this cable right away. And I suggest another to the Yard to get them moving on querying the domestic service agencies first thing in the morning. Put my name to it."

In the car, Isabel asked, "We're still suspects, aren't we?"

"Strictly speaking, yes. Don't let it worry you. None of you is under serious consideration."

"Because of Daisy?"

"Good heavens no! We're not allowed to take that sort of thing into account." A certain amount of bias was inevitable, however. Perhaps they ought to have subjected the three women to closer scrutiny? Perhaps they would have to, if they eliminated both Cartwright and Vaughn. Alec changed the subject. "Were the cleaners you found for the cellar satisfactory?"

"Excellent. It looks clean as a whistle and the smell is barely perceptible. I'm so sorry for them. They both fought in the war and haven't been able to find steady employment since. Their wives both work to make ends meet. The men feel inadequate, not being able to provide for their families. I'm going to have them back to build shelves in the cellar for storing apples, as soon as I've worked out just what I want."

"It sounds as if you're quite comfortable moving back in."

Isabel grinned. "None of us believes in ghosts! Vera isn't altogether happy about being in a house where someone was murdered, but I pointed out that we lived for a fortnight with the body actually present. Anyway, she has plenty to occupy her thoughts. I can't tell you how grateful we are for what Daisy's done for her."

"She has a penchant for combining helping people with interfering in police investigations," Alec said dryly, drawing up in front of Cherry Trees. "You don't mind if I come in for a minute?"

"Not at all."

Willie and Vera were drinking coffee in the sitting room. Despite Alec's refusal, Isabel bustled off to fetch cups for him and herself.

"Miss Chandler—Willie—" It was difficult to decide how he ought to address the ladies. "I'd like you to confirm the date Miss Sutcliffe passed on to us, the last day's work Mrs. Hedger was paid for."

"Or so she claimed. It was the seventeenth. Of last month, of course."

"You're certain?"

"Absolutely. I never forget a number."

"And will you confirm that today you completed an audit of the accounts of Langridge's, the estate agent?"

"Who told you? Neither I nor Isabel!"

"Just putting together hints from your boss—"

"Mr. Davis talked about it?"

"Indirectly. Isabel said you'd finished a big job today, so I assumed . . . What I really need to know is when you or Mr. Davis intend to give Langridge the results of the audit."

Willie considered, her blond head tilted, eyes narrowed. "I suppose there's no harm, since you already know so much. Mr. Davis is going to ask Mr. Langridge to call at our offices tomorrow morning, whenever convenient to him." Unexpectedly, she giggled. "If you ask me, it would be much easier for him to go to Langridge's. When Mr. Langridge came in to request the audit, it was touch and go whether he'd make it up the stairs to Mr. Davis's room."

"I take it Mr. Langridge had his suspicions that something was amiss?"

"Sole proprietorships—one owner and one or more employees—rarely call for an audit until they're fairly sure something's wrong. They'd do better to get an outside audit regularly, like big companies."

"Did you know what or whom Langridge suspected?"

"No. Mr. Langridge has four employees. He probably didn't tell Mr. Davis if he suspected one person in particular. It could bias the audit. I discovered pretty quickly whom he ought to have suspected. I won't confirm your guess, though."

"Very proper," said Alec, grinning.

Isabel came in with the coffee. As they were drinking from demitasses, Alec relented and accepted. He emptied the tiny cup rather quicker than was strictly polite, made his adieux, and went out to the car. On the way back to the police station, he reflected that he was indubitably biased in their favour. He could only hope it wouldn't come to arresting one or more of them. Given his ambiguous position in the case, though, he'd be able to leave that dismaying task to DI Underwood.

Who wouldn't be any happier about it than Alec.

Happily, another suspect had moved up the list. Alec had been interrupted before telling Underwood about the interesting second item in Tom Tring's note.

THIRTY

"*Miss Chandler* confirmed the seventeenth," Alec announced.

"Seventeenth?" said Underwood, taking out a pocket diary. "A Monday. Mrs. Hedger went in three days a week—Monday, Wednesday, Friday, as she does now, I expect. If she was paid on the Monday, likely she was usually paid each day that she worked, rather than weekly. She wasn't paid on Wednesday. So the victim died Monday night or sometime Tuesday."

"Not that it helps us much."

"No, people don't remember what they were doing on a particular day a month ago, unless they had an appointment or an engagement, something worth noting down. What about Miss Chandler's audit?"

"Davis, her boss, is seeing Langridge tomorrow to give him the results. Miss Chandler naturally refused to confirm the name of the embezzler. I'm reluctant to tackle Vaughn about it, to-night. We might queer their pitch."

"Yes, better avoid the subject. It doesn't seem to have any bearing on our business, anyway."

"Agreed. If we do need the actual figures gone over at some

point, it's a job for Piper." Alec retrieved Tom's note from his inside breast pocket. "You didn't hear the last part of this. It should be more immediately useful than the rest."

"Vaughn?"

"Mrs. Vaughn, according to report. She had a flaming row with Mrs. Gray, at Cherry Trees."

"From the housekeeper via the gardener?"

"From the housekeeper originally, I expect, but rather more roundabout." Tom had been cautious in his note, in case it fell into the wrong hands, but Alec knew him well enough to guess he was hinting that the story had been overheard in a tea shop by Mrs. Tring.

"Fourth or fifth hand," Underwood said gloomily. "Everyone in Beaconsfield is talking about the murder, exaggerating and adding to any little scrap they can possibly claim to know about the Grays. Though with the gardener's name and him being local, we shouldn't have any trouble finding him tomorrow. I'll send a man to Seer Green. When did this row happen?"

"Unknown. We might do worse than making that our first question. Something on the lines of: 'On what date did your quarrel with Mrs. Gray take place?'"

"Leading the witness."

"We won't have a judge watching us."

They continued to discuss tactics, and then every conceivable permutation of the scanty evidence and the theoretical possibilities, with Pennicuik venturing a few words now and then. In spite of yet more coffee, by the time Ernie Piper's call came through at last, at a quarter to midnight, all three were somnolent.

Alec, more accustomed than the local men to working through the night, was first to reach for the ringing phone.

"Fletcher."

"It's me, Chief. The car just turned into the drive."

"Don't let the bloody woman go to bed."

"I'll see what I can do." Ernie sounded remarkably cheery. The Vaughns' servants must have been good hosts.

"We're on our way."

260

Twenty minutes later, the Austin Twelve swung into the drive and stopped just short of the garage doors, next to the new wing behind the house. Light showed dimly through the heavy curtains of its ground-floor windows.

A curtain twitched. A man's face looked out, the electric light making a halo of the corn-gold hair Alec recalled from their encounter in the bar of the Saracen's Head. Donald Vaughn.

They walked back to the front door. It was already open and Ernie welcomed them with relief.

"I don't know how much longer I could have kept her downstairs."

"Twitchy, is she?" Underwood asked.

"That's not quite the word I had in mind," Ernie said primly. "Close, but not quite. No, he's the one that's twitching."

He led the way along a narrow corridor, past a couple of closed doors and one standing open to the dark, silent kitchen. Stairs rose on their left. They came to a last door, probably once the back door of the old house, beyond which was the light, warmth, comfort, and colour of a modern sitting room. Alec noted radiators as well as a good fire. Decidedly there was money, whether or not its distribution was as they had been told.

Ernie ushered them in and announced them butler fashion: "Detective Chief Inspector Fletcher. Detective Inspector Underwood."

Goggling at Alec, Vaughn started up from the depths of an easy chair, spilling the drink in his hand on his dress trousers. "You!" he yelped. "You're a policeman?"

"I am. I've got a few questions I'd like to put to you. Is there somewhere we can go?"

"Stay here," commanded Mrs. Vaughn. She was a formidable figure of a woman, large, well-corseted in her plum-coloured velvet evening frock, well-coiffed and discreetly made-up, and wearing what appeared to be good jewellery. A few years older than her husband, Alec guessed. "Donald has nothing to say that cannot be said in my presence." Her voice had no trace of the local accent.

"The front room," Vaughn gabbled. "It'll be better, Myra. We won't disturb you. This way, Mr. . . . Inspector." He scurried towards the four policemen, who parted to let him through the door.

Alec followed, with Pennicuik bringing up the rear, as arranged earlier. Ernie Piper stayed with Underwood and Mrs. Vaughn. Alec hoped they could cope with her.

The "front room" had probably been the sitting room of the old house. Now it was furnished as an office, rather feminine in style, with an inlaid escritoire, a couple of dusky-rose plush armchairs, and some near-Hepplewhite side chairs, including one at the desk. Alec glanced into the glass-fronted bookcase and saw fashionable novels where one might expect calfskin-bound editions of venerable classics—Michael Arlen, Charles Morgan, Woolf, Waugh, and Rosamond Lehmann's *succès de scandale*, *Dusty Answer*.

Alec sat down on the desk chair. It wasn't quite the position of power offered by a seat behind a good solid kneehole desk, but it would do. Vaughn looked round vaguely before sinking into an armchair. He remembered the drink still in his hand, what was left of it, and emptied the glass at one gulp. Pennicuik took his stance by the door, slightly to Vaughn's rear.

With a gesture at the bookcase, Alec asked, "Yours?"

"No, I'm not a reader. Besides, I don't have time. I often have to work in the evenings, and when I'm free, as often as not she drags me up to town to rotten highbrow plays, or concerts. And she doesn't like me going to the pub." Once begun, his grievances poured out. "She has pots of money, but she's so stingy I have to work if I want any sort of life. I'm a good salesman. I'd do much better as a commercial traveller, but no, she wants me right here under her bloody thumb. I tell you, I'm sick of it!"

If the victim were Myra Vaughn, the chief suspect would not be far to seek. A motive for killing Judith Gray was less clear-cut.

"You hate your wife, so you had an affair with Mrs. Gray."

"I don't *hate* her. I just want to get away from her. Judith was beautiful, gay, fun to be with, and she'd been in the same posi-tion as me, with a penny-pinching husband. We were in love."

"You use the past tense, Mr. Vaughn."

"She's dead." He sounded defeated. Then the implication of Alec's words sank in. His eyes blazed with hope. "Isn't she?"

"Almost certainly. But not quite. We should know by tomor-row."

"She might be alive? Somewhere in France? How can I find her?" His shoulders slumped. "No, she wouldn't have gone without me."

He was very convincing. Could he be acting? Not inconceiv-able. All salesmen were essentially actors, putting on a persuasive show of enthusiasm for whatever they were touting.

"You intended to go to France with her?"

"She was going to buy a house. We were going to live to-gether as man and wife. She was a modern woman. She didn't care about outdated conventions, and she didn't want ever to marry again. If Myra wanted a divorce, I wouldn't contest it. What am I going to do?"

Spend a good long stretch in clink for fraud, Alec suspected. "She was more willing to support you in idleness than Mrs. Vaughn is?"

"I wasn't going empty-handed." Injured innocence played less well than the previous changeable emotions. "I've managed to save a bit."

Alec didn't ask about the provenance of the "savings." No hurry: This was a preliminary interview, and there would be more, whether Vaughn was still at liberty or not. They still had no firm evidence implicating him in the homicide.

"Either Mrs. Gray deserted you, or she's dead. Did your wife know about the affair?"

"No, of course not."

"According to information received—"

"Well, she might have. All right, she did. I don't know how the deuce she found out. We were bloody careful not to be seen together, and you wouldn't think gossip would travel this far, anyway. Myra knows people in High Wycombe, not Beaconsfield, but she heard somehow. She drove over to Cherry Trees and had an almighty row with Judith."

"You were present?"

"Good lord no! It wasn't that easy to get over there, actually. We don't do a lot of business in Beaconsfield. Judith goes—went—to London almost every weekend, unless prospective buyers had an appointment to view her house. Of course, if Myra hadn't made plans for an evening, I could always say I had to show a house and dash over for a couple of hours. The evening bus service is rotten but not impossible. Sometimes I could even talk Myra into letting me use the car to get to a country property." He snickered, amused at having used his wife's car to deceive her.

"The presence of the Jowett was noted."

"Nosy neighbours? I can't imagine why they should care. Judith certainly doesn't—didn't—care for them." Suddenly, embarrassingly, he broke down in sobs, his face hidden in his hands. "Oh, God, leave me alone, can't you?"

"Just one more question. What was Mrs. Gray's reaction to your wife's incursion?"

"She was bloody furious! What do you think? After that she wouldn't . . . do anything. She said it would have to wait till we reached France. She didn't abandon me. Oh, God, she's dead!"

Alec slipped out of the room, on the way signalling to Pennicuik to stay. The behaviour of someone in that sort of semi-hysterical state could not be predicted.

The old exterior door between the house and the new wing was too solid to let him hear what was going on beyond. He pictured the position of the chair Mrs. Vaughn had been sitting in when he left. It was turned slightly away from the door. He was less certain whether the hinges had creaked when the door closed behind him. He had been concentrating on Vaughn, ahead of him.

Standing there wasn't getting him anywhere. Cautiously he turned the handle and pulled the door towards him till there was a gap of a couple of inches. Now he heard Mrs. Gray's indignant voice.

". . . May have remonstrated with the woman. We did not have a vulgar row. If one speaks firmly and does not back down, people realise one means what one says. I forced her—by force of character—to acknowledge that she ought not to have led a married man astray. I exacted a promise that relations between them would cease. Except on a business level, naturally. I wouldn't want to deprive poor Donald of his little job."

"And did 'relations' cease?" Underwood asked. Alec guessed from his slightly raised voice that he was aware of the listener at the door.

"Yes. Whenever he went out on business in the evening, I watched her house. He never came."

"You never spoke to her again?"

"Certainly not."

"And what did your husband think of your interference?"

"I never spoke to him about it. I saw no need. The matter was settled."

"When did you settle it? On what date did you call on Mrs. Gray?"

"I don't recall the date. It's not the sort of appointment one puts in one's diary."

"Roughly."

"Really, Officer, I've told you I don't recall. I will not be badgered!"

Alec decided his time had come. He went in. Neither Underwood nor Ernie Piper was taken by surprise. Myra Vaughn reacted with outrage. She rose to her feet with a majestic surge and declaimed, "Three of you! You may bully me, but you can't—"

"Madam, I have no intention of bullying anyone. Inspector, may I have a quick word with you?"

They stepped into the old house and shut the door. "You heard the fairy-tale version of the quarrel?" said Underwood. "That's the first she's said to the purpose. We had a diatribe about how her family lived in the manor forever and always been respected and respectable, with a family tree back to her great-great-grandfather, and the respected professions of every respectable male. If any were less than respectable she didn't mention them. I couldn't shut her up! I hope you had better luck?"

"Vaughn was dying to talk. About Judith Gray, not his putative peculations. I'm steering clear of that subject for the present, as we agreed."

"Don't want to throw a spanner in the works of the fraud people."

"I'll tell you the rest later. Just one point you ought to know right away: He saw her after her quarrel with his wife, so she was still alive at that point. You may want to concentrate on whether there was a second encounter."

"Right. Are you done with him?"

"He's had an apparent emotional breakdown. If he's pulled himself together, I'll keep going. If not, there's always tomorrow. I doubt he'll be arrested on the other charge before late afternoon." Langridge had to talk to Davis, then they had to prove their case to the fraud division of the Bucks police, if such existed, or their outside experts. Doubtless Davis's partner, Mrs. Vaughn's brother, would also have to be consulted, or at least warned.

Alec returned to Vaughn. He had dried his eyes—now red, whether from weeping or rubbing—and looked defiant.

"I don't believe she's dead! Something has prevented her writing to me. Perhaps she lost the accommodation address I gave her in all the upheaval of packing and travelling, don't you think?" he appealed to Alec. "Or her letter could have been lost in the post."

"Quite possible."

"She might have written to Cherry Trees 'to be called for,' and those women who bought her house threw it away. If she addressed it to the office—everything is so disorganised it could be anywhere. She knows better than to send it here. . . ."

His almost feverish cataloguing of the ways Judith Gray's letter might have gone astray was damnably persuasive.

Alec suppressed a yawn. He was too tired to judge. "Did Mrs. Vaughn call on Mrs. Gray a second time?"

"No. Judith would have told me."

If she had survived the encounter. "When did you last see Mrs. Gray? The date, or even just the day of the week could help us trace her."

"Saturday. It was a Saturday morning. She was about to leave for London. I told you she spent most weekends in town. She usually went up on a Friday and came back Monday or Tuesday but she said she was going to return on Sunday because she had so much to do."

"Had she much luggage with her?"

"Just an overnight bag. She kept some clothes at her friend's flat. Mrs. Knox, not a man, in case you were wondering. I offered to carry the bag to the station for her, but she still didn't want us to be seen together, even though we were very soon going away together. I'll find her somehow. Mrs. Knox—Elizabeth—will know where she is."

"You have Mrs. Knox's address?"

"No. Do you?" Vaughn asked eagerly.

"Sorry, it's my business to ask questions, not answer them." In any case, Mrs. Knox wasn't at her London address.

"It's in Belgravia. I know that much. And her husband's name is Freddie—Frederick. I'll get hold of a directory. How many Frederick Knoxes can there be in Belgravia?" It was a rhetorical question.

Alec said sharply, "You're not to leave the area without providing an address to the police." He decided to call it a day. "One more question for now: Do you or did you ever have in your possession a key to the cellar?"

"Never. I *never* had any keys. She wouldn't let me show the house when she wasn't at home."

"Very well. We'll want to talk to you again tomorrow, and have you sign a statement. What time would suit you to come into the police station, in either Beaconsfield or High Wycombe?"

"Beaconsfield! If Mr. Langridge heard I'd been seen going into the police station in Wycombe . . . I'm showing a house in Penn tomorrow so I'll have the car in the morning. Noon. I'll be there at noon. Not that I have anything else to tell you. But you said you'll know by tomorrow if . . . if Judith is still alive?"

"I said we *ought* to know. Good night, Mr. Vaughn."

Underwood was also ready to leave. Alec let Ernie Piper take the wheel to drive the inspector and Pennicuik to their homes in High Wycombe. On the way, they discussed the interviews. Underwood hadn't learned anything more from Mrs. Vaughn than what Alec had overheard.

"If you ask me, she didn't do it," Underwood said ironically. "Murder isn't respectable."

"By accident?"

"Getting into a pushing-shoving match isn't respectable, either."

"Neither is a shouting match," Ernie pointed out.

"Which she doesn't admit to," said Underwood. "I don't think she's exactly lying. It's more a matter of editing the facts in her own mind and persuading herself her own behaviour was irreproachably . . . well, respectable."

"Editing out raised voices is one thing," Alec said. "Convincing herself she didn't kill Judith Gray—if she did—would be a bit of a stretch. Her husband, on the other hand, is either a plausible liar or genuinely grief-stricken, or both."

"You've known more murderers than I have, I imagine. Don't they sometimes bitterly regret the deed and mourn for the victim?"

"Yes indeed, and that could be the explanation. But I confess I can't make him out."

"We'll have another go at them tomorrow." Underwood sighed. "I suppose it's about time I tried my wiles on Mrs. Hedger. Tomorrow's Wednesday. She'll be at Cherry Trees and maybe less impregnable than on her own ground."

"Good luck."

"Sergeant, once we find the gardener's whereabouts, you can go and talk to him, if that's all right, Mr. Fletcher? We can't wait till we turn up the housekeeper and the maid."

"Though they're the ones most likely to provide us with new names," said Alec. "The Vaughns and the Cartwrights are all very well, but there must be dozens of people who knew Judith Gray of whom we have no inkling."

THIRTY-ONE

Daisy was already awake when Sally tapped on the door and came in with the early morning tea tray. Alec was sound asleep at her side. She hadn't roused when he came in last night.

She was inclined to let him sleep, but Sally said, "Mr. Piper left a message at the desk, Mrs. Fletcher, to wake him and Mr. Fletcher at half past seven."

"I'll take care of Alec, Sally. You can deal with Ernie."

"I already did." She grinned. "He groaned a bit, but he thanked me ever so politely." She went out.

Daisy sat up, leaned over, and kissed Alec. He didn't stir. She shook his shoulder. He grunted, rolled over, and put his arms about her waist.

"Darling, it's time to wake up."

"Noooo."

"According to Ernie, via Sally."

"I only just got to bed." Alec sat up.

She poured and passed him his cup of tea. "Did you find out anything worth staying up late for?"

"Not really. The Vaughns and the Cartwrights are still in

the picture. Besides them, the note Tom gave you is our best lead, though it could take a few days to lead anywhere."

"How much longer will the super let you stay on the case?"

He shrugged. "Anyone's guess. Until he needs me for something more important. I still think you should go home after the inquest."

"Perhaps." Daisy sighed. "I'll go and see Isabel this morning."

"Not too early. Underwood's going to have a chat—try to have a chat, I should say—with Mrs. Hedger at about half past nine."

"I'll aim for half past ten. What are you doing this morning?"

"It depends on what information comes in from various feelers."

"The Hotel Majestic? And the woman in St. Tropez?"

"Among others." Dressing-gowned and sponge bag in hand, he went off to take a bath.

The sun shone in through the east-facing window. Daisy decided to go for a walk in the country after breakfast. In the latter days of October, fine days were not to be wasted.

Alec and Ernie were long gone when she went down. Only two couples remained in the dining room, so Sally was at leisure to chat. She brought Daisy's scrambled eggs and toast, then stood leaning on the back of the other chair at the table.

"Mr. Piper wouldn't tell me: Do they know yet who did it?"

"No." Daisy was sure of that after what Alec had said. "They're having a difficult time finding out about Mrs. Gray's friends and acquaintances, because she didn't really have any in Beaconsfield. I'm sorry to speak ill of a relative of yours, but your aunt isn't at all helpful."

"I doubt she knows much. She's always been one to mind her own business. Whenever I gave her a hand at Cherry Trees, she'd keep telling me not to poke my nose in where I shouldn't. As if I would! But I'd notice and remember visitors if I'd seen any.

There wasn't none came while I was there," Sally said regretfully. "I wish I could help Mr. Piper. And Mr. Fletcher, of course."

She departed to answer a call for fresh coffee.

Daisy took a pleasant walk through fields and woods. The predominant beeches still enhanced the golden sunlight, though many leaves had fallen to crackle underfoot. Silvery old man's beard and the yellow and red berries of bryony wreathed the field hedges, with here and there a spindle tree flaunting its pink and orange fruit.

Rabbits popped out of their burrows to watch Daisy's approach and disappeared underground as she came closer. Squirrels chittered at her from the safety of high branches. She wished she had Nana with her to have fun chasing them.

She remembered advising Isabel to get a watchdog. It still seemed a good idea. Now the three of them were back at home, they should start looking for a puppy.

On her return to the fringes of the town, Daisy passed a garden where someone was attempting to burn a pile of damp leaves and rubbish. Clouds of smoke billowed across the road and grabbed her by the throat. She tried not to inhale as she hurried past, but she started to cough, bringing on the nightmarish choking sensation that had made her bout of bronchitis so beastly.

She emerged from the haze gasping. A few yards ahead was a bus stop with a bench. She sat down, and after a few minutes recovered her breath and her equanimity. The doctor had warned that her lungs would be abnormally sensitive to irritants for a while, though with care they should recover completely.

Her chest still ached a bit, but slowly she walked on. By the time she reached Cherry Trees, she felt much better.

Isabel, naturally, was hoping for news of the investigation.

"Sorry," said Daisy. "Alec was out very late last night but he didn't tell me anything this morning. Not much at least. Just that they were expecting to hear from the Majestic and Mrs. Gray's friend in St. Tropez."

"Mr. Underwood told me they'd already had a telegram from the Sûreté."

"Police and hoteliers never sleep. What did it say?"

"The hotel has the trunks in storage and wants to know what to do with them, since madame didn't take up her reservation."

"Did Mr. Underwood get anything out of Mrs. Hedger?"

"No more than you and I did. What's more, she marched out in a huff, saying she wouldn't come back till I could promise she wouldn't be pestered while she was trying to do her job."

"Oh dear!"

"Mr. Underwood said he wasn't going to try that again. They'll let her cool off and then, if they still need her, take her over to the station. They have a lead to the Grays' gardener, and they found out the names of the maid and housekeeper, so they're looking for them. When they find them, they may not have to bother with Mrs. Hedger. She's more trouble than she's worth."

"He told you much more than Alec told me!"

Isabel smiled. "He stayed for a cup of coffee." While she and Daisy talked, she had made a fresh pot of coffee and moved a few gingersnaps from a cooling rack onto a plate, and they had adjourned from kitchen to sitting room. "I'm not sure Mrs. Hedger isn't more trouble to me than she's worth, too. I'm really fed up with her. Have another biscuit."

"Thanks. They're delicious. You must have been up early baking."

"No earlier than usual. They're very quick to make."

"You must be busy, though. I don't want to keep you from what you were going to do." Daisy started to get up.

"No, wait." Isabel glanced at the window. "I was going to work in the garden, but judging by the gloom, it's going to start pouring any minute. I thought the sunshine wouldn't last. I wonder if you'd mind lending a hand. . . ."

"Anything I can do to help."

"Just keeping me company for half an hour, really. The thing is, I want to work out what needs doing in the cellar to make it suitable for storing apples. Jams and bottled fruit, too, and root vegetables. And— Well, to tell the truth, I don't want to be down there alone."

"I don't blame you!"

"When I went down to inspect the cleaning, the workmen were with me, you see. Not that I believe in ghosts, but I'd just rather not . . ."

"Of course I'll come. You're bound to need someone to hold one end of a tape measure or something."

"I'll borrow Vera's tape measure. Dressmaking is not one of my domestic skills." Isabel went over to a Victorian sewing table.

"I'll get my notebook from my coat pocket."

Isabel dropped off the coffee tray in the kitchen on the way. The door to the cellar stood ajar, as she had been airing it since it was cleaned. She stepped on to the landing and reached to her right to click on the electric light.

"The men nailed a lath across the broken rail, but I don't know how strong it is. Be careful."

"I won't touch it." Daisy sniffed as she stepped through the door. All she could smell was ginger biscuits. "I'm glad I didn't actually see the body."

"So am I! I don't think I'd ever have been able to use the cellar if I had. It will smell wonderful when it's full of apples."

Leaving the door wide open, they cautiously descended the steep, narrow stairs. The handrail bolted to the wall seemed sound enough. Daisy tried to avoid looking at the shallow, rectangular excavation where the body had lain.

Apart from a few ordinary shelves in one corner, the wine racks were obviously unsuitable for the kind of storage Isabel needed. "You'll be able to reuse the side pieces, won't you?"

"I should think so."

"Heavens, if these racks were all filled with bottles, he could have tippled day and night for years." Hearing a heavy thud in the house above, Daisy glanced up at the doorway. "What was that?"

"I don't know," Isabel said with a frown. "I can't think of anything left in a position where it might fall. Unless Vera stacked her books in a tall, untidy pile—but I doubt we'd hear that down here, all the way from her bedroom. It sounded like the front door slamming."

"I'm sure you shut it. Did you lock it?"

"No. I really must get in the habit of—"

"Hello? Where are you?" A male voice, on the edge of hysteria. It was vaguely familiar to Daisy.

"Oh blast!" Isabel exclaimed. "It's Vaughn. I suppose he's—"

"I know you're at home. Where are you?"

"Should I tell him about the Majestic?"

"If it'll get rid of him," Daisy advised.

Isabel moved towards the staircase, but before she reached it Vaughn appeared at the top. Dressed in an overcoat of a rather too vivid blue, he hadn't doffed his hat on entering the house so unceremoniously. In one hand he held the strap of a leather satchel, in the other a dripping umbrella. His face was very pale.

"You know where Judith went," he shouted at Isabel. "The copper wouldn't tell me, but it was obvious he knew and only you could have told him."

"I found out since last time you asked me," Isabel said soothingly. "The police are pretty certain she's dead, but she seems to have made plans to stay at the Hotel Majestic in Paris."

"The Majestic? I'll find it. But I can't have you setting the coppers on my trail. I'm going to lock you in."

"You said you never had the keys!" Isabel took a couple of swift strides towards the stairs.

"Keep back!" Vaughn wielded his steel-ferruled umbrella like a spear. "One jab and you'd go flying." Without turning his head, he chucked the satchel behind him in the passage. Taking a jangling bunch of keys from his coat pocket, he stepped backward, pulling the door shut.

As it thumped into its frame, Isabel bounded up the steps. Daisy heard the click of the lock. Isabel turned the handle and tugged, but she was too late.

"Blast!" said Daisy.

Isabel sat down on the top step and looked at her watch. "Half past eleven. Five hours till Vera comes home. But Alec will miss you."

"Not if he's busy. Vera won't be able to let us out without a key, unless Vaughn's left it in the lock. But she won't know we're stuck here and she has no reason to try the door."

"She'll go to the kitchen for a cuppa. We'll shout through the keyhole."

"There's those little flap things. And he *may* have left the key in the hole."

"The first thing is to find out. I brought a pocket torch to get a good look at how the shelves are put together. That'll help." Isabel ascended the stairs. Daisy, standing at the foot, watched her kneel down on the landing and fiddle with the flap. "It's not very strong. I may be able to lever it off."

"I have a nail file in my pocket. Would that help?"

"Yes."

Daisy trod carefully up the steps, one hand on the wall rail. "Here you are. I'll hold the torch, shall I?"

The ceiling light was centrally placed so as to illuminate the racks, and the landing was murky. Daisy trained the torch beam on the keyhole. Isabel easily prised off the little oval piece of brass. She put it in her pocket and stuck the nail file into the hole.

"It goes in quite a way. I don't think he left the key."

"In any case, the door fits too tight for us to slide a paper under it and catch the key as it falls, the way they do in thrillers."

"Let me have the torch a minute." Isabel tried to shine the light into the keyhole while peering past it and her hand. "I can't see very well but I'm pretty sure it's not there."

"See if you can twist the flap to the side."

Isabel handed the torch back, stuck the nail file in again, and wiggled it. "That's not getting anywhere. I'll try to push it hard enough to bend it. No, I can't get a good enough grip on the file."

"I have a propelling pencil. That might work. Just a mo."

Daisy went down to where she had left her notebook. Alec had given her a leather notebook case, with a loop inside to hold a writing implement and a gold propelling pencil to fit in the loop. "Here, use this."

"It'd get scratched."

"I'd rather have a little bit of fresh air than a pristine pencil!" Daisy's suffocating nightmare hovered on the edge of her consciousness. Feeling less casual than she hoped she sounded, she asked, "How long do you think the air in a room this size would last two people?"

"Ages, I'm sure." Isabel poked the pencil into the keyhole and jabbed. "A hammer . . . I know, my shoe." With the heel of her shoe she bashed the end of the pencil. The heel hit the keyhole plate with a thump. She lowered the shoe and peered into the hole again. "Oh dear, your pencil went all the way through. The flap is bent right out of the way."

"Good! Not only can we breathe through the hole if the air in here gets bad, but Vera is bound to see the pencil. I wonder if a rolled-up note could be pushed through. Oh, botheration, now I haven't got anything to write with."

"Just several pieces of paper would draw attention, even if it's all blank."

"True." Inspiration struck. "I know, we can write SOS in Morse code by making holes with the nail file."

They found by experiment that a half sheet of paper from Daisy's notebook could easily be folded small enough to fit through the keyhole. So they sat on the steps "writing" SOS messages, Daisy with the nail file, Isabel with one of Vera's kirby grips that she found in her pocket, having picked it up off the floor or some piece of furniture.

A dozen bits of paper would more than suffice, they decided. Isabel pushed them through. Then she sat back on her heels and contemplated the hair grip.

"I'm going to have a go at picking the lock with this. Alec made it look so easy. A little hook at the end, I think."

Straightening the grip was easy; making a hook at the end

not much harder. But the narrow strip of metal was even more difficult to grasp firmly than the nail file. Isabel poked and prodded, until it snapped at the point where she had straightened it.

"It was worth a try," said Daisy. "Unless you have any more tricks up your sleeve, we might as well get on with your measuring."

"Except we can't write down the measurements."

"What a bore." She sighed, then wondered if sighing used up more oxygen than just breathing. Her chest felt tight. It must be her imagination. They couldn't possibly be running short of air yet.

She could smell the carbolic now, and beneath it a faint, barely perceptible sickly sweetness. Her throat closed against it. She coughed, gasped, struggled to inhale.

"Daisy, what's the matter? What's wrong?"

With an effort, Daisy pulled herself together and forced herself to relax. "It's . . . nothing," she wheezed. "Sorry. Just an . . . aftereffect of being ill. I breathed some nasty smoke from a rubbish fire on the way here . . . but now it's all in my imagination. The disinfectant . . ."

Isabel sniffed. "I can't smell it. I suppose I'm used to it. If Mrs. Hedger ever comes back, I really must persuade her to stop using so much. Are you going to be all right?"

"Yes, quite all right. Let's talk about something else. What do you make of Vaughn's behaviour?"

"Isn't it obvious? He killed Mrs. Gray and he knows Mr. Underwood and Alec are hot on his trail, so he's making his escape."

"I've spent too much time with detectives to believe anything is obvious. If he killed her, why persist in trying to find out where she intended to go? Before, it could have been an act to disarm suspicion, but that doesn't explain why he came here just before bolting. He'd have done better simply to leave with all possible haste."

"I suppose so."

"And then there's Willie's side of it. Clearly he's been involved in something nefarious at work."

"Cooking the books, expected to boil over today."

"I'd guess that's why he's hopping it. Coming here delayed his departure. Unless he believes, or at least hopes, she's still alive, it makes no sense."

"None of it makes sense," Isabel said crossly. "I hope the police have a better idea of what's going on. I wish they didn't have such a mania for secrecy!"

"Let's check the shelves for a nail we can extract, and I'll have a go at picking the lock. I really don't want to spend five hours in here, plus however long it would take Vera to get help." Daisy glanced around. The room seemed to have shrunk. "And even if breathing through the keyhole helps, we can't be sure we won't run out of air."

THIRTY-TWO

"*Half past* twelve," the inspector fumed. "Vaughn's not coming."

"He may have been held up," said Alec. "Or locked up, though I doubt it. Your county fraud people would have to go over all the figures first, and in my experience the fraud chappies are not usually so quick off the mark."

"I'd better find out. I'll ring my super."

"If it were my super, I'd make sure of my ground and talk to the accountants first. None of those concerned has confirmed directly that Vaughn was under suspicion. Even assuming our conjectures are correct, Langridge and Davis may not even have laid a charge yet. You know your own superintendent best, of course . . ."

Underwood grinned. "From what you've said, Mr. Crane is much more ferocious than Parry."

"Crane's bark is worse than his bite."

"You're right, though. I'll get on to the accountants." He put through the call. "Not in the office? . . . No, I don't want to talk to Mr. Spencer. Is Miss Chandler available? . . . Thank you . . . Good morning, Miss Chandler . . . Yes, DI Underwood." Mindful of the capacity of country operators for listening in, the inspector avoided naming names. "I hope you're now free to confirm that the accounts you were auditing concerned the business and the specific person we were enquiring about . . ." He listened.

Alec could hear Willie's voice, but not what she was saying. She spoke at some length before Underwood asked a couple of clarifying questions, thanked her, and hung up, frowning.

"Well? Don't tell me we've been barking up the wrong tree?"

"Not at all. We've been spot on. I didn't quite grasp the details of how Vaughn did it, but he's been helping himself, all right. Davis and Langridge went off half an hour ago to present the evidence to the accountant who deals with such matters for the county force. Apparently, Langridge hadn't decided whether to prosecute or to try to recover the monies without undesirable publicity."

"Is Vaughn aware that he's in trouble?"

"She didn't say so. From what she did say, Langridge had no time to go back to his office and confront Vaughn."

"He could hardly have expected to get away with it forever. If he's chosen this particular moment to take to his heels, why?" Alec could see more than one answer, but it was officially Underwood's case and he ought to have a chance to do his share of speculating.

"The secretary must have known Langridge was going to see the accountants. Suppose Vaughn went to the office after his appointment this morning, asked to see the boss, and she told him. On top of the pressure we've applied over the murder . . . It's enough to make anyone take to his heels, let alone a hysteric like Vaughn."

"Unless the hysteria is all an act. It's one of the easier emotions to fake. The trouble is, he hasn't been charged on the misappropriation, and we haven't the evidence to charge him with manslaughter, far less murder."

"So, at present, we aren't justified in asking other forces to detain him on any grounds other than wanted for questioning.

Damnation. He could go to ground before we— No! I'll bet you a fiver he's heading for France!"

"No takers. If he killed her, he'll want to keep up the pretence of looking for her for as long as possible, trying to bamboozle us. If he didn't, if he honestly still hopes to find her alive—"

"Then he'll go on trying till the last possible moment to find out where she is," Underwood said grimly, jumping to his feet, "and he's been pestering Isabel—Miss Sutcliffe about it. I'm going to Cherry Trees."

He grabbed his hat from the stand and jammed it onto his head. His overcoat half on, he charged through the door. Alec, amused at his would-be knight errantry, retrieved his hat and coat and followed at a more sedate pace. After all, he had no reason to suppose Daisy was in peril from the abominable Vaughn. He stopped to leave a message for Ernie and Pennicuik, who had gone to see the gardener.

Then Alec recalled that Daisy had been going to call on Isabel. He speeded his pace.

Through the wet streets they dashed in the Austin Twelve. Alec pulled up in front of Cherry Trees, Underwood jumping out before the car came to a halt. No sign of Vaughn's black Jowett, Alec noted.

The front gate hung open. The inspector hurried up the path. When Alec caught up with him, he was banging on the door with one hand and holding down the doorbell button with the other. He stopped. They listened. Not a sound from within.

"She's upstairs at the back," Alec proposed, "or gone to the shops."

"Not in this downpour."

"If she set out before— Never mind. Try again, and I'll go round the house snooping in the windows."

No one in the sitting room, nothing out of place. Likewise the den and the dining room at the back. With the solidly built house between them, he couldn't hear Underwood's banging. The next window was the half-glazed side door. When he looked through, he blocked much of the grey daylight, so that the passage within was in obscurity. It wasn't so dark he could have failed to see a person, however. He was about to move away when something on the floor a few feet inside the door caught his eye.

He stood to one side and craned his neck. The "something" was a small heap of rubbish. Presumably Mrs. Hedger had left it there when she stormed out on being accosted by Underwood. But Isabel, an orderly person, would never have left it lying. She was the sort who would have cleared it away the moment she noticed it.

Alec peered. Paper, splinters of wood—was that a glint of gold? He tried the door. Locked, but he could break the glass and open it.

He hesitated. This was Underwood's case and Underwood's manor. He should be consulted. Alec went on, glancing in at the kitchen windows as he passed. The small size of the windows obstructed his view, but unless someone was under the table, the room was empty.

He caught the inspector trying the front door. "It's not locked. Should we go in?"

"Yes. But hold your horses a moment." He told what he'd seen. "It may be just rubbish, but it's right beside the cellar door."

"Vaughn pushed Isabel down the stairs!" Underwood gasped, horrified, swinging back to the front door.

"Great Scott, no! That wouldn't explain the stuff. I think he does have keys. It would be natural to deny it with a body found in the locked cellar, whether he killed her or not. My guess is that he's somehow managed to lock Isabel in the cellar and she's pushed everything she could find through the keyhole to attract Miss Leighton's attention when she comes home."

"Ingenious! She's a resourceful woman. Let's go and release her."

"Have you a skeleton key on you?" Alec asked as he followed Underwood into the entrance hall.

"No. They're . . . frowned upon. We're supposed to get a warrant and a locksmith. I rather glossed over your lock-picking in my report. 'Gained access,' method unspecified."

"You'd better shut your eyes this time. I just hope Isabel hasn't tried to master the trick of it and damaged the wards. Anyone at home?" he called.

Turning into the cross-passage, they immediately heard a muffled noise ahead, compounded of thumps and whistles, interspersed with yelps that might have been cries of "help!" Alec recognised the piercing, unladylike whistle that Daisy had been taught by her late brother; she used it—on rare occasions—to summon Nana. He sighed. Of course she was here, had been present at precisely the wrong moment, as usual. He went to the cupboard under the stairs as Underwood hurried forward to reassure the captives.

The contents of the cupboard were neatly arrayed, whether a tribute to Isabel's orderliness or because the ladies had only resided in the house for a couple of weeks. Alec found the bent clothes hanger at once, hung on a hook.

Crouched by the door, the inspector was speaking soothingly into the keyhole. "We'll have you out in two ticks, Miss Sutcliffe. Here's Mr. Fletcher with the wire. You'd better move down the stairs a bit out of the way of the door." He switched his ear to the hole, then stood up with a nod to Alec. "It was Vaughn all right."

"Is Daisy down there, too? Oh yes, that's her propelling pencil among the rubbish." He picked it up and put it in his pocket, then stooped to probe the keyhole with the hook. The inside of the lock felt different. He twisted and turned and jiggled the wire, but nothing clicked. "Damn. Daisy!" he called mouth to hole. "Did you mess about with this lock?"

He turned his head to listen. After a moment, Isabel's voice said, "We both did. We prised a nail out of the shelves, a nice long one, and tried to open it. Unsuccessfully. Why?"

"Because, between the pair of you, you've mucked it up. Bent the wards or knocked one crooked, or something. We're going to have to get a locksmith." Much as he'd prefer to, he couldn't stay and deal with Daisy's predicament. The hunt for Vaughn must be set in motion. Alec and Underwood had another interview scheduled with the Cartwrights. Ernie and Pennicuik were expected back with whatever they had gleaned from the gardener, White. Depending on their information, Mrs. Hedger might have to be hauled in to the police station. "Are you all right? Over to you."

"Oh yes, we've only been here . . ." Faintly: "Daisy, how long have we been here? . . . No, it hasn't been forever! About an hour, since Vaughn shut the door . . . Uh, over to you."

"The air is still good for a long time, then. Tell me what Vaughn said to you and what you told him. Over." He knelt on the floor, the easier to apply his ear to the hole.

"I told him about the Hotel Majestic. I'm sorry, but he was looking quite wild-eyed. He locked us in to stop us raising the alarm before he could get away. The rotter had the keys all the time. I expect you and Mr. Underwood are anxious to get on his trail. We'll be all right, but tell the locksmith to hurry! Over."

"We'll send a constable with an axe in case the locksmith has any difficulty. Tell Daisy I have her gold pencil safe; I'll leave it on the hall table. And give her my love, would you? We're off now. See you later."

"Give my . . . thanks to Mr. Underwood. See you later."

Alec stood up, with a crick in his neck and another in his lower back. Underwood had disappeared at the mention of a locksmith. Now he returned with a bunch of keys dangling from his forefinger.

"I rifled Miss Sutcliffe's handbag," he explained in a low voice. "We oughtn't to leave the house unlocked. I hope she'll forgive me."

"Seeing you rifled the entire house a couple of days ago," said Alec, "I doubt she'll mind. We can put out that alert now. We've got him for false imprisonment at the least."

"You mean they just went away and left us here?" Daisy asked indignantly.

"They have to chase after Vaughn. I suppose I could have asked them to fetch my hatchet and chop down the door, but I didn't think of it in time. Besides, I'd really rather not have to replace the whole door."

"No, sorry, of course not. I just hope they can find a lock-smith who'll come right away."

"You're not getting the wind up again, are you, Daisy?"

"Certainly not. Don't harp on that."

"My turn to apologise. I didn't mean to. I know it was just because you were ill."

"Being locked in a cellar doesn't improve one's disposition! Alec wouldn't have left if there were any danger. He may even think we're safer locked up. At worst, his axe bearer will come along and let us out for a late lunch."

Isabel grinned. "Hungry again?"

"I went for a long walk this morning. Nana would have loved it. You really must get a dog. Vaughn wouldn't have taken us by surprise if you had a nice mastiff sleeping in the front hall."

"I was thinking of a bulldog. I've always liked the look of them, and someone told me they're not half as fierce as they look."

"More likely to slobber a burglar to death than to bite him."

"What's your Nana?"

" 'Heinz Fifty-seven. She's a farm dog, part sheepdog, prob-ably part terrier. My stepdaughter fell for her when she was a puppy."

They talked about different breeds, Daisy having known a good many dogs while growing up in the country, at Fairacres. Then they talked about gardens, flowers, fruit and vegetables, and raising chickens. Isabel hoped for better harvests here in the temperate south than she had achieved in the suburbs of Hud-dersfield.

The natural sequel was food. Daisy was ravenous, as well as dying of thirst, by the time a knocking on the cellar door an-nounced the arrival of a bobby, axe in hand.

The constable was perfectly willing to chop down the door, if that was what Miss Sutcliffe required. "Howsumdever," a lock-smith was on the way from High Wycombe. If the ladies would bide just a wee bit longer, they would be released with no damage done.

Daisy would have opted for immediate release, but it was for Isabel to decide. They bided a wee bit longer.

An hour later, they were sitting in the kitchen, finishing the last bites of a lunch of toasted cheese and apples, when the doorbell rang. Isabel got up and peeked out of the window.

"A black umbrella—I think it's Mrs. Barnes. I don't feel like entertaining, but it's the first time she's called. And I want to see if she has any suggestions about someone to take Mrs. Hedger's place."

"Offer a cup of coffee. I could do with one. I'll put it on while you answer the door."

An explanation of why they were having after-lunch coffee so late inevitably turned into an account of the morning's excitements. The doctor's wife was properly sympathetic as well as much entertained.

"I won't breathe a word to a soul," she promised. "Goodness, I never dreamt the life of a policeman's wife was so exciting."

"It's not supposed to be," Daisy assured her.

When Mrs. Barnes left, Daisy helped Isabel wash the few dishes, then went back to the hotel. She had intended to take a nap, but she wasn't really sleepy and her typewriter sat in silent reproach on the table in the window. . . .

Once she started transforming her notes on the Inns of Court into an article, she became absorbed in manipulating words. Time passed without her noticing, until a knock on the door made her surface.

"Mrs. Fletcher, it's Sally. You didn't come down to tea, so I brought you some."

"You spoil me, Sally. Put it here, will you? I've fallen behind in my work, so I'll just keep at it while it's going smoothly."

"I don't want to interrupt." Sally hesitated. "But do you mind if I ask you a question?"

Daisy tore her thoughts away from the Inns of Court, which the arrival of tea had scarcely disrupted. "Yes?"

"It's Auntie May. Someone told me she was at home, not out at work, so I went round this afternoon. She's upset: angry for sure, and maybe afraid. But she won't tell me what the trouble is. She just sits there in her rocking chair, rocking and rocking. Do you know what's wrong, Mrs. Fletcher? What happened to upset her so?"

"The police went round to Cherry Trees this morning to ask her a few questions, that's all. You know my husband and DI Underwood. You know they wouldn't bully her. She wouldn't talk to them, just stormed out of the house, I was told. Older people without much education tend to be afraid of the police, I'm afraid," Daisy added tactfully.

"Auntie left school at twelve to go into service."

"There you are, then. I wouldn't worry about it. She's just being awkward."

"I know she can be difficult. She likes to keep herself to herself, you see, and questions always upset her. Oh dear, I suppose she'll get over it."

"I'm sure she will." Daisy didn't mention that Mrs. Hedger might have lost her job at Cherry Trees in the meantime. "Try not to worry, Sally."

"Thanks, Mrs. Fletcher. I'll pop round after supper and make sure she's all right. It's just that she's the only relative I've got left in these parts."

Daisy went on with her work. It was going well. She let her tea grow cold and got crumbs in her typewriter, but by the time she went down to dinner, she had finished the draft.

The dining room was busy, and buzzing with chatter. Sally had saved Daisy a small table in a comparatively quiet corner.

"Sorry, Mrs. Fletcher, we're out of everything 'cepting the ham."

"Then ham let it be. What's brought the crowd out?"

"Hasn't Mr. Fletcher told you yet? They've arrested Mr. Vaughn. I've got to run. I'll bring your soup in just a minute."

Sally had no time to stop and chat. Eavesdropping on nearby diners supplied "arrested for murder," but offered no further credible details. Daisy went back up to the bedroom without much food for speculation. She sat on the bed with her type-script, trying to concentrate on editing.

Alec came in before she had finished, wresting off his tie as he closed the door.

"Darling, you look exhausted. Sally says you've arrested Vaughn."

"I suppose Sergeant Harris has been talking again. I'm go-ing to write a strongly worded suggestion that he be sacked, or at least demoted. Yes, Vaughn was easy to catch, driving his wife's car. She's furious—she wanted it for some errand this afternoon. Once we were fairly sure he was heading for Paris, and had good reason for stopping him, it didn't take long to pull him in." Alec grinned. "We're grateful to you and Isabel for the information and for being stuck in the cellar."

"What do you mean? You arrested him for kidnapping us, not for murder?"

"False imprisonment, as he didn't run off with you. We'll need your statements tomorrow. Still no grounds for homicide. We can hope for a confession." Wearily he sat down on the edge of the bed. "But I'm not inclined to believe he killed her. We've found Judith Gray's maid and housekeeper, one in London, one in Bath, so tomorrow we'll have local lads ask them a few ques-tions. Between them, they should be able to confirm the quar-rel Mrs. Tom heard about, and identify the second woman for certain."

"Mrs. Tom? You didn't tell me . . . I'm glad she had some suc-cess for her trouble."

"Yes, it may reconcile her to Tom's notion of a nice outing to the countryside. The maid used to go up to town with Mrs. Gray, so we're hoping for the names of London friends."

"What about the one in St. Tropez? Elizabeth Knox?"

"She wired. She and her husband and Geegee, who turns out to be Sir George Gantry, are devastated. A *flic* is going round to talk to them."

"The inquest is tomorrow afternoon?"

"Yes. I doubt you and your friends will be called upon. Underwood's going to request an adjournment as early as possible in the proceedings, and he says the coroner's a reasonable man. Enough, Daisy. I didn't get much sleep last night and I'll be up early again in the morning."

THIRTY-THREE

Once again Daisy awoke to the arrival of Sally with early morning tea, to find Alec already gone. She snatched at the fading wisps of a dream and missed. A glance at the clock showed that she had missed breakfast, too. However, as well as a little pot of not very early tea, Sally set a plate of bread and butter and a hardboiled egg on the bedside table.

"Thank you so much, Sally." The sight of her set questions buzzing in Daisy's brain. "Are you in a hurry?"

"No, Mrs. Fletcher. I'm finished serving breakfasts for this morning. Mr. Fletcher and Mr. Piper had theirs ages ago and went out."

"Pull up a chair. I'd like to ask a couple of questions, if you don't mind?"

"Course not. Anything I can do to help."

"I was just wondering if your aunt was very upset that she wasn't paid for the time she worked while no one was living at Cherry Trees."

"She wasn't happy about it. Well, who would be? But she didn't really expect to be. I don't blame Miss Sutcliffe, mind.

She didn't ask Auntie to do it, and there can't have been much needed doing, with the house empty."

"Why do you think she bothered, then, if she didn't expect to be paid?"

Sally considered, her head tilted. "Partly habit. She's ever so set in her ways, Auntie May. And she could always hope, couldn't she? When you make just enough to scrape by, sometimes you've just got to hope."

Remembering her own less-than-affluent days, Daisy could only agree. She persevered. "Yet yesterday she went off in a huff in the middle of her work. That was more of an interruption than spending a few minutes answering a few questions would have been. Even for someone as . . . crotchety as Mrs. Hedger, it seems a bit silly. Against her own interests."

"She's always been contrary. It is odd, though. She's not been properly herself recently."

"In what way?"

"Sort of like as if . . ." Sally frowned. "As if she's got a secret. Something she won't tell even me, and I'm the only person she ever talks to."

"A pleasant secret, would you guess, or unpleasant?"

"I . . . I'm not sure. Sometimes she seemed pleased. Not happy-pleased, more sort of smug. But sometimes . . . sometimes it seemed as if she was almost afraid, like I told you yesterday. Do you think she knew who killed Mrs. Gray?"

"It's possible. Do *you* think she'd be likely to withhold that information from the police?"

"I don't know, Mrs. Fletcher, and that's the truth. She'll be in awful trouble if she did, won't she?" Tears sprang up in Sally's eyes.

Luckily the hankie under Daisy's pillow was unused. She handed it over. Afraid that Mrs. Hedger might be in much more serious trouble than withholding information, she had no words of comfort to offer.

Mopping her eyes, Sally cheered up. "But maybe now Mr.

Vaughn's been arrested, it won't matter much. She really cheered up when I told her they caught the murderer."

So Sally believed Vaughn had been charged with murder, as, no doubt, did most or all of those who heard of the arrest. It was not for Daisy to enlighten them. She moved on to the last question that must have revolved and evolved in her dreams.

"Did your aunt ever mention getting a letter of recommendation—a character—from Mrs. Gray?"

"Not that I remember. Oh, wait, she did say—ages ago—that Mrs. Gray didn't like her and would likely give her a reference that wasn't fit to show. But Mrs. Clark, that was housekeeper at Cherry Trees, always said she was a hard worker even if she had her ways, so she'd ask her for a character."

Mrs. Clark, thought Daisy—all that running about after the gardener, and all the time Sally could have revealed the housekeeper's name if anyone had thought to ask her. "Did Mrs. Clark write her a letter?"

"Auntie didn't say. Is it important? I could ask her."

"No, no, it doesn't matter. Gosh, look at the time. I'd better get up! Thanks again for my breakfast."

Sally went off looking puzzled and unhappy.

Daisy decided to take a bath, a good place for thinking. Chin-deep in hot water, she considered Sally's opinions on her aunt's state of mind.

Mrs. Hedger knew who had killed her employer, so much seemed pretty clear. It was not at all improbable that she should have seen or heard something that gave his—or her—identity away, or she might have actually witnessed the incident. Then why not tell the police?

Sheer bloody-mindedness was not an adequate explanation. She might have been threatened with harm if she didn't hold her tongue, but in that case, whence the pleasure Sally had noted?

Blackmail sprang to mind. Blackmail, with its prospect of gain and risk of retaliation, would account for Mrs. Hedger's mingled smugness and fearfulness. Could it also explain her cheering up when she heard about Vaughn's arrest, supposedly for murder?

Daisy reached for her flannel. Washing disturbed her train of thought, so she didn't anwer her own question until she was clean, dry, enveloped in her warm blue dressing gown, and back in the bedroom. Knickers, suspender belt, stockings—warm lisle for the country. As she drew them on, her thoughts returned to Vaughn's arrest.

Why had the news pleased Mrs. Hedger? It put paid to any hope of money from blackmail—at least, it would have if he actually had been charged with Mrs. Gray's death. She might be relieved of anxiety, but wouldn't she also have regretted a lost opportunity? Sally had not spoken of regret.

Perhaps Sally had simply failed to notice it. Or perhaps Mrs. Hedger had realised by then just how dangerous blackmailing a murderer would be.

Daisy shied away from the third possibility that dawned on her. The general populace was naturally relieved that the murderer had supposedly been arrested, but the person who had most to gain from the police ending their enquiries was the actual killer. Was Mrs. Hedger the one who had pushed Mrs. Gray down the stairs?

A cleaning woman bumping off her employer? Unheard of, and a singularly unsettling idea.

Daisy wondered whether she was arguing in circles. Alec was bound to point out that her train of thought was pure speculation, based on nothing more substantial than Sally's opinions of her aunt's state of mind. Or he'd say they had already come up with the theory and dismissed it. Nonetheless, she had to tell him.

Sighing, she finished dressing. It wasn't even a pleasant morning for a stroll. Outside the window, rain bucketed down. Umbrella in hand, Daisy set out.

She hoped to see Alec alone but she was out of luck. All four detectives were together and none showed any sign of departing when she said she wanted to speak to Alec. He and Under-wood exchanged "what now?" glances while Pennicuik took her dripping umbrella and Ernie set a chair for her.

"Go ahead, Daisy." Alec wore his infuriating patient look. "You've got a revelation for us?"

"I didn't claim a revelation," Daisy said defensively. "I just woke up wondering . . . and I asked Sally Hedger—"

"You've already discussed this matter with Miss Hedger?"

"Miss Hedger!" Ernie was upset.

"It wasn't till I'd asked her a few questions that I worked it out."

"Mrs. Fletcher," said DI Underwood, "could you perhaps start with your conclusion and then explain how you reached it?"

"Oh yes, much easier than trying to start at the beginning. I think it's more than likely Mrs. Hedger killed Mrs. Gray."

The silence that followed had a surprised quality.

Then Underwood said, "Well, why not? I, for one, have been considering her as a balky witness. I've barely given her a pass-ing thought as a suspect."

"Nor have I," Alec admitted.

"Y'know, Chief," said Ernie, "I did wonder about that disin-fectant smell. My landlady uses the stuff. The smell fades in a couple of hours. Mrs. Hedger must have used gallons for you to be able to detect it a couple of days later."

"Drains and mucky boots," Underwood recalled. "That's what she told Miss Sutcliffe."

"Isabel always puts her gardening boots by the back door," said Daisy, "and I haven't caught the least whiff of bad drains. I've been in and out of the house for days."

"Is that all you're going on, Daisy?"

"No, darling. Though I do think it's significant. Drains and manure don't smell the least bit like that awful sickly stench when you opened the cellar door, so it's hard to believe she mistook it."

Ernie backed her up. "More like she knew the body was there and expected it to start smelling."

"I did wonder whether she knew about it and kept quiet because she was blackmailing the murderer."

The detectives considered the theory. Underwood rejected it. "That wouldn't work. The body was bound to be discovered sooner or later, and once the murderer was arrested he'd have no incentive not to denounce her. She's not the sort to run off abroad with her ill-gotten gains. I doubt she's ever been farther than High Wycombe in her life."

"Sally said she was pleased to hear about Mr. Vaughn's arrest. As far as I can make out, everyone believes he was arrested for murder. So I dropped the blackmail idea."

"What else did Miss Hedger have to say, Mrs. Fletcher?"

Daisy recounted the conversation. It sounded very thin, without a shred of actual evidence. She was glad Ernie had brought up the question of disinfectant to add a bit of solidity to her tissue of conjectured emotions—if one could describe a smell as solid.

"And then she said her aunt cheered up when she heard of the arrest, as I told you. I asked if she'd talked about a reference letter from Mrs. Gray. Apparently she hadn't expected a recommendation worth showing a prospective employer but thought the housekeeper might give her one. Sally doesn't know whether she did. She can't have, though, because Isabel would have told you if she'd seen it."

"I'm sure she would," said the detective. "Anything more?"

"No, that's it." Daisy felt flattened. "It doesn't sound like very much, but I thought I ought to tell you."

"I—we appreciate it. We'll certainly follow up. In fact, if it's all right with you, Mr. Fletcher, Sergeant Piper can go right now and have a chat with Miss Hedger. Just to confirm what you've told us, Mrs. Fletcher—not that I doubt it!—and to see if she has anything to add that she didn't think to mention to you."

Walking back to the Saracen's Head with Ernie holding her umbrella above her head, Daisy felt better. Surely Ernie's time was too valuable for Underwood to waste it on a wild goose chase, which meant he didn't think her theory was utter bosh. And Alec had smiled at her as she left. She hoped that meant his silence was only because he was deferring to the inspector.

"Well done, Mrs. Fletcher," said Ernie. "The chief would have cottoned on to Mrs. Hedger sooner or later, but you may have saved us days of following false leads. I'm awfully sorry for Miss Hedger, though. Does she realise where your questions were leading?"

"Not at the time. She may have put two and two together by now. The best thing you can do for Sally is make sure she understands you won't drop her if her aunt turns out to be guilty."

Blushing, Ernie said hotly, "I wouldn't do that! But maybe she'll hate me if we have to arrest her auntie."

"I doubt it. My impression is that she's not all that fond of Mrs. Hedger. She sticks by her because she's the only family she has in this district, and she helps her because it's her nature to be helpful."

"She's wonderful, isn't she?"

"I like her very much," Daisy assured him.

The church clock was striking six when Alec and Underwood, followed by Ernie and Pennicuik, turned off Wycombe End into the murky, muddy alley. The rain had stopped and the temperature had dropped, threatening a frost. The mud would be glazed with ice by morning.

The inspector took the search warrant from his pocket. "This is all very well, but if she won't open the door, we can't serve it."

"Let's worry about that if it happens." Alec had a contingency plan involving windows and Ernie's slight stature, but the less Underwood knew about it the better.

A dim light was visible through the curtain at the downstairs window of Mrs. Hedger's one-up, one-down cottage. Underwood stationed Ernie and Pennicuik on the opposite side of the alley, eight or ten feet away, less because the suspect might try to flee than because her tiny space had no room for them.

Underwood knocked.

An angry voice was heard from within. Then the door was opened, by Sally Hedger. She was in tears.

"Mr. Underwood," she choked out, standing aside to let them pass. "She thinks now you arrested Mr. Vaughn it's all right to wear her things. She says it's not stealing because she was dead. I can't make her understand—"

"Sally," said Alec, "go out to Sergeant Piper. He's just across the way. I'll call you if your aunt asks for you."

She fled as Alec turned to see the inspector gaping at the old woman in the rocking chair. Mrs. Hedger's short, stout body was enveloped in a glossy fur coat. On a slimmer woman, it would have been a loose, comfortable travelling coat. On her, it barely met across the bosom and completely enveloped her feet.

"Wotcha staring at? I di'n' steal it." She bristled with self-righteousness. "She was dead, she ha'n' got no more use for it. 'Sides, she weren't no better'n a doxy."

"May Hedger, I must advise you . . ."

As Underwood proceeded with the Judges' Rules warning, Alec went up the stairs, ducking under a low beam. He didn't have to exercise the searching skills Tom Tring had taught him years ago. The beam of his torch picked out the expensive overnight suitcase in one corner of the tiny room. On top of it was a stylish leather handbag.

Careful to protect fingerprints with a handkerchief, he moved the bag to the bed, an iron bedstead with a thin mattress covered with a faded, patched counterpane. The clasp clicked open easily. Alec turned the torch beam on the contents.

A silver cigarette case with the monogram JJG—Judith Jane Gray. Had she wanted gold and given in to her elderly husband's notorious frugality? A bunch of keys—Alec hooked it out with his little finger. The pasteboard tag, "Cherry Trees," removed any remaining doubt. He took them downstairs.

Mrs. Hedger was glaring at the inspector in malevolent silence.

Underwood looked at the bunch of keys and went straight to the salient fact. "You knew Mrs. Gray was dead."

"I could tell right off. I've laid out many a corpse in my time."

"You locked the cellar and didn't report her death to the police."

"Who'd invite that busybody Abel Harris to come sticking his nose in! It were an accident, any road."

"An accident, was it?"

"Tha's right, seeing she pushed me first. 'Go away,' she said. 'I haven't got time now for writing letters.' And she give me a shove so I shoved back. I weren't to know she'd lose her balance and go tumbling down. It wasn't like I murdered her. An accident it were."

"That's for a jury to decide," said Underwood. "You're under arrest, Mrs. Hedger, and must come with us to the station to be charged. Please take off that coat. It will be used in evidence."

"It's cold out," said Alec, struck by an unexpected wave of compassion for the stubborn, ignorant, cross-grained old woman. "Let her keep it on."

On Friday evening, Alec came home to Hampstead. Daisy hurried down to greet him in the hall.

"Darling, I'm so glad you've made it in time for dinner. When I got your wire, I invited Tom and Mrs. Tring. It seemed only fair that they should hear all about the case."

He handed his hat and coat to the parlourmaid, who bore them away for a good brushing. "Thank you, Elsie. I take it, Daisy, you expect to get more information out of me if Tom's helping?"

"Naturally. They're up in the nursery with the twins. Tom's on hands and knees with his godson on his back, being a rhinoceros as far as I could make out. Oliver has a penchant for exotic steeds since last time we went to the zoo. I do hope he won't become a big game hunter."

"And Mirrie?"

"She's on Mrs. Tom's lap, reading a picture book while Mrs.

299

Tom and Nurse Gilpin chat. Mrs. Tom gets on with Nurse much better than I do. Go and have a wash and brush up, darling. I'll tell Mrs. Dobson to dish up in fifteen minutes, unless you want a whisky first, or a beer with Tom."

"Beer sounds good. Make it half an hour. I'll say good night to the twins and bring the Trings down. With luck, I'll get the story over with and eat my dinner in peace."

When they were all settled in the sitting room with drinks to hand, Tom rumbled, "You had the inquest yesterday, Chief?"

"Yesterday afternoon. It was just as well the coroner couldn't sit sooner, gave us time to get it pretty much all wrapped up for him. His jury brought in homicide by May Hedger. Manslaughter or murder is up to a criminal jury, of course. Sally Hedger made an excellent witness, Daisy, clear and concise in spite of floods of tears throughout the proceedings."

"Poor Sally! I wish I'd been there to support her."

Alec grinned. "Ernie managed that, in his usual unobtrusive style. Not quite holding her hand, but being stalwart at her side with a supply of clean handkerchiefs, while behaving in a properly policemanlike manner."

"He's a good lad," Tom observed.

"I left him there for another day, to help Underwood with reports and tying up loose ends."

"That's nice," said Mrs. Tring placidly. "She sounds like a nice young woman. Didn't you say that she's wanting to move to London, Mrs. Fletcher? Me and Tom have been thinking of renting out a room, now he's retired, if we could find a nice, reliable lodger."

"She's very reliable," Daisy assured her. "I'd be glad to know she has a safe place to stay with good people when she comes to the big bad city."

"And young Ernie knows he's always welcome to take potluck with us." She exchanged a glance of complicity with Daisy.

Tom wanted to hear about Daisy and her friend being locked in the cellar where the body was found. She gave him a highly coloured account that made him chuckle, while his missus tut-tutted.

"It's funny now," said Daisy, "but it was quite frightening at the time."

Mrs. Tring was confused. "Well I never! And the man who shut you up turned out not to be the murderer after all?"

"He had other matters on his conscience. Apart from the cellar business, his crime was financial fraud."

"Tell us the whole story, Chief," Tom requested. "First of all, I assume you were able to present the coroner with a definitive identification of the body?"

"Oh yes, it was Judith Gray all right. The coroner would probably have accepted Sally Hedger's evidence, along with what we found in her aunt's attic: the luggage and handbag, contents intact. As it happened, Mrs. Gray's friend Mrs. Knox was able to give us the name of their mutual dentist. You know how people recommend their medical practitioners to their friends. He's a Harley Street man, as we supposed. When we explained our difficulty, he came right down to Beaconsfield, records in hand. Ghoulish curiosity, as DI Underwood said."

"Ah," said Tom, grinning behind his magnificent moustache.

"He found the reality a great deal more unpleasant than he anticipated. He managed to identify her faster than I'd have believed possible."

"I don't blame him," said Daisy.

"As for the rest, Tom, to tell the truth, the case was a barrel of red herrings. And we couldn't shoot them, we had to fish for them. The stepson—he had the best motive, two excellent motives in fact: money and revenge. The victim was his father's second wife and treated the old man abominably, by all accounts. Unfortunately, he has an unassailable alibi. It's no good looking at me like that, Tom. I know unassailable alibis are made to be assailed. But this is truly untouchable."

"If you say so, Chief."

"Then there were Donald Vaughn and Roger Cartwright.

Either or both may have been the victim's lovers. Both their wives assumed they were."

"Both of them!" Mrs. Tring was shocked.

"And a London friend now in France. She seems to have been rather free and easy with her favours, and Vaughn may have been her lover; Cartwright probably not. Anyway, each of their wives suspected a liaison and thus had a motive for hating her. Whether or not they were correct in their assumptions turns out to be irrelevant."

"Vaughn's the one," Tom rumbled, "the house agent, that shut up Mrs. Fletcher and t'other young lady in the cellar."

"That's right. Financial fraud, as Daisy said. He'd been appropriating his employer's money, quite a bit of it, but no large sums at one time. As he was saving—stuffing cash under a loose floorboard—he didn't give himself away by excessive expenditure."

"My friend Willie—Miss Chandler—was auditing the books but wasn't allowed to tell anyone. At the last minute, he found out. That's why he was running away, nothing to do with the murder. His trouble was, he was under the impression that Mrs. Gray expected him to join her in France to start a new life together with the help of his loot, but he didn't know where she was. He turned up at Cherry Trees in a final attempt to get her address out of Isabel. Hence our ordeal in the cellar."

"Ah," said Tom. "And Cartwright, Chief? That's the headmaster, ducks."

"Cartwright behaved in a suspicious manner because he had . . . er . . . attempted to misbehave with the young women teachers at his school, the latest of whom was one of Daisy's friends."

"Has he been sacked yet, darling?"

"I had a word with the rector before I left. Cartwright has been given notice for the end of term, and the board is considering making Vera Leighton headmistress. In the meantime, Mr. Turnbull will keep a close eye on things at the school."

"Good."

"Any more red herrings in that barrel, Chief?"

"Plenty. Miss Chandler, Miss Sutcliffe, and Miss Leighton for a start. Miss Sutcliffe spent the most time at the house during the buying and selling process. Miss Leighton jumped like a startled rabbit when Cartwright was mentioned and Miss Chandler displayed a pronounced aversion to Vaughn, and neither was willing to explain."

"Those are Mrs. Fletcher's friends," said Mrs. Tring indignantly. "You can't have suspected them."

"Can't make exceptions, ducks, you know that."

"I didn't suspect them much, nor for long. Naturally DI Underwood was slower to trust them, but none of them had any apparent motive. Miss Sutcliffe is a transparently forthright person, and she and Daisy together came up with the name of the hotel Mrs. Gray had intended to stay at in Paris, as well as the address of Mrs. Gray's friends in France—"

"That's noble of you, darling. I'll take credit for the hotel, but you would have got the address as soon as Isabel handed over the letter."

"True. Once we'd found out why the other two were so secretive, all three were more or less out of the picture."

"So the young ladies," Mrs. Tring pondered aloud, "they never had anything to do with the case?"

"Nothing but the misfortune of moving into a house with a body in the cellar."

"And inheriting a murderous cleaning woman!" Daisy exclaimed. It might be good fortune in the end, she thought, as it had brought Mr. Underwood into Isabel's life—but if they made a match of it, what about the other two? Life was so complicated!

"More likely," Alec went on, "were Judith Gray's ex-servants, and her London friends and enemies. You two found the servants for us, and I'm sorry I couldn't give you credit."

"Were they any use to you, Chief?"

"They were very helpful with regard to the friends and enemies, but in fact they were so many more red herrings. We never had to track down most of them because the real culprit came to light. I have to admit I never seriously considered the char-woman."

"I don't believe I've ever heard of such a case," Tom observed. "Might have saved you a lot of trouble if the missus and I had managed to scrape up an aquaintance with Mrs. Hedger."

"Mrs. Hedger is not the sort with whom anyone could scrape up an acquaintance. She keeps herself to herself, even now she's in a cell. When we walked in on her at home, she was wearing Mrs. Gray's fur coat. Even to her it was obvious she couldn't get away with refusing to explain."

"What was her excuse?"

"Nothing new. You've heard it before: It wasn't stealing, because the owner was dead. Of course, that required an explanation of how she knew Mrs. Gray was dead. The whole story came out then. I don't think she realised how much she was saying."

"Ah." Tom nodded. "That kind that don't talk much, once they get going you never know what'll spill out. So how did Mrs. Gray end up with a broken neck?"

"A silly squabble over a reference. She didn't have the common courtesy to spend a minute writing one for the old woman. She tried to push past her. Mrs. Hedger didn't care for being shoved out of the way and pushed back. Unfortunately Mrs. Gray happened to be standing on the cellar stairs at the time. The railing is not a sturdy one."

"Ah."

"In any other place, I'm sure nothing would have come of it beyond a bit of name-calling. Whether she was really in a hurry or just being obnoxious, we'll never know."

"She might have been in a hurry," Daisy proposed, "because she wanted to evade Vaughn and avoid a row about not giving him her address. Whatever he believed, I'm sure he wasn't part of her plans for the future, not with Sir George Gantry waiting for her in St. Tropez."

"We'll never know," Alec repeated.

"One more question, darling. Did you ever find the cellar key?

That's what brought us—you—into the investigation in the first place."

"Yes. All the house keys, including the cellar key, were in Mrs. Gray's handbag."

"Ah. If Mrs. H. had thrown them out and kept her mouth shut, she might have got away with a charge of theft."

"She's keeping her mouth shut now, when it's too late. One question is still bothering me, one she can't or won't answer: Why Mrs. Gray went down to the cellar in the first place. It was empty."

"I can guess," said Mrs. Tring. "It's like me checking to make sure the gas is out on the kitchen stove before I go round the shops. She was about to leave the house forever, and she went down to make sure everything was as it should be. I expect she went all over the rest of the house, too."

"Could be," Alec agreed, smiling. "That hadn't dawned on me. As DI Underwood remarked, we could do with more detecting ladies on the force."